MOTLEY TALES
AND A PLAY

The New York Public Library Collector's Editions are illustrated with original art and handwritten letters, diaries, and manuscripts from the collections of the Library. They are designed to evoke the world of the writer and the book, and to enhance the pleasure of reading the great works of literature.

THE NEW YORK PUBLIC LIBRARY

*Collector's
Edition*

MOTLEY TALES
AND A PLAY

ANTON CHEKHOV

DOUBLEDAY

New York   London   Toronto

Sydney   Auckland

FRONTISPIECE: *Photograph of Anton Chekhov, n.d., from* Izbrannye proizvedeniia *(Moscow/Leningrad, 1928).*

PUBLISHED BY DOUBLEDAY
a division of Bantam Doubleday Dell Publishing Group, Inc.
1540 Broadway, New York, New York 10036

DOUBLEDAY and the portrayal of an anchor with a dolphin
are trademarks of Doubleday, a division of
Bantam Doubleday Dell Publishing Group, Inc.

Permissions are to be found on page 386.

Book design by Marysarah Quinn

Library of Congress Cataloging-in-Publication Data
Chekhov, Anton Pavlovich, 1860–1904.
[Selections. English. 1998]
Motley tales and a play / Anton Chekhov.
p.   cm. — (New York Public Library collector's edition)
Tales translated by Constance Garnett, play adapted by David Mamet
from a literal translation by Vlada Chernomordik.
Includes bibliographical references.
Contents: The student—Anna on the neck—The beauties—The chorus
girl—Misery—A happy ending—The darling—The huntsman—Sleepy—
Peasants—The teacher of literature—Easter eve—Happiness—Anyuta—
The witch—The two Volodyas—Ward no. 6—The three sisters.
1. Chekhov, Anton Pavlovich, 1860–1904—Translations into English.
I. Garnett, Constance Black, 1862-1946.   II. Chernomordik, Vlada.
III. Mamet, David. Three sisters.   IV. Title.   V. Series.
PG3456.A13G38   1998
891.72'3—dc21   97-40220
                                                                          CIP

ISBN 0-385-48730-4

This edition is printed on acid-free paper

Printed in the United States of America

First New York Public Library Collector's Edition: March 1998

1   3   5   7   9   10   8   6   4   2

ACKNOWLEDGMENTS

This volume was created with the participation of many people throughout The New York Public Library. For their help in developing *Motley Tales and a Play* by Anton Chekhov, we are grateful for the contributions of the curators and staffs of the Slavic and Baltic Divisions, the Henry W. and Albert A. Berg Collection of English and American Literature, and the Billy Rose Theatre Collection of the Library for the Performing Arts. Special recognition and thanks go to researcher and writer Lara Merlin; Anne Skillion, Series Editor; and Karen Van Westering, Manager of Publications.

The New York Public Library wishes to extend thanks to its trustees Catherine Marron and Marshall Rose, as well as to Morton Janklow, for their early support and help in initiating this project.

Paul LeClerc, President

Michael Zavelle, Senior Vice President

CONTENTS

A PLAY

Suggestions for Further Reading

Checklist of Illustrations

Permissions

ABOUT ANTON CHEKHOV

The grandson of a former serf, Anton Pavlovich Chekhov became one of the greatest and most beloved figures of Russian literature. While attending medical school on a scholarship, he began writing short stories and humorous sketches to support his family. By the time of his graduation, he had focused his prodigious talents on literature. Like Leo Tolstoy and Fyodor Dostoyevsky, he had a sharp eye for the complicated workings of the human soul; yet, unlike his older compatriots, he viewed human weaknesses not with contempt or despair but with affection, humor, and compassion.

Commenting on Chekhov's peculiar genius and his role as an innovator, Tolstoy remarked, "What intellect! What an incomparable artist! He has created new art forms, literary forms the like of which I have never come across elsewhere." Chekhov helped to re-create both the modern short story and the modern play by directing the radiant light of his art on a stark and beautiful moment of truth. As E. M. Forster noted, "His only aim is to describe certain things and people in a way that shall be interesting and beautiful . . . Nothing has happened that might not happen in the world of daily life . . . but the particular sequence of the events is not to be experienced this side of poetry."

Anton Chekhov as a young man.

By purchasing his own and his children's freedom from their master twenty years before the emancipation of the serfs, Chekhov's grandfather saved the future writer from being born into slavery. The most brilliant member of an exceptionally talented—though unfocused—family, Chekhov was born in 1860 in the provincial southern Russian town of Taganrog. His father, Pavel Jegorovich Chekhov, a strict and fanatical Christian, believed in severely disciplining children and frequently whipped his sons; Chekhov later compared the beatings he received from his father to his grandfather's treatment as a serf, adding that his own childhood consisted of "nothing but suffering." His father owned a small drafty shop and required his three eldest sons to staff it from 5 A.M. until 11 P.M., in addition to keeping up with their schoolwork and attending all-night Orthodox church services. The little grocery was never successful, and his father went bankrupt the year Chekhov turned sixteen. Pavel Jegorovich fled to Moscow to escape debtors' prison, taking with him his two eldest sons. The rest of the family, consisting of Chekhov's mother, two younger brothers, and his beloved sister, Maria, soon followed, leaving Chekhov behind to complete his studies before rejoining the family in the capital. For three years, while preparing for his examinations, he gave private lessons for the pittance of a few rubles to support himself. Despite these difficulties, the young scholar did well enough to win a fellowship of twenty-five rubles a month, and decided to use the money to study medicine.

According to his lifelong friend and publisher, Aleksei Suvorin, the impetus for Chekhov's first story came from the medical student's need to earn enough money to buy his mother a birthday cake. With the sale of that story, Chekhov added the role of family breadwinner to that of student. Over the next seven years, he wrote more than four hundred short stories, sketches, tales, and one-act plays. It was not an easy life for a young man: on one occasion he had to make ten

A rare photograph of Chekhov's mother, Evgenia, who tried to restrain her husband's often brutal treatment of their children.

visits to a reluctant editor to collect his fee of three rubles. Yet, while still in medical school, he came to understand the crucial role literature would play in his life. But he never abandoned medicine, claiming, "Medicine is my lawful wife, literature my mistress. When I tire of the one, I spend the night with the other. As long as it does not become a regular habit, it is not humdrum and neither of them suffers from my infidelity. If I did not have my medical pursuits, I should find it difficult to devote my random thoughts and spare time to literature."

Chekhov suffered from chronic poor health, hemorrhaging from tuberculosis for the first time when he was only twenty-four years old. His family and friends were therefore greatly surprised when he undertook a visit to the penal colony of Sakhalin, a desolate island off the Pacific coast of Siberia, in 1890. The trip involved a grueling three-month journey across the Siberian plains. Once there, he made the first complete census of Sakhalin, and later produced a book documenting the miserable conditions he witnessed.

Throughout his life, Chekhov's writing was criticized for lack of social engagement, which perhaps resulted from a misreading of his detached, though not indifferent, style. In fact, starting with the trip to Sakhalin, he demonstrated his dedication to the welfare of others in one endeavor after another. He established the first library in his native town of Taganrog, purchasing 319 volumes for it on one trip to France alone and eventually donating the bulk of his personal collection of books. He labored earnestly to improve public education in the villages. Although never free from financial worries and still burdened with providing for his family, he spent over ten thousand rubles to build three primary schools in Melikhovo, where he had settled, and in the neighboring towns of Talezh and Novoselki. Although Chekhov never referred to it, even in his journal, Tsar Nicholas II granted this serf's grandson a "hereditary nobility" in honor of his "exemplary zeal and exertions directed toward the education of the people." He raised money to build a tuberculosis sanatorium in Yalta for the indigent and helped organize relief efforts during the

A finely wrought line drawing by Sergei Bekhonen of Chekhov's dacha, the country house at Melikhovo in which he wrote The Three Sisters, *used as a headpiece in the 1919 album commemorating the original production of the play.*

disastrous famine of 1891–92. As a man of medicine, he served without recompense on a Sanitary Council established to combat a threatening cholera epidemic, and was always on call to local peasants requiring his services in rural areas, where doctors were few.

A kind man—Lillian Hellman said, in her introduction to a collection of his letters, that if she could choose a famous writer to have dinner with, she would eschew the cantankerous Tolstoy for the genial Chekhov—he was also an incomparable artist. He transformed the short story from little more than a shortened novel into a sketch—a carefully rendered slice of life—giving it the distinct form

that we know today. He had a knack for turning the mundane into art; his brother Mikhail recalled that "somebody said in front of him that it was difficult to find material for stories. 'What nonsense!' Anton exclaimed. 'I can write about anyone or anything . . .' His eyes sparkled, he glanced round for some object or other and caught sight of an ashtray: 'There, now! Look at that! Tomorrow I could write a story called "The Ashtray." ' "

Chekhov's writings can be considered a literary analogue to photography—an art form coeval with the modern short story—in which the emphasis is on an instantaneous glimpse of reality. Indeed, his fellow writers described his technique in particularly visual terms. Tolstoy said, "Like the impressionists, Chekhov possesses his own particular style. One watches him daub on such colors as he has by him with apparent carelessness, and one imagines that all these splashes of paint have nothing in common between them. But as soon as one stands back and looks from a distance, the effect is extraordinary. Before one, there emerges a picture that is striking and irresistible." And Leonard Woolf, who helped popularize Chekhov in the English-speaking world, offered that his stories seem "to be the work of a man who has delicately, fastidiously, and ironically picked up with the extreme tips of his fingers a little piece of real life, and then with minute care and skill pinned it by means of words into a book." Young writers the world over quickly adopted Chekhovian methods. John Galsworthy noted in 1932 that "Chekhov has been the most potent magnet to young writers in several countries for the last twenty years." Twenty years later, Elizabeth Bowen contended that without him "a large body of English stories might have remained unwritten."

Chekhov displayed unusual artistic versatility in becoming not only a fiction writer but an accomplished dramatist. His love of the theater developed early; at age thirteen, he started to attend plays, buying the cheapest tickets and arriving two hours before performances for a good seat. His school required that students obtain permission to attend a show, and so he would don disguises consisting of makeup, glasses, and a fake beard. As a dramatist, he combined a youthful fascination with the magic of the theater with the wisdom of his fiction, leading Graham Greene to say, "Into our old nineteenth-century theater, with its melodramas and adulteries and the morality of the endless Sundays, the [Chekhov] play broke like youth . . . But there lies the trap, for Chekhov's work is not young: it is as old as the strange land from which it emerged."

Chekhov's plays continue in the naturalistic vein of his fiction, presenting a somewhat removed view of his characters that nonetheless intimates the author's affection for their humanity. Still, his work seemed such a departure from the prevailing level of artifice that audiences needed time to fully appreciate it. He nearly abandoned writing plays after the dismal failure of *The Seagull* in 1896; however,

Chekhov with three friends, from left: P. M. Svobodin, Vladimir Davidov, Chekhov, Aleksei Suvorin. In his capacity of editor, Suvorin, who became a close personal friend, launched Chekhov's literary career.

Chekhov's great love and wife, the talented and passionate actress Olga Knipper, for whom he wrote The Three Sisters.

that play's revival by Konstantin Stanislavsky's Moscow Art Theater two years later was wildly successful, and Chekhov's collaboration with the renowned director is now legendary. Founded in 1898, the Moscow Art Theater made a tremendous splash in the theatrical world, abolishing the star system and focusing on ensemble playing—Stanislavsky originated the idea that "there are no small parts, just small actors"—and making the high theatricality of the nineteenth-century stage taboo. Honoring simplicity and the art of quiet truths, Stanislavsky's company provided an ideal venue for presenting Chekhov's naturalistic portraits. Superb productions were mounted of *Uncle Vanya* in 1899, *The Three Sisters* in 1901, and *The Cherry Orchard* (his last masterpiece) in 1904.

Another important reason for Chekhov's connection to the Moscow Art Theater came from his growing relationship with one of its most talented members, Olga Knipper, whom he married in 1901. Chekhov was often forced by his failing health to live in the south, and thus away from Knipper, whose career kept her in Moscow for extended periods of time. Deeply in love, he wrote *The Three Sisters* with Knipper in mind for the pivotal role of Masha. The play addresses the theme of a passionate woman trapped by the boredom and numbing senselessness of her existence. As in all of Chekhov's plays, the characters seem unable to truly converse with one another, speaking only in short soliloquies addressed to no one, not even themselves. The pregnant pauses and slow pacing of the play are crucial to our being able to feel the monotony that weighs upon the title characters. Actress Lynn Fontanne commented on the evocative richness of Chekhov's spare writing: "There is as much action between the lines as there is in the spoken words. There is a great deal between the speeches, a great deal between the acts, and, I sometimes think, between the performances!" Writing this play may have been Chekhov's own way of enduring the difficult separation from his beloved. As the French biographer Sophie Laffitte suggested, *"The Three Sisters* consists of a sort of long message, a long inner dialogue between the author and the faraway Olga Knipper. It is the most

"He was suddenly silent, coughed, looked at me out of the corners of his eyes, and smiled that tender, charming smile of his which attracted one so irresistibly to him and made one listen so attentively to his words." —Russian writer Maksim Gorky on Chekhov

'Chekhovian,' the most nostalgic, the most harmonious of his plays. The audiences proved it: the play beat all previous records in the number of its performances."

Toward the end of his short life, Chekhov stopped writing and focused instead on selecting and editing the stories that he wanted to include in an edition of his complete works. It is from these works that we have selected the stories for this edition, each remarkable in its own way: "Sleepy" shows the author experimenting with innovative narrative techniques to represent various stages of consciousness, from full wakefulness to dreaming, and much of the gray area in between. "Anyuta" and "The Chorus Girl" offer sensitive portrayals of women who live outside traditional sexual norms, as "Easter Eve," with its homoerotic impulses, does for men. "Ward No. 6," one of Chekhov's longer pieces, is also among the earlier literary works to treat mental illness without demonizing the afflicted. Chekhov's own favorite from among all his stories is the sweet, inspirational tale "The Student." Each story included here shows a different aspect of Chekhov's mastery.

Anton Chekhov died of tuberculosis in 1904. A family friend, Tatiana Shchepkina-Kupernik, reported, "Sometimes Chekhov would remark in conversation that he would soon be forgotten. 'I shall be read for seven or seven and a half years,' he would say, 'and then they'll forget me.' However, on one occasion he added, 'But then a little time will pass, and they'll begin to read me again, and for a long time.'" Once again, this gentle and soft-spoken artist showed a remarkable knack for seeing into the human heart.

А. П. ЧЕХОВ.

The elegant wreath designed by Sergei Bekhonen for the album commemorating the original production of The Three Sisters.

◆ ◆ ◆ ◆ ◆ ◆ ◆ ◆ ◆ ◆ ◆ ◆ ◆ ◆ ◆ ◆ ◆ ◆ ◆

ABOUT THIS EDITION

Anton Chekhov's fiction touches readers by offering them the opportunity to enter for the space of a moment into a fanciful yet genuine world of his creation. The acclaimed American critic Edmund Wilson praised Chekhov, in whose work "the beauty and poignancy of an atmosphere, of an idea, a person, a moment are caught and put before us without emphasis, without anything which we recognize as theatrical, but with the brightness of the highest art." In keeping with this method, this Collector's Edition seeks to evoke the charm of Chekhov's stories and plays. Including a unique assortment of paintings and photographs from The New York Public Library's collections, this volume invites readers to experience the artistry of Anton Chekhov in the context of some exceptional Russian artworks of his time.

POSTCARD IN ANTON CHEKHOV'S HAND

The same whimsical spirit that suffuses his writing marks Chekhov's correspondence. One of the treasures of The New York Public Library's Slavic and Baltic Division is a charming handwritten postcard to Nikolai Nikolaevich Obolensky. Obolensky (whom Chekhov nicknamed "Stiva" because of the similarity of his last name to that of

Anna Karenina's dissolute brother, Stiva Oblonsky) served as both friend and doctor to Chekhov. In this short epistle, Chekhov takes advantage of being laid up with the flu to write to his friend about having dedicated a new short story to him.

Although a doctor himself, Chekhov displayed a peculiar blindness to the state of his own health. He professed to be unaware of the tuberculosis that killed him at such an early age; he may have hoped to spare his family and friends by not naming the mortal disease, or perhaps needed to shield himself from the threat it implied. In true Chekhovian style, he ends this short note to a fellow physician by cursing influenza and cheering great people, in whose ranks he includes his friend and himself.

PAINTINGS BY ISAAK LEVITAN AND ILIA REPIN

Chekhov was closely acquainted with many important Russian cultural and artistic figures. With none of these was he more intimate than the renowned artist Isaak Ilich Levitan (1861–1900), widely considered the greatest Russian landscape painter of the nineteenth century. Like Chekhov, Levitan overcame a difficult childhood: born into a poor Jewish family and orphaned at an early age, he enrolled in the Moscow School of Painting at thirteen. There he became acquainted with Nikolai Chekhov, the writer's elder brother. Jews, among them Levitan, were forced to move outside the city limits of Moscow in 1879 after the unsuccessful assassination attempt on Tsar Alexander II. Although he was already acclaimed by some of the leading figures in the art world, stress and poverty weighed heavily upon the eighteen-year-old artist. Over the next few years, he frequently required Chekhov's services as a physician, and the two became close friends. They often lived near each other, and during many long visits shared their deepest thoughts.

Levitan, who once proposed to Chekhov's sister, Maria, never married, but had a number of romantic affairs. Chekhov's all-too-accurate depiction of one such liaison in his story "The Grasshopper" led to a bitter estrangement between the two artists in 1892. Three years later, the poet and Chekhov family friend Tatiana Shchepkina-Kupernik effected a joyful reconciliation between the pair.

Levitan and Chekhov shared many attitudes toward life and art, including an abiding love of nature. Chekhov frequently said that when he could no longer write, he would become a gardener. Levitan's tender and elegiac landscapes provide an appropriate complement to his stories. Shortly before Levitan's early death, Chekhov, who was compelled by his own poor health to live in the south, expressed a longing for his native central Russia. Levitan asked for a piece of cardboard and immediately began painting Chekhov's beloved countryside. Thereafter, the work held a place of honor over Chekhov's fireplace.

Ilia Efimovich Repin (1844–1930), a popular painter identified with the Society for Traveling Artists, was another acquaintance of Chekhov's. Interested in representing literary figures, Repin executed a famous portrait of Tolstoy plowing a field, underscoring the affinity of Count Tolstoy—a member of the highest Russian nobility—with the peasantry. Impressed with Chekhov's poignant depiction of country life in "The Peasants," Repin created illustrations for that controversial story. (Tolstoy, however, did not share Repin's enthusiasm for this story, which depicted the Russian peasantry not as salt-of-the-earth, simple folk who enjoyed their poverty and squalor—as Tolstoy viewed them—but rather as bitter and struggling former serfs like Chekhov's own family. Ironically, the count denounced the story as "a sin," adding that the "author doesn't know the common people." The official state censor agreed with Tolstoy, opposing Chekhov's representations of the government's and clergy's role in the peasants' sufferings. Despite his disapproval of this particular story, Tolstoy was a great admirer of Chekhov, and the two met several times. Chekhov liked to tell of his first visit to Tolstoy's estate at Iasnia Poliana, where he arrived just as the great elder of Russian

ОТКРЫТОЕ ПИСЬМО.

3 мсд

Петровка, д. Кабанова

Доктору

Николаю Николаевичу

Оболонскому

от признательной пациентки.

На этой сторонѣ пишется только адресъ.

In this postcard (above and opposite) to his friend and doctor Nikolai Nikolaevich Obolensky, Chekhov proclaims, "To the death of influenza and to the health of great people, in whose numbers are both you and I!"

Influenza, овладевши

всем моим существом, лишает

от меня возможности посетить

Вас и рекомендовать Вам

возможно скорее прочесть 4940

№ Нового Времени (вторник),

где напечатан рассказ, украшен-

ный инициалами Вашего имени.

Да погибнет influenza и да здрав-

ствуют великие люди, в том числе

и мы с Вами! А в каком положении

Ваша любовь?

А. Ч.

"Birch Grove" by the great Russian landscape painter Isaak Levitan, a close friend of Chekhov's.

literature was heading to the lake for a bath. He invited Chekhov to join him, and thus, at their first encounter, both writers were naked and up to their necks in water.)

Additional paintings by Repin, in which he characteristically drew upon both contemporary figures and his Cossack background to portray Russian life in his time and Chekhov's, lend the unique flavor of his quintessentially Russian art to this edition.

VLADIMIR NABOKOV'S LECTURE NOTES ON CHEKHOV

The idiosyncratic author and flamboyant literature professor Vladimir Nabokov taught a survey course on Russian literature in translation at each of the three colleges—Stanford University, Wellesley College, and Cornell University—with which he was associated after his arrival in the United States in 1940, giving up teaching only when the success of *Lolita* in 1958 allowed him to devote himself to writing. In planning for this course, he drafted one hundred lectures on Russian literature, or about 2,000 pages, between the time of his immigration and his first class at Stanford in the summer of 1941. Interestingly, despite his abundant preparations, the lecture notes on Chekhov, as well as those on Tolstoy's *The Death of Ivan Ilich*, are less complete than usual for Nabokov. The editor of the lectures, Fredson Bowers, suggests that because of his great familiarity with Chekhov's stories, Nabokov may have felt comfortable extemporizing his presentations.

Nabokov held Chekhov's work in great esteem, even mentioning that a person's appreciation for Chekhov can be a reliable litmus test for his or her worth as a friend. As Bowers points out, "He is tireless in illustrating how Chekhov made the ordinary seem of supreme value to the reader." In a typically playful comment, Nabokov stated, "Chekhov's books are sad books for humorous people; that is, only a reader with a sense of humor can really appreciate their sadness."

Chukovski. -- Friend Chekhov (Atlantic Monthly)

Chekhov .... enjoyed practical jokes, masquerading, and *all this*
buffoonery. He wuld ~~throw a~~ *once he is said to have handed a* heavy round watermelon wrapped up in a
thick paper ~~into the hands~~ of a *To* Moscow policeman and confided to
him in a worried manner: "Bomb! Take into the police station --
be careful!" etc. ~~One his practical joke~~ *~~Burton at Yalta~~*

Without this phenomenal sociability of his; without his
constant readiness to hobnob with anyone at all, to sing with
singers and to get drunk with drunkards; without that burning
interest in the lives, habits, conversations, and occupations of
hundreds and thousands of people, he would *hardly* ~~certainly never~~ have
been able to create that colossal, encyclopedically detailed
Russian world of the 1880's and 1890's which goes by the name
of Chekhov's <u>Short Stories</u>.

In his lecture notes, Vladimir Nabokov speaks of Chekhov's "burning interest in the lives, habits, conversations, and occupations of hundreds and thousands of people."

right temperament is there, — but he does not mind ~~mind them~~ because his temperament is quite foreign to ~~creative~~ verbal inventiveness. Even a bit of bad grammar or a slack newspaper ~~cliché~~ sentence - left him less concerned, than for instance Conrad was, when ~~au dire de according~~ to Ford Madox Ford, he tried to find a word of two syllables and a half - not merely two syllables and not merely three, but exactly two and a half - which (was absolutely ~~- and~~ he said he was purposely sought. - but was the nature of his talent necessary to end a certain description. Chekhov would have ended ~~it~~ with an "oo" or an "or" - and never have noticed it his ending — the magical part of it is that inspite of his tolerating flaws ~~that~~ a which beginner would have avoided, inspite of his being quite ~~content~~ satisfying with the word in the street, ~~I mean~~ the man in the street among words, Chekhov managed to convey an impression of artistic beauty far surpassing that of ~~Cæsar~~ many who thought they knew what rich beautiful writing is. He did it by keeping all his words of the same exact tint of grey, ~~rather old double~~ a tint between the colors of an old fence and a ~~delicate~~ that of a low cloud, ~~a~~ The variety of his moods, the ~~em~~ flicker of his charming wit, the deeply artistic economy of characterisation, the vivid details and the fade-out of human ~~sadness~~ life - all the peculiar Chekovian features are enhanced by being ~~of~~ suffused and surrounded by a verbal ~~dimness~~ haziness ~~which his~~ personality ~~explained the use of a form of alchemy~~ His quiet and subtle humor pervade the grayness of the lives he creates. For the Russian philosophical or social minded critic he was the unique exponent of a unique Russian type of character. It is rather difficult to explain what that type was or is, because it is all so linked up with the general psychological and social history of the Russian 19th century. It is not quite exact to say that Chekhov dealt in charming

Nabokov told his students, "Chekhov managed to convey an impression of artistic beauty far surpassing that of many writers who thought they knew what rich, beautiful prose was."

Honoring the stories, he advised his students, "I heartily recommend taking as often as possible Chekhov's books . . . and dreaming through them as they are intended to be dreamed through."

RANDALL JARRELL'S MANUSCRIPT NOTES FOR A TRANSLATION OF *THE THREE SISTERS*

The eminent American poet and critic Randall Jarrell was just one of the many authors compelled by the power of Chekhov's drama to undertake a translation of *The Three Sisters*. The manuscript of Jarrell's attempt is in The New York Public Library's special collections. His papers relating to this work suggest the tremendous amount of feeling, thought, and art that go into a successful translation. To prepare for the task of putting English words into the mouths of Chekhov's Russian characters, he composed character sketches for many of the play's personae. This Collector's Edition reproduces Jarrell's penetrating analysis of Olga, the eldest and quietest of the sisters, who relinquishes her dreams in order to care for someone else.

PHOTOGRAPHS OF CHEKHOV AND HIS FAMILY

Throughout his life, Chekhov remained extremely close to his family. Despite the early tyrannical treatment he received from his father, he chose to understand, if not excuse, his father's abuse by seeing it as a legacy of the slavery he had barely escaped. He was also quite devoted to his mother, who he feared was greatly dispirited by Pavel Chekhov's bankruptcy and the family's miserable living conditions in Moscow. While staying on his own in Taganrog to finish his studies, Chekhov asked his cousin Misha to console his "physically and morally crushed" mother, adding that in "this archmalicious world there is nothing dearer to us than our mother, and therefore you will much oblige your humble servant by comforting his half-moribund mother."

Perhaps another reason for Chekhov's attachment to his family lay in their near-complete dependence upon him from an early age. When he joined the family in Moscow at age nineteen, he brought with him two boarders to help supplement the family income, moved the family from its damp and dismal basement apartment to more livable quarters (though still located in a poverty-ridden red-light district), and assumed the responsibility for financing the education of his two younger brothers and sister, none of whom were enrolled in school because the family could not afford the registration fees. He and his sister, Maria (affectionately known as Masha), remained devoted to each other, and lived together with their parents until Chekhov's death. The photographs in this volume—of Chekhov, his mother and sister—offer the reader a glimpse not only of the writer but also of the beloved relations whose needs first led him into a literary career.

ARCHIVES FROM THE MOSCOW ART THEATER

To commemorate the debut performance of *The Three Sisters*, Nikolai Efros, a Russian theater critic and contemporary of the author, gathered an album of photographs and other theatrical memorabilia. Including publicity stills, reminiscences, and even a letter in Chekhov's hand, this extraordinary album brings together a unique assortment of materials related to the most famous production of the play. A number of items from Efros's collection, including cast photographs (some with Chekhov's wife, Olga Knipper, who played the role of Masha) and a portrait of the playwright, grace this edition of Chekhov's works.

The photographs in this album, held in the Library's Slavic and

Chekhov's devoted sister, Maria, a schoolteacher who kept house for the author until his untimely death.

Ivan, one of Chekhov's brothers. The brilliance of Chekhov's successes often eclipsed the achievements of other members of his family.

XXXVIII ♦ ABOUT THIS EDITION

Baltic Division, and an unusual set of photostatic negatives (not reproduced here) from the Moscow Art Theater productions of Chekhov's plays (including *The Three Sisters*) held in the Billy Rose Theatre Collection, provide fascinating visual documentation of the play as it was produced during Chekhov's own time. The costumes and sets take us right into the home—thus, the very world—that each sister finds so stifling. And by studying the expressive faces of the original Russian cast members, many of whom Chekhov presumably had in mind while writing the play, we glean a whole set of clues to aid in understanding his sensitive, despairing characters.

THE TITLE OF THIS ANTHOLOGY

In deciding upon a name for this volume, we deferred to Chekhov himself, who explained in a letter the difficulties he had in titling his second volume of stories:

> By the way, we tried to find . . . a name for my book. We tried hard, but could not hit on anything better than "Cats and Pikes," or "Flowers and Dogs." I considered a name, "Buy this book, to get a wallop in the jaw," or "Step in; what will you have?" but the poet [Liodor Ivanovich Palmin, also a humorist] found these titles hackneyed and commonplace . . . As far as I am concerned, I think all titles that have a grammatically collective meaning, stupid and cheap. I should prefer one that [Nikolai Aleksandrovich] Leikin [another writer] suggests, namely, "A. Chekhonte. Stories and Tales"; nothing more, although such titles are fit for celebrities and are not for such as I.

After thus struggling, Chekhov finally settled upon a title that pleased him, "Motley Tales," and the anthology was so named. This Collector's Edition takes his idea one step further, adding a play to a collection of short stories.

A NOTE ON THE TRANSLATIONS

Over the years, numerous artists have been enticed by the beauty and elegance of Chekhov's prose to undertake translations of his fiction and plays, and thus there existed an exceptional pool of translations from which to select the contents of this edition. Clearly, Chekhov's works continue to exert a powerful influence on talented poets and translators.

The short stories presented here are the works of the British translator Constance Garnett (1862–1946), a literary powerhouse who translated many of the greatest masterpieces of nineteenth-century Russian literature, including the most important novels of Tolstoy and Dostoevsky, as well as a thirteen-volume collection of Chekhov's short stories, two volumes of his plays, and a selection of his letters. Garnett's renditions of Chekhov's fiction required the dedication of many years of her life; she produced approximately two volumes of stories per year, which included all those stories that Chekhov considered worth republishing during his lifetime. The resulting versions of Chekhov's masterpieces show her labor of love to have been well worth the effort. In Garnett's translations, we still find the closest English renderings of Chekhov's colloquial and subdued language, giving the English-speaking reader a genuine sense of his artistry.

The list of American, English, and Irish writers who have devoted themselves to the task of bringing *The Three Sisters* to an English-speaking audience boasts some major names in the literary world, including Randall Jarrell, Lanford Wilson, Jean-Claude van Itallie, Frank McGuinness, and Brian Friel. The translation chosen for this edition is the work of contemporary American playwright David Mamet (1947–), who is considered by some to have the finest ear for dialogue in drama today. Working from a literal translation by Vlada Chernomordik, Mamet has brilliantly rendered Chekhov's drama in vivid and dynamic language that is sure to delight.

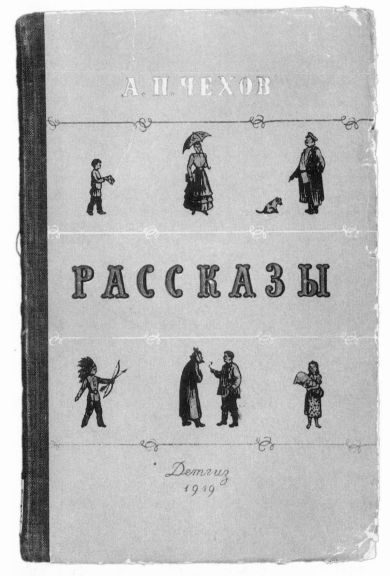

The whimsical cover of a 1949 Soviet edition of Chekhov's short stories.

MOTLEY TALES

THE STUDENT

At first the weather was fine and still. The thrushes were calling, and in the swamps close by something alive droned pitifully with a sound like blowing into an empty bottle. A snipe flew by, and the shot aimed at it rang out with a gay, resounding note in the spring air. But when it began to get dark in the forest a cold, penetrating wind blew inappropriately from the east, and everything sank into silence. Needles of ice stretched across the pools, and it felt cheerless, remote, and lonely in the forest. There was a whiff of winter.

Ivan Velikopolsky, the son of a sacristan, and a student of the clerical academy, returning home from shooting, kept walking on the path by the waterlogged meadows. His fingers were numb and his face was burning with the wind. It seemed to him that the cold that had suddenly come on had destroyed the order and harmony of things, that nature itself felt ill at ease, and that was why the evening darkness was falling more rapidly than usual. All around it was deserted and peculiarly gloomy. The only light was one gleaming in the widows' gardens near the river; the village, over three miles away, and everything in the distance all round, was plunged in the cold evening mist. The student remembered that, as he had left the house, his mother was sitting barefoot on the floor in the entryway, cleaning the samovar, while his father lay on the stove coughing; as it was Good Friday nothing had been cooked, and the student was terribly hungry. And now, shrinking from the cold, he thought that just such a wind had blown in the days of Rurik and in the time of Ivan the Terrible and Peter, and in their time there had been just the same desperate poverty and hunger, the same thatched roofs with holes in them, ignorance, misery, the same desolation around, the same darkness, the same feeling of oppression—all these had existed, did exist, and would exist, and the lapse of a thousand years would make life no better. And he did not want to go home.

The gardens were called the widows' because they were kept by two widows, mother and daughter. A campfire was burning brightly with a crackling sound, throwing out light far around on the ploughed earth. The widow Vasilisa, a tall, fat old woman in a man's coat, was standing by and looking thoughtfully into the fire; her daughter Lukerya, a little pockmarked woman with a stupid-looking face, was sitting on the ground, washing a cauldron and spoons. Apparently they had just had supper. There was a sound of men's voices; it was the laborers watering their horses at the river.

"Here you have winter back again," said the student, going up to the campfire. "Good evening."

Vasilisa started, but at once recognized him and smiled cordially.

"I did not know you; God bless you," she said. "You'll be rich."

They talked. Vasilisa, a woman of experience who had been in service with the gentry, first as a wet nurse, afterward as a children's nurse, expressed herself with refinement, and a soft, sedate smile never left her face; her daughter Lukerya, a village peasant woman who had been crushed by her husband, simply screwed up her eyes at the student and said nothing, and she had a strange expression like that of a deaf-mute.

"At just such a fire the Apostle Peter warmed himself," said the student, stretching out his hands to the fire, "so it must have been cold then, too. Ah, what a terrible night it must have been, granny! An utterly dismal long night!"

He looked round at the darkness, shook his head abruptly, and asked:

"No doubt you have heard the reading of the Twelve Apostles?"

"Yes, I have," answered Vasilisa.

"If you remember, at the Last Supper Peter said to Jesus, 'I am ready to go with Thee into darkness and unto death.' And our Lord answered him thus: 'I say unto thee, Peter, before the cock croweth thou wilt have denied Me thrice.' After the supper Jesus went through the agony of death in the garden and prayed, and poor Peter was weary in spirit and faint, his eyelids were heavy and he could not struggle against sleep. He fell asleep. Then you heard how Judas the same night kissed Jesus and betrayed Him to His tormentors. They took Him bound to the high priest and beat Him, while Peter, exhausted, worn out with misery and alarm, hardly awake, you know, feeling that something awful was just going to happen on earth, followed behind. . . . He loved Jesus passionately, intensely, and now he saw from far off how He was beaten. . . ."

Lukerya left the spoons and fixed an immovable stare upon the student.

"They came to the high priest's," he went on; "they began to question Jesus, and meantime the laborers made a fire in the yard as it was cold, and warmed themselves. Peter, too, stood with them near the fire and warmed himself as I am doing. A woman, seeing him, said: 'He was with Jesus, too'—that is as much as to say that he, too, should be taken to be questioned. And all the laborers that were standing near the fire must have looked sourly and suspiciously at him, because he was confused and said: 'I don't know Him.' A little while after, again someone recognized him as one of Jesus' disciples and said: 'Thou, too, art one of them,' but again he denied it. And for the third time someone turned to him: 'Why, did I not see thee with Him in the garden today?' For the third time he denied it. And immediately after that time the cock crowed, and Peter, looking from afar off at Jesus, remembered the words He had said to him in the evening. . . . He remembered, he came to himself, went out of the yard and wept bitterly—bitterly. In the Gospel it is written: 'He went out and wept bitterly.' I imagine it: the still, still, dark, dark garden, and in the stillness, faintly audible, smothered sobbing. . . ."

The student sighed and sank into thought. Still smiling, Vasilisa suddenly gave a gulp, big tears flowed freely down her cheeks, and she screened her face from the fire with her sleeve as though ashamed of her tears, and Lukerya, staring immovably at the student, flushed crimson, and her expression became strained and heavy like that of someone enduring intense pain.

The laborers came back from the river, and one of them riding a horse was quite near, and the light from the fire quivered upon him. The student said good night to the widows and went on. And again the darkness was about him and his fingers began to be numb. A cruel wind was blowing, winter really had come back, and it did not feel as though Easter would be the day after tomorrow.

Now the student was thinking about Vasilisa: since she had shed tears, all that had happened to Peter the night before the Crucifixion must have some relation to her. . . .

He looked round. The solitary light was still gleaming in the darkness and no figures could be seen near it now. The student thought again that if Vasilisa had shed tears, and her daughter had been troubled, it was evident that what he had just been telling them about, which had happened nineteen centuries ago, had a relation to the present—to both women, to the desolate village, to himself, to all people. The old woman had wept, not because he could tell the story touchingly, but because Peter was near to her, because her whole being was interested in what was passing in Peter's soul.

And joy suddenly stirred in his soul, and he even stopped for a minute to take breath. "The past," he thought, "is linked with the present by an unbroken chain of events flowing one out of another."

And it seemed to him that he had just seen both ends of that chain; that when he touched one end the other quivered.

When he crossed the river by the ferryboat, and afterward, mounting the hill, looked at his village and toward the west where the cold purple sunset lay a narrow streak of light, he thought that truth and beauty, which had guided human life there in the garden and in the yard of the high priest, had continued without interruption to this day, and had evidently always been the chief thing in human life and in all earthly life, indeed; and the feeling of youth, health, vigor—he was only twenty-two—and the inexpressible sweet expectation of happiness, of unknown mysterious happiness, took possession of him little by little, and life seemed to him enchanting, marvelous, and full of lofty meaning.

1894

ANNA ON THE NECK

I

After the wedding they did not even have light refreshments; the happy pair simply drank a glass of champagne, changed into their traveling things, and drove to the station. Instead of a gay wedding ball and supper, instead of music and dancing, they went on a journey to pray at a shrine a hundred and fifty miles away. Many people commended this, saying that Modest Alekseich was a man high up in the service and no longer young, and that a noisy wedding might not have seemed quite suitable; and music is apt to sound dreary when a government official of fifty-two marries a girl who is only just eighteen. People said, too, that Modest Alekseich, being a man of principle, had arranged this visit to the monastery expressly in order to make his young bride realize that even in marriage he put religion and morality above everything.

The happy pair were seen off at the station. The crowd of relations and colleagues in the service stood, with glasses in their hands, waiting for the train to start to shout "Hurrah!" and the bride's father, Pyotr Leontich, wearing a top hat and the uniform of a teacher, already drunk and very pale, kept craning toward the window, glass in hand, and saying in an imploring voice:

"Anyuta! Anya, Anya! one word!"

Anna bent out of the window to him, and he whispered something to her, enveloping her in a stale smell of alcohol, blew into her ear—she could make out nothing—and made the sign of the cross over her face, her bosom, and her hands; meanwhile he was breathing in gasps and tears were shining in his eyes. And the schoolboys, Anna's brothers, Petya and Andrusha, pulled at his coat from behind, whispering in confusion:

"Father, hush! . . . Father, that's enough. . . ."

When the train started, Anna saw her father run a little way after the train, staggering and spilling his wine, and what a kind, guilty, pitiful face he had:

"Hurra—ah!" he shouted.

The happy pair were left alone. Modest Alekseich looked about the compartment, arranged their things on the shelves, and sat down, smiling, opposite his young wife. He was an official of medium height, rather stout and puffy, who looked exceedingly well nourished, with long whiskers and no mustache. His cleanshaven, round, sharply defined chin looked like the heel of a foot. The most characteristic point in his face was the absence of mustache, the bare, freshly shaven place, which gradually passed into the fat cheeks, quivering like jelly. His deportment was dignified, his movements were deliberate, his manner was soft.

"I cannot help remembering now one circumstance," he said, smiling. "When, five years ago, Kosorotov received the order of St. Anna of the second grade, and went to thank His Excellency, His Excellency expressed himself as follows: 'So now you have three Annas: one in your buttonhole and two on your neck.' And it must be explained that at that time Kosorotov's wife, a quarrelsome and frivolous person, had just returned to him, and that her name was Anna. I trust that when I receive the Anna of the second grade His Excellency will not have occasion to say the same thing to me."

He smiled with his little eyes. And she, too, smiled, troubled at the thought that at any moment this man might kiss her with his thick damp lips, and that she had no right to prevent his doing so.

The soft movements of his fat person frightened her; she felt both fear and disgust. He got up, without haste took the order off his neck, took off his coat and waistcoat, and put on his dressing gown.

"That's better," he said, sitting down beside Anna.

Anna remembered what agony the wedding had been, when it had seemed to her that the priest, and the guests, and everyone in church had been looking at her sorrowfully and asking why, why was she, such a sweet, nice girl, marrying such an elderly, uninteresting gentleman. Only that morning she was delighted that everything had been satisfactorily arranged, but at the time of the wedding, and now in the railway carriage, she felt cheated, guilty, and ridiculous. Here she had married a rich man and yet she had no money, her wedding dress had been bought on credit, and when her father and brothers had been saying goodbye, she could see from their faces that they had not a penny. Would they have any supper that day? And tomorrow? And for some reason it seemed to her that her father and the boys were sitting tonight hungry without her, and feeling the same misery as they had the day after their mother's funeral.

"Oh, how unhappy I am!" she thought. "Why am I so unhappy?"

With the awkwardness of a man with settled habits, unaccustomed to dealing with women, Modest Alekseich touched her on the waist and patted her on the shoulder, while she went on thinking about money, about her mother and her mother's death. When her mother died, her father, Pyotr Leontich, a teacher of drawing and writing at the high school, had taken to drink; impoverishment had followed, the boys had not had boots or galoshes, their father had been hauled up before the magistrate, the warrant officer had come and made an inventory of the furniture. . . . What a disgrace! Anna had had to look after her drunken father, darn her brothers' stockings, go to market, and when she was complimented on her youth, her beauty, and her elegant manners, it seemed to her that everyone was looking at her cheap hat and the holes in her boots that were inked over. And at night there had been tears and a haunting dread that her father would soon, very soon, be dismissed from the school for his weakness, and that he would not survive it, but would die, too, like their mother. But ladies of their acquaintance had taken the matter in hand and looked about for a good match for Anna. This Modest Alekseich, who was neither young nor good-looking but had money, was soon found. He had a hundred thousand in the bank and the family estate, which he had rented out. He was a man of principle and stood well with His Excellency; it would be nothing to him, so they told Anna, to get a note from His Excellency to the directors of the high school, or even to the Education Commissioner, to prevent Pyotr Leontich from being dismissed.

While she was recalling these details, she suddenly heard strains of music which floated in at the window, together with the sound of voices. The train was stopping at a station. In the crowd beyond the platform an accordion and a cheap squeaky fiddle were being briskly played, and the sound of a military band came from beyond the villas and the tall birches and poplars that lay bathed in the moonlight; there must have been a dance in the place. Summer visitors and townspeople, who used to come out here by train in fine weather for a breath of fresh air, were parading up and down on the platform. Among them was the wealthy owner of all the summer villas—a tall, stout, dark man called Artynov. He had prominent eyes and looked like an Armenian. He wore a strange costume; his shirt was unbuttoned, showing his chest; he wore high boots with spurs, and a black cloak hung from his shoulders and dragged on the ground like a train. Two boar-hounds followed him with their sharp noses to the ground.

Tears were still shining in Anna's eyes, but she was not thinking now of her mother, nor of money, nor of her marriage; but shaking hands with schoolboys and officers she knew, she laughed gaily and said quickly:

"How do you do? How are you?"

She went out onto the platform between the carriages into the moonlight, and stood so that they could all see her in her new splendid dress and hat.

"Why are we stopping here?" she asked.

"This is a junction. They are waiting for the mail train to pass."

Seeing that Artynov was looking at her, she screwed up her eyes coquettishly and began talking aloud in French; and because her voice sounded so pleasant, and because she heard music and the moon was reflected in the pond, and because Artynov, the notorious Don Juan and spoiled child of fortune, was looking at her eagerly and with curiosity, and because everyone was in good spirits—she suddenly felt joyful, and when the train started and the officers of her acquaintance saluted her, she was humming the polka, the strains of which reached her from the military band playing beyond the trees; and she returned to her compartment feeling as though it had been proved to her at the station that she would certainly be happy in spite of everything.

The happy pair spent two days at the monastery, then went back to town. They lived in a rent-free apartment. When Modest Alekseich had gone to the office, Anna played the piano, or shed tears of depression, or lay down on a couch and read novels or looked through fashion papers. At dinner Modest Alekseich ate a great deal and talked about politics, about appointments, transfers, and promotions in the service, about the necessity of hard work, and said that, family life not being a pleasure but a duty, if you took care of the kopeks the rubles would take care of themselves, and that he put religion and morality before everything else in the world. And holding his knife in his fist as though it were a sword, he would say:

"Everyone ought to have his duties!"

And Anna listened to him, was frightened, and could not eat, and she usually got up from the table hungry. After dinner her husband lay down for a nap and snored loudly, while Anna went to see her own family. Her father and the boys looked at her in a peculiar way, as though just before she came in they had been blaming her for having married for money a tedious, wearisome man she did not love; her rustling skirts, her bracelets, and her general air of a married lady offended them and made them uncomfortable. In her presence they felt a little embarrassed and did not know what to talk to her about; but yet they still loved her as before, and were not used to having dinner without her. She sat down with them to cabbage soup, porridge, and fried potatoes, smelling of mutton dripping. Pyotr Leontich filled his glass from the decanter with a trembling hand and drank it off hurriedly, greedily, with repulsion, then poured out a second glass and then a third. Petya and Andrusha, thin, pale boys with big eyes, would take the decanter and say desperately:

"You mustn't, father. . . . Enough, father. . . ."

And Anna, too, was troubled and entreated him to drink no more; and he would suddenly fly into a rage and beat the table with his fists:

"I won't allow anyone to dictate to me!" he would shout. "Wretched boys! wretched girl! I'll turn you all out!"

But there was a note of weakness, of good nature in his voice, and no one was afraid of him. After dinner he usually dressed in his best. Pale, with a cut on his chin from shaving, craning his thin neck, he would stand for half an hour before the glass, prinking, combing his hair, twisting his black mustache, sprinkling himself with scent, tying his cravat in a bow; then he would put on his gloves and his top hat, and go off to give his private lessons. Or if it was a holiday he would stay at home and paint, or play the harmonium, which wheezed and growled; he would try to wrest from it pure, harmonious sounds and would sing to it; or would storm at the boys:

"Wretches! Good-for-nothing boys! You have spoiled the instrument!"

In the evening Anna's husband played cards with his colleagues, who lived under the same roof in the government quarters. The wives of these gentlemen would come in—ugly, tastelessly dressed women, as coarse as cooks—and in the apartment gossip would begin, as tasteless and unattractive as the ladies themselves. Sometimes Modest Alekseich would take Anna to the theater. In the intermissions he would never let her stir a step from his side, but walked about arm in arm with her through the corridors and the foyer. When he bowed to someone, he immediately whispered to Anna: "A civil councilor . . . visits at His Excellency's," or "A man of means . . . has a house of his own." When they passed the buffet Anna had a great longing for something sweet; she was fond of chocolate and apple cakes, but she had no money, and she did not like to ask her husband. He would take a pear, pinch it with his fingers, and ask uncertainly:

"How much?"

"Twenty-five kopeks!"

"I say!" he would reply, and put it down; but as it was awkward to leave the buffet without buying anything, he would order some seltzer water and drink the whole bottle himself, and tears would come into his eyes. And Anna hated him at such times.

And, suddenly flushing crimson, he would say to her rapidly:

"Bow to that old lady!"

"But I don't know her."

"No matter. That's the wife of the director of the local treasury! Bow, I tell you," he would grumble insistently. "Your head won't drop off."

Anna bowed, and her head certainly did not drop off, but it was agonizing. She did everything her husband wanted her to, and was furious with herself for having let him deceive her like the merest idiot. She had married him only for his money, and yet she had less money now than before her marriage. In the old days her father would sometimes give her twenty kopeks, but now she had not a farthing. To take money by stealth or ask for it, she could not; she was afraid of her husband, she trembled before him. She felt as though she had been afraid of him for years. In her childhood the director of the high school had always seemed the most impressive and terrifying force in the world, sweeping down like a thunderstorm or a steam engine ready to crush her; another similar force of which the whole family talked, and of which they were for some reason afraid, was His Excellency; then there were a dozen others, less formidable, and among them the teachers at the high school, with shaven upper lips, stern, implacable; and now finally, there was Modest Alekseich, a man of principle, who even resembled the director in the face. And in Anna's imagination all these forces blended together into one, and, in the form of a terrible, huge white bear, menaced the weak and erring such as her father. And she was afraid to say anything in opposition to her husband, and gave a forced smile, and tried to make a show of pleasure when she was coarsely caressed and defiled by embraces that terrified her.

Only once Pyotr Leontich had the temerity to ask for a loan of fifty rubles in order to pay some very irksome debt, but what an agony it had been!

"Very good; I'll give it to you," said Modest Alekseich after a moment's thought; "but I warn you I won't help you again till you give up drinking. Such a failing is disgraceful in a man in the government service! I must remind you of the well-known fact that many capable people have been ruined by that passion, though they might possibly, with temperance, have risen in time to a very high position."

And long-winded phrases followed: "inasmuch as . . ." "following upon which proposition . . ." "in view of the aforesaid contention . . ."; and Pyotr Leontich was in agonies of humiliation and felt an intense craving for alcohol.

And when the boys came to visit Anna, generally in broken boots and threadbare trousers, they, too, had to listen to sermons.

"Every man ought to have his duties!" Modest Alekseich would say to them.

And he did not give them money. But he did give Anna bracelets, rings, and brooches, saying that these things would come in useful for a rainy day. And he often unlocked her drawer and made an inspection to see whether they were all safe.

II

Meanwhile winter came on. Long before Christmas there was an announcement in the local papers that the usual winter ball would take place on the twenty-ninth of December in the Hall of Nobility. Every evening after cards Modest Alekseich was excitedly whispering with his colleagues' wives and glancing at Anna, and then paced up and down the room for a long while, thinking. At last, late one evening, he stood still, facing Anna, and said:

"You ought to get yourself a ball dress. Do you understand? Only please consult Marya Grigoryevna and Natalya Kuzminishna."

And he gave her a hundred rubles. She took the money, but she did not consult anyone when she ordered the ball dress; she spoke to no one but her father, and tried to imagine how her mother would have dressed for a ball. Her mother had always dressed in the latest fashion and had always taken trouble over Anna, dressing her elegantly like a doll, and had taught her to speak French and dance the mazurka superbly (she had been a governess for five years before her marriage). Like her mother, Anna could make a new dress out of an old one, clean gloves with benzine, rent jewels; and, like her mother, she knew how to screw up her eyes, lisp, assume graceful attitudes, fly into raptures when necessary, and throw a mournful and enigmatic look into her eyes. And from her father she had inherited the dark color of her hair and eyes, her highly strung nerves, and the habit of always making herself look her best.

When, half an hour before setting off for the ball, Modest Alekseich went into her room without his coat on, to put his order round his neck before her mirror, dazzled by her beauty and the splendor of her fresh, ethereal dress, he combed his whiskers complacently and said:

"So that's what my wife can look like . . . so that's what you can look like! Anyuta!" he went on, dropping into a tone of solemnity, "I have made your fortune, and now I beg you to do something for mine. I beg you to get introduced to the wife of His Excellency!

For God's sake, do! Through her I may get the post of senior reporting clerk!"

They went to the ball. They reached the Hall of Nobility, the entrance with the hall porter. They came to the vestibule with the hat stands, the fur coats; footmen scurrying about, and ladies with low necklines putting up their fans to screen themselves from the drafts. There was a smell of gas and of soldiers. When Anna, walking upstairs on her husband's arm, heard the music and saw herself full length in the looking glass in the full glow of the lights, there was a rush of joy in her heart, and she felt the same presentiment of happiness as in the moonlight at the station. She walked in proudly, confidently, for the first time feeling herself not a girl but a lady, and unconsciously imitating her mother in her walk and in her manner. And for the first time in her life she felt rich and free. Even her husband's presence did not oppress her, for as she crossed the threshold of the hall she had guessed instinctively that the proximity of an old husband did not detract from her in the least, but, on the contrary, gave her that shade of piquant mystery that is so attractive to men. The orchestra was already playing and the dances had begun. After their flat Anna was overwhelmed by the lights, the bright colors, the music, the noise, and looking round the room, thought, "Oh, how lovely!" She at once distinguished in the crowd all her acquaintances, everyone she had met before at parties or on picnics— all the officers, the teachers, the lawyers, the officials, the landowners, His Excellency, Artynov, and the ladies of the highest standing, dressed up and very *décolletées*, handsome and ugly, who had already taken up their positions in the stalls and pavilions of the charity bazaar, to begin selling things for the benefit of the poor. A huge officer in epaulettes—she had been introduced to him in Staro-Kievsky Street when she was a schoolgirl, but now she could not remember his name—seemed to spring from out of the ground, begging her for a waltz, and she flew away from her husband, feeling as though she were floating away in a sailing boat in a violent storm, while her husband was left far away on the shore. She danced passionately, with fervor, a waltz, then a polka and a quadrille, being snatched by one partner as soon as she was left by another, dizzy with music and the noise, mixing Russian with French, lisping, laughing, and with no thought of her husband or anything else. She excited great admiration among the men—that was evident, and indeed it could not have been otherwise; she was breathless with excitement, felt thirsty, and convulsively clutched her fan. Pyotr Leontich, her father, in a crumpled dress coat that smelled of benzine, came up to her, offering her a plate of pink ices.

"You are enchanting this evening," he said, looking at her rapturously, "and I have never so much regretted that you were in such a hurry to get married. . . . What was it for? I know you did it for our sake, but . . ." With a shaking hand he drew out a roll of notes and said: "I got the money for my lessons today, and can pay your husband what I owe him."

She put the plate back into his hand, and was pounced upon by someone and borne off to a distance. She caught a glimpse over her partner's shoulder of her father gliding over the floor, putting his arm round a lady and whirling down the ballroom with her.

"How sweet he is when he is sober!" she thought.

She danced the mazurka with the same huge officer; he moved gravely, as heavily as a dead carcass in a uniform, twitched his shoulders and his chest, stamped his feet very languidly—he felt fearfully disinclined to dance. She fluttered round him, provoking him by her beauty, her bare neck; her eyes glowed defiantly, her movements were passionate, while he became more and more indifferent, and held out his hands to her as graciously as a king.

"Bravo, bravo!" said people watching them.

But little by little the huge officer, too, broke out; he grew lively, excited, and, overcome by her fascination, was carried away and danced lightly, youthfully, while she merely moved her shoulders and looked slyly at him as though she were now the queen and he were her slave; and at that moment it seemed to her that the whole room was looking at them, and that everybody was thrilled and envied them. The huge officer had hardly had time to thank her for the dance, when the crowd suddenly parted and the men drew themselves up in a strange way, with their hands at their sides. His Excellency, with two stars on his dress coat, was walking up to her. Yes, His Excellency was walking straight toward her, for he was staring directly at her with a sugary smile, while he licked his lips as he always did when he saw a pretty woman.

"Delighted, delighted . . ." he began. "I shall order your husband to be clapped in a lockup for keeping such a treasure hidden from us till now. I've come to you with a message from my wife," he went on, offering her his arm. "You must help us. . . . M-m-yes. . . . We ought to give you the prize for beauty as they do in America. . . . M-m-yes. . . . The Americans. . . . My wife is expecting you impatiently."

He led her to a stall and presented her to a middle-aged lady, the lower part of whose face was disproportionately large, so that she looked as though she were holding a big stone in her mouth.

"You must help us," she said through her nose in a singsong voice. "All the pretty women are working for our charity bazaar, and you are the only one enjoying yourself. Why won't you help us?"

She went away, and Anna took her place by the cups and the silver samovar. She was soon doing a lively trade. Anna asked no less than a ruble for a cup of tea, and made the huge officer drink three cups. Artynov, the rich man with prominent eyes, who suffered from asthma, came up, too; he was not dressed in the strange costume in which Anna had seen him in the summer at the station, but wore a dress coat like everyone else. Keeping his eyes fixed on Anna, he drank a glass of champagne and paid a hundred rubles for it, then drank some tea and gave another hundred—all this without saying a word, as he was short of breath because of asthma. . . . Anna invited purchasers and got money out of them, firmly convinced by now that her smiles and glances could not fail to afford these people great pleasure. She realized now that she was created exclusively for this noisy, brilliant, laughing life, with its music, its dancers, its adorers, and her old terror of a force that was sweeping down upon her and menacing to crush her seemed to her ridiculous: she was afraid of no one now, and regretted only that her mother could not be there to rejoice at her success.

Pyotr Leontich, pale by now but still steady on his legs, came up to the stall and asked for a glass of brandy. Anna turned crimson, expecting him to say something inappropriate (she was already ashamed of having such a poor and ordinary father); but he emptied his glass, took ten rubles out of his roll of notes, flung it down, and walked away with dignity without uttering a word. A little later she saw him dancing in the grand chain, and by now he was staggering and kept shouting something, to the great confusion of his partner; and Anna remembered how at the ball three years before he had staggered and shouted in the same way, and it had ended in the police sergeant's taking him home to bed, and next day the director had threatened to dismiss him from his post. How inappropriate that memory was!

When the samovars were put out in the stalls and the exhausted ladies handed over their takings to the middle-aged lady with the stone in her mouth, Artynov took Anna on his arm to the hall where supper was served to all who had assisted at the bazaar. There were some twenty people at supper, not more, but it was very noisy. His Excellency proposed a toast:

"In this magnificent dining room it will be appropriate to drink to the success of the cheap dining rooms, which are the object of today's bazaar."

The brigadier general proposed the toast: "To the power by which even the artillery is vanquished," and all the company clinked glasses with the ladies. It was very, very gay.

When Anna was escorted home it was daylight and the cooks were going to market. Joyful, intoxicated, full of new sensations, exhausted, she undressed, dropped into bed, and at once fell asleep. . . .

It was past one in the afternoon when the servant waked her and announced that M. Artynov had called. She dressed quickly and went down into the drawing room. Soon after Artynov, His Excellency called to thank her for her assistance in the bazaar. With a sugary smile, chewing his lips, he kissed her hand, and asking her permission to come again, took his leave, while she remained standing in the middle of the drawing room, amazed, enchanted, unable to believe that this change in her life, this marvelous change, had taken place so quickly; and at that moment Modest Alekseich walked in . . . and he, too, stood before her now with the same ingratiating, sugary, cringingly respectful expression which she was accustomed to see on his face in the presence of the great and powerful; and with rapture, with indignation, with contempt, convinced that no harm would come to her from it, she said, articulating distinctly each word:

"Be off, you blockhead!"

From this time forward Anna never had one day free, as she was always taking part in picnics, expeditions, performances. She returned home every day after midnight, and went to bed on the floor in the drawing room, and afterward used to tell everyone, touchingly, how she slept under flowers. She needed a very great deal of money, but she was no longer afraid of Modest Alekseich, and spent his money as though it were her own; and she did not ask, did not demand it, simply sent him in the bills: "Give bearer two hundred rubles," or "Pay one hundred rubles at once."

At Easter Modest Alekseich received the Anna of the second grade. When he went to offer his thanks, His Excellency put aside the paper he was reading and settled himself more comfortably in his chair.

"So now you have three Annas," he said, scrutinizing his white hands and pink nails—"one on your buttonhole and two on your neck."

Modest Alekseich put two fingers to his lips as a precaution against laughing too loud and said:

"Now I have only to look forward to the arrival of a little Vladimir. I make bold to beg Your Excellency to stand godfather."

He was alluding to Vladimir of the fourth grade, and was already imagining how he would tell everywhere the story of this pun, so apt in its readiness and audacity, and he wanted to say something equally apt, but His Excellency was buried again in his newspaper, and merely gave him a nod.

And Anna went on driving about with three horses, going out hunting with Artynov, playing in one-act dramas, going out to supper, and was more and more rarely with her own family; they dined now alone. Pyotr Leontich was drinking more heavily than ever; there was no money, and the harmonium had been sold long ago for debt. The boys did not let him go out alone in the street now, but looked after him for fear he might fall down; and whenever they met Anna driving in Staro-Kievsky Street with a pair of horses and Artynov on the box instead of a coachman, Pyotr Leontich took off his top hat, and was about to shout to her, but Petya and Andrusha took him by the arm, and said imploringly:

"You mustn't, father. Hush, father!"

1895

THE BEAUTIES

I

I remember, when I was a high-school boy in the fifth or sixth class, I was driving with my grandfather from the village of Bolshoe Kryepkoe in the Don region to Rostov-on-the-Don. It was a sultry, languidly dreary day of August. Our eyes were glued together, and our mouths were parched from the heat and the dry burning wind which drove clouds of dust to meet us; one did not want to look or speak or think, and when our drowsy driver, a Little Russian called Karpo, swung his whip at the horses and lashed me on my cap, I did not protest or utter a sound, but only, rousing myself from half-slumber, gazed mildly and dejectedly into the distance to see whether there was a village visible through the dust. We stopped to feed the horses in a big Armenian village at a rich Armenian's whom my grandfather knew. Never in my life have I seen a greater caricature than that Armenian. Imagine a little shaven head with thick overhanging eyebrows, a beak of a nose, long gray mustaches, and a wide mouth with a long cherry-wood chibouk sticking out of it. This little head was clumsily attached to a lean hunchback carcass attired in a fantastic garb, a short red jacket, and full bright blue trousers. This figure walked straddling its legs and shuffling with its slippers, spoke without taking the chibouk out of its mouth, and behaved with truly Armenian dignity, not smiling, but staring with wide-open eyes and trying to take as little notice as possible of its guests.

There was neither wind nor dust in the Armenian's rooms, but it was just as unpleasant, stifling, and dreary as in the steppe and on the road. I remember, dusty and exhausted by the heat, I sat in the corner on a green box. The unpainted wooden walls, the furniture, and the floors colored with yellow ocher, smelt of dry wood baked by the sun. Wherever I looked there were flies and flies and flies. . . . Grandfather and the Armenian were talking about grazing, about manure, and about oats. . . . I knew that they would be a good hour getting the samovar; that grandfather would be not less than an hour drinking his tea, and then would lie down to sleep for two or three hours; that I should waste a quarter of the day waiting, after which there would be again the heat, the dust, the jolting cart. I heard the muttering of the two voices, and it began to seem to me that I had been seeing the Armenian, the cupboard with the crockery, the flies, the windows with the burning sun beating on them, for ages and ages, and should only cease to see them in the far-off future, and I was seized with hatred for the steppe, the sun, the flies. . . .

A Little Russian peasant woman in a kerchief brought in a tray of tea things, then the samovar. The Armenian went slowly out into the passage and shouted: "Mashya, come and pour out tea! Where are you, Mashya?"

Hurried footsteps were heard, and there came into the room a girl of sixteen in a simple cotton dress and a white kerchief. As she washed the crockery and poured out the tea, she was standing with her back to me, and all I could see was that she was of a slender figure, barefooted, and that her little bare heels were covered by long trousers.

The Armenian invited me to have tea. Sitting down to the table, I glanced at the girl, who was handing me a glass of tea, and felt all at once as though a wind were blowing over my soul and blowing away all the impressions of the day with their dust and dreariness. I saw the

bewitching features of the most beautiful face I have ever met in real
life or in my dreams. Before me stood a beauty, and I recognized that
at the first glance as I should have recognized lightning.

I am ready to swear that Masha—or, as her father called her,
Mashya—was a real beauty, but I don't know how to prove it. It
sometimes happens that clouds are huddled together in disorder on
the horizon, and the sun hiding behind them colors them and the sky
with tints of every possible shade—crimson, orange, gold, lilac,
muddy pink; one cloud is like a monk, another like a fish, a third like
a Turk in a turban. The glow of sunset enveloping a third of the sky
gleams on the cross on the church, flashes on the windows of the
manor house, is reflected in the river and the puddles, quivers on the
trees; far, far away against the background of the sunset, a flock of
wild ducks is flying homeward. . . . And the boy herding the cows,
and the surveyor driving in his chaise over the dam, and the gentleman out for a walk, all gaze at the sunset, and every one of them
thinks it terribly beautiful, but no one knows or can say in what its
beauty lies.

I was not the only one to think the Armenian girl beautiful. My
grandfather, an old man of seventy, gruff and indifferent to women
and the beauties of nature, looked caressingly at Masha for a full
minute, and asked:

"Is that your daughter, Avert Nazaritch?"

"Yes, she is my daughter," answered the Armenian.

"A fine young lady," said my grandfather approvingly.

An artist would have called the Armenian girl's beauty classical
and severe; it was just that beauty the contemplation of which—God
knows why!—inspires in one the conviction that one is seeing correct
features; that hair, eyes, nose, mouth, neck, bosom, and every movement of the young body all go together in one complete harmonious
accord in which nature has not blundered over the smallest line. You
fancy for some reason that the ideally beautiful woman must have
such a nose as Masha's, straight and slightly aquiline, just such great
dark eyes, such long lashes, such a languid glance; you fancy that her

black curly hair and eyebrows go with the soft white tint of her brow and cheeks as the green reeds go with the quiet stream. Masha's white neck and her youthful bosom were not fully developed, but you fancy the sculptor would need a great creative genius to mold them. You gaze, and little by little the desire comes over you to say to Masha something extraordinarily pleasant, sincere, beautiful, as beautiful as she herself was.

At first I felt hurt and abashed that Masha took no notice of me, but was all the time looking down; it seemed to me as though a peculiar atmosphere, proud and happy, separated her from me and jealously screened her from my eyes.

"That's because I am covered with dust," I thought, "am sunburnt, and am still a boy."

But little by little I forgot myself, and gave myself up entirely to the consciousness of beauty. I thought no more now of the dreary steppe, of the dust, no longer heard the buzzing of the flies, no longer tasted the tea, and felt nothing except that a beautiful girl was standing only the other side of the table.

I felt this beauty rather strangely. It was not desire, nor ecstasy, nor enjoyment that Masha excited in me, but a painful though pleasant sadness. It was a sadness vague and undefined as a dream. For some reason I felt sorry for myself, for my grandfather and for the Armenian, even for the girl herself, and I had a feeling as though we all four had lost something important and essential to life which we should never find again. My grandfather, too, grew melancholy; he talked no more about manure or about oats, but sat silent, looking pensively at Masha.

After tea my grandfather lay down for a nap while I went out of the house into the porch. The house, like all the houses in the Armenian village, stood in the full sun; there was not a tree, not an awning, no shade. The Armenian's great courtyard, overgrown with goosefoot and wild mallows, was lively and full of gaiety in spite of the great heat. Threshing was going on behind one of the low hurdles which intersected the big yard here and there. Round a post stuck into the middle of the threshing-floor ran a dozen horses harnessed side by side, so that they formed one long radius. A Little Russian in a long waistcoat and full trousers was walking beside them, cracking a whip and shouting in a tone that sounded as though he were jeering at the horses and showing off his power over them.

"A—a—a, you damned brutes! . . . A—a—a, plague take you! Are you frightened?"

The horses, sorrel, white, and piebald, not understanding why they were made to run round in one place and to crush the wheat straw, ran unwillingly, as though with effort, swinging their tails with an offended air. The wind raised up perfect clouds of golden chaff from under their hoofs and carried it away far beyond the hurdle. Near the tall fresh stacks peasant women were swarming with rakes, and carts were moving, and beyond the stacks in another yard another dozen similar horses were running round a post, and a similar Little Russian was cracking his whip and jeering at the horses.

The steps on which I was sitting were hot; on the thin rails and here and there on the window frames sap was oozing out of the wood from the heat; red ladybirds were huddling together in the streaks of shadow under the steps and under the shutters. The sun was baking me on my head, on my chest, and on my back, but I did not notice it, and was conscious only of the thud of bare feet on the uneven floor in the passage and in the rooms behind me. After clearing away the tea things, Masha ran down the steps, fluttering the air as she passed, and like a bird flew into a little grimy outhouse—I suppose the kitchen—from which came the smell of roast mutton and the sound of angry talk in Armenian. She vanished into the dark doorway, and in her place there appeared on the threshold an old, bent, red-faced Armenian woman wearing green trousers. The old woman was angry and was scolding someone. Soon afterward Masha appeared in the doorway, flushed with the heat of the kitchen and carrying a big black loaf on her shoulder; swaying gracefully under the weight of the bread, she ran across the yard to the threshing-floor, darted over the hurdle, and, wrapt in a cloud of golden chaff, vanished behind the carts. The Little Russian who was driving the horses lowered his whip, sank into silence, and gazed for a minute in the direction of the carts. Then when the Armenian girl darted again by the horses and leaped over the hurdle, he followed her with his eyes, and shouted to the horses in a tone as though he were greatly disappointed:

"Plague take you, unclean devils!"

And all the while I was unceasingly hearing her bare feet, and seeing how she walked across the yard with a grave, preoccupied face. She ran now down the steps, swishing the air about me, now into the kitchen, now to the threshing-floor, now through the gate, and I could hardly turn my head quickly enough to watch her.

And the oftener she fluttered by me with her beauty, the more acute became my sadness. I felt sorry both for her and for myself and for the Little Russian, who mournfully watched her every time she ran through the cloud of chaff to the carts. Whether it was envy of her beauty, or that I was regretting that the girl was not mine, and never would be, or that I was a stranger to her; or whether I vaguely felt that her rare beauty was accidental, unnecessary, and, like everything on earth, of short duration; or whether, perhaps, my sadness was that peculiar feeling which is excited in man by the contemplation of real beauty, God only knows.

The three hours of waiting passed unnoticed. It seemed to me that I had not had time to look properly at Masha when Karpo drove up to the river, bathed the horse, and began to put it in the shafts. The wet horse snorted with pleasure and kicked his hoofs against the shafts. Karpo shouted to it: "Ba-ack!" My grandfather woke up. Masha opened the creaking gates for us, we got into the chaise and drove out of the yard. We drove in silence as though we were angry with one another.

When, two or three hours later, Rostov and Nahitchevan appeared in the distance, Karpo, who had been silent the whole time, looked round quickly, and said:

"A fine wench, that at the Armenian's."

And he lashed his horses.

"And the oftener she fluttered by me with her beauty, the more acute became my sadness." In this landscape by Chekhov's close friend Isaak Levitan, the figure of a woman walking was added by Chekhov's elder brother Nikolai.

II

Another time, after I had become a student, I was traveling by rail to the south. It was May. At one of the stations, I believe it was between Byelgorod and Harkov, I got out of the train to walk about the platform.

The shades of evening were already lying on the station garden, on the platform, and on the fields; the station screened off the sunset, but on the topmost clouds of smoke from the engine, which were tinged with rosy light, one could see the sun had not yet quite vanished.

As I walked up and down the platform I noticed that the greater number of the passengers were standing or walking near a second-class compartment, and that they looked as though some celebrated person were in that compartment. Among the curious whom I met near this compartment I saw, however, an artillery officer who had been my fellow traveler, an intelligent, cordial, and sympathetic fellow—as people mostly are whom we meet on our travels by chance and with whom we are not long acquainted.

"What are you looking at there?" I asked.

He made no answer, but only indicated with his eyes a feminine figure. It was a young girl of seventeen or eighteen, wearing a Russian dress, with her head bare and a little shawl flung carelessly on one shoulder; not a passenger, but I suppose a sister or daughter of the stationmaster. She was standing near the carriage window, talking to an elderly woman who was in the train. Before I had time to realize what I was seeing, I was suddenly overwhelmed by the feeling I had once experienced in the Armenian village.

The girl was remarkably beautiful, and that was unmistakable to me and to those who were looking at her as I was.

If one is to describe her appearance feature by feature, as the practice is, the only really lovely thing was her thick wavy fair hair, which hung loose with a black ribbon tied round her head; all the other features were either irregular or very ordinary. Either from a peculiar form of coquettishness, or from shortsightedness, her eyes were screwed up, her nose had an undecided tilt, her mouth was small, her profile was feebly and insipidly drawn, her shoulders were narrow and undeveloped for her age—and yet the girl made the impression of being really beautiful, and looking at her, I was able to feel convinced that the Russian face does not need strict regularity in order to be lovely; what is more, that if instead of her turnup nose the girl had been given a different one, correct and plastically irreproachable like the Armenian girl's, I fancy her face would have lost all its charm from the change.

Standing at the window talking, the girl, shrugging at the evening damp, continually looking round at us, at one moment put her arms akimbo, at the next raised her hands to her head to straighten her hair, talked, laughed, while her face at one moment wore an expression of wonder, the next of horror, and I don't remember a moment when her face and body were at rest. The whole secret and magic of her beauty lay just in these tiny, infinitely elegant movements, in her smile, in the play of her face, in her rapid glances at us, in the combination of the subtle grace of her movements with her youth, her freshness, the purity of her soul that sounded in her laugh and voice, and with the weakness we love so much in children, in birds, in fawns, and in young trees.

It was that butterfly's beauty so in keeping with waltzing, darting about the garden, laughter and gaiety, and incongruous with serious thought, grief, and repose; and it seemed as though a gust of wind blowing over the platform, or a fall of rain, would be enough to wither the fragile body and scatter the capricious beauty like the pollen of a flower.

"So—o! . . ." the officer muttered with a sigh when, after the second bell, we went back to our compartment.

And what that "So—o" meant I will not undertake to decide.

Perhaps he was sad, and did not want to go away from the beauty and the spring evening into the stuffy train; or perhaps he, like me, was unaccountably sorry for the beauty, for himself, and for me, and for all the passengers, who were listlessly and reluctantly sauntering back to their compartments. As we passed the station window, at which a pale, red-haired telegraphist with upstanding curls and a faded, broad-cheeked face was sitting beside his apparatus, the officer heaved a sigh and said:

"I bet that telegraphist is in love with that pretty girl. To live out in the wilds under one roof with that ethereal creature and not fall in love is beyond the power of man. And what a calamity, my friend! what an ironical fate, to be stooping, unkempt, gray, a decent fellow and not a fool, and to be in love with that pretty, stupid little girl who would never take a scrap of notice of you! Or worse still: imagine that telegraphist is in love, and at the same time married, and that his wife is as stooping, as unkempt, and as decent a person as himself."

On the platform between our carriage and the next the guard was standing with his elbows on the railing, looking in the direction of the beautiful girl, and his battered, wrinkled, unpleasantly beefy face, exhausted by sleepless nights and the jolting of the train, wore a look of tenderness and of the deepest sadness, as though in that girl he saw happiness, his own youth, soberness, purity, wife, children; as though he were repenting and feeling in his whole being that that girl was not his, and that for him, with his premature old age, his uncouthness, and his beefy face, the ordinary happiness of a man and a passenger was as far away as heaven. . . .

The third bell rang, the whistles sounded, and the train slowly moved off. First the guard, the stationmaster, then the garden, the beautiful girl with her exquisitely sly smile, passed before our windows. . . .

Putting my head out and looking back, I saw how, looking after the train, she walked along the platform by the window where the telegraph clerk was sitting, smoothed her hair, and ran into the garden. The station no longer screened off the sunset, the plain lay open before us, but the sun had already set and the smoke lay in black clouds over the green, velvety young corn. It was melancholy in the spring air, and in the darkening sky, and in the railway carriage.

The familiar figure of the guard came into the carriage, and he began lighting the candles.

1888

THE CHORUS GIRL

One day while she was still pretty and young and her voice was sweet, Nikolai Kolpakov, an admirer of hers, was sitting in a room on the second floor of her cottage. The afternoon was unbearably sultry and hot. Kolpakov, who had just dined and drunk a whole bottle of vile port, felt thoroughly ill and out of sorts. Both he and she were bored, and were waiting for the heat to abate so that they might go for a stroll.

Suddenly a bell rang in the hall. Kolpakov, who was sitting in his slippers without a coat, jumped up and looked at Pasha with a question in his eyes.

"It is probably the postman or one of the girls," said the singer.

Kolpakov was not afraid of the postman or of Pasha's girl friends, but nevertheless he snatched up his coat and disappeared into the next room while Pasha ran to open the door. What was her astonishment when she saw on the threshold, not the postman nor a girl friend, but an unknown woman, beautiful and young! Her dress was distinguished and she was evidently a lady.

The stranger was pale and was breathing heavily, as if she were out of breath from climbing the stairs.

"What can I do for you?" Pasha inquired.

The lady did not reply at once. She took a step forward, looked slowly around the room, and sank into a chair as if her legs had collapsed under her from faintness or fatigue. Her pale lips moved silently, trying to utter words which would not come.

"Is my husband here?" she asked at last, raising her large eyes with their red and swollen lids to Pasha's face.

"What husband do you mean?" Pasha whispered, suddenly taking such violent fright that her hands and feet grew as cold as ice. "What husband?" she repeated beginning to tremble.

"My husband—Nikolai Kolpakov."

"N-no, my lady. I don't know your husband."

A minute passed in silence. The stranger drew her handkerchief several times across her pale lips, and held her breath in an effort to subdue an inward trembling, while Pasha stood before her as motionless as a statue, gazing at her full of uncertainty and fear.

"So you say he is not here?" asked the lady. Her voice was firm now and a strange smile had twisted her lips.

"I—I—don't know whom you mean!"

"You are a revolting, filthy, vile creature!" muttered the stranger looking at Pasha with hatred and disgust. "Yes, yes, you are revolting. I am glad indeed that an opportunity has come at last for me to tell you this!"

Pasha felt that she was producing the effect of something indecent and foul on this lady in black, with the angry eyes and the long, slender fingers, and she was ashamed of her fat, red cheeks, the pockmark on her nose, and the lock of hair on her forehead that would never stay up. She thought that if she were thin and her face were not powdered, and she had not that curl on her forehead, she would not feel so afraid and ashamed standing there before this mysterious, unknown lady.

"Where is my husband?" the lady went on. "However it makes no difference to me whether he is here or not, I only want you to know that he has been caught embezzling funds entrusted to him, and that the police are looking for him. He is going to be arrested. Now see what you have done!"

The lady rose and began to walk up and down in violent agitation. Pasha stared at her; fear rendered her uncomprehending.

"He will be found today and arrested," the lady repeated with a sob full of bitterness and rage. "I know who has brought this horror upon him! Disgusting, abominable woman. Horrible, corrupt creature! (Here the lady's lips curled and her nose wrinkled with aversion.) I am powerless. Listen to me, you low woman. I am powerless and you are stronger than I, but there is One who will avenge me and my children. God's eyes see all things. He is just. He will call you to account for every tear I have shed, every sleepless night I have passed. The time will come when you will remember me!"

Once more silence fell. The lady walked to and fro wringing her hands. Pasha continued to watch her dully, uncomprehendingly, dazed with doubt, waiting for her to do something terrible.

"I don't know what you mean, my lady!" she suddenly cried, and burst into tears.

"That's a lie!" screamed the lady, her eyes flashing with anger. "I know all about it! I have known about you for a long time. I know that he has been coming here every day for the last month."

"Yes—and what if he has? Is it my fault? I have a great many visitors, but I don't force anyone to come. They are free to do as they please."

"I tell you he is accused of embezzlement! He has taken money that didn't belong to him, and for the sake of a woman like you—for your sake, he has brought himself to commit a crime! Listen to me," the lady said sternly, halting before Pasha. "You are an unprincipled woman, I know. You exist to bring misfortune to men, that is the object of your life, but I cannot believe that you have fallen so low as not to have one spark of humanity left in your breast. He has a wife, he has children, oh, remember that! There is one means of saving us from poverty and shame; if I can find nine hundred rubles today he will be left in peace. Only nine hundred rubles!"

"What nine hundred rubles?" asked Pasha feebly. "I—I don't know—I didn't take—"

"I am not asking you to give me nine hundred rubles; you have no money, and I don't want anything that belongs to you. It is something else that I ask. Men generally give presents of jewelry to women like you. All I ask is that you should give me back the things that my husband has given you."

"My lady, he has never given me anything!" wailed Pasha, beginning to understand.

"Then where is the money he has wasted? He has squandered in some way his own fortune, and mine, and the fortunes of others. Where has the money gone? Listen, I implore you! I was excited just now and said some unpleasant things, but I ask you to forgive me! I know you must hate me, but if pity exists for you, oh, put yourself in my place! I implore you to give me the jewelry!"

"H'm—" said Pasha, shrugging her shoulders. "I should do it with pleasure, only I swear before God he never gave me a thing. He didn't, indeed. But, no, you are right," the singer suddenly stammered in confusion. "He did give me two little things. Wait a minute, I'll fetch them for you if you want them."

Pasha pulled out one of the drawers of her bureau, and took from it a bracelet of hollow gold and a narrow ring set with a ruby.

"Here they are!" she said, handing them to her visitor.

The lady grew angry and a spasm passed over her features. She felt that she was being insulted.

"What is this you are giving me?" she cried. "I'm not asking for alms, but for the things that do not belong to you, for the things that you have extracted from my weak and unhappy husband by your position. When I saw you on the wharf with him on Thursday you were wearing costly brooches and bracelets. Do you think you can play the innocent child with me? I ask you for the last time: will you give me those presents or not?"

"You are strange, I declare," Pasha exclaimed, beginning to take offense. "I swear to you that I have never had a thing from your Nikolai, except this bracelet and ring. He has never given me anything, but these and some little cakes."

"Little cakes!" the stranger laughed suddenly. "His children are starving at home, and he brings you little cakes! So you won't give up the things?"

Receiving no answer, the lady sat down, her eyes grew fixed, and she seemed to be debating something.

"What shall I do?" she murmured. "If I can't get nine hundred rubles he will be ruined as well as the children and myself. Shall I kill this creature, or shall I go down on my knees to her?"

The lady pressed her handkerchief to her eyes and burst into tears.

"Oh, I beseech you!" she sobbed. "It is you who have disgraced and ruined my husband; now save him! You can have no pity for him, I know; but the children, remember the children! What have they done to deserve this?"

Pasha imagined his little children standing on the street corner weeping with hunger, and she, too, burst into tears.

"What can I do, my lady?" she cried. "You say I am a wicked creature who has ruined your husband, but I swear to you before God I have never had the least benefit from him! Mota is the only girl in our chorus who has a rich friend, the rest of us all live on bread and water. Your husband is an educated, pleasant gentleman, that's why I received him. We can't pick and choose."

"I want the jewelry; give me the jewelry! I am weeping, I am humiliating myself; see, I shall fall on my knees before you!"

Pasha screamed with terror and waved her arms. She felt that this pale, beautiful lady, who spoke the same refined language that people did in plays, might really fall on her knees before her, and for the very reason that she was so proud and highbred, she would exalt herself by doing this, and degrade the little singer.

"Yes, yes, I'll give you the jewelry!" Pasha cried hastily, wiping her eyes. "Take it, but it did not come from your husband! I got it from other visitors. But take it, if you want it!"

Pasha pulled out an upper drawer of the bureau, and took from it a diamond brooch, a string of corals, two or three rings, and a bracelet. These she handed to the lady.

"Here is the jewelry, but I tell you again your husband never gave me a thing. Take it, and may you be the richer for having it!" Pasha went on, offended by the lady's threat that she would go down on her knees. "You are a lady and his lawful wife—keep him at home then! The idea of it! As if I had asked him to come here! He came because he wanted to!"

The lady looked through her tears at the jewelry that Pasha had handed her and said:

"This isn't all. There is scarcely five hundred rubles' worth here."

Pasha violently snatched a gold watch, a cigarette case, and a set of studs out of the drawer and flung up her arms, exclaiming:

"Now I am cleaned out! Look for yourself!"

Her visitor sighed. With trembling hands she wrapped the trinkets in her handkerchief, and went out without a word, without even a nod.

The door of the adjoining room opened and Kolpakov came out. His face was pale and his head was shaking nervously, as if he had just swallowed a very bitter draft. His eyes were full of tears.

"I'd like to know what you ever gave me!" Pasha attacked him vehemently. "When did you ever give me the smallest present?"

"Presents—they are a detail, presents!" Kolpakov cried, his head still shaking. "Oh, my God, she wept before you, she abased herself!"

"I ask you again: what have you ever given me?" screamed Pasha.

"My God, she—a respectable, a proud woman, was actually ready to fall on her knees before—before this—wench! And I have brought her to this! I allowed it!"

He seized his head in his hands.

"No," he groaned out, "I shall never forgive myself for this—never! Get away from me, wretch!" he cried, backing away from Pasha with horror, and keeping her off with outstretched, trembling hands. "She was ready to go down on her knees, and before whom?—Before you! Oh, my God!"

He threw on his coat and, pushing Pasha contemptuously aside, strode to the door and went out.

Pasha flung herself down on the sofa and burst into loud wails. She already regretted the things she had given away so impulsively, and her feelings were hurt. She remembered that a merchant had beaten her three years ago for nothing, yes, absolutely for nothing, and at that thought she wept louder than ever.

1886

MISERY

"To whom shall I tell my grief?"

Twilight. Big flakes of wet snow are whirling lazily about the street lamps, which have just been lighted, and lie in a thin soft layer on roofs, horses' backs, shoulders, caps. Iona Potapov, the sleigh driver, is all white like a ghost. He sits on the box without stirring, bent as double as the living body can be bent. If a regular snowdrift fell on him it seems as though even then he would not think it necessary to shake it off. . . . His little mare is white and motionless too. Her stillness, the angularity of her lines, and the sticklike straightness of her legs make her look like a halfpenny gingerbread horse. She is probably lost in thought. Anyone who has been torn away from the plough, from the familiar gray landscapes, and cast into this slough, full of monstrous lights, of unceasing uproar and hurrying people, is bound to think.

It is a long time since Iona and his nag have budged. They came out of the yard before dinnertime and not a single fare yet. But now the shades of evening are falling on the town. The pale light of the street lamps changes to a vivid color, and the bustle of the street grows noiser.

"Cabby, to the Vyborgskaya!" Iona hears. "Cabby!"

Iona starts, and through his snow-plastered eyelashes he sees an officer in a military overcoat with a hood over his head.

"To the Vyborgskaya," repeats the officer. "Are you asleep? To the Vyborgskaya!"

In token of assent Iona gives a tug at the reins, which sends cakes of snow flying from the horse's back and shoulders. The officer gets into the sleigh. Iona clicks to the horse, cranes his neck like a swan, rises in his seat, and, more from habit than necessity, brandishes his whip. The mare cranes her neck, too, crooks her sticklike legs, and hesitatingly sets off.

"Where are you shoving, you devil?" Iona immediately hears shouts from the dark mass shifting to and fro before him. "Where the devil are you going? Keep to the r-right!"

"You don't know how to drive! Keep to the right," says the officer angrily.

A coachman driving a carriage swears at him; a pedestrian crossing the road and brushing the horse's nose with his shoulder looks at him angrily and shakes the snow off his sleeve. Iona fidgets on the box as though he were sitting on thorns, jerks his elbows, and turns his eyes about like one possessed, as though he does not know where he is or why he is there.

"What rascals they all are!" says the officer jocosely. "They are simply doing their best to run up against you or fall under the horse's feet. They must be doing it on purpose."

Iona looks at his fare and moves his lips. Apparently he means to say something, but only a sniff comes out.

"What?" inquires the officer.

Iona gives a wry smile and, straining his throat, brings out huskily: "My son . . . er . . . my son died this week, sir."

"H'm! What did he die of?"

Iona turns his whole body round to his passenger and says:

"Who can tell! It must have been from fever. . . . He lay three days in the hospital and then he died. . . . God's will."

"Turn round, you devil!" comes out of the darkness. "Have you gone off your head, you old dog? Look where you are going!"

"Drive on! drive on!" says the officer. "We won't get there till tomorrow at this rate. Hurry up!"

Iona cranes his neck again, rises in his seat, and with heavy grace swings his whip. Several times he looks round at the officer, but the latter keeps his eyes shut and is apparently disinclined to listen. Putting his fare down at the Vyborgskaya, Iona stops by a restaurant, and again sits huddled up on the box. . . . Again the wet snow paints him and his horse white. One hour passes, and then another.

Three young men, two tall and thin, one short and hunchbacked, come up, railing at each other and loudly stamping on the pavement with their galoshes.

"Cabby, to the Police Bridge," the hunchback shouts in a cracked voice. "The three of us . . . twenty kopecks!"

Iona tugs at the reins and clicks to his horse. Twenty kopecks is not a fair price, but he has no thoughts for that. Whether it is a ruble or whether it is five kopecks does not matter to him now so long as he has a fare. . . . The three young men, shoving each other and using bad language, go up to the sleigh, and all three try to sit down at once. The question remains to be settled: Which are to sit down and which one is to stand? After a long altercation, ill temper, and abuse, they come to the conclusion that the hunchback must stand because he is the shortest.

"Well, drive on," says the hunchback in his cracked voice, settling himself and breathing down Iona's neck. "Cut along! What a cap you've got, my friend! You wouldn't find a worse one in all Petersburg. . . ."

"He-he! . . . he-he! . . ." laughs Iona. "It's nothing to boast of!"

"Well, then, nothing to boast of, drive on! Are you going to drive like this all the way? Eh? Shall I give you one in the neck?"

"My head aches," says one of the tall ones. "At the Dukmasovs' yesterday Vaska and I drank four bottles of brandy between us."

"I can't make out why you talk such stuff," says the other tall one angrily. "You lie like a brute."

"Strike me dead, it's the truth! . . ."

"It's about as true as that a louse coughs."

"He-he!" grins Iona. "Me-er-ry gentlemen!"

"Tfoo! the devil take you!" cries the hunchback indignantly. "Will you get on, you old plague, or won't you? Is that the way to drive? Give her one with the whip. Hang it all, give it her well."

Iona feels behind his back the jolting person and quivering voice of the hunchback. He hears abuse addressed to him, he sees people, and the feeling of loneliness begins little by little to be less heavy on his heart. The hunchback swears at him, till he chokes over some elaborately whimsical string of epithets and is overpowered by his cough. His tall companions begin talking of a certain Nadezhda Petrovna. Iona looks round at them. Waiting till there is a brief pause, he looks round once more and says:

"This week . . . er . . . my . . . er . . . son died!"

"We shall all die . . ." says the hunchback with a sigh, wiping his lips after coughing. "Come, drive on! Drive on! My friends, I simply cannot stand crawling like this! When will he get us there?"

"Well, you give him a little encouragement . . . one in the neck!"

"Do you hear, you old plague? I'll make you smart. If one stands on ceremony with fellows like you one may as well walk. Do you hear, you old dragon? Or don't you care a hang what we say?"

And Iona hears rather than feels a slap on the back of his neck.

"He-he! . . ." he laughs. "Merry gentlemen . . . God give you health!"

"Cabman, are you married?" asks one of the tall ones.

"I? He-he! Me-er-ry gentlemen. The only wife for me now is the damp earth. . . . He-ho-ho! . . . The grave that is! . . . Here my son's dead and I am alive. . . . It's a strange thing, death has come in at the wrong door. . . . Instead of coming for me it went for my son. . . ."

And Iona turns round to tell them how his son died, but at that point the hunchback gives a faint sigh and announces that, thank God! they have arrived at last. After taking his twenty kopecks, Iona gazes for a long while after the revelers, who disappear into a dark entry. Again he is alone and again there is silence for him. . . . The misery which has been for a brief space eased comes back again and tears his heart more cruelly than ever. With a look of anxiety and suffering Iona's eyes stray restlessly among the crowds moving to and fro on both sides of the street: can he not find among those thousands someone who will listen to him? But the crowds flit by heedless of him and his misery. . . . His misery is immense, beyond all bounds. If Iona's heart were to burst and his misery to flow out, it would flood the whole world, it seems, but yet it is not seen. It has found a hiding place in such an insignificant shell that one would not have found it with a candle by daylight. . . .

Iona sees a house porter with a parcel and makes up his mind to address him.

"What time will it be, friend?" he asks.

"Going on for ten. . . . Why have you stopped here? Drive on!"

Iona drives a few paces away, bends himself double, and gives himself up to his misery. He feels it is no good to appeal to people. But before five minutes have passed he draws himself up, shakes his head as though he feels a sharp pain, and tugs at the reins. . . . He can bear it no longer.

"Back to the yard!" he thinks. "To the yard!"

And his little mare, as though she knew his thoughts, falls to trotting. An hour and a half later Iona is sitting by a big dirty stove. On the stove, on the floor, and on the benches are people snoring. The air is full of smells and stuffiness. Iona looks at the sleeping figures, scratches himself, and regrets that he has come home so early. . . .

"His misery is immense, beyond all bounds. If Iona's heart were to burst and his misery to flow out, it would flood the whole world . . ."

"I have not earned enough to pay for the oats, even," he thinks. "That's why I am so miserable. A man who knows how to do his work, . . . who has had enough to eat, and whose horse has had enough to eat, is always at ease. . . ."

In one of the corners a young cabman gets up, clears his throat sleepily, and makes for the water bucket.

"Want a drink?" Iona asks him.

"Seems so."

"May it do you good. . . . But my son is dead, mate. . . . Do you hear? This week in the hospital. . . . It's a queer business. . . ."

Iona looks to see the effect produced by his words, but he sees nothing. The young man has covered his head over and is already asleep. The old man sighs and scratches himself. . . . Just as the young man had been thirsty for water, he thirsts for speech. His son will soon have been dead a week, and he has not really talked to anybody yet. . . . He wants to talk of it properly, with deliberation. . . . He wants to tell how his son was taken ill, how he suffered, what he said before he died, how he died. . . . He wants to describe the funeral, and how he went to the hospital to get his son's clothes. He still has his daughter Anisya in the country. . . . And he wants to talk about her too. . . . Yes, he has plenty to talk about now. His listener ought to sigh and exclaim and lament. . . . It would be even better to talk to women. Though they are silly creatures, they blubber at the first word.

"Let's go out and have a look at the mare," Iona thinks. "There is always time for sleep. . . . You'll have sleep enough, no fear. . . ."

He puts on his coat and goes into the stables where his mare is standing. He thinks about oats, about hay, about the weather. . . . He cannot think about his son when he is alone. . . . To talk about him with someone is possible, but to think of him and picture him is insufferable anguish. . . .

"Are you munching?" Iona asks his mare, seeing her shining

eyes. "There, munch away, munch away. . . . Since we have not earned enough for oats, we will eat hay. . . . Yes, . . . I have grown too old to drive. . . . My son ought to be driving, not I. . . . He was a real cabman. . . . He ought to have lived. . . ."

Iona is silent for a while, and then he goes on:

"That's how it is, old girl. . . . Kuzma Ionich is gone. . . . He said goodbye to me. . . . He went and died for no reason. . . . Now, suppose you had a little colt, and you were own mother to that little colt. . . . And all at once that same little colt went and died. . . . You'd be sorry, wouldn't you? . . ."

The little mare munches, listens, and breathes on her master's hands. Iona is carried away and tells her all about it.

1886

A HAPPY ENDING

Lyubov Grigoryevna, a substantial, buxom lady of forty who undertook matchmaking and many other matters of which it is usual to speak only in whispers, had come to see Stytchkin, the head guard, on a day when he was off duty. Stytchkin, somewhat embarrassed, but, as always, grave, practical, and severe, was walking up and down the room, smoking a cigar and saying:

"Very pleased to make your acquaintance. Semyon Ivanovitch recommended you on the ground that you may be able to assist me in a delicate and very important matter affecting the happiness of my life. I have, Lyubov Grigoryevna, reached the age of fifty-two; that is a period of life at which very many have already grown-up children. My position is a secure one. Though my fortune is not large, yet I am in a position to support a beloved being and children at my side. I may tell you between ourselves that apart from my salary I have also money in the bank which my manner of living has enabled me to save. I am a practical and sober man, I lead a sensible and consistent life, so that I may hold myself up as an example to many. But one thing I lack—a domestic hearth of my own and a partner in life, and I live like a wandering Magyar, moving from place to place without any satisfaction. I have no one with whom to take counsel, and when

I am ill no one to give me water, and so on. Apart from that, Lyubov Grigoryevna, a married man has always more weight in society than a bachelor. . . . I am a man of the educated class, with money, but if you look at me from a point of view, what am I? A man with no kith and kin, no better than some Polish priest. And therefore I should be very desirous to be united in the bonds of Hymen—that is, to enter into matrimony with some worthy person."

"An excellent thing," said the matchmaker, with a sigh.

"I am a solitary man and in this town I know no one. Where can I go, and to whom can I apply, since all the people here are strangers to me? That is why Semyon Ivanovitch advised me to address myself to a person who is a specialist in this line, and makes the arrangement of the happiness of others her profession. And therefore I most earnestly beg you, Lyubov Grigoryevna, to assist me in ordering my future. You know all the marriageable young ladies in the town, and it is easy for you to accommodate me."

"I can. . . ."

"A glass of wine, I beg you. . . ."

With an habitual gesture the matchmaker raised her glass to her mouth and tossed it off without winking.

"I can," she repeated. "And what sort of bride would you like, Nikolay Nikolayitch?"

"Should I like? The bride fate sends me."

"Well, of course it depends on your fate, but everyone has his own taste, you know. One likes dark ladies, the other prefers fair ones."

"You see, Lyubov Grigoryevna," said Stytchkin, sighing sedately, "I am a practical man and a man of character; for me beauty and external appearance generally take a secondary place, for, as you know yourself, beauty is neither bowl nor platter, and a pretty wife involves a great deal of anxiety. The way I look at it is, what matters most in a woman is not what is external, but what lies within—that is, that she should have soul and all the qualities. A glass of wine, I beg. . . . Of course, it would be very agreeable that one's wife should be rather plump, but for mutual happiness it is not of great consequence; what matters is the mind. Properly speaking, a woman does not need mind either, for if she has brains she will have too high an opinion of herself, and take all sorts of ideas into her head. One cannot do without education nowadays, of course, but education is of different kinds. It would be pleasing for one's wife to know French and German, to speak various languages, very pleasing; but what's the use of that if she can't sew on one's buttons, perhaps? I am a man of the educated class; I am just as much at home, I may say, with Prince Kanitelin as I am with you here now. But my habits are simple, and I want a girl who is not too much a fine lady. Above all, she must have respect for me and feel that I have made her happiness."

"To be sure."

"Well, now as regards the essential. . . . I do not want a wealthy bride; I would never condescend to anything so low as to marry for money. I desire not to be kept by my wife, but to keep her, and that she may be sensible of it. But I do not want a poor girl either. Though I am a man of means, and am marrying not from mercenary motives, but from love, yet I cannot take a poor girl, for, as you know yourself, prices have gone up so, and there will be children."

"One might find one with a dowry," said the matchmaker.

"A glass of wine, I beg. . . ."

There was a pause of five minutes.

The matchmaker heaved a sigh, took a sidelong glance at the guard, and asked:

"Well, now, my good sir . . . do you want anything in the bachelor line? I have some fine bargains. One is a French girl and one is a Greek. Well worth the money."

The guard thought a moment and said:

"No, I thank you. In view of your favorable disposition, allow me to inquire now how much you ask for your exertions in regard to a bride?"

"I don't ask much. Give me twenty-five rubles and the stuff for a dress, as is usual, and I will say thank you . . . but for the dowry, that's a different account."

Stytchkin folded his arms over his chest and fell to pondering in silence. After some thought he heaved a sigh and said:

"That's dear. . . ."

"It's not at all dear, Nikolay Nikolayitch! In old days when there were lots of weddings one did do it cheaper, but nowadays what are our earnings? If you make fifty rubles in a month, that is not a fast, you may be thankful. It's not on weddings we make our money, my good sir."

Stytchkin looked at the matchmaker in amazement and shrugged his shoulders.

"H'm! . . . Do you call fifty rubles little?" he asked.

"Of course it is little! In old days we sometimes made more than a hundred."

"H'm! I should never have thought it was possible to earn such a sum by these jobs. Fifty rubles! It is not every man that earns as much! Pray drink your wine. . . ."

The matchmaker drained her glass without winking. Stytchkin looked her over from head to foot in silence, then said:

"Fifty rubles. . . . Why, that is six hundred rubles a year. . . . Please take some more. . . . With such dividends, you know, Lyubov Grigoryevna, you would have no difficulty in making a match for yourself. . . ."

"For myself," laughed the matchmaker, "I am an old woman."

"Not at all. . . . You have such a figure, and your face is plump and fair, and all the rest of it."

The matchmaker was embarrassed. Stytchkin was also embarrassed and sat down beside her.

"You are still very attractive," said he; "if you met with a practical, steady, careful husband, with his salary and your earnings you might even attract him very much, and you'd get on very well together. . . ."

"Goodness knows what you are saying, Nikolay Nikolayitch."

"Well, I meant no harm. . . ."

A silence followed. Stytchkin began loudly blowing his nose, while the matchmaker turned crimson, and looking bashfully at him, asked:

"And how much do you get, Nikolay Nikolayitch?"

"I? Seventy-five rubles, besides tips. . . . Apart from that we make something out of candles and hares."

"You go hunting, then?"

"No. Passengers who travel without tickets are called hares with us."

Another minute passed in silence. Stytchkin got up and walked about the room in excitement.

"I don't want a young wife," said he. "I am a middle-aged man, and I want someone who . . . as it might be like you . . . staid and settled . . . and a figure something like yours. . . ."

"Goodness knows what you are saying . . ." giggled the match-maker, hiding her crimson face in her kerchief.

"There is no need to be long thinking about it. You are after my own heart, and you suit me in your qualities. I am a practical, sober man, and if you like me . . . what could be better? Allow me to make you a proposal!"

The matchmaker dropped a tear, laughed, and, in token of her consent, clinked glasses with Stytchkin.

"Well," said the happy railway guard, "now allow me to explain to you the behavior and manner of life I desire from you. . . . I am a strict, respectable, practical man. I take a gentlemanly view of everything. And I desire that my wife should be strict also, and should understand that to her I am a benefactor and the foremost person in the world."

He sat down, and, heaving a deep sigh, began expounding to his bride-elect his views on domestic life and a wife's duties.

1887

THE DARLING

Olenka, the daughter of the retired collegiate assessor Plemyan-niakov, was sitting on her back porch, lost in thought. It was hot, the flies were persistent and teasing, and it was pleasant to reflect that it would soon be evening. Dark rainclouds were gathering from the east, and bringing from time to time a breath of moisture in the air.

Kukin, who was the manager of an open-air theater called the Tivoli, and who lived in the lodge, was standing in the middle of the garden looking at the sky.

"Again!" he observed despairingly. "It's going to rain again! Rain every day, as though to spite me. I might as well hang myself! It's ruin! Fearful losses every day."

He flung up his hands, and went on, addressing Olenka:

"There! that's the life we lead, Olga Semyonovna. It's enough to make one cry. One works and does one's utmost; one wears oneself out, getting no sleep at night, and racks one's brain what to do for the best. And then what happens? To begin with, one's public is ignorant, boorish. I give them the very best operetta, a dainty masque, first-rate music-hall artists. But do you suppose that's what they want? They don't understand anything of that sort. They want a clown; what they ask for is vulgarity. And then look at the weather! Almost every evening it rains. It started on the tenth of May, and it's kept it up all May and June. It's simply awful! The public doesn't come, but I've to pay the rent just the same, and pay the artists."

The next evening the clouds would gather again, and Kukin would say with an hysterical laugh:

"Well, rain away, then! Flood the garden, drown me! Damn my luck in this world and the next! Let the artists drag me into court! Send me to prison—to Siberia!—the scaffold! Ha, ha, ha!"

And the next day the same thing.

Olenka listened to Kukin with silent gravity, and sometimes tears came into her eyes. In the end his misfortunes touched her; she grew to love him. He was a small thin man, with a yellow face, and curls combed forward on his forehead. He spoke in a thin tenor; as he talked his mouth worked on one side, and there was always an expression of despair on his face; yet he aroused a deep and genuine affection in her. She was always fond of someone, and could not exist without loving. In earlier days she had loved her Papa, who now sat in a darkened room, breathing with difficulty; she had loved her aunt who used to come every other year from Bryansk; and before that, when she was at school, she had loved her French master. She was a gentle, softhearted, compassionate girl, with mild, tender eyes and very good health. At the sight of her full rosy cheeks, her soft white neck with a little dark mole on it, and the kind, naive smile which came into her face when she listened to anything pleasant, men thought, "Yes, not half bad," and smiled too, while lady visitors could not refrain from seizing her hand in the middle of a conversation, exclaiming in a gush of delight, "You darling!"

The house in which she had lived since her birth, and which was left her in her father's will, was at the extreme end of the town, not far from the Tivoli. In the evenings and at night she could hear the band playing, and the crackling and banging of fireworks, and it seemed to her that it was Kukin struggling with his destiny, storming the entrenchments of his chief foe, the indifferent public; there was a

"She was always fond of someone, and could not exist without loving."

sweet thrill at her heart, she had no desire to sleep, and when he returned home at daybreak, she tapped softly at her bedroom window and, showing him only her face and one shoulder through the curtain, she gave him a friendly smile. . . .

He proposed to her, and they were married. And when he had a closer view of her neck and her plump, fine shoulders, he threw up his hands, and said:

"You darling!"

He was happy, but as it rained on the day and night of his wedding, his face still retained an expression of despair.

They got on very well together. She used to sit in his office, to look after things in the Tivoli, to put down the accounts and pay the wages. And her rosy cheeks, her sweet, naive, radiant smile, were to be seen now at the office window, now in the refreshment bar or behind the scenes of the theater. And already she used to say to her acquaintances that the theater was the chief and most important thing in life, and that it was only through the drama that one could derive true enjoyment and become cultivated and humane.

"But do you suppose the public understands that?" she used to say. "What they want is a clown. Yesterday we gave *Faust Inside Out,* and almost all the boxes were empty; but if Vanichka and I had been producing some vulgar thing, I assure you the theater would have been packed. Tomorrow Vanichka and I are doing *Orpheus in the Underworld.* Do come."

And what Kukin said about the theater and the actors she repeated. Like him she despised the public for their ignorance and their indifference to art; she took part in the rehearsals, she corrected the actors, she kept an eye on the behavior of the musicians, and when there was an unfavorable notice in the local paper, she shed tears, and then went to the editor's office to set things right.

The actors were fond of her and used to call her "Vanichka and I," and "the darling"; she was sorry for them and used to lend them small sums of money, and if they deceived her, she used to shed a few tears in private, but did not complain to her husband.

They got on well in the winter too. They took the theater in the town for the whole winter, and let it for short terms to a troupe from Little Russia, or to a conjurer, or to a local dramatic society. Olenka grew stouter, and was always beaming with satisfaction, while Kukin grew thinner and yellower, and continually complained of their terrible losses, although he had not done badly all the winter. He used to cough at night, and she used to give him hot raspberry tea or lime-flower water, to rub him with eau-de-Cologne, and to wrap him in her warm shawls.

"You're such a sweet pet!" she used to say with perfect sincerity, stroking his hair. "You're such a pretty dear!"

Toward Lent he went to Moscow to collect a new troupe, and without him she could not sleep, but sat all night at her window, looking at the stars, and she compared herself with the hens, who are awake all night and uneasy when the cock is not in the henhouse. Kukin was detained in Moscow, and wrote that he would be back at Easter, adding some instructions about the Tivoli. But on the Sunday before Easter, late in the evening, came a sudden ominous knock at the gate; someone was hammering on the gate as though on a barrel—boom, boom, boom! The drowsy cook went flopping with her bare feet through the puddles, as she ran to open the gate.

"Please open," said someone outside in a thick bass. "There is a telegram for you."

Olenka had received telegrams from her husband before, but this time for some reason she felt numb with terror. With shaking hands she opened the telegram and read as follows:

IVAN PETROVICH DIED SUDDENLY TODAY. AWAITING IMMATE INSTRUCTIONS FUFUNERAL TUESDAY.

That was how it was written in the telegram—"fufuneral," and the utterly incomprehensible word "immate." It was signed by the stage manager of the operatic company.

"My darling!" sobbed Olenka. "Vanichka, my precious, my darling! Why did I ever meet you! Why did I know you and love you! Your poor heartbroken Olenka is all alone without you!"

Kukin's funeral took place on Tuesday in Moscow, Olenka returned home on Wednesday, and as soon as she got indoors she threw herself on her bed and sobbed so loudly that it could be heard next door, and in the street.

"Poor darling!" the neighbors said, as they crossed themselves. "Olga Semyonovna, poor darling! How she does take on!"

Three months later Olenka was coming home from mass, melancholy and in deep mourning. It happened that one of her neighbors, Vassily Andreich Pustovalov, returning home from church, walked back beside her. He was the manager at Babakayev's, the timber merchant's. He wore a straw hat, a white waistcoat, and a gold watch-chain, and looked more like a country gentleman than a man in trade.

"Everything happens as it is ordained, Olga Semyonovna," he said gravely, with a sympathetic note in his voice; "and if any of our dear ones die, it must be because it is the will of God, so we ought to have fortitude and bear it submissively."

After seeing Olenka to her gate, he said goodbye and went on. All day afterward she heard his sedately dignified voice, and whenever she shut her eyes she saw his dark beard. She liked him very much. And apparently she had made an impression on him too, for not long afterward an elderly lady, with whom she was only slightly acquainted, came to drink coffee with her, and as soon as she was seated at table began to talk about Pustovalov, saying that he was an excellent man whom one could thoroughly depend upon, and that any girl would be glad to marry him. Three days later Pustovalov himself came. He did not stay long, only about ten minutes, and he did not say much, but when he left, Olenka loved him—loved him so much that she lay awake all night in a perfect fever, and in the morning she sent for the elderly lady. The match was quickly arranged, and then came the wedding.

Pustovalov and Olenka got on very well together when they were married.

Usually he sat in the office till dinnertime, then he went out on business, while Olenka took his place, and sat in the office till evening, making up accounts and booking orders.

"Timber gets dearer every year; the price rises twenty percent," she would say to her customers and friends. "Only fancy we used to sell local timber, and now Vassichka always has to go for wood to the Mogilev district. And the freight!" she would add, covering her cheeks with her hands in horror. "The freight!"

It seemed to her that she had been in the timber trade for ages and ages, and that the most important and necessary thing in life was timber; and there was something intimate and touching to her in the very sound of words such as "balk," "post," "beam," "pole," "scantling," "batten," "lath," "plank," etc.

At night when she was asleep she dreamed of perfect mountains of planks and boards, and long strings of wagons carting timber somewhere far away. She dreamed that a whole regiment of six-inch beams forty feet high, standing on end, was marching upon the timberyard; that logs, beams, and boards knocked together with the resounding crash of dry wood, kept falling and getting up again, piling themselves on each other. Olenka cried out in her sleep, and Pustovalov said to her tenderly: "Olenka, what's the matter, darling? Cross yourself!"

Her husband's ideas were hers. If he thought the room was too hot, or that business was slack, she thought the same. Her husband did not care for entertainments, and on holidays he stayed at home. She did likewise.

"You are always at home or in the office," her friends said to her. "You should go to the theater, darling, or to the circus."

"Vassichka and I have no time to go to theaters," she would answer sedately. "We have no time for nonsense. What's the use of these theaters?"

On Saturdays Pustovalov and she used to go to the evening

service; on holidays to early mass, and they walked side by side with softened faces as they came home from church. There was a pleasant fragrance about them both, and her silk dress rustled agreeably. At home they drank tea, with fancy bread and jams of various kinds, and afterward they ate pie. Every day at twelve o'clock there was a savory smell of beet-root soup and of mutton or duck in their yard, and on fast days of fish, and no one could pass the gate without feeling hungry. In the office the samovar was always boiling, and customers were regaled with tea and biscuits. Once a week the couple went to the baths and returned side by side, both red in the face.

"Yes, we have nothing to complain of, thank God," Olenka used to say to her acquaintances. "I wish everyone were as well off as Vassichka and I."

When Pustovalov went away to buy wood in the Mogilev district, she missed him dreadfully, lay awake, and cried. A young veterinary surgeon in the army, called Smirnin, to whom they had let their lodge, used sometimes to come in in the evening. He used to talk to her and play cards with her, and this entertained her in her husband's absence. She was particularly interested in what he told her of his home life. He was married and had a little boy, but was separated from his wife because she had been unfaithful to him, and now he hated her and sent her forty rubles a month for the maintenance of their son. And hearing of all this, Olenka sighed and shook her head. She was sorry for him.

"Well, God keep you," she used to say to him at parting, as she lighted him down the stairs with a candle. "Thank you for coming to cheer me up, and may the Mother of God give you health."

And she always expressed herself with the same sedateness and dignity, the same reasonableness, in imitation of her husband. As the veterinary surgeon was disappearing behind the door below, she would say:

"You know, Vladimir Platonich, you'd better make it up with your wife. You should forgive her for the sake of your son. You may be sure the little fellow understands."

And when Pustovalov came back, she told him in a low voice about the veterinary surgeon and his unhappy home life, and both sighed and shook their heads and talked about the boy, who, no doubt, missed his father, and by some strange connection of ideas, they went up to the holy icons, bowed to the ground before them, and prayed that God would give them children.

And so the Pustovalovs lived for six years quietly and peaceably in love and complete harmony.

But behold! one winter day after drinking hot tea in the office, Vassily Andreich went out into the yard without his cap on to see about sending off some timber, caught cold, and was taken ill. He had the best doctors, but he grew worse and died after four months' illness. And Olenka was a widow once more.

"I've nobody, now you've left me, my darling," she sobbed, after her husband's funeral. "How can I live without you, in wretchedness and misery! Pity me, good people, all alone in the world!"

She went about dressed in black with "weepers," and gave up wearing hat and gloves for good. She hardly ever went out, except to church, or to her husband's grave, and led the life of a nun. It was not till six months later that she took off the weepers and opened the shutters of the windows. She was sometimes seen in the mornings, going with her cook to market for provisions, but what went on in her house and how she lived now could only be surmised. People guessed, from seeing her drinking tea in her garden with the veterinary surgeon, who read the newspaper aloud to her, and from the fact that, meeting a lady she knew at the post office, she said to her:

"There is no proper veterinary inspection in our town, and that's the cause of all sorts of epidemics. One is always hearing of people's getting infection from the milk supply, or catching diseases from horses and cows. The health of domestic animals ought to be as well cared for as the health of human beings."

She repeated the veterinary surgeon's words, and was of the same opinion as he about everything. It was evident that she could not live a year without some attachment, and had found new happiness in the lodge. In anyone else this would have been censured, but no one could think ill of Olenka; everything she did was so natural. Neither she nor the veterinary surgeon said anything to other people of the change in their relations, and tried, indeed, to conceal it, but without success, for Olenka could not keep a secret. When he had visitors, men serving in his regiment, and she poured out tea or served the supper, she would begin talking of the cattle plague, of the foot and mouth disease, and of the municipal slaughterhouses. He was dreadfully embarrassed, and when the guests had gone, he would seize her by the hand and hiss angrily:

"I've asked you before not to talk about what you don't understand. When we veterinary surgeons are talking among ourselves, please don't put your word in. It's really annoying."

And she would look at him with astonishment and dismay, and ask him in alarm: "But Volodichka, what *am* I to talk about?"

And with tears in her eyes she would embrace him, begging him not to be angry, and they were both happy.

But this happiness did not last long. The veterinary surgeon departed, departed forever with his regiment, when it was transferred to a distant place—to Siberia, perhaps. And Olenka was left alone.

Now she was absolutely alone. Her father had long been dead, and his armchair lay in the attic, covered with dust and lame of one leg. She got thinner and plainer, and when people met her in the street they did not look at her as they used to, and did not smile to her; evidently her best years were over and left behind, and now a new sort of life had begun for her, which did not bear thinking about. In the evening Olenka sat in the porch, and heard the band playing and the fireworks popping in the Tivoli, but now the sound stirred no response. She looked into her yard without interest, thought of nothing, wished for nothing, and afterward, when night came on, she went to bed and dreamed of her empty yard. She ate and drank as it were unwillingly.

And what was worst of all, she had no opinions of any sort. She saw the objects about her and understood what she saw, but could not form any opinion about them, and did not know what to talk about. And how awful it is not to have any opinions! One sees a bottle, for instance, or the rain, or a peasant driving in his cart, but what the bottle is for, or the rain, or the peasant, and what is the meaning of it, one can't say, and could not even for a thousand rubles. When she had Kukin, or Pustovalov, or the veterinary surgeon, Olenka could explain everything, and give her opinion about anything you like, but now there was the same emptiness in her brain and in her heart as there was in her yard outside. And it was as harsh and as bitter as wormwood in the mouth.

Little by little the town grew in all directions. The road became a street, and where the Tivoli and the timberyard had been, there were new turnings and houses. How rapidly time passes! Olenka's house grew dingy, the roof got rusty, the shed sank on one side, and the whole yard was overgrown with docks and stinging nettles. Olenka herself had grown plain and elderly; in summer she sat in the porch, and her soul, as before, was empty and dreary and full of bitterness. In winter she sat at her window and looked at the snow. When she caught the scent of spring, or heard the chime of the church bells, a sudden rush of memories from the past came over her, there was a tender ache in her heart, and her eyes brimmed over with tears; but this was only for a minute, and then came emptiness again and the sense of the futility of life. The black kitten, Briska, rubbed against her and purred softly, but Olenka was not touched by these feline caresses. That was not what she needed. She wanted a love that would absorb her whole being, her whole soul and reason—that would give her ideas and an object in life, and would warm her old blood. And she would shake the kitten off her skirt and say with vexation:

"Get along; I don't want you!"

And so it was, day after day and year after year, and no joy, and no opinions. Whatever Mavra, the cook, said, she accepted.

One hot July day, toward evening, just as the cattle were being driven away, and the whole yard was full of dust, someone suddenly

knocked at the gate. Olenka went to open it herself and was dumb-
founded when she looked out: she saw Smirnin, the veterinary surgeon, gray-headed, and dressed as a civilian. She suddenly remembered everything. She could not help crying and letting her head fall
on his breast without uttering a word, and in the violence of her
feeling she did not notice how they both walked into the house and
sat down to tea.

"My dear Vladimir Platonich! What fate has brought you?" she
muttered, trembling with joy.

"I want to settle here for good, Olga Semyonovna," he told her.
"I have resigned my post, and have come to settle down and try my
luck on my own account. Besides, it's time for my boy to go to
school. He's a big boy. I am reconciled with my wife, you know."

"Where is she?" asked Olenka.

"She's at the hotel with the boy, and I'm looking for lodgings."

"Good gracious, my dear soul! Lodgings? Why not have my
house? Why shouldn't that suit you? Why, my goodness, I wouldn't
take any rent!" cried Olenka in a flutter, beginning to cry again.
"You live here, and the lodge will do nicely for me. Oh dear! how
glad I am!"

Next day the roof was painted and the walls were whitewashed,
and Olenka, with her arms akimbo, walked about the yard giving
directions. Her face was beaming with her old smile, and she was
brisk and alert as though she had waked from a long sleep. The
veterinary's wife arrived—a thin, plain lady, with short hair and a
peevish expression. With her was her little Sasha, a boy of ten, small
for his age, blue-eyed, chubby, with dimples in his cheeks. And
scarcely had the boy walked into the yard when he ran after the cat,
and at once there was the sound of his gay, joyous laugh.

"Is that your puss, Auntie?" he asked Olenka. "When she has
little ones, do give us a kitten. Mamma is awfully afraid of mice."

Olenka talked to him, and gave him tea. Her heart warmed and
there was a sweet ache in her bosom, as though the boy had been her
own child. And when he sat at the table in the evening, going over

his lessons, she looked at him with deep tenderness and pity as she murmured to herself:

"You pretty pet! . . . my precious! . . . Such a fair little thing, and so clever."

" 'An island is a piece of land which is entirely surrounded by water,' " he read aloud.

"An island is a piece of land," she repeated, and this was the first opinion to which she gave utterance with positive conviction after so many years of silence and dearth of ideas.

Now she had opinions of her own, and at supper she talked to Sasha's parents, saying how difficult the lessons were at the high schools, but that yet the high school was better than a commercial one, since with a high-school education all careers were open to one, such as being a doctor or an engineer.

Sasha began going to the high school. His mother departed to Kharkov to her sister's and did not return; his father used to go off every day to inspect cattle, and would often be away from home for three days together, and it seemed to Olenka as though Sasha was entirely abandoned, that he was not wanted at home, that he was being starved, and she carried him off to her lodge and gave him a little room there.

And for six months Sasha had lived in the lodge with her. Every morning Olenka came into his bedroom and found him fast asleep, sleeping noiselessly with his hand under his cheek. She was sorry to wake him.

"Sashenka," she would say mournfully, "get up, darling. It's time for school."

He would get up, dress and say his prayers, and then sit down to breakfast, drink three glasses of tea, and eat two large biscuits and half a buttered roll. All this time he was hardly awake and a little ill-humored in consequence.

"You don't quite know your fable, Sashenka," Olenka would say, looking at him as though he were about to set off on a long journey.

"What a lot of trouble I have with you! You must work and do your best, darling, and obey your teachers."

"Oh, do leave me alone!" Sasha would say.

Then he would go down the street to school, a little figure, wearing a big cap and carrying a satchel on his shoulder. Olenka would follow him noiselessly.

"Sashenka!" she would call after him, and she would pop into his hand a date or a caramel. When he reached the street where the school was, he would feel ashamed of being followed by a tall, stout woman; he would turn round and say:

"You'd better go home, Auntie. I can go the rest of the way alone."

She would stand still and look after him fixedly till he had disappeared at the school gate.

Ah, how she loved him! Of her former attachments not one had been so deep; never had her soul surrendered to any feeling so spontaneously, so disinterestedly, and so joyously as now that her maternal instincts were aroused. For this little boy with the dimple in his cheek and the big school cap, she would have given her whole life, she would have given it with joy and tears of tenderness. Why? Who can tell why?

When she had seen the last of Sasha, she returned home, contented and serene, brimming over with love; her face, which had grown younger during the last six months, smiled and beamed; people meeting her looked at her with pleasure.

"Good morning, Olga Semyonovna, darling. How are you, darling?"

"The lessons at the high school are very difficult now," she would relate at the market. "It's too much; in the first class yesterday they gave him a fable to learn by heart, and a Latin translation and a problem. You know it's too much for a little chap."

And she would begin talking about the teachers, the lessons, and the schoolbooks, saying just what Sasha said.

At three o'clock they had dinner together: in the evening they learned their lessons together and cried. When she put him to bed, she would stay a long time making the Cross over him and murmuring a prayer; then she would go to bed and dream of that faraway misty future when Sasha would finish his studies and become a doctor or an engineer, would have a big house of his own with horses and a carriage, would get married and have children. . . . She would fall asleep still thinking of the same thing, and tears would run down her cheeks from her closed eyes, while the black cat lay purring beside her: "Mrr, mrr, mrr."

Suddenly there would come a loud knock at the gate.

Olenka would wake up breathless with alarm, her heart throbbing. Half a minute later would come another knock.

"It must be a telegram from Kharkov," she would think, beginning to tremble from head to foot. "Sasha's mother is sending for him from Kharkov. . . . Oh, mercy on us!"

She was in despair. Her head, her hands, and her feet would turn chill, and she would feel that she was the most unhappy woman in the world. But another minute would pass, voices would be heard: it would turn out to be the veterinary surgeon coming home from the club.

"Well, thank God!" she would think.

And gradually the load in her heart would pass off, and she would feel at ease. She would go back to bed thinking of Sasha, who lay sound asleep in the next room, sometimes crying out in his sleep:

"I'll give it to you! Get away! Shut up!"

1899

THE HUNTSMAN

A sultry, stifling midday. Not a cloudlet in the sky. . . . The sun-baked glass had a disconsolate, hopeless look: even if there were rain, it could never be green again. . . . The forest stood silent, motionless, as though it were looking at something with its treetops or expecting something.

At the edge of the clearing a tall, narrow-shouldered man of forty in a red shirt, in patched trousers that had been a gentleman's, and in high boots, was slouching along with a lazy, shambling step. He was sauntering along the road. On the right was the green of the clearing, on the left a golden sea of ripe rye stretched to the very horizon. He was red and perspiring, a white cap with a straight jockey peak, evidently a gift from some openhanded young gentleman, perched jauntily on his handsome flaxen head. Across his shoulder hung a game bag with a blackcock lying in it. The man held a double-barreled gun cocked in his hand, and screwed up his eyes in the direction of his lean old dog, who was running on ahead sniffing the bushes. There was stillness all round, not a sound . . . everything living was hiding away from the heat.

"Yegor Vlassich!" The huntsman suddenly heard a soft voice.

He started and, looking round, scowled. Beside him, as though she had sprung out of the earth, stood a pale-faced woman of thirty with a sickle in her hand. She was trying to look into his face, and was smiling diffidently.

"Oh, it is you, Pelagea!" said the huntsman, stopping and deliberately uncocking the gun. "H'm! . . . How have you come here?"

"The women from our village are working here, so I have come with them. . . . As a laborer, Yegor Vlassich."

"Oh . . ." growled Yegor Vlassich, and slowly walked on.

Pelagea followed him. They walked in silence for twenty paces.

"I have not seen you for a long time, Yegor Vlassich . . ." said Pelagea looking tenderly at the huntsman's moving shoulders. "I have not seen you since you came into our hut at Easter for a drink of water . . . you came in at Easter for a minute and then God knows how . . . drunk . . . you scolded and beat me and went away. . . . I have been waiting and waiting. . . . I've tired my eyes out looking for you. Ah, Yegor Vlassich, Yegor Vlassich! You might look in just once!"

"What is there for me to do there?"

"Of course there is nothing for you to do . . . though to be sure . . . there is the place to look after. . . . To see how things are going. . . . You are the master. . . . I say, you have shot a blackcock, Yegor Vlassich! You ought to sit down and rest!"

As she said all this Pelagea laughed like a silly girl and looked up at Yegor's face. Her face was simply radiant with happiness.

"Sit down? If you like . . ." said Yegor in a tone of indifference, and he chose a spot between two fir trees. "Why are you standing? You sit down too."

Pelagea sat a little way off in the sun and, ashamed of her joy, put her hand over her smiling mouth. Two minutes passed in silence.

"You might come for once," said Pelagea.

"What for?" sighed Yegor, taking off his cap and wiping his red forehead with his hand. "There is no object in my coming. To go for an hour or two is only waste of time, it's simply upsetting you, and to live continually in the village my soul could not endure. . . . You know yourself I am a pampered man. . . . I want a bed to sleep in, good tea to drink, and refined conversation. . . . I want all the niceties, while you live in poverty and dirt in the village. . . . I couldn't stand it for a day. Suppose there were an edict that I must live with you, I should either set fire to the hut or lay hands on myself. Since childhood I've had this love for ease; there is no help for it."

"Where are you living now?"

"With the gentleman here, Dmitry Ivanich, as a huntsman. I furnish his table with game, but he keeps me . . . more for his pleasure than anything."

"That's not proper work you're doing, Yegor Vlassich. . . . For other people it's a pastime, but with you it's like a trade . . . like real work."

"You don't understand, you silly," said Yegor, gazing gloomily at the sky. "You have never understood, and as long as you live you will never understand what sort of man I am. . . . You think of me as a foolish man, gone to the bad, but to anyone who understands, I am the best shot there is in the whole district. The gentry feel that, and they have even printed things about me in a magazine. There isn't a man to be compared with me as a sportsman. . . . And it is not because I am pampered and proud that I look down upon your village work. From my childhood, you know, I have never had any calling apart from guns and dogs. If they took away my gun, I used to go out with the fishing hook, if they took the hook I caught things with my hands. And I went in for horse dealing too, I used to go to the fairs when I had the money, and you know that if a peasant goes in for being a sportsman, or a horse dealer, it's goodbye to the plough. Once the spirit of freedom has taken a man you will never root it out of him. In the same way, if a gentleman goes in for being an actor or for any other art, he will never make an official or a landowner. You are a woman, and you do not understand, but one must understand that."

"I understand, Yegor Vlassich."

"You don't understand if you are going to cry. . . ."

"I . . . I'm not crying," said Pelagea, turning away. "It's a sin, Yegor Vlassich! You might stay a day with luckless me, anyway. It's twelve years since I was married to you, and . . . and . . . there has never once been love between us! . . . I . . . I am not crying."

"Love . . ." muttered Yegor, scratching his arm. "There can't be any love. It's only in name we are husband and wife; we aren't really. In your eyes I am a wild man, and in mine you are a simple peasant woman with no understanding. Are we well matched? I am a free, pampered, profligate man, while you are a working woman, going in bast shoes and never straightening your back. The way I think of myself is that I am the foremost man in every kind of sport, and you look at me with pity. . . . Is that being well matched?"

"But we are married, you know, Yegor Vlassich," sobbed Pelagea.

"Not married of our free will. . . . Have you forgotten? You have to thank Count Sergey Pavlovich and yourself. Out of envy, because I shot better than he did, the count kept giving me wine for a whole month, and when a man's drunk you could make him change his religion, let alone getting married. To pay me out he married me to you when I was drunk. . . . A huntsman to a herd-girl! You saw I was drunk, why did you marry me? You were not a serf, you know; you could have resisted. Of course it was a bit of luck for a herd-girl to marry a huntsman, but you ought to have thought about it. Well, now be miserable, cry. It's a joke for the count, but a crying matter for you. . . . Beat yourself against the wall."

A silence followed. Three wild ducks flew over the clearing. Yegor followed them with his eyes till, transformed into three scarcely visible dots, they sank down far beyond the forest.

"How do you live?" he asked, moving his eyes from the ducks to Pelagea.

"Now I am going out to work, and in the winter I take a child from the Foundling Hospital and bring it up on the bottle. They give me a ruble and a half a month."

"Oh. . . ."

Again a silence. From the strip that had been reaped floated a soft song which broke off at the very beginning. It was too hot to sing.

"They say you have put up a new hut for Akulina," said Pelagea. Yegor did not speak.

"So she is dear to you. . . ."

"It's your luck, it's fate!" said the huntsman, stretching. "You must put up with it, poor thing. But goodbye, I've been chattering long enough. . . . I must be at Boltovo by the evening."

Yegor rose, stretched himself, and slung his gun over his shoulder; Pelagea got up.

"And when are you coming to the village?" she asked softly.

"I have no reason to, I shall never come sober, and you have little to gain from me drunk; I am spiteful when I am drunk. Goodbye!"

"Goodbye, Yegor Vlassich."

Yegor put his cap on the back of his head and, clicking to his dog, went on his way. Pelagea stood still looking after him. . . . She saw his moving shoulder blades, his jaunty cap, his lazy, careless step, and her eyes were full of sadness and tender affection. . . . Her gaze flitted over her husband's tall, lean figure and caressed and fondled it. . . . He, as though he felt that gaze, stopped and looked round. . . . He did not speak, but from his face, from his shrugged shoulders, Pelagea could see that he wanted to say something to her. She went up to him timidly and looked at him with imploring eyes.

"Take it," he said, turning round.

He gave her a crumpled ruble note and walked quickly away.

"Goodbye, Yegor Vlassich," she said, mechanically taking the ruble.

He walked by a long road, straight as a taut strap. She, pale and motionless as a statue, stood, her eyes seizing every step he took. But the red of his shirt melted into the dark color of his trousers, his step could not be seen, and the dog could not be distinguished from the boots. Nothing could be seen but the cap, and . . . suddenly Yegor turned off sharply into the clearing and the cap vanished in the greenness.

"Goodbye, Yegor Vlassich," whispered Pelagea, and she stood on tiptoe to see the white cap once more.

1885

SLEEPY

Night. Varka, the little nurse, a girl of thirteen, is rocking the cradle in which the baby is lying, and humming hardly audibly:

> "*Hush-a-bye, my baby wee,*
> *While I sing a song for thee.*"

A little green lamp is burning before the icon; there is a string stretched from one end of the room to the other, on which baby clothes and a pair of big black trousers are hanging. There is a big patch of green on the ceiling from the icon lamp, and the baby clothes and the trousers throw long shadows on the stove, on the cradle, and on Varka. . . . When the lamp begins to flicker, the green patch and the shadows come to life, and are set in motion, as though by the wind. It is stuffy. There is a smell of cabbage soup, and of the inside of a boot shop.

The baby is crying. For a long while he has been hoarse and exhausted with crying; but he still goes on screaming, and there is no knowing when he will stop. And Varka is sleepy. Her eyes are glued together, her head droops, her neck aches. She cannot move her eyelids or her lips, and she feels as though her face is dried and wooden, as though her head has become as small as the head of a pin.

"Hush-a-bye, my baby wee," she hums, "while I cook the groats for thee. . . ."

A cricket is churring in the stove. Through the door in the next room the master and the apprentice Afanasy are snoring. . . . The cradle creaks plaintively, Varka murmurs—and it all blends into that soothing music of the night to which it is so sweet to listen, when one is lying in bed. Now that music is merely irritating and oppressive, because it goads her to sleep, and she must not sleep; if Varka—God forbid!—should fall asleep, her master and mistress would beat her.

The lamp flickers. The patch of green and the shadows are set in motion, forcing themselves on Varka's fixed, half-open eyes, and in her half slumbering brain are fashioned into misty visions. She sees dark clouds chasing one another over the sky, and screaming like the baby. But then the wind blows, the clouds are gone, and Varka sees a broad high road covered with liquid mud; along the high road stretch files of wagons, while people with wallets on their backs are trudging along and shadows flit backward and forward; on both sides she can see forests through the cold harsh mist. All at once the people with their wallets and their shadows fall on the ground in the liquid mud. "What is that for?" Varka asks. "To sleep, to sleep!" they answer her. And they fall sound asleep, and sleep sweetly, while crows and magpies sit on the telegraph wires, scream like the baby, and try to wake them.

"Hush-a-bye, my baby wee, and I will sing a song to thee," murmurs Varka, and now she sees herself in a dark stuffy hut.

Her dead father, Yefim Stepanov, is tossing from side to side on the floor. She does not see him, but she hears him moaning and rolling on the floor from pain. "His guts have burst," as he says; the pain is so violent that he cannot utter a single word, and can only draw in his breath and clack his teeth like the rattling of a drum:

"Boo—boo—boo—boo. . . ."

Her mother, Pelagea, has run to the master's house to say that

". . . if Varka—God forbid!—should fall asleep, her master and mistress would beat her."

Yefim is dying. She has been gone a long time, and ought to be back. Varka lies awake on the stove, and hears her father's "boo—boo—boo." And then she hears someone has driven up to the hut. It is a young doctor from the town, who has been sent from the big house where he is staying on a visit. The doctor comes into the hut; he cannot be seen in the darkness, but he can be heard coughing and rattling the door.

"Light a candle," he says.

"Boo—boo—boo," answers Yefim.

Pelagea rushes to the stove and begins looking for the broken pot with the matches. A minute passes in silence. The doctor, feeling in his pocket, lights a match.

"In a minute, sir, in a minute," says Pelagea. She rushes out of the hut, and soon afterward comes back with a bit of candle.

Yefim's cheeks are rosy and his eyes are shining, and there is a peculiar keenness in his glance, as though he were seeing right through the hut and the doctor.

"Come, what is it? What are you thinking about?" says the doctor, bending down to him. "Aha! have you had this long?"

"What? Dying, Your Honor, my hour has come. . . . I am not to stay among the living. . . ."

"Don't talk nonsense! We will cure you!"

"That's as you please, Your Honor, we humbly thank you, only we understand. . . . Since death has come, there it is."

The doctor spends a quarter of an hour over Yefim, then he gets up and says:

"I can do nothing. You must go into the hospital, there they will operate on you. Go at once. . . . You must go! It's rather late, they will all be asleep in the hospital, but that doesn't matter, I will give you a note. Do you hear?"

"Kind sir, but what can he go in?" says Pelagea. "We have no horse."

"Never mind. I'll ask your master, he'll let you have a horse."

The doctor goes away, the candle goes out, and again there is the sound of "boo—boo—boo." Half an hour later someone drives up to the hut. A cart has been sent to take Yefim to the hospital. He gets ready and goes. . . .

But now it is a clear bright morning. Pelagea is not at home; she has gone to the hospital to find what is being done to Yefim. Somewhere there is a baby crying, and Varka hears someone singing with her own voice:

"Hush-a-bye, my baby wee, I will sing a song to thee."

Pelagea comes back; she crosses herself and whispers:

"They put him to rights in the night, but toward morning he gave up his soul to God. . . . The Kingdom of Heaven be his and peace everlasting. . . . They say he was taken too late. . . . He ought to have gone sooner. . . ."

Varka goes out into the road and cries there, but all at once someone hits her on the back of her head so hard that her forehead knocks against a birch tree. She raises her eyes and sees, facing her, her master, the shoemaker.

"What are you about, you scabby slut?" he says. "The child is crying, and you are asleep!"

He gives her a sharp slap behind the ear, and she shakes her head, rocks the cradle, and murmurs her song. The green patch and the shadows from the trousers and the baby clothes move up and down, nod to her, and soon take possession of her brain again. Again she sees the high road covered with liquid mud. The people with wallets on their backs and the shadows have lain down and are fast asleep. Looking at them, Varka has a passionate longing for sleep; she would lie down with enjoyment, but her mother Pelagea is walking beside her, hurrying her on. They are hastening together to the town to find jobs.

"Give alms, for Christ's sake!" her mother begs of the people they meet. "Show us the divine mercy, kindhearted gentlefolk!"

"Give the baby here!" a familiar voice answers. "Give the baby here!" the same voice repeats, this time harshly and angrily. "Are you asleep, you wretched girl?"

Varka jumps up, and looking around grasps what is the matter: there is no high road, no Pelagea, no people meeting them, there is only her mistress, who has come to feed the baby, and is standing in the middle of the room. While the stout, broad-shouldered woman nurses the child and soothes it, Varka stands looking at her and waiting till she has done. And outside the windows the air is already turning blue, the shadows and the green patch on the ceiling are visibly growing pale, it will soon be morning.

"Take him," says her mistress, buttoning up her chemise over her bosom; "he is crying. He must be bewitched."

Varka takes the baby, puts him in the cradle, and begins rocking it again. The green patch and the shadows gradually disappear, and now there is nothing to force itself on her eyes and cloud her brain. But she is as sleepy as before, fearfully sleepy! Varka lays her head on the edge of the cradle, and rocks her whole body to overcome her sleepiness, but yet her eyes are glued together, and her head is heavy.

"Varka, heat the stove!" she hears the master's voice through the door.

So it is time to get up and set to work. Varka leaves the cradle, and runs to the shed for firewood. She is glad. When one moves and runs about, one is not so sleepy as when one is sitting down. She brings the wood, heats the stove, and feels that her wooden face is getting supple again, and that her thoughts are growing clearer.

"Varka, set the samovar!" shouts her mistress.

Varka splits a piece of wood, but has scarcely time to light the splinters and put them in the samovar, when she hears a fresh order:

"Varka, clean the master's galoshes!"

She sits down on the floor, cleans the galoshes, and thinks how nice it would be to put her head into a big deep galosh, and have a little nap in it. . . . And all at once the galosh grows, swells, fills up the whole room. Varka drops the brush, but at once shakes her head, opens her eyes wide, and tries to look at things so that they may not grow big and move before her eyes.

"Varka, wash the steps outside; I am ashamed for the customers to see them!"

Varka washes the steps, sweeps and dusts the rooms, then heats another stove and runs to the shop. There is a great deal of work: she hasn't one minute free.

But nothing is so hard as standing in the same place at the kitchen table peeling potatoes. Her head droops over the table, the potatoes dance before her eyes, the knife tumbles out of her hand while her fat, angry mistress is moving about near her with her sleeves tucked up, talking so loud that it makes a ringing in Varka's ears. It is agonizing, too, to wait at dinner, to wash, to sew, there are minutes when she longs to flop on to the floor regardless of everything, and to sleep.

The day passes. Seeing the windows getting dark, Varka presses her temples, which feel as though they were made of wood, and smiles, though she does not know why. The dusk of evening caresses her eyes that will hardly keep open, and promises her sound sleep soon. In the evening visitors come.

"Varka, set the samovar!" shouts her mistress.

The samovar is a little one, and before the visitors have drunk all the tea they want, she has to heat it five times. After tea Varka stands for a whole hour on the same spot, looking at the visitors, and waiting for orders.

"Varka, run and buy three bottles of beer!"

She starts off, and tries to run as quickly as she can, to drive away sleep.

"Varka, fetch some vodka! Varka, where's the corkscrew? Varka, clean a herring!"

But now, at last, the visitors have gone; the lights are put out, the master and mistress go to bed.

"Varka, rock the baby!" she hears the last order.

The cricket churrs in the stove; the green patch on the ceiling and the shadows from the trousers and the baby clothes force themselves on Varka's half-opened eyes again, wink at her and cloud her mind.

"Hush-a-bye, my baby wee," she murmurs, "and I will sing a song to thee."

And the baby screams, and is worn out with screaming. Again Varka sees the muddy high road, the people with wallets, her mother Pelageya, her father Yefim. She understands everything, she recognizes everyone, but through her half sleep she cannot understand the force which binds her, hand and foot, weighs upon her, and prevents her from living. She looks round, searches for that force that she may escape from it, but she cannot find it. At last, tired to death, she does her very utmost, strains her eyes, looks up at the flickering green patch, and listening to the screaming, finds the foe who will not let her live.

That foe is the baby.

She laughs. It seems strange to her that she has failed to grasp such a simple thing before. The green patch, the shadows, and the cricket seem to laugh and wonder too.

The hallucination takes possession of Varka. She gets up from her stool, and with a broad smile on her face and wide unblinking eyes, she walks up and down the room. She feels pleased and tickled at the thought that she will be rid directly of the baby that binds her hand and foot. . . . Kill the baby and then sleep, sleep, sleep. . . .

Laughing and winking and shaking her fingers at the green patch, Varka steals up to the cradle and bends over the baby. When she has strangled him, she quickly lies down on the floor, laughs with delight that she can sleep, and in a minute is sleeping as soundly as the dead.

1888

PEASANTS

Nikolay Tchikildyeev, a waiter in the Moscow hotel Slavyansky Bazaar, was taken ill. His legs went numb and his gait was affected, so that on one occasion, as he was going along the corridor, he tumbled and fell down with a tray full of ham and peas. He had to leave his job. All his own savings and his wife's were spent on doctors and medicines; they had nothing left to live upon. He felt dull with no work to do, and he made up his mind he must go home to the village. It is better to be ill at home, and living there is cheaper; and it is a true saying that the walls of home are a help.

He reached Zhukovo toward evening. In his memories of childhood he had pictured his home as bright, snug, comfortable. Now, going into the hut, he was positively frightened; it was so dark, so crowded, so unclean. His wife, Olga, and his daughter, Sasha, who had come with him, kept looking in bewilderment at the big untidy stove, which filled up almost half the hut and was black with soot and flies. What lots of flies! The stove was on one side, the beams lay slanting on the walls, and it looked as though the hut were just going to fall to pieces. In the corner, facing the door, under the holy images, bottle labels and newspaper cuttings were stuck on the walls instead of pictures. The poverty, the poverty! Of the grown-up people there were none at home; all were at work at the harvest. On the stove was sitting a white-headed girl of eight, unwashed and apathetic; she did not even glance at them as they came in. On the floor a white cat was rubbing itself against the oven fork.

"Puss, puss!" Sasha called to her. "Puss!"

"She can't hear," said the little girl; "she has gone deaf."

"How is that?"

"Oh, she was beaten."

Nikolay and Olga realized from the first glance what life was like here, but said nothing to one another; in silence they put down their bundles, and went out into the village street. Their hut was the third from the end, and seemed the very poorest and oldest-looking; the second was not much better; but the last one had an iron roof, and curtains in the windows. That hut stood apart, not enclosed; it was a tavern. The huts were in a single row, and the whole of the little village—quiet and dreamy, with willows, elders, and mountain ash trees peeping out from the yards—had an attractive look.

Beyond the peasants' homesteads there was a slope down to the river, so steep and precipitous that huge stones jutted out bare here and there through the clay. Down the slope, among the stones and holes dug by the potters, ran winding paths; bits of broken pottery, some brown, some red, lay piled up in heaps, and below there stretched a broad, level, bright green meadow, from which the hay had been already carried, and in which the peasants' cattle were wandering. The river, three quarters of a mile from the village, ran twisting and turning, with beautiful leafy banks; beyond it was again a broad meadow, a herd of cattle, long strings of white geese; then, just as on the near side, a steep ascent uphill, and on the top of the hill a hamlet, and a church with five domes, and at a little distance the manor house.

"It's lovely here in your parts!" said Olga, crossing herself at the sight of the church. "What space, oh Lord!"

Just at that moment the bell began ringing for service (it was

Saturday evening). Two little girls, down below, who were dragging up a pail of water, looked round at the church to listen to the bell.

"At this time they are serving the dinners at the Slavyansky Bazaar," said Nikolay dreamily.

Sitting on the edge of the slope, Nikolay and Olga watched the sun setting, watched the gold and crimson sky reflected in the river, in the church windows, and in the whole air—which was soft and still and unutterably pure as it never was in Moscow. And when the sun had set the flocks and herds passed, bleating and lowing; geese flew across from the further side of the river, and all sank into silence; the soft light died away in the air, and the dusk of evening began quickly moving down upon them.

Meanwhile Nikolay's father and mother, two gaunt, bent, toothless old people, just of the same height, came back. The women—the sisters-in-law Marya and Fyokla—who had been working on the landowner's estate beyond the river, arrived home, too. Marya, the wife of Nikolay's brother Kiryak, had six children, and Fyokla, the wife of Nikolay's brother Denis—who had gone for a soldier—had two; and when Nikolay, going into the hut, saw all the family, all those bodies big and little moving about on the lockers, in the hanging cradles and in all the corners, and when he saw the greed with which the old father and the women ate the black bread, dipping it in water, he realized he had made a mistake in coming here, sick, penniless, and with a family, too—a great mistake!

"And where is Kiryak?" he asked after they had exchanged greetings.

"He is in service at the merchant's," answered his father; "a keeper in the woods. He is not a bad peasant, but too fond of his glass."

"He is no great help!" said the old woman tearfully. "Our men are a grievous lot; they bring nothing into the house, but take plenty out. Kiryak drinks, and so does the old man; it is no use hiding a sin; he knows his way to the tavern. The Heavenly Mother is wroth."

In honor of the visitors they brought out the samovar. The tea smelt of fish; the sugar was gray and looked as though it had been nibbled; cockroaches ran to and fro over the bread and among the crockery. It was disgusting to drink, and the conversation was disgusting, too—about nothing but poverty and illnesses. But before they had time to empty their first cups there came a loud, prolonged drunken shout from the yard:

"Ma-arya!"

"It looks as though Kiryak were coming," said the old man. "Speak of the devil."

All were hushed. And again, soon afterward, the same shout, coarse and drawn out as though it came out of the earth:

"Ma-arya!"

Marya, the elder sister-in-law, turned pale and huddled against the stove, and it was strange to see the look of terror on the face of the strong, broad-shouldered, ugly woman. Her daughter, the child who had been sitting on the stove and looked so apathetic, suddenly broke into loud weeping.

"What are you howling for, you plague?" Fyokla, a handsome woman, also strong and broad-shouldered, shouted to her. "He won't kill you, no fear!"

From his old father Nikolay learned that Marya was afraid to live in the forest with Kiryak, and that when he was drunk he always came for her, made a row, and beat her mercilessly.

"Ma-arya!" the shout sounded close to the door.

"Protect me, for Christ's sake, good people!" faltered Marya, breathing as though she had been plunged into very cold water. "Protect me, kind people. . . ."

All the children in the hut began crying, and looking at them; Sasha, too, began to cry. They heard a drunken cough, and a tall, black-bearded peasant wearing a winter cap came into the hut, and was the more terrible because his face could not be seen in the dim light of the little lamp. It was Kiryak. Going up to his wife, he swung his arm and punched her in the face with his fist. Stunned by the blow, she did not utter a sound, but sat down, and her nose instantly began bleeding.

"What a disgrace! What a disgrace!" muttered the old man, clambering up onto the stove. "Before visitors, too! It's a sin!"

The old mother sat silent, bowed, lost in thought; Fyokla rocked the cradle.

Evidently conscious of inspiring fear, and pleased at doing so, Kiryak seized Marya by the arm, dragged her toward the door, and bellowed like an animal in order to seem still more terrible; but at that moment he suddenly caught sight of the visitors and stopped.

"Oh, they have come . . ." he said, letting his wife go; "my own brother and his family. . . ."

Staggering and opening wide his red, drunken eyes, he said his prayer before the image and went on:

"My brother and his family have come to the parental home . . . from Moscow, I suppose. The great capital Moscow, to be sure, the mother of cities. . . . Excuse me."

He sank down on the bench near the samovar and began drinking tea, sipping it loudly from the saucer in the midst of general silence. . . . He drank off a dozen cups, then reclined on the bench and began snoring.

They began going to bed. Nikolay, as an invalid, was put on the stove with his old father; Sasha lay down on the floor, while Olga went with the other women into the barn.

"Aye, aye, dearie," she said, lying down on the hay beside Marya; "you won't mend your trouble with tears. Bear it in patience, that is all. It is written in the Scriptures: 'If anyone smite thee on the right cheek, offer him the left one also.' . . . Aye, aye, dearie."

Then in a low singsong murmur she told them about Moscow, about her own life, how she had been a servant in furnished lodgings.

"And in Moscow the houses are big, built of brick," she said; "and there are ever so many churches, forty times forty, dearie; and they are all gentry in the houses, so handsome and so proper!"

Marya told her that she had not only never been in Moscow, but had not even been in their own district town; she could not read or write, and knew no prayers, not even "Our Father." Both she and Fyokla, the other sister-in-law, who was sitting a little way off listening, were extremely ignorant and could understand nothing. They both disliked their husbands; Marya was afraid of Kiryak, and whenever he stayed with her she was shaking with fear, and always got a headache from the fumes of vodka and tobacco with which he reeked. And in answer to the question whether she did not miss her husband, Fyokla answered with vexation:

"Miss him!"

They talked a little and sank into silence.

It was cool and a cock crowed at the top of his voice near the barn, preventing them from sleeping. When the bluish morning light was already peeping through all the crevices, Fyokla got up stealthily and went out, and then they heard the sound of her bare feet running off somewhere.

II

Olga went to church, and took Marya with her. As they went down the path toward the meadow both were in good spirits. Olga liked the wide view, and Marya felt that in her sister-in-law she had someone near and akin to her. The sun was rising. Low down over the meadow floated a drowsy hawk. The river looked gloomy; there was a haze hovering over it here and there, but on the further bank a streak of light already stretched across the hill. The church was gleaming, and in the manor garden the rooks were cawing furiously.

"The old man is all right," Marya told her, "but Granny is strict; she is continually nagging. Our own grain lasted till Carnival. We buy flour now at the tavern. She is angry about it; she says we eat too much."

"Aye, aye, dearie! Bear it in patience, that is all. It is written: 'Come unto Me, all ye that labor and are heavy laden.'"

Olga spoke sedately, rhythmically, and she walked like a pilgrim woman, with a rapid, anxious step. Every day she read the Gospel, read it aloud like a deacon; a great deal of it she did not understand but the words of the Gospel moved her to tears, and words like "forasmuch as" and "verily" she pronounced with a sweet flutter at her heart. She believed in God, in the Holy Mother, in the Saints; she believed one must not offend anyone in the world—not simple folks, nor Germans, nor gypsies, nor Jews—and woe even to those who have no compassion on the beasts. She believed this was written in the Holy Scriptures; and so, when she pronounced phrases from Holy Writ, even though she did not understand them, her face grew softened, compassionate, and radiant.

"What part do you come from?" Marya asked her.

"I am from Vladimir. Only I was taken to Moscow long ago, when I was eight years old."

They reached the river. On the further side a woman was standing at the water's edge, undressing.

"It's our Fyokla," said Marya, recognizing her. "She has been over the river to the manor yard. To the stewards. She is a shameless hussy and foulmouthed—fearfully!"

Fyokla, young and vigorous as a girl, with her black eyebrows and her loose hair, jumped off the bank and began splashing the water with her feet, and waves ran in all directions from her.

"Shameless—dreadfully!" repeated Marya.

The river was crossed by a rickety little bridge of logs, and exactly below it in the clear, limpid water was a shoal of broad-headed mullets. The dew was glistening on the green bushes that looked into the water. There was a feeling of warmth; it was comforting! What a lovely morning! And how lovely life would have been in this world, in all likelihood, if it were not for poverty, horrible, hopeless poverty, from which one can find no refuge! One had only to look round at the village to remember vividly all that had happened the day before, and the illusion of happiness which seemed to surround them vanished instantly.

They reached the church. Marya stood at the entrance, and did not dare to go farther. She did not dare to sit down either. Though they only began ringing for mass between eight and nine, she remained standing the whole time.

While the Gospel was being read the crowd suddenly parted to make way for the family from the great house. Two young girls in white frocks and wide-brimmed hats walked in; with them a chubby, rosy boy in a sailor suit. Their appearance touched Olga; she made up her mind from the first glance that they were refined, well educated, handsome people. Marya looked at them from under her brows, sullenly, dejectedly, as though they were not human beings coming in, but monsters who might crush her if she did not make way for them.

And every time the deacon boomed out something in his bass voice she fancied she heard "Ma-arya!" and she shuddered.

III

The arrival of the visitors was already known in the village, and directly after mass a number of people gathered together in the hut. The Leonytchevs and Matvyeitchevs and the Ilyitchovs came to inquire about their relations who were in service in Moscow. All the lads of Zhukovo who could read and write were packed off to Moscow and hired out as butlers or waiters (while from the village on the other side of the river the boys all became bakers), and that had been the custom from the days of serfdom long ago when a certain Luka Ivanitch, a peasant from Zhukovo, now a legendary figure, who had been a waiter in one of the Moscow clubs, would take none but his fellow villagers into his service, and found jobs for them in taverns and restaurants; and from that time the village of Zhukovo was always called among the inhabitants of the surrounding districts Slaveytown. Nikolay had been taken to Moscow when he was eleven, and Ivan Makaritch, one of the Matvyeitchevs, at that time a headwaiter in the "Hermitage" garden, had put him into a situation. And now, addressing the Matvyeitchevs, Nikolay said emphatically:

"Ivan Makaritch was my benefactor, and I am bound to pray for him day and night, as it is owing to him I have become a good man."

"My good soul!" a tall old woman, the sister of Ivan Makaritch, said tearfully, "and not a word have we heard about him, poor dear."

"In the winter he was in service at Omon's, and this season there was a rumor he was somewhere out of town, in gardens. . . . He has aged! In old days he would bring home as much as ten rubles a day in the summertime, but now things are very quiet everywhere. The old man frets."

The women looked at Nikolay's feet, shod in felt boots, and at his pale face, and said mournfully:

"You are not one to get on, Nikolay Osipitch; you are not one to get on! No, indeed!"

And they all made much of Sasha. She was ten years old, but she was little and very thin, and might have been taken for no more than seven. Among the other little girls, with their sunburnt faces and roughly cropped hair, dressed in long faded smocks, she with her white little face, with her big dark eyes, with a red ribbon in her hair, looked funny, as though she were some little wild creature that had been caught and brought into the hut.

"She can read, too," Olga said in her praise, looking tenderly at her daughter. "Read a little, child!" she said, taking the Gospel from the corner. You read, and the good Christian people will listen."

The testament was an old and heavy one in leather binding, with dog-eared edges, and it exhaled a smell as though monks had come into the hut. Sasha raised her eyebrows and began in a loud rhythmic chant:

" 'And the angel of the Lord . . . appeared unto Joseph, saying unto him: Rise up, and take the Babe and His mother.' "

"The Babe and His mother," Olga repeated, and flushed all over with emotion.

" 'And flee into Egypt . . . and tarry there until such time as . . .' "

At the word "tarry" Olga could not refrain from tears. Looking at her, Marya began to whimper, and after her Ivan Makaritch's sister. The old father cleared his throat, and bustled about to find something to give his granddaughter, but, finding nothing, gave it up with a wave of his hand. And when the reading was over the neighbors dispersed to their homes, feeling touched and very much pleased with Olga and Sasha.

As it was a holiday, the family spent the whole day at home. The old woman, whom her husband, her daughters-in-law, her grandchildren all alike called Granny, tried to do everything herself; she heated the stove and set the samovar with her own hands, even waited at the midday meal, and then complained that she was worn out with work. And all the time she was uneasy for fear someone should eat a piece too much, or that her husband and daughters-in-law would sit idle. At one time she would hear the tavern keeper's geese going at the back of the huts to her kitchen garden, and she would run out of the hut with a long stick and spend half an hour screaming shrilly by her cabbages, which were as gaunt and scraggy as herself; at another time she fancied that a crow had designs on her chickens, and she rushed to attack it with loud words of abuse. She was cross and grumbling from morning till night. And often she raised such an outcry that passersby stopped in the street.

She was not affectionate toward the old man, reviling him as a lazybones and a plague. He was not a responsible, reliable peasant, and perhaps if she had not been continually nagging at him he would not have worked at all, but would have simply sat on the stove and talked. He talked to his son at great length about certain enemies of his, complained of the insults he said he had to put up with every day from the neighbors, and it was tedious to listen to him.

"Yes," he would say, standing with his arms akimbo, "yes. . . . A week after the Exaltation of the Cross I sold my hay willingly at thirty kopecks a pood. . . . Well and good. . . . So you see I was taking the hay in the morning with a good will; I was interfering with no one. In an unlucky hour I see the village elder, Antip Syedelnikov, coming out of the tavern. 'Where are you taking it, you ruffian?' says he, and takes me by the ear."

Kiryak had a fearful headache after his drinking bout, and was ashamed to face his brother.

"What vodka does! Ah, my God!" he muttered, shaking his aching head. "For Christ's sake, forgive me, brother and sister; I'm not happy myself."

As it was a holiday, they bought a herring at the tavern and made a soup of the herring's head. At midday they all sat down to drink tea, and went on drinking it for a long time, till they were all perspiring; they looked positively swollen from the tea drinking, and after it began sipping the broth from the herring's head, all helping themselves out of one bowl. But the herring itself Granny had hidden.

In the evening a potter began firing pots on the ravine. In the meadow below the girls got up a choral dance and sang songs. They played the concertina. And on the other side of the river a kiln for baking pots was lighted, too, and the girls sang songs, and in the distance the singing sounded soft and musical. The peasants were noisy in and about the tavern. They were singing with drunken voices, each on his own account, and swearing at one another, so that Olga could only shudder and say:

"Oh, holy Saints!"

She was amazed that the abuse was incessant, and those who were loudest and most persistent in this foul language were the old men who were so near their end. And the girls and children heard the swearing, and were not in the least disturbed by it, and it was evident that they were used to it from their cradles.

It was past midnight, the kilns on both sides of the river were put out, but in the meadow below and in the tavern the merrymaking still went on. The old father and Kiryak, both drunk, walking arm-in-arm and jostling against each other's shoulders, went to the barn where Olga and Marya were lying.

"Let her alone," the old man persuaded him; "let her alone. . . . She is a harmless woman. . . . It's a sin. . . ."

"Ma-arya!" shouted Kiryak.

"Let her be. . . . It's a sin. . . . She is not a bad woman."

Both stopped by the barn and went on.

"I lo-ove the flowers of the fi-ield," the old man began singing suddenly in a high, piercing tenor. "I lo-ove to gather them in the meadows!"

Then he spat, and with a filthy oath went into the hut.

IV

Granny put Sasha by her kitchen garden and told her to keep watch that the geese did not go in. It was a hot August day. The tavern keeper's geese could make their way into the kitchen garden by the backs of the huts, but now they were busily engaged picking up oats by the tavern, peacefully conversing together, and only the gander craned his head high as though trying to see whether the old woman were coming with her stick. The other geese might come up from below, but they were now grazing far away the other side of the river, stretched out in a long white garland about the meadow. Sasha stood about a little, grew weary, and, seeing that the geese were not coming, went away to the ravine.

There she saw Marya's eldest daughter, Motka, who was standing motionless on a big stone, staring at the church. Marya had given birth to thirteen children, but she only had six living, all girls, not one boy, and the eldest was eight. Motka, in a long smock, was standing barefooted in the full sunshine; the sun was blazing down right on her head, but she did not notice that, and seemed as though turned to stone. Sasha stood beside her and said, looking at the church:

"God lives in the church. Men have lamps and candles, but God has little green and red and blue lamps like little eyes. At night God walks about the church, and with Him the Holy Mother of God and Saint Nikolay, thud, thud, thud! . . . And the watchman is terrified, terrified! Aye, aye, dearie," she added, imitating her mother. "And when the end of the world comes all the churches will be carried up to heaven."

"With the-ir be-ells?" Motka asked in her deep voice, drawling every syllable.

"With their bells. And when the end of the world comes the good will go to Paradise, but the angry will burn in fire eternal and unquenchable, dearie. To my mother as well as to Marya God will say: 'You never offended anyone, and for that go to the right to Paradise'; but to Kiryak and Granny He will say: 'You go to the left into the fire.' And anyone who has eaten meat in Lent will go into the fire, too."

She looked upward at the sky, opening wide her eyes, and said:

"Look at the sky without winking, you will see angels."

Motka began looking at the sky, too, and a minute passed in silence.

"Do you see them?" asked Sasha.

"I don't," said Motka in her deep voice.

"But I do. Little angels are flying about the sky and flap, flap with their little wings as though they were gnats."

Motka thought for a little, with her eyes on the ground, and asked:

"Will Granny burn?"

"She will, dearie."

From the stone an even gentle slope ran down to the bottom, covered with soft green grass, which one longed to lie down on or to touch with one's hands. . . . Sasha lay down and rolled to the bottom. Motka with a grave, severe face, taking a deep breath, lay down too, and rolled to the bottom, and in doing so tore her smock from the hem to the shoulder.

"What fun it is!" said Sasha, delighted.

They walked up to the top to roll down again, but at that moment they heard a shrill, familiar voice. Oh, how awful it was! Granny, a toothless, bony, hunchbacked figure, with short gray hair which was fluttering in the wind, was driving the geese out of the kitchen garden with a long stick, shouting.

"They have trampled all the cabbages, the damned brutes! I'll cut your throats, thrice accursed plagues! Bad luck to you!"

She saw the little girls, flung down the stick and picked up a switch, and, seizing Sasha by the neck with her fingers, thin and hard as the gnarled branches of a tree, began whipping her. Sasha cried with pain and terror, while the gander, waddling and stretching his neck, went up to the old woman and hissed at her, and when he went back to his flock all the geese greeted him approvingly with "Ga-ga-ga!" Then Granny proceeded to whip Motka, and in this Motka's smock was torn again. Feeling in despair, and crying loudly, Sasha went to the hut to complain. Motka followed her; she, too, was crying on a deeper note, without wiping her tears, and her face was as wet as though it had been dipped in water.

"Holy Saints!" cried Olga, aghast, as the two came into the hut. "Queen of Heaven!"

Sasha began telling her story, while at the same time Granny walked in with a storm of shrill cries and abuse; then Fyokla flew into a rage, and there was an uproar in the hut.

"Never mind, never mind!" Olga, pale and upset, tried to comfort them, stroking Sasha's head. "She is your grandmother; it's a sin to be angry with her. Never mind, my child."

Nikolay, who was worn out already by the everlasting hubbub, hunger, stifling fumes, filth, who hated and despised the poverty, who was ashamed for his wife and daughter to see his father and mother, swung his legs off the stove and said in an irritable, tearful voice, addressing his mother:

"You must not beat her! You have no right to beat her!"

"You lie rotting on the stove, you wretched creature!" Fyokla shouted at him spitefully. "The devil brought you all on us, eating us out of house and home."

"*Nikolay, who was worn out already by the everlasting hubbub, hunger, stifling fumes, filth, who hated and despised the poverty, who was ashamed for his wife and daughter to see his father and mother, swung his legs off the stove . . .*"

Sasha and Motka and all the little girls in the hut huddled on the stove in the corner behind Nikolay's back, and from that refuge listened in silent terror, and the beating of their little hearts could be distinctly heard. Whenever there is someone in a family who has long been ill, and hopelessly ill, there come painful moments when all timidly, secretly, at the bottom of their hearts long for his death; and only the children fear the death of someone near them, and always feel horrified at the thought of it. And now the children, with bated breath, with a mournful look on their faces, gazed at Nikolay and thought that he was soon to die; and they wanted to cry and to say something friendly and compassionate to him.

He pressed close to Olga, as though seeking protection, and said to her softly in a quavering voice:

"Olya darling, I can't stay here longer. It's more than I can bear. For God's sake, for Christ's sake, write to your sister Klavdia Abramovna. Let her sell and pawn everything she has; let her send us the money. We will go away from here. Oh Lord," he went on miserably, "to have one peep at Moscow! If I could see it in my dreams, the dear place!"

And when the evening came on, and it was dark in the hut, it was so dismal that it was hard to utter a word. Granny, very ill-tempered, soaked some crusts of rye bread in a cup, and was a long time, a whole hour, sucking at them. Marya, after milking the cow, brought in a pail of milk and set it on a bench; then Granny poured it from the pail into a jug just as slowly and deliberately, evidently pleased that it was now the Fast of the Assumption, so that no one would drink milk and it would be left untouched. And she only poured out a very little in a saucer for Fyokla's baby. When Marya and she carried the jug down to the cellar Motka suddenly stirred, clambered down from the stove, and going to the bench where stood the wooden cup full of crusts, sprinkled into it some milk from the saucer.

Granny, coming back into the hut, sat down to her soaked crusts again, while Sasha and Motka, sitting on the stove, gazed at her, and they were glad that she had broken her fast and now would go to hell. They were comforted and lay down to sleep, and Sasha as she dozed off to sleep imagined the Day of Judgment: a huge fire was burning, somewhat like a potter's kiln, and the Evil One, with horns like a cow's, and black all over, was driving Granny into the fire with a long stick, just as Granny herself had been driving the geese.

V

On the day of the Feast of the Assumption, between ten and eleven in the evening, the girls and lads who were merrymaking in the meadow suddenly raised a clamor and outcry, and ran in the direction of the village; and those who were above on the edge of the ravine could not for the first moment make out what was the matter.

"Fire! Fire!" they heard desperate shouts from below. "The village is on fire!"

Those who were sitting above looked round, and a terrible and extraordinary spectacle met their eyes. On the thatched roof of one of the end cottages stood a column of flame, seven feet high, which curled round and scattered sparks in all directions as though it were a fountain. And all at once the whole roof burst into bright flame, and the crackling of the fire was audible.

The light of the moon was dimmed, and the whole village was by now bathed in a red quivering glow: black shadows moved over the ground, there was a smell of burning, and those who ran up from below were all gasping and could not speak for trembling; they jostled against each other, fell down, and they could hardly see in the unaccustomed light, and did not recognize each other. It was terrible. What seemed particularly dreadful was that doves were flying over the fire in the smoke; and in the tavern, where they did not yet know of the fire, they were still singing and playing the concertina as though there were nothing the matter.

"Uncle Semyon's on fire," shouted a loud, coarse voice.

Marya was fussing about round her hut, weeping and wringing her hands, while her teeth chattered, though the fire was a long way off at the other end of the village. Nikolay came out in high felt boots, the children ran out in their little smocks. Near the village constable's hut an iron sheet was struck. Boom, boom, boom! . . . floated through the air, and this repeated, persistent sound sent a pang to the heart and turned one cold. The old women stood with the holy icons. Sheep, calves, cows were driven out of the backyards into the street; boxes, sheepskins, tubs were carried out. A black stallion, who was kept apart from the drove of horses because he kicked and injured them, on being set free ran once or twice up and down the village, neighing and pawing the ground; then suddenly stopped short near a cart and began kicking it with his hind legs.

They began ringing the bells in the church on the other side of the river.

Near the burning hut it was hot and so light that one could distinctly see every blade of grass. Semyon, a red-haired peasant with a long nose, wearing a reefer jacket and a cap pulled down right over his ears, sat on one of the boxes which they had succeeded in bringing out: his wife was lying on her face, moaning and unconscious. A little old man of eighty, with a big beard, who looked like a gnome—not one of the villagers, though obviously connected in some way with the fire—walked about bareheaded, with a white bundle in his arms. The glare was reflected on his bald head. The village elder, Antip Syedelnikov, as swarthy and black-haired as a gypsy, went up to the hut with an axe, and hacked out the windows one after another—no one knew why—then began chopping up the roof.

"Women, water!" he shouted. "Bring the engine! Look sharp!"

The peasants, who had been drinking in the tavern just before, dragged the engine up. They were all drunk; they kept stumbling and falling down, and all had a helpless expression and tears in their eyes.

"Wenches, water!" shouted the elder, who was drunk, too. "Look sharp, wenches!"

The women and the girls ran downhill to where there was a

spring, and kept hauling pails and buckets of water up the hill, and, pouring it into the engine, ran down again. Olga and Marya and Sasha and Motka all brought water. The women and the boys pumped the water; the pipe hissed, and the elder, directing it now at the door, now at the windows, held back the stream with his finger, which made it hiss more sharply still.

"Bravo, Antip!" voices shouted approvingly. "Do your best."

Antip went inside the hut into the fire and shouted from within.

"Pump! Bestir yourselves, good Christian folk, in such a terrible mischance!"

The peasants stood round in a crowd, doing nothing but staring at the fire. No one knew what to do, no one had the sense to do anything, though there were stacks of wheat, hay, barns, and piles of faggots standing all round. Kiryak and old Osip, his father, both tipsy, were standing there, too. And as though to justify his doing nothing, old Osip said, addressing the woman who lay on the ground:

"What is there to trouble about, old girl! The hut is insured—why are you taking on?"

Semyon, addressing himself first to one person and then to another, kept describing how the fire had started.

"That old man, the one with the bundle, a house serf of General Zhukov's. . . . He was cook at our general's, God rest his soul! He came over this evening: 'Let me stay the night,' says he. . . . Well, we had a glass, to be sure. . . . The wife got the samovar—she was going to give the old fellow a cup of tea, and in an unlucky hour she set the samovar in the entrance. The sparks from the chimney must have blown straight up to the thatch; that's how it was. We were almost burnt ourselves. And the old fellow's cap has been burnt; what a shame!"

And the sheet of iron was struck indefatigably, and the bells kept ringing in the church the other side of the river. In the glow of the fire Olga, breathless, looking with horror at the red sheep and the pink doves flying in the smoke, kept running down the hill and up again. It seemed to her that the ringing went to her heart with a sharp stab, that the fire would never be over, that Sasha was lost. . . . And when the ceiling of the hut fell in with a crash, the thought that now the whole village would be burnt made her weak and faint, and she could not go on fetching water, but sat down on the ravine, setting the pail down near her; beside her and below her, the peasant women sat wailing as though at a funeral.

Then the stewards and watchmen from the estate the other side of the river arrived in two carts, bringing with them a fire engine. A very young student in an unbuttoned white tunic rode up on horseback. There was the thud of axes. They put a ladder to the burning framework of the house, and five men ran up it at once. Foremost of them all was the student, who was red in the face and shouting in a harsh, hoarse voice, and in a tone as though putting out fires was a thing he was used to. They pulled the house to pieces, a beam at a time; they dragged away the corn, the hurdles, and the stacks that were near.

"Don't let them break it up!" cried stern voices in the crowd. "Don't let them."

Kiryak made his way up to the hut with a resolute air, as though he meant to prevent the newcomers from breaking up the hut, but one of the workmen turned him back with a blow in his neck. There was the sound of laughter, the workman dealt him another blow, Kiryak fell down, and crawled back into the crowd on his hands and knees.

Two handsome girls in hats, probably the student's sisters, came from the other side of the river. They stood a little way off, looking at the fire. The beams that had been dragged apart were no longer burning, but were smoking vigorously; the student, who was working the hose, turned the water, first on the beams, then on the peasants, then on the women who were bringing the water.

"George!" the girls called to him reproachfully in anxiety, "George!"

The fire was over. And only when they began to disperse they noticed that the day was breaking, that everyone was pale and rather dark in the face, as it always seems in the early morning when the last stars are going out. As they separated, the peasants laughed and made jokes about General Zhukov's cook and his cap which had been burnt; they already wanted to turn the fire into a joke, and even seemed sorry that it had so soon been put out.

"How well you extinguished the fire, sir!" said Olga to the student. "You ought to come to us in Moscow: there we have a fire every day."

"Why, do you come from Moscow?" asked one of the young ladies.

"Yes, miss. My husband was a waiter at the Slavyansky Bazaar. And this is my daughter," she said, indicating Sasha, who was cold and huddling up to her. "She is a Moscow girl, too."

The two young ladies said something in French to the student, and he gave Sasha a twenty-kopeck piece.

Old Father Osip saw this, and there was a gleam of hope in his face.

"We must thank God, Your Honor, there was no wind," he said, addressing the student, "or else we should have been all burnt up together. Your Honor, kind gentlefolks," he added in embarrassment in a lower tone, "the morning's chilly . . . something to warm one . . . half a bottle to Your Honor's health."

Nothing was given him, and clearing his throat he slouched home. Olga stood afterward at the end of the street and watched the two carts crossing the river by the ford and the gentlefolks walking across the meadow; a carriage was waiting for them the other side of the river. Going into the hut, she described to her husband with enthusiasm:

"Such good people! And so beautiful! The young ladies were like cherubim."

"Plague take them!" Fyokla, sleepy, said spitefully.

VI

Marya thought herself unhappy, and said that she would be very glad to die; Fyokla, on the other hand, found all this life to her taste: the poverty, the uncleanliness, and the incessant quarreling. She ate what was given her without discrimination; slept anywhere, on whatever came to hand. She would empty the slops just at the porch, would splash them out from the doorway, and then walk barefoot through the puddle. And from the very first day she took a dislike to Olga and Nikolay just because they did not like this life.

"We shall see what you'll find to eat here, you Moscow gentry!" she said malignantly. "We shall see!"

One morning, it was at the beginning of September, Fyokla, vigorous, good-looking, and rosy from the cold, brought up two pails of water; Marya and Olga were sitting meanwhile at the table drinking tea.

"Tea and sugar," said Fyokla sarcastically. "The fine ladies!" she added, setting down the pails. "You have taken to the fashion of tea every day. You better look out that you don't burst with your tea drinking," she went on, looking with hatred at Olga. "That's how you have come by your fat mug, having a good time in Moscow, you lump of flesh!" She swung the yoke and hit Olga such a blow on the shoulder that the two sisters-in-law could only clasp their hands and say:

"Oh, holy Saints!"

Then Fyokla went down to the river to wash the clothes, swearing all the time so loudly that she could be heard in the hut.

The day passed and was followed by the long autumn evening. They wound silk in the hut; everyone did it except Fyokla; she had gone over the river. They got the silk from a factory close by, and the whole family working together earned next to nothing, twenty kopecks a week.

"Things were better in the old days under the gentry," said the old father as he wound silk. "You worked and ate and slept, everything in its turn. At dinner you had cabbage soup and boiled grain, and at supper the same again. Cucumbers and cabbage in plenty: you could eat to your heart's content, as much as you wanted. And there was more strictness. Everyone minded what he was about."

The hut was lighted by a single little lamp, which burned dimly and smoked. When someone screened the lamp and a big shadow fell across the window, the bright moonlight could be seen. Old Osip, speaking slowly, told them how they used to live before the emancipation; how in those very parts, where life was now so poor and so dreary, they used to hunt with harriers, greyhounds, retrievers, and when they went out as beaters the peasants were given vodka; how whole wagonloads of game used to be sent to Moscow for the young masters; how the bad were beaten with rods or sent away to the Tver estate, while the good were rewarded. And Granny told them something, too. She remembered everything, positively everything. She described her mistress, a kind, God-fearing woman, whose husband was a profligate and a rake, and all of whose daughters made unlucky marriages: one married a drunkard, another married a workman, the other eloped secretly (Granny herself, at that time a young girl, helped in the elopement), and they had all three as well as their mother died early from grief. And remembering all this, Granny positively began to shed tears.

All at once someone knocked at the door, and they all started.

"Uncle Osip, give me a night's lodging."

The little bald old man, General Zhukov's cook, the one whose cap had been burnt, walked in. He sat down and listened, then he, too, began telling stories of all sorts. Nikolay, sitting on the stove with his legs hanging down, listened and asked questions about the dishes that were prepared in the old days for the gentry. They talked of rissoles, cutlets, various soups and sauces, and the cook, who remembered everything very well, mentioned dishes that are no longer served. There was one, for instance—a dish made of bulls' eyes, which was called "waking up in the morning."

"And used you to do cutlets *à la maréchal?*" asked Nikolay.

"No."

Nikolay shook his head reproachfully and said:

"Tut, tut! You were not much of a cook!"

The little girls sitting and lying on the stove stared down without blinking; it seemed as though there were a great many of them, like cherubim in the clouds. They liked the stories: they were breathless; they shuddered and turned pale with alternate rapture and terror, and they listened breathlessly, afraid to stir, to Granny, whose stories were the most interesting of all.

They lay down to sleep in silence; and the old people, troubled and excited by their reminiscences, thought how precious was youth, of which, whatever it might have been like, nothing was left in the memory but what was living, joyful, touching, and how terribly cold was death, which was not far off, better not think of it! The lamp died down. And the dusk, and the two little windows sharply defined by the moonlight, and the stillness and the creak of the cradle, reminded them for some reason that life was over, that nothing one could do would bring it back. . . . You doze off, you forget yourself, and suddenly someone touches your shoulder or breathes on your cheek—and sleep is gone; your body feels cramped, and thoughts of death keep creeping into your mind. You turn on the other side: death is forgotten, but old dreary, sickening thoughts of poverty, of food, of how dear flour is getting, stray through the mind, and a little later again you remember that life is over and you cannot bring it back. . . .

"Oh, Lord!" sighed the cook.

Someone gave a soft, soft tap at the window. It must be Fyokla come back. Olga got up, and yawning and whispering a prayer, opened the door, then drew the bolt in the outer room, but no one came in; only from the street came a cold draft and a sudden brightness from the moonlight. The street, still and deserted, and the moon itself floating across the sky, could be seen at the open door.

"Who is there?" called Olga.

"I," she heard the answer—"it is I."

Near the door, crouching against the wall, stood Fyokla, absolutely naked. She was shivering with cold, her teeth were chattering, and in the bright moonlight she looked very pale, strange, and beautiful. The shadows on her, and the bright moonlight on her skin, stood out vividly, and her dark eyebrows and firm, youthful bosom were defined with peculiar distinctness.

"The ruffians over there undressed me and turned me out like this," she said. "I've come home without my clothes . . . naked as my mother bore me. Bring me something to put on."

"But go inside!" Olga said softly, beginning to shiver, too.

"I don't want the old folks to see." Granny was, in fact, already stirring and muttering, and the old father asked: "Who is there?" Olga brought her own smock and skirt, dressed Fyokla, and then both went softly into the inner room, trying not to make a noise with the door.

"Is that you, you sleek one?" Granny grumbled angrily, guessing who it was. "Fie upon you, nightwalker! . . . Bad luck to you!"

"It's all right, it's all right," whispered Olga, wrapping Fyokla up; "it's all right, dearie."

All was stillness again. They always slept badly; everyone was kept awake by something worrying and persistent: the old man by the pain in his back, Granny by anxiety and anger, Marya by terror, the children by itch and hunger. Now, too, their sleep was troubled; they kept turning over from one side to the other, talking in their sleep, getting up for a drink.

Fyokla suddenly broke into a loud, coarse howl, but immediately checked herself, and only uttered sobs from time to time, growing softer and on a lower note, until she relapsed into silence. From time to time from the other side of the river there floated the sound of the beating of the hours; but the time seemed somehow strange—five was struck and then three.

"Oh, Lord!" sighed the cook.

Looking at the windows, it was difficult to tell whether it was still moonlight or whether the dawn had begun. Marya got up and went out, and she could be heard milking the cows and saying, "Stea-dy!" Granny went out, too. It was still dark in the hut, but all the objects in it could be discerned.

Nikolay, who had not slept all night, got down from the stove. He took his dress coat out of a green box, put it on, and going to the window, stroked the sleeves and took hold of the coattails—and smiled. Then he carefully took off the coat, put it away in his box, and lay down again.

Marya came in again and began lighting the stove. She was evidently hardly awake, and seemed dropping asleep as she walked. Probably she had had some dream, or the stories of the night before came into her mind as, stretching luxuriously before the stove, she said:

"No, freedom is better."

VII

The master arrived—that was what they called the police inspector. When he would come and what he was coming for had been known for the last week. There were only forty households in Zhukovo, but more than two thousand rubles of arrears of rates and taxes had accumulated.

The police inspector stopped at the tavern. He drank there two glasses of tea, and then went on foot to the village elder's hut, near which a crowd of those who were in debt stood waiting. The elder, Antip Syedelnikov, was, in spite of his youth—he was only a little over thirty—strict and always on the side of the authorities, though he himself was poor and did not pay his taxes regularly. Evidently he enjoyed being elder, and liked the sense of authority, which he could only display by strictness. In the village council the peasants were afraid of him and obeyed him. It would sometimes happen that he would pounce on a drunken man in the street or near the tavern, tie his hands behind him, and put him in the lockup. On one occasion he even put Granny in the lockup because she went to the village council instead of Osip, and began swearing, and he kept her there for a whole day and night. He had never lived in a town or read a book, but somewhere or other had picked up various learned expressions, and loved to make use of them in conversation, and he was respected for this though he was not always understood.

When Osip came into the village elder's hut with his tax book, the police inspector, a lean old man with a long gray beard, in a gray tunic, was sitting at a table in the passage, writing something. It was clean in the hut; all the walls were dotted with pictures cut out of the illustrated papers, and in the most conspicuous place near the icon there was a portrait of the Battenburg who was the Prince of Bulgaria. By the table stood Antip Syedelnikov with his arms folded.

"There is one hundred and nineteen rubles standing against him," he said when it came to Osip's turn. "Before Easter he paid a ruble, and he has not paid a kopeck since."

The police inspector raised his eyes to Osip and asked:

"Why is this, brother?"

"Show Divine mercy, Your Honor," Osip began, growing agitated. "Allow me to say last year the gentleman at Lutorydsky said to me, 'Osip,' he said, 'sell your hay . . . you sell it,' he said. Well, I had a hundred poods for sale; the women mowed it on the watermeadow. Well, we struck a bargain all right, willingly. . . ."

He complained of the elder, and kept turning round to the peasants as though inviting them to bear witness; his face flushed red and perspired, and his eyes grew sharp and angry.

"I don't know why you are saying all this," said the police inspector. "I am asking you . . . I am asking you why you don't pay your arrears. You don't pay, any of you, and am I to be responsible for you?"

"I can't do it."

"His words have no sequel, Your Honor," said the elder. "The

Tchikildyeevs certainly are of a defective class, but if you will just ask the others, the root of it all is vodka, and they are a very bad lot. With no sort of understanding."

The police inspector wrote something down, and said to Osip quietly, in an even tone, as though he were asking him for water:

"Be off."

Soon he went away; and when he got into his cheap chaise and cleared his throat, it could be seen from the very expression of his long thin back that he was no longer thinking of Osip or of the village elder, nor of the Zhukovo arrears, but was thinking of his own affairs. Before he had gone three quarters of a mile Antip was already carrying off the samovar from the Tchikildyeevs' cottage, followed by Granny, screaming shrilly and straining her throat:

"I won't let you have it, I won't let you have it, damn you!"

He walked rapidly with long steps, and she pursued him panting, almost falling over, a bent, ferocious figure; her kerchief slipped onto her shoulders, her gray hair with greenish lights on it was blown about in the wind. She suddenly stopped short, and like a genuine rebel, fell to beating her breast with her fists and shouting louder than ever in a singsong voice, as though she were sobbing:

"Good Christians and believers in God! Neighbors, they have ill-treated me! Kind friends, they have oppressed me! Oh, oh! dear people, take my part."

"Granny, Granny!" said the village elder sternly, "have some sense in your head!"

It was hopelessly dreary in the Tchikildyeevs' hut without the samovar; there was something humiliating in this loss, insulting, as though the honor of the hut had been outraged. Better if the elder had carried off the table, all the benches, all the pots—it would not have seemed so empty. Granny screamed, Marya cried, and the little girls, looking at her, cried, too. The old father, feeling guilty, sat in the corner with bowed head and said nothing. And Nikolay, too, was silent. Granny loved him and was sorry for him, but now, forgetting her pity, she fell upon him with abuse, with reproaches, shaking her

fist right in his face. She shouted that it was all his fault; why had he
sent them so little when he boasted in his letters that he was getting
fifty rubles a month at the Slavyansky Bazaar? Why had he come,
and with his family, too? If he died, where was the money to come
from for his funeral . . . ? And it was pitiful to look at Nikolay,
Olga, and Sasha.

The old father cleared his throat, took his cap, and went off to
the village elder. Antip was soldering something by the stove, puffing
out his cheeks; there was a smell of burning. His children, emaciated
and unwashed, no better than the Tchikildyeevs, were scrambling
about the floor; his wife, an ugly, freckled woman with a prominent
stomach, was winding silk. They were a poor, unlucky family, and
Antip was the only one who looked vigorous and handsome. On a
bench there were five samovars standing in a row. The old man said
his prayer to Battenburg and said:

"Antip, show the Divine mercy. Give me back the samovar, for
Christ's sake!"

"Bring three rubles, then you shall have it."

"I can't do it!"

Antip puffed out his cheeks, the fire roared and hissed, and the
glow was reflected in the samovar. The old man crumpled up his cap
and said after a moment's thought:

"You give it me back."

The swarthy elder looked quite black, and was like a magician; he
turned round to Osip and said sternly and rapidly:

"It all depends on the rural captain. On the twenty-sixth instant
you can state the grounds for your dissatisfaction before the adminis-
trative session, verbally or in writing."

Osip did not understand a word, but he was satisfied with that
and went home.

Ten days later the police inspector came again, stayed an hour
and went away. During those days the weather had changed to cold
and windy; the river had been frozen for some time past, but still
there was no snow, and people found it difficult to get about. On the

eve of a holiday some of the neighbors came into Osip's to sit and have a talk. They did not light the lamp, as it would have been a sin to work, but talked in the darkness. There were some items of news, all rather unpleasant. In two or three households hens had been taken for the arrears, and had been sent to the district police station, and there they had died because no one had fed them; they had taken sheep, and while they were being driven away tied to one another, shifted into another cart at each village, one of them had died. And now they were discussing the question, who was to blame?

"The Zemstvo," said Osip. "Who else?"

"Of course it is the Zemstvo."

The Zemstvo was blamed for everything—for the arrears, and for the oppressions, and for the failure of the crops, though no one of them knew what was meant by the Zemstvo. And this dated from the time when well-to-do peasants who had factories, shops, and inns of their own were members of the Zemstvos, were dissatisfied with them, and took to swearing at the Zemstvos in their factories and inns.

They talked of God's not sending the snow; they had to bring in wood for fuel, and there was no driving nor walking in the frozen ruts. In old days fifteen to twenty years ago conversation was much more interesting in Zhukovo. In those days every old man looked as though he were treasuring some secret; as though he knew something and was expecting something. They used to talk about an edict in golden letters, about the division of lands, about new land, about treasures; they hinted at something. Now the people of Zhukovo had no mystery at all; their whole life was bare and open in the sight of all, and they could talk of nothing but poverty, food, there being no snow yet. . . .

There was a pause. Then they thought again of the hens, of the sheep, and began discussing whose fault it was.

"The Zemstvo," said Osip wearily. "Who else?"

VIII

The parish church was nearly five miles away at Kosogorovo, and the peasants only attended it when they had to do so for baptisms, weddings, or funerals; they went to the services at the church across the river. On holidays in fine weather the girls dressed up in their best and went in a crowd together to church, and it was a cheering sight to see them in their red, yellow, and green dresses cross the meadow; in bad weather they all stayed at home. They went for the sacrament to the parish church. From each of those who did not manage in Lent to go to confession in readiness for the sacrament the parish priest, going the round of the huts with the cross at Easter, took fifteen kopecks.

The old father did not believe in God, for he hardly ever thought about Him; he recognized the supernatural, but considered it was entirely the women's concern, and when religion or miracles were discussed before him, or a question was put to him, he would say reluctantly, scratching himself:

"Who can tell!"

Granny believed, but her faith was somewhat hazy; everything was mixed up in her memory, and she could scarcely begin to think of sins, of death, of the salvation of the soul, before poverty and her daily cares took possession of her mind, and she instantly forgot what she was thinking about. She did not remember the prayers, and usually in the evenings, before lying down to sleep, she would stand before the icons and whisper:

"Holy Mother of Kazan, Holy Mother of Smolensk, Holy Mother of Troerutchitsy. . . ."

Marya and Fyokla crossed themselves, fasted and took the sacrament every year, but understood nothing. The children were not taught their prayers, nothing was told them about God, and no moral principles were instilled into them; they were only forbidden to eat meat or milk in Lent. In the other families it was much the same: there were few who believed, few who understood. At the same time everyone loved the Holy Scripture, loved it with a tender, reverent love; but they had no Bible, there was no one to read it and explain it, and because Olga sometimes read them the Gospel, they respected her, and they all addressed her and Sasha as though they were superior to themselves.

For church holidays and services Olga often went to neighboring villages, and to the district town, in which there were two monasteries and twenty-seven churches. She was dreamy, and when she was on these pilgrimages she quite forgot her family, and only when she got home again suddenly made the joyful discovery that she had a husband and daughter, and then would say, smiling and radiant:

"God has sent me blessings!"

What went on in the village worried her and seemed to her revolting. On Elijah's Day they drank, at the Assumption they drank, at the Ascension they drank. The Feast of the Intercession was the parish holiday for Zhukovo, and the peasants used to drink then for three days; they squandered on drink fifty rubles of money belonging to the Mir, and then collected more for vodka from all the households. On the first day of the feast the Tchikildyeevs killed a sheep and ate of it in the morning, at dinner-time, and in the evening; they ate it ravenously, and the children got up at night to eat more. Kiryak was fearfully drunk for three whole days; he drank up everything, even his boots and cap, and beat Marya so terribly that they had to pour water over her. And then they were all ashamed and sick.

However, even in Zhukovo, in this "Slaveytown," there was once an outburst of genuine religious enthusiasm. It was in August, when throughout the district they carried from village to village the Holy Mother, the giver of life. It was still and overcast on the day when they expected *Her* at Zhukovo. The girls set off in the morning to meet the icon, in their bright holiday dresses, and brought Her toward the evening, in procession with the Cross and with singing, while the bells pealed in the church across the river. An immense crowd of villagers and strangers flooded the street; there was noise, dust, a great crush. . . . And the old father and Granny and

Kiryak—all stretched out their hands to the icon, looked eagerly at it and said, weeping:

"Defender! Mother! Defender!"

All seemed suddenly to realize that there was not an empty void between earth and heaven, that the rich and the powerful had not taken possession of everything, that there was still a refuge from injury, from slavish bondage, from crushing, unendurable poverty, from the terrible vodka.

"Defender! Mother!" sobbed Marya. "Mother!"

But the thanksgiving service ended and the icon was carried away, and everything went on as before; and again there was a sound of coarse drunken oaths from the tavern.

Only the well-to-do peasants were afraid of death; the richer they were the less they believed in God, and in the salvation of souls, and only through fear of the end of the world put up candles and had services said for them, to be on the safe side. The peasants who were rather poorer were not afraid of death. The old father and Granny were told to their faces that they had lived too long, that it was time they were dead, and they did not mind. They did not hinder Fyokla from saying in Nikolay's presence that when Nikolay died her husband Denis would get exemption to return home from the army. And Marya, far from fearing death, regretted that it was so slow in coming, and was glad when her children died.

Death they did not fear, but of every disease they had an exaggerated terror. The merest trifle was enough—a stomach upset, a slight chill, and Granny would be wrapped up on the stove, and would begin moaning loudly and incessantly:

"I am dy-ing!"

The old father hurried off for the priest, and Granny received the sacrament and extreme unction. They often talked of colds, of worms, of tumors which move in the stomach and coil round to the heart. Above all, they were afraid of catching cold, and so put on thick clothes even in the summer and warmed themselves at the stove. Granny was fond of being doctored, and often went to the hospital, where she used to say she was not seventy, but fifty-eight; she supposed that if the doctor knew her real age he would not treat her, but would say it was time she died instead of taking medicine. She usually went to the hospital early in the morning, taking with her two or three of the little girls, and came back in the evening, hungry and ill-tempered—with drops for herself and ointments for the little girls. Once she took Nikolay, who swallowed drops for a fortnight afterward, and said he felt better.

Granny knew all the doctors and their assistants and the wise men for twenty miles round, and not one of them she liked. At the Intercession, when the priest made the round of the huts with the cross, the deacon told her that in the town near the prison lived an old man who had been a medical orderly in the army, and who made wonderful cures, and advised her to try him. Granny took his advice. When the first snow fell she drove to the town and fetched an old man with a big beard, a converted Jew, in a long gown, whose face was covered with blue veins. There were outsiders at work in the hut at the time: an old tailor, in terrible spectacles, was cutting a waistcoat out of some rags, and two young men were making felt boots out of wool; Kiryak, who had been dismissed from his place for drunkenness, and now lived at home, was sitting beside the tailor mending a bridle. And it was crowded, stifling, and noisome in the hut. The converted Jew examined Nikolay and said that it was necessary to try cupping.

He put on the cups, and the old tailor, Kiryak, and the little girls stood round and looked on, and it seemed to them that they saw the disease being drawn out of Nikolay; and Nikolay, too, watched how the cups suckling at his breast gradually filled with dark blood, and felt as though there really were something coming out of him, and smiled with pleasure.

"It's a good thing," said the tailor. "Please God, it will do you good."

The Jew put on twelve cups and then another twelve, drank some tea, and went away. Nikolay began shivering; his face looked drawn, and, as the women expressed it, shrank up like a fist; his fingers turned blue. He wrapped himself up in a quilt and in a sheepskin, but got colder and colder. Toward the evening he began to be in great distress; asked to be laid on the ground, asked the tailor not to smoke; then he subsided under the sheepskin and toward morning he died.

IX

Oh, what a grim, what a long winter!

Their own grain did not last beyond Christmas, and they had to buy flour. Kiryak, who lived at home now, was noisy in the evenings, inspiring terror in everyone, and in the mornings he suffered from headache and was ashamed; and he was a pitiful sight. In the stall the starved cows bellowed day and night—a heartrending sound to Granny and Marya. And as ill luck would have it, there was a sharp frost all the winter, the snow drifted in high heaps, and the winter dragged on. At Annunciation there was a regular blizzard, and there was a fall of snow at Easter.

But in spite of it all the winter did end. At the beginning of April there came warm days and frosty nights. Winter would not give way, but one warm day overpowered it at last, and the streams began to flow and the birds began to sing. The whole meadow and the bushes near the river were drowned in the spring floods, and all the space between Zhukovo and the further side was filled up with a vast sheet of water, from which wild ducks rose up in flocks here and there. The spring sunset, flaming among gorgeous clouds, gave every evening something new, extraordinary, incredible—just what one does not believe in afterward, when one sees those very colors and those very clouds in a picture.

The cranes flew swiftly, swiftly, with mournful cries, as though they were calling themselves. Standing on the edge of the ravine, Olga looked a long time at the flooded meadow, at the sunshine, at the bright church, that looked as though it had grown younger; and her tears flowed and her breath came in gasps from her passionate longing to go away, to go far away to the end of the world. It was already settled that she should go back to Moscow to be a servant, and that Kiryak should set off with her to get a job as a porter or something. Oh, to get away quickly!

As soon as it dried up and grew warm they got ready to set off. Olga and Sasha, with wallets on their backs and shoes of plaited bark on their feet, came out before daybreak: Marya came out, too, to see them on their way. Kiryak was not well, and was kept at home for another week. For the last time Olga prayed at the church and thought of her husband, and though she did not shed tears, her face puckered up and looked ugly like an old woman's. During the winter she had grown thinner and plainer, and her hair had gone a little gray, and instead of the old look of sweetness and the pleasant smile on her face, she had the resigned, mournful expression left by the sorrows she had been through, and there was something blank and irresponsive in her eyes, as though she did not hear what was said. She was sorry to part from the village and the peasants. She remembered how they had carried out Nikolay, and how a requiem had been ordered for him at almost every hut, and all had shed tears in sympathy with her grief. In the course of the summer and the winter there had been hours and days when it seemed as though these people lived worse than the beasts, and to live with them was terrible; they were coarse, dishonest, filthy, and drunken; they did not live in harmony, but quarreled continually, because they distrusted and feared and did not respect one another. Who keeps the tavern and makes the people drunken? A peasant. Who wastes and spends on drink the funds of the commune, of the schools, of the church? A peasant. Who stole from his neighbors, set fire to their property, gave false witness at the court for a bottle of vodka? At the meetings of the Zemstvo and other local bodies, who was the first to fall foul of the peasants? A peasant. Yes, to live with them was terrible; but yet, they were human beings, they suffered and wept like human beings, and there was nothing in their lives for which one could not find excuse. Hard labor that made the whole body ache at night, the cruel winters, the scanty harvests, the overcrowding; and they had no help and none to whom they could look for help. Those of them who were a little stronger and better off could be no help, as they were themselves coarse, dishonest, drunken, and abused one another just as revoltingly; the paltriest little clerk or official treated the peasants as though they were tramps, and addressed even the village elders and church wardens as inferiors, and considered they had a right to do so. And, indeed, can any sort of help or good example be given by mercenary, greedy, depraved, and idle persons who only visit the village in order to insult, to despoil, and to terrorize? Olga remembered the pitiful, humiliated look of the old people when in the winter Kiryak had been taken to be flogged. . . . And now she felt sorry for all these people, painfully so, and as she walked on she kept looking back at the huts.

After walking two miles with them Marya said goodbye, then kneeling, and falling forward with her face on the earth, she began wailing:

"Again I am left alone. Alas, for poor me! poor, unhappy! . . ."

And she wailed like this for a long time, and for a long way Olga and Sasha could still see her on her knees, bowing down to someone at the side and clutching her head in her hands, while the rooks flew over her head.

The sun rose high; it began to get hot. Zhukovo was left far behind. Walking was pleasant. Olga and Sasha soon forgot both the village and Marya; they were gay and everything entertained them. Now they came upon an ancient barrow, now upon a row of telegraph posts running one after another into the distance and disappearing into the horizon, and the wires hummed mysteriously. Then they saw a homestead, all wreathed in green foliage; there came a scent from it of dampness, of hemp, and it seemed for some reason that happy people lived there. Then they came upon a horse's skele-

"*After walking two miles with them Marya said goodbye, then kneeling, and falling forward with her face on the earth, she began wailing: 'Again I am left alone. Alas, for poor me! . . .'*"

ton whitening in solitude in the open fields. And the larks trilled unceasingly, the corncrakes called to one another, and the land-rail cried as though someone were really scraping at an old iron rail.

At midday Olga and Sasha reached a big village. There in the broad street they met the little old man who was General Zhukov's cook. He was hot, and his red, perspiring bald head shone in the sunshine. Olga and he did not recognize each other, then looked round at the same moment, recognized each other, and went their separate ways without saying a word. Stopping near the hut which looked newest and most prosperous, Olga bowed down before the open windows, and said in a loud, thin chanting voice:

"Good Christian folk, give alms, for Christ's sake, that God's blessing may be upon you, and that your parents may be in the Kingdom of Heaven in peace eternal."

"Good Christian folk," Sasha began chanting, "give, for Christ's sake, that God's blessing, the Heavenly Kingdom . . ."

1897

THE TEACHER OF
LITERATURE

I

There was the thud of horses' hoofs on the wooden floor; they brought out of the stable the black horse, Count Nulin; then the white, Giant; then his sister Maika. They were all magnificent, expensive horses. Old Shelestov saddled Giant and said, addressing his daughter Masha:

"Well, Maria Godefroy, come, get on! Hopla!"

Masha Shelestov was the youngest of the family; she was eighteen, but her family could not get used to thinking that she was not a little girl, and so they still called her Manya and Manyusa; and after there had been a circus in the town which she had eagerly visited, everyone began to call her Maria Godefroy.

"Hop-la!" she cried, mounting Giant. Her sister Varya got on Maika, Nikitin on Count Nulin, the officers on their horses, and the long picturesque cavalcade, with the officers in white tunics and the ladies in their riding habits, moved at a walking pace out of the yard.

Nikitin noticed that when they were mounting the horses and afterward riding out into the street, Masha for some reason paid attention to no one but himself. She looked anxiously at him and at Count Nulin and said:

"You must hold him on the curb all the time, Sergey Vassilich. Don't let him shy. He's pretending."

And either because her Giant was very friendly with Count Nulin, or perhaps by chance, she rode all the time beside Nikitin, as she had done the day before, and the day before that. And he looked at her graceful little figure sitting on the proud white beast, at her delicate profile, at the chimney-pot hat, which did not suit her at all and made her look older than her age—looked at her with joy, with tenderness, with rapture; listened to her, taking in little of what she said, and thought:

"I promise on my honor, I swear to God, I won't be afraid and I'll speak to her today."

It was seven o'clock in the evening—the time when the scent of white acacia and lilac is so strong that the air and the very trees seem heavy with the fragrance. The band was already playing in the town gardens. The horses made a resounding thud on the pavement, on all sides there were sounds of laughter, talk, and the banging of gates. The soldiers they met saluted the officers, the schoolboys bowed to Nikitin, and all the people who were hurrying to the gardens to hear the band were pleased at the sight of the party. And how warm it was! How soft-looking were the clouds scattered carelessly about the sky, how kindly and comforting the shadows of the poplars and the acacias, which stretched across the street and reached as far as the balconies and second stories of the houses on the other side.

They rode on out of town and set off at a trot along the high road. Here there was no scent of lilac and acacia, no music of the band, but there was the fragrance of the fields, there was the green of young rye and wheat, the marmots were squeaking, the rooks were cawing. Wherever one looked it was green, with only here and there black patches of bare ground, and far away to the left in the cemetery a white streak of apple blossom.

They passed the slaughterhouses, then the brewery, and overtook a military band hastening to the suburban gardens.

"Polyansky has a very fine horse, I don't deny that," Masha said to Nikitin, with a glance toward the officer who was riding beside Varya. "But it has blemishes. That white patch on its left leg ought not to be there, and, look, it tosses its head. You can't train it not to now; it will toss its head till the end of its days."

Masha was as passionate a lover of horses as her father. She felt a pang when she saw other people with fine horses, and was pleased when she saw defects in them. Nikitin knew nothing about horses; it made absolutely no difference to him whether he held his horse on the bridle or on the curb, whether he trotted or galloped; he only felt that his position was strained and unnatural, and that consequently the officers who knew how to sit in their saddles must please Masha more than he could. And he was jealous of the officers.

As they rode by the suburban gardens someone suggested their going in and getting some seltzer-water. They went in. There were no trees but oaks in the gardens; they had only just come into leaf, so that through the young foliage the whole garden could still be seen with its platform, little tables, and swings, and the crows' nests were visible, looking like big hats. The party dismounted near a table and asked for seltzer-water. People they knew, walking about the garden, came up to them. Among them were the army doctor, in high boots, and the conductor of the band, waiting for the musicians. The doctor must have taken Nikitin for a student, for he asked:

"Have you come for the summer holidays?"

"No, I am here permanently," answered Nikitin. "I am a teacher at the school."

"You don't say so?" said the doctor, with surprise. "So young and already a teacher?"

"Young, indeed! My goodness, I'm twenty-six!"

"You have a beard and mustache, but yet one would never guess you were more than twenty-two or twenty-three. How young-looking you are!"

"What a beast!" thought Nikitin. "He, too, takes me for a whippersnapper!"

He disliked it extremely when people referred to his youth, especially in the presence of women or the schoolboys. Ever since he had come to the town as a master in the school he had detested his own youthful appearance. The schoolboys were not afraid of him, old people called him "young man," ladies preferred dancing with him to listening to his long arguments, and he would have given a great deal to be ten years older.

From the garden they went on to the Shelestovs' farm. There they stopped at the gate and asked the bailiff's wife, Praskovya, to bring some fresh milk. Nobody drank the milk; they all looked at one another, laughed, and galloped back. As they rode back the band was playing in the suburban garden; the sun was setting behind the cemetery, and half the sky was crimson from the sunset.

Masha again rode beside Nikitin. He wanted to tell her how passionately he loved her, but he was afraid he would be overheard by the officers and Varya, and he was silent. Masha was silent, too, and he felt why she was silent and why she was riding beside him, and was so happy that the earth, the sky, the lights of the town, the black outline of the brewery—all blended for him into something very pleasant and comforting, and it seemed to him as though Count Nulin were stepping on air and would climb up into the crimson sky.

They arrived home. The samovar was already boiling on the table, old Shelestov was sitting with his friends, officials in the Circuit Court, and as usual he was criticizing something.

"It's loutishness!" he said. "Loutishness and nothing more. Yes!"

Since Nikitin had been in love with Masha, everything at the Shelestovs' pleased him: the house, the garden, and the evening tea, and the wickerwork chairs, and the old nurse, and even the word "loutishness," which the old man was fond of using. The only thing he did not like was the number of cats and dogs and the Egyptian pigeons, who moaned disconsolately in a big cage in the veranda. There were so many house dogs and yard dogs that he had learned to recognize only two of them in the course of his acquaintance with the Shelestovs: Mushka and Som. Mushka was a little mangy dog with a shaggy face, spiteful and spoiled. She hated Nikitin: when she saw him she put her head on one side, showed her teeth, and began to growl: "Rrr . . . ga-nga-nga . . . rrr . . . !" Then she would get under his chair, and when he would try to drive her away she would go off into piercing yaps, and the family would say: "Don't be frightened. She doesn't bite. She is a good dog."

Som was a tall black dog with long legs and a tail as hard as a stick. At dinner and tea he usually moved about under the table, and thumped on people's boots and on the legs of the table with his tail. He was a good-natured, stupid dog, but Nikitin could not endure him because he had the habit of putting his head on people's knees at dinner and messing their trousers with saliva. Nikitin had more than once tried to hit him on his head with a knife handle, to flip him on the nose; he had abused him, had complained of him, but nothing saved his trousers.

After their ride the tea, jam, rusks, and butter seemed very nice. They all drank their first glass in silence and with great relish; over the second they began an argument. It was always Varya who started the arguments at tea; she was good-looking, handsomer than Masha, and was considered the cleverest and most cultured person in the house, and she behaved with dignity and severity, as an eldest daughter should who has taken the place of her dead mother in the house. As the mistress of the house, she felt herself entitled to wear a dressing gown in the presence of her guests, and to call the officers by their surnames; she looked on Masha as a little girl, and talked to her as though she were a schoolmistress. She used to speak of herself as an old maid—so she was certain she would marry.

Every conversation, even about the weather, she invariably turned into an argument. She had a passion for catching at words, pouncing on contradictions, quibbling over phrases. You would begin talking to her, and she would stare at you and suddenly interrupt: "Excuse me, excuse me, Petrov, the other day you said the very opposite!"

Or she would smile ironically and say: "I notice, though, you begin to advocate the principles of the secret police. I congratulate you."

If you jested or made a pun, you would hear her voice at once: "That's stale," "That's pointless." If an officer ventured on a joke, she would make a contemptuous grimace and say, "An army joke!"

And she rolled the *r* so impressively that Mushka invariably answered from under a chair, "Rrr . . . nga-nga-nga . . . !"

On this occasion at tea the argument began with Nikitin's mentioning the school examinations:

"Excuse me, Sergey Vassilich," Varya interrupted him. "You say it's difficult for the boys. And whose fault is that, let me ask you? For instance, you set the boys in the eighth class an essay on 'Pushkin as a Psychologist.' To begin with, you shouldn't set such a difficult subject; and, secondly, Pushkin was not a psychologist. Shchedrin now, or Dostoevsky let us say, is a different matter, but Pushkin is a great poet and nothing more."

"Shchedrin is one thing, and Pushkin is another," Nikitin answered sulkily.

"I know you don't think much of Shchedrin at the high school, but that's not the point. Tell me, in what sense is Pushkin a psychologist?"

"Why, do you mean to say he was not a psychologist? If you like, I'll give you examples."

And Nikitin recited several passages from *Onegin* and then from *Boris Godunov*.

"I see no psychology in that." Varya sighed. "The psychologist is the man who describes the recesses of the human soul, and that's fine poetry and nothing more."

"I know the sort of psychology you want," said Nikitin, offended. "You want someone to saw my finger with a blunt saw while I howl at the top of my voice—that's what you mean by psychology."

"That's poor! But still you haven't shown me in what sense Push-kin is a psychologist."

When Nikitin had to argue against anything that seemed to him narrow, conventional, or something of that kind, he usually leaped up from his seat, clutched at his head with both hands, and began, with a moan, running from one end of the room to another. And it was the same now: he jumped up, clutched his head in his hands, and with a moan walked round the table; then he sat down a little way off.

The officers took his part. Captain Polyansky began assuring Varya that Pushkin really was a psychologist, and to prove it quoted two lines from Lermontov; Lieutenant Gernet said that if Pushkin had not been a psychologist they would not have erected a monu-ment to him in Moscow.

"That's loutishness!" was heard from the other end of the table. "I said as much to the governor: 'It's loutishness, Your Excellency,' I said."

"I won't argue anymore," cried Nikitin. "It's unending. . . . Enough! Ach, get away, you nasty dog!" he cried to Som, who laid his head and paw on his knee.

"Rrr . . . nga-nga-nga!" came from under the table.

"Admit that you are wrong!" cried Varya. "Own up!"

But some young ladies came in, and the argument dropped of itself. They all went into the drawing room. Varya sat down at the piano and began playing dances. They danced first a waltz, then a polka, then a quadrille with a grand chain which Captain Polyansky led through all the rooms, then a waltz again.

During the dancing the old men sat in the drawing room, smok-ing and looking at the young people. Among them was Shebaldin, the director of the municipal bank, who was famed for his love of literature and dramatic art. He had founded the local Musical and Dramatic Society, and took part in the performances himself, confin-ing himself, for some reason, to playing comic footmen or to reading in a singsong voice "The Woman Sinner." His nickname in the town was "the Mummy," as he was tall, very lean and scraggy, and always had a solemn air and a fixed, lusterless eye. He was so devoted to the dramatic art that he even shaved his mustache and beard, and this made him still more like a mummy.

After the grand chain, he shuffled up to Nikitin sideways, coughed, and said:

"I had the pleasure of being present during the argument at tea. I fully share your opinion. We are of one mind, and it would be a great pleasure to me to talk to you. Have you read Lessing's *Hamburg Dramaturgy*?"

"No, I haven't."

Shebaldin was horrified, and, waving his hands as though he had burned his fingers, and saying nothing more, he staggered back from Nikitin. Shebaldin's appearance, his question, and his surprise, struck Nikitin as funny, but he thought nonetheless:

"It really is awkward. I am a teacher of literature, and to this day I've not read Lessing. I must read him."

Before supper the whole company, old and young, sat down to play "fate." They took two packs of cards: one pack was dealt round to the company, the other was laid on the table face downward.

"The one who has his card in his hand," old Shelestov began solemnly, lifting the top card of the second pack, "is fated to go into the nursery and kiss nurse."

The pleasure of kissing the nurse fell to the lot of Shebaldin. They all crowded around him, took him to the nursery, and laughing and clapping their hands, made him kiss the nurse. There was a great uproar and shouting.

"Not so ardently!" cried Shelestov with tears of laughter. "Not so ardently!"

It was Nikitin's "fate" to hear the confessions of all. He sat on a chair in the middle of the drawing room. A shawl was brought and put over his head. The first who came to confess to him was Varya.

"I know your sins," Nikitin began, looking in the darkness at her stern profile. "Tell me, madam, how do you explain your walking with Polyansky every day? Oh, it's not for nothing she walks with an hussar!"

"That's poor," said Varya, and walked away.

Then under the shawl he saw the shine of big motionless eyes, caught the lines of a dear profile in the dark, together with a familiar, precious fragrance which reminded Nikitin of Masha's room.

"Maria Godefroy," he said, and did not know his own voice, it was so soft and tender, "what are your sins?"

Masha screwed up her eyes and put out the tip of her tongue at him, then she laughed and went away. And a minute later she was standing in the middle of the room, clapping her hands and crying:

"Supper, supper, supper!"

And they all streamed into the dining room. At supper Varya had another argument, and this time with her father. Polyansky ate stolidly, drank red wine, and described to Nikitin how once in a winter campaign he had stood all night up to his knees in a bog; the enemy was so near that they were not allowed to speak or smoke, the night was cold and dark, a piercing wind was blowing. Nikitin listened and stole side glances at Masha. She was gazing at him immovably, without blinking, as though she was pondering something or was lost in a reverie. . . . It was pleasure and agony to him both at once.

"Why does she look at me like that?" was the question that fretted him. "It's awkward. People may notice it. Oh, how young, how naive she is!"

The party broke up at midnight. When Nikitin went out at the gate, a window opened on the first floor, and Masha showed herself at it.

"Sergey Vassilich!" she called.

"What is it?"

"I tell you what . . ." said Masha, evidently thinking of something to say. "I tell you what. . . . Polyansky said he would come in a day or two with his camera and take us all. We must meet here."

"Very well."

Masha vanished, the window was slammed, and someone immediately began playing the piano in the house.

"Well, it is a house!" thought Nikitin while he crossed the street. "A house in which there is no moaning except from Egyptian pigeons, and they only do it because they have no other means of expressing their joy!"

But the Shelestovs were not the only festive household. Nikitin had not gone two hundred paces before he heard the strains of a piano from another house. A little further he met a peasant playing the balalaika at the gate. In the gardens the band struck up a potpourri of Russian songs.

Nikitin lived nearly half a mile from the Shelestovs' in a flat of eight rooms at the rent of three hundred rubles a year, which he shared with his colleague Ippolit Ippolitich, a teacher of geography and history. When Nikitin went in, this Ippolit Ippolitich, a snub-nosed, middle-aged man with a reddish beard and a coarse, good-natured, un-intellectual face like a workman's, was sitting at the table correcting his pupils' maps. He considered that the most important and necessary part of the study of geography was the drawing of maps, and of the study of history the learning of dates: he would sit for nights together correcting in blue pencil the maps drawn by the boys and girls he taught, or making chronological tables.

"What a lovely day it has been!" said Nikitin, going in to him. "I wonder at you—how can you sit indoors?"

Ippolit Ippolitich was not a talkative person; he either remained silent or talked of things which everybody knew already. Now what he answered was:

"Yes, very fine weather. It's May now; we soon shall have real summer. And summer's a very different thing from winter. In the winter you have to heat the stoves, but in summer you can keep warm without. In summer you have your window open at night and still are warm, and in winter you are cold even with the double frames in."

Nikitin had not sat at the table for more than one minute before he was bored.

"Good night!" he said, getting up and yawning. "I wanted to tell you something romantic concerning myself, but you are—geography! If one talks to you of love, you will ask one at once, 'What was the date of the Battle of Kalka?' Confound you, with your battles and your capes in Siberia!"

"What are you cross about?"

"Why, it is vexatious!"

And vexed that he had not spoken to Masha, and that he had no one to talk to of his love, he went to his study and lay down upon the sofa. It was dark and still in the study. Lying gazing into the darkness, Nikitin for some reason began thinking how in two or three years he would go to Petersburg, how Masha would see him off at the station and would cry; in Petersburg he would get a long letter from her in which she would entreat him to come home as quickly as possible. And he would write to her. . . . He would begin his letter like that: "My dear little rat!"

"Yes, my dear little rat!" he said, and he laughed.

He was lying in an uncomfortable position. He put his arms under his head and put his left leg over the back of the sofa. He felt more comfortable. Meanwhile a pale light was more and more perceptible at the windows, sleepy cocks crowed in the yard. Nikitin went on thinking how he would come back from Petersburg, how Masha would meet him at the station, and with a shriek of delight would fling herself on his neck; or, better still, he would surprise her and come home by stealth late at night: the cook would open the door, then he would go on tiptoe to the bedroom, undress noiselessly, and jump into bed! And she would wake up and be overjoyed.

It was beginning to get quite light. By now there were no windows, no study. On the steps of the brewery by which they had ridden that day Masha was sitting, saying something. Then she took Nikitin by the arm and went with him to the suburban garden. There he saw the oaks and the crows' nests like hats. One of the nests rocked; out of it peeped Shebaldin, shouting loudly: "You have not read Lessing!"

Nikitin shuddered all over and opened his eyes. Ippolit Ippolitich was standing before the sofa and, throwing back his head, was putting on his cravat.

"Get up; it's time for school," he said. "You shouldn't sleep in your clothes; it spoils your clothes. You should sleep in your bed, undressed."

And as usual he began slowly and emphatically saying what everybody knew.

Nikitin's first lesson was on Russian language in the second class. When at nine o'clock punctually he went into the classroom, he saw written on the blackboard two large letters—M.S. That, no doubt, meant Masha Shelestov.

"They've scented it out already, the rascals . . ." thought Nikitin. "How is it they know everything?"

The second lesson was in the fifth class. And there two letters, M.S., were written on the blackboard; and when he went out of the classroom at the end of the lesson, he heard the shout behind him as though from a theater gallery:

"Hurrah for Masha Shelestov!"

His head was heavy from sleeping in his clothes, his limbs were weighted down with inertia. The boys, who were expecting every day to break up before the examinations, did nothing, were restless, and so bored that they got into mischief. Nikitin, too, was restless, did not notice their pranks, and was continually going to the window. He could see the street brilliantly lighted up with the sun; above the houses the blue limpid sky, the birds, and far, far away, beyond the gardens and the houses, vast indefinite distance, the forests in the blue haze, the smoke from a passing train. . . .

Here two officers in white tunics, playing with their whips, passed in the street in the shade of the acacias. Here a lot of Jews, with gray beards, and caps on, drove past in a wagonette. . . . The governess walked by with the director's granddaughter. Som ran by in the company of two other dogs. . . . And then Varya, wearing a simple gray dress and red stockings, carrying the *European Herald* in her hand, passed by. She must have been to the town library. . . .

And it would be a long time before lessons were over at three o'clock! And after school he could not go home nor to the Shelestovs', but must go to give a lesson at Wolf's. This Wolf, a wealthy Jew who had turned Lutheran, did not send his children to the high school, but had them taught at home by the high-school masters, and paid five rubles a lesson.

He was bored, bored, bored.

At three o'clock he went to Wolf's and spent there, as it seemed to him, an eternity. He left there at five o'clock, and before seven he had to be at the high school again to a meeting of the masters—to draw up the plan for the oral examination of the fourth and sixth classes.

When late in the evening he left the high school and went to the Shelestovs', his heart was beating and his face was flushed. A month before, even a week before, he had, every time that he made up his mind to speak to her, prepared a whole speech, with an introduction and a conclusion. Now he had not one word ready; everything was in a muddle in his head, and all he knew was that today he would *certainly* declare himself, and that it was utterly impossible to wait any longer.

"I will ask her to come to the garden," he thought; "we'll walk about a little and I'll speak."

There was not a soul in the hall; he went into the dining room and then into the drawing room. . . . There was no one there either. He could hear Varya arguing with someone upstairs and the clink of the dressmaker's scissors in the nursery.

There was a little room in the house which had three names: the little room, the passage room, and the dark room. There was a big cupboard in it where they kept medicines, gunpowder, and their hunting gear. Leading from this room to the first floor was a narrow wooden staircase where cats were always asleep. There were two doors in it—one leading to the nursery, one to the drawing room. When Nikitin went into this room to go upstairs, the door from the nursery opened and shut with such a bang that it made the stairs and the cupboard tremble; Masha, in a dark dress, ran in with a piece of blue material in her hand, and, not noticing Nikitin, darted toward the stairs.

"Stay . . ." said Nikitin, stopping her. "Good evening, Godefroy. . . . Allow me. . . ."

He gasped, he did not know what to say; with one hand he held her hand and with the other the blue material. And she was half frightened, half surprised, and looked at him with big eyes.

"Allow me . . ." Nikitin went on, afraid she would go away. "There's something I must say to you. . . . Only . . . it's inconvenient here. I cannot, I am incapable. . . . Understand, Godefroy, I can't—that's all. . . ."

The blue material slipped onto the floor, and Nikitin took Masha by the other hand. She turned pale, moved her lips, then stepped back from Nikitin and found herself in the corner between the wall and the cupboard.

"On my honor, I assure you . . ." he said softly. "Masha, on my honor. . . ."

She threw back her head and he kissed her lips, and that the kiss might last longer he put his fingers to her cheeks; and it somehow happened that he found himself in the corner between the cupboard and the wall, and she put her arms round his neck and pressed her head against his chin.

Then they both ran into the garden. The Shelestovs had a garden of nine acres. There were a score of old maples and lime trees in it; there was one fir tree, and all the rest were fruit trees: cherries, apples, pears, chestnuts, silvery olive trees. . . . There were masses of flowers, too.

Nikitin and Masha ran along the avenues in silence, laughed, asked each other from time to time disconnected questions which they did not answer. A crescent moon was shining over the garden, and drowsy tulips and irises were stretching up from the dark grass in its faint light, as though begging for words of love for themselves, too.

When Nikitin and Masha went back to the house, the officers and the young ladies were already assembled and dancing the mazurka. Again Polyansky led the grand chain through all the rooms, again after dancing they played "fate." Before supper, when the visitors had gone into the dining room, Masha, left alone with Nikitin, pressed close to him and said:

"You must speak to Papa and Varya yourself; I am embarrassed."

After supper he talked to the old father. After listening to him, Shelestov thought a little and said:

"I am very grateful for the honor you do me and my daughter, but let me speak to you as a friend. I will speak to you, not as a father, but as one gentleman to another. Tell me, why do you want to be married so young? Only peasants are married so young, and that, of course, is loutishness. But why should you? Where's the satisfaction of putting on the fetters at your age?"

"I am not young!" said Nikitin, offended. "I am in my twenty-seventh year."

"Papa, the farrier has come!" cried Varya from the other room.

And the conversation broke off. Varya, Masha, and Polyansky saw Nikitin home. When they reached his gate, Varya said:

"Why is it your mysterious Metropolit Metropolitich never shows himself anywhere? He might come and see us."

The mysterious Ippolit Ippolitich was sitting on his bed, taking off his trousers, when Nikitin went in to him.

"Don't go to bed, my dear fellow," said Nikitin breathlessly. "Stop a minute; don't go to bed!"

Ippolit Ippolitich put on his trousers hurriedly and asked in a flutter:

"What is it?"

"I am going to be married."

Nikitin sat down beside his companion and looking at him wonderingly, as though surprised at himself, said:

"Only fancy, I am going to be married! To Masha Shelestov! I made an offer today."

"Well? She seems a good sort of girl. Only she is very young."

"Yes, she is young," sighed Nikitin, and shrugged his shoulders with a careworn air. "Very, very young!"

"She was my pupil at the high school. I know her. She wasn't bad at geography, but she was no good at history. And she was inattentive in class, too."

Nikitin for some reason felt suddenly sorry for his companion, and longed to say something kind and comforting to him.

"My dear fellow, why don't you get married?" he asked. "Why don't you marry Varya, for instance? She is a splendid, first-rate girl! It's true she is very fond of arguing, but a heart . . . what a heart! She was just asking about you. Marry her, my dear boy! Eh?"

He knew perfectly well that Varya would not marry this dull, snub-nosed man, but still he urged him to marry her—why?

"Marriage is a serious step," said Ippolit Ippolitich after a moment's thought. "One has to look at it all round and weigh things thoroughly; it's not to be done rashly. Prudence is always a good thing, and especially in marriage, when a man, ceasing to be a bachelor, begins a new life."

And he talked of what everyone has known for ages. Nikitin did not stay to listen, said good night, and went to his own room. He undressed quickly and quickly got into bed, in order to be able to think the sooner of his happiness, of Masha, of the future; he smiled, then suddenly recalled that he had not read Lessing.

"I must read him," he thought. "Though, after all, why should I? To hell with him!"

And exhausted by his happiness, he fell asleep at once and went on smiling till the morning.

He dreamed of the thud of horses' hoofs on a wooden floor; he dreamed of the black horse Count Nulin, then of the white Giant and its sister Maika, being led out of the stable.

II

"It was very crowded and noisy in the church, and once someone cried out, and the head priest, who was marrying Masha and me, looked through his spectacles at the crowd, and said severely: 'Don't move about the church, and don't make a noise, but stand quietly and pray. You should have the fear of God in your hearts.'

"My best men were two of my colleagues, and Masha's best men were Captain Polyansky and Lieutenant Gernet. The bishop's choir sang superbly. The sputtering of the candles, the brilliant light, the gorgeous dresses, the officers, the numbers of gay, happy faces, and a special ethereal look in Masha, everything together—the surroundings and the words of the wedding prayers—moved me to tears and filled me with triumph. I thought how my life had blossomed, how poetically it was shaping itself! Two years ago I was still a student, I was living in cheap furnished rooms, without money, without relations, and, as I fancied then, with nothing to look forward to. Now I am a teacher in the high school in one of the best provincial towns, with a secure income, loved, spoiled. It is for my sake, I thought, this crowd is collected, for my sake three candelabra have been lighted, the deacon is booming, the choir is doing its best; and it's for my sake that this young creature, whom I soon shall call my wife, is so young, so elegant, and so joyful. I recalled our first meetings, our rides into the country, my declaration of love and the weather, which, as though expressly, was so exquisitely fine all the summer; and the happiness which at one time in my old rooms seemed to me possible only in novels and stories, I was now experiencing in reality—I was now, as it were, holding it in my hands.

"After the ceremony they all crowded in disorder round Masha and me, expressed their genuine pleasure, congratulated us and wished us joy. The brigadier general, an old man of seventy, confined himself to congratulating Masha, and said to her in a squeaky, aged voice, so loud that it could be heard all over the church:

" 'I hope that even after you are married you may remain the rose you are now, my dear.'

"The officers, the director, and all the teachers smiled from politeness, and I was conscious of an agreeable artificial smile on my face, too. Dear Ippolit Ippolitich, the teacher of history and geography, who always says what everyone has heard before, pressed my hand warmly and said with feeling:

" 'Hitherto you have been unmarried and have lived alone, and now you are married and no longer single.'

"From the church we went to a two-story house which I am receiving as part of the dowry. Besides that house Masha is bringing me twenty thousand rubles, as well as a piece of wasteland with a shanty on it, where I am told there are numbers of hens and ducks which are not looked after and are turning wild. When I got home from the church, I stretched myself at full length on the low sofa in my new study and began to smoke; I felt snug, cosy, and comfortable, as I never had in my life before. And meanwhile the wedding party were shouting 'Hurrah!' while a wretched band in the hall played flourishes and all sorts of trash. Varya, Masha's sister, ran into the study with a wineglass in her hand, and with a queer, strained expression, as though her mouth were full of water; apparently she had meant to go on further, but she suddenly burst out laughing and sobbing, and the wineglass crashed on the floor. We took her by the arms and led her away.

" 'Nobody can understand!' she muttered afterward, lying on the old nurse's bed in a back room. 'Nobody, nobody! My God, nobody can understand!'

"But everyone understood very well that she was four years older than her sister Masha, and still unmarried, and that she was crying, not from envy, but from the melancholy consciousness that her time was passing, and perhaps had passed. When they danced the quadrille, she was back in the drawing room with a tear-stained and heavily powdered face, and I saw Captain Polyansky holding a plate of ice before her while she ate it with a spoon.

"It is past five o'clock in the morning. I took up my diary to describe my complete and perfect happiness, and thought I would write a good six pages, and read it tomorrow to Masha; but, strange to say, everything is muddled in my head and as misty as a dream, and I can remember vividly nothing but that episode with Varya, and I want to write, 'Poor Varya!' I could go on sitting here and writing 'Poor Varya!' By the way, the trees have begun rustling; it will rain. The crows are cawing, and my Masha, who has just gone to sleep, has for some reason a sorrowful face."

For a long while afterward Nikitin did not write his diary. At the beginning of August he had school examinations, and after the fifteenth classes began. As a rule he set off for school before nine in the morning, and before ten o'clock he was looking at his watch and pining for his Masha and his new house. In the lower forms he would set some boy to dictate, and while the boys were writing, would sit in the window with his eyes shut, dreaming; whether he dreamed of the future or recalled the past, everything seemed to him equally delightful, like a fairy tale. In the senior classes they were reading aloud Gogol or Pushkin's prose works, and that made him sleepy; people, trees, fields, horses, rose before his imagination, and he would say with a sigh, as though fascinated by the author:

"How lovely!"

At the midday recess Masha used to send him lunch in a snow-white napkin, and he would eat it slowly, with pauses, to prolong the enjoyment of it; and Ippolit Ippolitich, whose lunch as a rule consisted of nothing but bread, looked at him with respect and envy, and gave expression to some familiar fact, such as:

"Men cannot live without food."

After school Nikitin went straight to give his private lessons, and when at last by six o'clock he got home, he felt excited and anxious, as though he had been away for a year. He would run upstairs breathless, find Masha, throw his arms round her, and kiss her and swear that he loved her, that he could not live without her, declare that he had missed her fearfully, and ask her in trepidation how she was and why she looked so depressed. Then they would dine together. After dinner he would lie on the sofa in his study and smoke, while she sat beside him and talked in a low voice.

His happiest days now were Sundays and holidays, when he was at home from morning till evening. On those days he took part in the naive but extraordinarily pleasant life which reminded him of a pastoral idyll. He was never weary of watching how his sensible and practical Masha was arranging her nest, and anxious to show that he was of some use in the house, he would do something useless—for instance, bring the chaise out of the stable and look at it from every side. Masha had installed a regular dairy with three cows, and in her cellar she had many jugs of milk and pots of sour cream, and she kept it all for butter. Sometimes, by way of a joke, Nikitin would ask her for a glass of milk, and she would be quite upset because it was against her rules; but he would laugh and throw his arms round her, saying:

"There, there; I was joking, my darling! I was joking!"

Or he would laugh at her strictness when, finding in the cupboard some stale bit of cheese or sausage as hard as a stone, she would say seriously:

"They will eat that in the kitchen."

He would observe that such a scrap was fit only for a mousetrap, and she would reply warmly that men knew nothing about housekeeping, and that it was just the same to the servants if you were to send down a hundredweight of savories to the kitchen. He would agree, and embrace her enthusiastically. Everything that was just in what she said seemed to him extraordinary and amazing; and what did not fit in with his convictions seemed to him naive and touching.

Sometimes he was in a philosophical mood, and he would begin to discuss some abstract subject while she listened and looked at his face with curiosity.

"I am immensely happy with you, my joy," he used to say, playing with her fingers or plaiting and unplaiting her hair. "But I don't look upon this happiness of mine as something that has come to me by chance, as though it had dropped from heaven. This happiness is a perfectly natural, consistent, logical consequence. I believe that man is the creator of his own happiness, and now I am enjoying just what I have myself created. Yes, I speak without false modesty: I have created this happiness myself and I have a right to it. You know my past. My unhappy childhood, without father or mother; my depressing youth, poverty—all this was a struggle, all this was the path by which I made my way to happiness. . . ."

In October the school sustained a heavy loss: Ippolit Ippolitich was taken ill with erysipelas on the head and died. For two days before his death he was unconscious and delirious, but even in his delirium he said nothing that was not perfectly well known to everyone.

"The Volga flows into the Caspian Sea. . . . Horses eat oats and hay. . . ."

There were no lessons at the high school on the day of his funeral. His colleagues and pupils were the coffin bearers, and the school choir sang all the way to the grave the anthem "Holy God." Three priests, two deacons, all his pupils and the staff of the boys' high school, and the bishop's choir in their best caftans, took part in the procession. And passersby who met the solemn procession crossed themselves and said:

"God grant us all such a death."

Returning home from the cemetery much moved, Nikitin got out his diary from the table and wrote:

"We have just consigned to the tomb Ippolit Ippolitich Ryzhitsky. Peace to your ashes, modest worker! Masha, Varya, and all the women at the funeral wept from genuine feeling, perhaps because they knew this uninteresting, humble man had never been loved by a woman. I wanted to say a warm word at my colleague's grave, but I was warned that this might displease the director, as he did not like our poor friend. I believe that this is the first day since my marriage that my heart has been heavy."

There was no other event of note in the scholastic year.

The winter was mild, with wet snow and no frost; on Epiphany Eve, for instance, the wind howled all night as though it were autumn, and water trickled off the roofs; and in the morning, at the ceremony of the blessing of the water, the police allowed no one to go on the river, because they said the ice was swelling up and looked dark. But in spite of bad weather Nikitin's life was as happy as in summer. And, indeed, he acquired another source of pleasure; he learned to play vint. Only one thing troubled him, moved him to anger, and seemed to prevent him from being perfectly happy: the cats and dogs which formed part of his wife's dowry. The rooms, especially in the morning, always smelt like a menagerie, and nothing could destroy the odor; the cats frequently fought with the dogs. The spiteful beast Mushka was fed a dozen times a day; she still refused to recognize Nikitin and growled at him: "Rrr . . . nga-nga-nga!"

One night in Lent he was returning home from the club where he had been playing cards. It was dark, raining, and muddy. Nikitin had an unpleasant feeling at the bottom of his heart and could not account for it. He did not know whether it was because he had lost twelve rubles at cards, or whether because one of the players, when they were settling up, had said that of course Nikitin had pots of money, with obvious reference to his wife's dowry. He did not regret the twelve rubles, and there was nothing offensive in what had been said; but, still, there was the unpleasant feeling. He did not even feel a desire to go home.

"Foo, how horrid!" he said, standing still at a lamppost.

It occurred to him that he did not regret the twelve rubles because he got them for nothing. If he had been a working man he would have known the value of every penny, and would not have been so careless whether he lost or won. And his good fortune had all, he reflected, come to him by chance, for nothing, and really was as superfluous for him as medicine for the healthy. If, like the vast majority of people, he had been harassed by anxiety for his daily bread, had been struggling for existence, if his back and chest had ached from work, then supper, a warm snug home, and domestic happiness, would have been the necessity, the compensation, the crown of his life; as it was, all this had a strange, indefinite significance for him.

"Foo, how horrid!" he repeated, knowing perfectly well that these reflections were in themselves a bad sign.

When he got home Masha was in bed: she was breathing evenly and smiling, and was evidently sleeping with great enjoyment. Near her the white cat lay curled up, purring. While Nikitin lit the candle and lighted his cigarette, Masha woke up and greedily drank a glass of water.

"I ate too many sweets," she said, and laughed. "Have you been to our house?" she asked after a pause.

"No."

Nikitin knew already that Captain Polyansky, on whom Varya had been building great hopes of late, was being transferred to one of the western provinces, and was already making his farewell visits in the town, and so it was depressing at his father-in-law's.

"Varya looked in this evening," said Masha, sitting up. "She did not say anything, but one could see from her face how wretched she is, poor darling! I can't bear Polyansky. He is fat and bloated, and when he walks or dances his cheeks shake. . . . He is not a man I would choose. But, still, I did think he was a decent person."

"I think he is a decent person now," said Nikitin.

"Then why has he treated Varya so badly?"

"Why badly?" asked Nikitin, beginning to feel irritation against the white cat, who was stretching and arching its back. "As far as I know, he has made no proposal and has given her no promises."

"Then why was he so often at the house? If he didn't mean to marry her, he oughtn't to have come."

Nikitin put out the candle and got into bed. But he felt disinclined to lie down and to sleep. He felt as though his head were immense and empty as a barn, and that new, peculiar thoughts were wandering about in it like tall shadows. He thought that, apart from the soft light of the icon lamp, that beamed upon their quiet domestic happiness, that apart from this little world in which he and this cat lived so peacefully and happily, there was another world. . . . And he had a passionate, poignant longing to be in that other world, to work himself at some factory or big workshop, to address big audiences, to write, to publish, to raise a stir, to exhaust himself, to suffer. . . . He wanted something that would engross him till he forgot himself, ceased to care for the personal happiness which yielded him only sensations so monotonous. And suddenly there rose vividly before his imagination the figure of Shebaldin with his clean-shaven face, saying to him with horror: "You haven't even read Lessing! You are quite behind the times! How you have gone to seed!"

Masha woke up and again drank some water. He glanced at her neck, at her plump shoulders and throat, and remembered the word the brigadier general had used in church—"rose."

"Rose," he muttered, and laughed.

His laugh was answered by a sleepy growl from Mushka under the bed: "Rrr . . . nga-nga-nga . . . !"

A heavy anger sank like a cold weight on his heart, and he felt tempted to say something rude to Masha, and even to jump up and hit her; his heart began throbbing.

"So then," he asked, restraining himself, "since I went to your house, I was obligated to marry you?"

"Of course. You know that very well."

"That's nice." And a minute later he repeated: "That's nice."

To relieve the throbbing of his heart, and to avoid saying too much, Nikitin went to his study and lay down on the sofa, without a pillow; then he lay on the floor on the carpet.

"What nonsense it is!" he said to reassure himself. "You are a teacher, you are working in the noblest of callings. . . . What need have you of any other world? What rubbish!"

But almost immediately he told himself with conviction that he was not a real teacher, but simply a government employee, as commonplace and mediocre as the Czech who taught Greek. He had never had a vocation for teaching, he knew nothing of the theory of teaching, and never had been interested in the subject; he did not know how to treat children; he did not understand the significance of what he taught, and perhaps did not teach the right things. Poor Ippolit Ippolitich had been frankly stupid, and all the boys, as well as his colleagues, knew what he was and what to expect from him; but he, Nikitin, like the Czech, knew how to conceal his stupidity and cleverly deceived everyone by pretending that, thank God, his teaching was a success. These new ideas frightened Nikitin; he rejected them, called them stupid, and believed that all this was due to his nerves, that he would laugh at himself.

And he did, in fact, by the morning laugh at himself and call himself an old woman; but it was clear to him that his peace of mind was lost, perhaps, forever, and that in that little two-story house happiness was henceforth impossible for him. He realized that the illusion had evaporated, and that a new life of unrest and clear sight was beginning which was incompatible with peace and personal happiness.

Next day, which was Sunday, he was at the school chapel, and there met his colleagues and the director. It seemed to him that they were entirely preoccupied with concealing their ignorance and discontent with life, and he, too, to conceal his uneasiness, smiled affably and talked of trivialities. Then he went to the station and saw the mail train come in and go out, and it was agreeable to him to be alone and not to have to talk to anyone.

At home he found Varya and his father-in-law, who had come to dinner. Varya's eyes were red with crying, and she complained of a headache, while Shelestov ate a great deal, saying that young men nowadays were unreliable, and that there was very little gentlemanly feeling among them.

"It's loutishness!" he said. "I shall tell him so to his face: 'It's loutishness, sir,' I shall say."

Nikitin smiled affably and helped Masha to look after their guests, but after dinner he went to his study and shut the door.

The March sun was shining brightly in at the windows and shedding its warm rays on the table. It was only the twentieth of the month, but already the cabmen were driving with wheels, and the starlings were noisy in the garden. It was just the weather in which Masha would come in, put one arm round his neck, tell him the horses were saddled or the chaise was at the door, and ask him what she should put on to keep warm. Spring was beginning as exquisitely as last spring, and it promised the same joys. . . . But Nikitin was thinking that it would be nice to take a holiday and go to Moscow, and stay at his old lodgings there. In the next room they were drinking coffee and talking of Captain Polyansky, while he tried not to listen and wrote in his diary: "Where am I, my God? I am surrounded by vulgarity and vulgarity. Wearisome, insignificant people, pots of sour cream, jugs of milk, cockroaches, stupid women. . . . There is nothing more terrible, mortifying, and distressing than vulgarity. I must escape from here, I must escape today, or I shall go out of my mind!"

1889–94

EASTER EVE

I was standing on the bank of the river Goltva, waiting for the ferryboat from the other side. At ordinary times the Goltva is a humble stream of moderate size, silent and pensive, gently glimmering from behind thick reeds; but now a regular lake lay stretched out before me. The waters of spring, running riot, had overflowed both banks and flooded both sides of the river for a long distance, submerging vegetable gardens, hayfields, and marshes, so that it was no unusual thing to meet poplars and bushes sticking out above the surface of the water and looking in the darkness like grim solitary crags.

The weather seemed to me magnificent. It was dark, yet I could see the trees, the water and the people. . . . The world was lighted by the stars, which were scattered thickly all over the sky. I don't remember ever seeing so many stars. Literally one could not have put a finger in between them. There were some as big as a goose's egg, others tiny as hempseed. . . . They had come out for the festival procession, every one of them, little and big, washed, renewed and joyful, and every one of them was softly twinkling its beams. The sky was reflected in the water; the stars were bathing in its dark depths and trembling with the quivering eddies. The air was warm and still. . . . Here and there, far away on the further bank in the impenetrable darkness, several bright red lights were gleaming. . . .

A couple of paces from me I saw the dark silhouette of a peasant in a high hat, with a thick knotted stick in his hand.

"How long the ferryboat is in coming!" I said.

"It is time it was here," the silhouette answered.

"You are waiting for the ferryboat, too?"

"No, I am not," yawned the peasant—"I am waiting for the illumination. I should have gone, but, to tell you the truth, I haven't the five kopecks for the ferry."

"I'll give you the five kopecks."

"No; I humbly thank you. . . . With that five kopecks put up a candle for me over there in the monastery. . . . That will be more interesting, and I will stand here. What can it mean, no ferryboat, as though it had sunk in the water!"

The peasant went up to the water's edge, took the rope in his hands, and shouted: "Ieronim! Ieron—im!"

As though in answer to his shout, the slow peal of a great bell floated across from the further bank. The note was deep and low, as from the thickest string of a double bass; it seemed as though the darkness itself had hoarsely uttered it. At once there was the sound of a cannon shot. It rolled away in the darkness and ended somewhere in the far distance behind me. The peasant took off his hat and crossed himself.

"Christ is risen," he said.

Before the vibrations of the first peal of the bell had time to die away in the air a second sounded, after it at once a third, and the darkness was filled with an unbroken quivering clamor. Near the red lights fresh lights flashed, and all began moving together and twinkling restlessly.

"Ieron—im!" we heard a hollow prolonged shout.

"They are shouting from the other bank," said the peasant, "so there is no ferry there either. Our Ieronim has gone to sleep."

The lights and the velvety chimes of the bell drew one toward them. . . . I was already beginning to lose patience and grow anxious, but behold at last, staring into the dark distance, I saw the outline of something very much like a gibbet. It was the long-expected ferry. It moved toward us with such deliberation that if it had not been that its lines grew gradually more definite, one might have supposed that it was standing still or moving to the other bank.

"Make haste! Ieronim!" shouted my peasant. "The gentleman's tired of waiting!"

The ferry crawled to the bank, gave a lurch, and stopped with a creak. A tall man in a monk's cassock and a conical cap stood on it, holding the rope.

"Why have you been so long?" I asked, jumping upon the ferry.

"Forgive me, for Christ's sake," Ieronim answered gently. "Is there no one else?"

"No one. . . ."

Ieronim took hold of the rope in both hands, bent himself to the figure of a mark of interrogation, and gasped. The ferryboat creaked and gave a lurch. The outline of the peasant in the high hat began slowly retreating from me—so the ferry was moving off. Ieronim soon drew himself up and began working with one hand only. We were silent, gazing toward the bank to which we were floating. There the illumination for which the peasant was waiting had begun. At the water's edge barrels of tar were flaring like huge campfires. Their reflections, crimson as the rising moon, crept to meet us in long, broad streaks. The burning barrels lighted up their own smoke and the long shadows of men flitting about the fire; but further to one side and behind them from where the velvety chime floated there was still the same unbroken black gloom. All at once, cleaving the darkness, a rocket zigzagged in a golden ribbon up the sky; it described an arc and, as though broken to pieces against the sky, was scattered crackling into sparks. There was a roar from the bank like a faraway hurrah.

"How beautiful!" I said.

"Beautiful beyond words!" sighed Ieronim. "Such a night, sir!

Another time one would pay no attention to the fireworks, but today one rejoices in every vanity. Where do you come from?"

I told him where I came from.

"To be sure . . . a joyful day today. . . ." Ieronim went on in a weak sighing tenor like the voice of a convalescent. "The sky is rejoicing and the earth and what is under the earth. All the creatures are keeping holiday. Only tell me, kind sir, why, even in the time of great rejoicing, a man cannot forget his sorrows?"

I fancied that this unexpected question was to draw me into one of those endless religious conversations which bored and idle monks are so fond of. I was not disposed to talk much, and so I only asked:

"What sorrows have you, Father?"

"As a rule only the same as all men, kind sir, but today a special sorrow has happened in the monastery: at mass, during the reading of the Bible, the monk and deacon Nikolay died."

"Well, it's God's will!" I said, falling into the monastic tone. "We must all die. To my mind, you ought to rejoice indeed. . . . They say if anyone dies at Easter he goes straight to the Kingdom of Heaven."

"That's true."

We sank into silence. The figure of the peasant in the high hat melted into the lines of the bank. The tar barrels were flaring up more and more.

"The Holy Scripture points clearly to the vanity of sorrow, and so does reflection," said Ieronim, breaking the silence; "but why does the heart grieve and refuse to listen to reason? Why does one want to weep bitterly?"

Ieronim shrugged his shoulders, turned to me, and said quickly:

"If I died, or anyone else, it would not be worth notice, perhaps; but, you see, Nikolay is dead! No one else but Nikolay! Indeed, it's hard to believe that he is no more! I stand here on my ferryboat and every minute I keep fancying that he will lift up his voice from the bank. He always used to come to the bank and call to me that I might not be afraid on the ferry. He used to get up from his bed at night on purpose for that. He was a kind soul. My God! how kindly and gracious! Many a mother is not so good to her child as Nikolay was to me! Lord, save his soul!"

Ieronim took hold of the rope, but turned to me again at once.

"And such a lofty intelligence, Your Honor," he said in a vibrating voice. "Such a sweet and harmonious tongue! Just as they will sing immediately at early matins: 'Oh lovely! oh sweet is Thy Voice!' Besides all other human qualities, he had, too, an extraordinary gift!"

"What gift?" I asked.

The monk scrutinized me, and as though he had convinced himself that he could trust me with a secret, he laughed good-humoredly.

"He had a gift for writing hymns of praise," he said. "It was a marvel, sir; you couldn't call it anything else! You will be amazed if I tell you about it. Our Father Archimandrite comes from Moscow, the Father Sub-Prior studied at the Kazan academy, we have wise monks and elders, but, would you believe it, no one could write them; while Nikolay, a simple monk, a deacon, had not studied anywhere, and had not even any outer appearance of it, but he wrote them! A marvel! a real marvel!" Ieronim clasped his hands and, completely forgetting the rope, went on eagerly:

"The Father Sub-Prior has great difficulty in composing sermons; when he wrote the history of the monastery he worried all the brotherhood and drove a dozen times to town, while Nikolay wrote canticles! Hymns of praise! That's a very different thing from a sermon or a history!"

"Is it difficult to write them?" I asked.

"There's great difficulty!" Ieronim wagged his head. "You can do nothing by wisdom and holiness if God has not given you the gift. The monks who don't understand argue that you only need to know the life of the saint for whom you are writing the hymn, and to make it harmonize with the other hymns of praise. But that's a mistake, sir. Of course, anyone who writes canticles must know the life of the saint to perfection, to the least trivial detail. To be sure, one must make them harmonize with the other canticles and know where to begin and what to write about. To give you an instance, the first response begins everywhere with 'the chosen' or 'the elect.' . . . The first line must always begin with the 'angel.' In the canticle of praise to Jesus the Most Sweet, if you are interested in the subject, it begins like this: 'Of angels Creator and Lord of all powers!' In the canticle to the Holy Mother of God: 'Of angels the foremost sent down from on high'; to Nikolay, the Wonder-worker—'An angel in semblance, though in substance a man,' and so on. Everywhere you begin with the angel. Of course, it would be impossible without making them harmonize, but the lives of the saints and conformity with the others is not what matters; what matters is the beauty and sweetness of it. Everything must be harmonious, brief, and complete. There must be in every line softness, graciousness, and tenderness; not one word should be harsh or rough or unsuitable. It must be written so that the worshiper may rejoice at heart and weep, while his mind is stirred and he is thrown into a tremor. In the canticle to the Holy Mother are the words: 'Rejoice, O Thou too high for human thought to reach! Rejoice, O Thou too deep for angels' eyes to fathom!' In another place in the same canticle: 'Rejoice, O tree that bearest the fair fruit of light that is the food of the faithful! Rejoice, O tree of gracious spreading shade, under which there is shelter for multitudes!' "

Ieronim hid his face in his hands, as though frightened at something or overcome with shame, and shook his head.

"Tree that bearest the fair fruit of light . . . tree of gracious spreading shade . . ." he muttered. "To think that a man should find words like those! Such a power is a gift from God! For brevity he packs many thoughts into one phrase, and how smooth and complete it all is! 'Light-radiating torch to all that be . . .' comes in the canticle to Jesus the Most Sweet. 'Light-radiating!' There is no such word in conversation or in books, but you see he invented it, he found it in his mind! Apart from the smoothness and grandeur of language, sir, every line must be beautified in every way; there must be flowers and lightning and wind and sun and all the objects of the visible world. And every exclamation ought to be put so as to be smooth and easy for the ear. 'Rejoice, thou flower of heavenly growth!' comes in the hymn to Nikolay the Wonder-worker. It's not simply 'heavenly flower,' but 'flower of heavenly growth.' It's smoother so and sweet to the ear. That was just as Nikolay wrote it! Exactly like that! I can't tell you how he used to write!"

"Well, in that case it is a pity he is dead," I said; "but let us get on, Father, or we shall be late."

Ieronim started and ran to the rope; they were beginning to peal all the bells. Probably the procession was already going on near the monastery, for all the dark space behind the tar barrels was now dotted with moving lights.

"Did Nikolay print his hymns?" I asked Ieronim.

"How could he print them?" he sighed. "And, indeed, it would be strange to print them. What would be the object? No one in the monastery takes any interest in them. They don't like them. They knew Nikolay wrote them, but they let it pass unnoticed. No one esteems new writings nowadays, sir!"

"Were they prejudiced against him?"

"Yes, indeed. If Nikolay had been an elder perhaps the brethren would have been interested, but he wasn't forty, you know. There were some who laughed and even thought his writing a sin."

"What did he write them for?"

"Chiefly for his own comfort. Of all the brotherhood, I was the only one who read his hymns. I used to go to him in secret, that no one else might know of it, and he was glad that I took an interest in them. He would embrace me, stroke my head, speak to me in caressing words as to a little child. He would shut his cell, make me sit down beside him, and begin to read. . . ."

Ieronim left the rope and came up to me.

"We were dear friends in a way," he whispered, looking at me with shining eyes. "Where he went I would go. If I were not there he would miss me. And he cared more for me than for anyone, and all because I used to weep over his hymns. It makes me sad to remember. Now I feel just like an orphan or a widow. You know, in our monastery they are all good people, kind and pious, but . . . there is no one with softness and refinement, they are just like peasants. They all speak loudly, and tramp heavily when they walk; they are noisy, they clear their throats, but Nikolay always talked softly, caressingly, and if he noticed that anyone was asleep or praying he would slip by like a fly or a gnat. His face was tender, compassionate. . . ."

Ieronim heaved a deep sigh and took hold of the rope again. We were by now approaching the bank. We floated straight out of the darkness and stillness of the river into an enchanted realm, full of stifling smoke, crackling lights, and uproar. By now one could distinctly see people moving near the tar barrels. The flickering of the lights gave a strange, almost fantastic, expression to their figures and red faces. From time to time one caught among the heads and faces a glimpse of a horse's head motionless as though cast in copper.

"They'll begin singing the Easter hymn directly . . ." said Ieronim, "and Nikolay is gone; there is no one to appreciate it. . . . There was nothing written dearer to him than that hymn. He used to take in every word! You'll be there, sir, so notice what is sung; it takes your breath away!"

"Won't you be in church, then?"

"I can't; . . . I have to work the ferry. . . ."

"But won't they relieve you?"

"I don't know. . . . I ought to have been relieved at eight; but, as you see, they don't come! . . . And I must own I should have liked to be in the church. . . ."

"Are you a monk?"

"Yes . . . that is, I am a lay brother."

The ferry ran into the bank and stopped. I thrust a five-kopeck piece into Ieronim's hand for taking me across, and jumped on land. Immediately a cart with a boy and a sleeping woman in it drove creaking onto the ferry. Ieronim, with a faint glow from the lights on his figure, pressed on the rope, bent down to it, and started the ferry back. . . .

I took a few steps through mud, but a little further walked on a soft, freshly trodden path. This path led to the dark monastery gates, that looked like a cavern through a cloud of smoke, through a disorderly crowd of people, unharnessed horses, carts, and chaises. All this crowd was rattling, snorting, laughing, and the crimson light and wavering shadows from the smoke flickered over it all. . . . A perfect chaos! And in this hubbub the people yet found room to load a little cannon and to sell cakes. There was no less commotion on the other side of the wall in the monastery precincts, but there was more regard for decorum and order. Here there was a smell of juniper and incense. They talked loudly, but there was no sound of laughter or snorting. Near the tombstones and crosses people pressed close to one another with Easter cakes and bundles in their arms. Apparently many had come from a long distance for their cakes to be blessed and now were exhausted. Young lay brothers, making a metallic sound with their boots, ran busily along the iron slabs that paved the way from the monastery gates to the church door. They were busy and shouting on the belfry, too.

"What a restless night!" I thought. "How nice!"

One was tempted to see the same unrest and sleeplessness in all nature, from the night darkness to the iron slabs, the crosses on the tombs and the trees under which the people were moving to and fro. But nowhere was the excitement and restlessness so marked as in the church. An unceasing struggle was going on in the entrance between the inflowing stream and the outflowing stream. Some were going in, others going out and soon coming back again to stand still for a little and begin moving again. People were scurrying from place to place, lounging about as though they were looking for something. The stream flowed from the entrance all round the church, disturbing even the front rows, where persons of weight and dignity were standing. There could be no thought of concentrated prayer. There were no prayers at all, but a sort of continuous, childishly irresponsible joy, seeking a pretext to break out and vent itself in some movement, even in senseless jostling and shoving.

The same unaccustomed movement is striking in the Easter service itself. The altar gates are flung wide open, thick clouds of incense float in the air near the candelabra; wherever one looks there are lights, the gleam and splutter of candles. . . . There is no reading; restless and lighthearted singing goes on to the end without ceasing. After each hymn the clergy change their vestments and come out to burn incense, which is repeated every ten minutes.

I had no sooner taken a place, when a wave rushed from in front and forced me back. A tall thickset deacon walked before me with a long red candle; the gray-headed archimandrite in his golden miter hurried after him with the censer. When they had vanished from sight the crowd squeezed me back to my former position. But ten minutes had not passed before a new wave burst on me, and again the deacon appeared. This time he was followed by the Father Sub-Prior, the man who, as Ieronim had told me, was writing the history of the monastery.

As I mingled with the crowd and caught the infection of the universal joyful excitement, I felt unbearably sore on Ieronim's account. Why did they not send someone to relieve him? Why could not someone of less feeling and less susceptibility go on the ferry? "Lift up thine eyes, O Sion, and look around," they sang in the choir, "for thy children have come to thee as to a beacon of divine light from north and south, and from east and from the sea. . . ."

I looked at the faces; they all had a lively expression of triumph, but no one was listening to what was being sung and taking it in, and not one was "holding his breath." Why was not Ieronim released? I could fancy Ieronim standing meekly somewhere by the wall, bending forward and hungrily drinking in the beauty of the holy phrase. All this that glided by the ears of people standing by me he would have eagerly drunk in with his delicately sensitive soul, and would have been spellbound to ecstasy, to holding his breath, and there

"*All this . . . he would have eagerly drunk in with his delicately sensitive soul, and would have been spellbound to ecstasy, to holding his breath, and there would not have been a man happier than he in all the church.*"

would not have been a man happier than he in all the church. Now he was plying to and fro over the dark river and grieving for his dead friend and brother.

The wave surged back. A stout, smiling monk, playing with his rosary and looking round behind him, squeezed sideways by me, making way for a lady in a hat and velvet cloak. A monastery servant hurried after the lady, holding a chair over our heads.

I came out of the church. I wanted to have a look at the dead Nikolay, the unknown canticle writer. I walked about the monastery wall, where there was a row of cells, peeped into several windows, and, seeing nothing, came back again. I do not regret now that I did not see Nikolay; God knows, perhaps if I had seen him I should have lost the picture my imagination paints for me now. I imagine that lovable poetical figure, solitary and not understood, who went out at nights to call to Ieronim over the water, and filled his hymns with flowers, stars, and sunbeams, as a pale timid man with soft, mild, melancholy features. His eyes must have shone, not only with intelligence, but with kindly tenderness and that hardly restrained childlike enthusiasm which I could hear in Ieronim's voice when he quoted to me passages from the hymns.

When we came out of church after mass it was no longer night. The morning was beginning. The stars had gone out and the sky was a morose grayish blue. The iron slabs, the tombstones, and the buds on the trees were covered with dew. There was a sharp freshness in the air. Outside the precincts I did not find the same animated scene as I had beheld in the night. Horses and men looked exhausted, drowsy, scarcely moved, while nothing was left of the tar barrels but heaps of black ash. When anyone is exhausted and sleepy he fancies that nature, too, is in the same condition. It seemed to me that the trees and the young grass were asleep. It seemed as though even the bells were not pealing so loudly and gaily as at night. The restlessness was over, and of the excitement nothing was left but a pleasant weariness, a longing for sleep and warmth.

Now I could see both banks of the river; a faint mist hovered over it in shifting masses. There was a harsh cold breath from the water. When I jumped onto the ferry, a chaise and some two dozen men and women were standing on it already. The rope, wet and as I fancied drowsy, stretched far away across the broad river and in places disappeared in the white mist.

"Christ is risen! Is there no one else?" asked a soft voice.

I recognized the voice of Ieronim. There was no darkness now to hinder me from seeing the monk. He was a tall narrow-shouldered man of five-and-thirty, with large rounded features, with half-closed listless-looking eyes and an unkempt wedge-shaped beard. He had an extraordinarily sad and exhausted look.

"They have not relieved you yet?" I asked in surprise.

"Me?" he answered, turning to me his chilled and dewy face with a smile. "There is no one to take my place now till morning. They'll all be going to the Father Archimandrite's to break the fast directly."

With the help of a little peasant in a hat of reddish fur that looked like the little wooden tubs in which honey is sold, he threw his weight on the rope; they gasped simultaneously, and the ferry started.

We floated across, disturbing on the way the lazily rising mist. Everyone was silent. Ieronim worked mechanically with one hand. He slowly passed his mild lusterless eyes over us; then his glance rested on the rosy face of a young merchant's wife with black eyebrows, who was standing on the ferry beside me silently shrinking from the mist that wrapped her about. He did not take his eyes off her face all the way.

There was little that was masculine in that prolonged gaze. It seemed to me that Ieronim was looking in the woman's face for the soft and tender features of his dead friend.

1886

HAPPINESS

A flock of sheep was spending the night on the broad steppe road that is called the great highway. Two shepherds were guarding it. One, a toothless old man of eighty, with a tremulous face, was lying on his stomach at the very edge of the road, leaning his elbows on the dusty leaves of a plantain; the other, a young fellow with thick black eyebrows and no mustache, dressed in the coarse canvas of which cheap sacks are made, was lying on his back, with his arms under his head, looking upward at the sky, where the stars were slumbering and the Milky Way lay stretched exactly above his face.

The shepherds were not alone. A couple of yards from them in the dusk that shrouded the road a horse made a patch of darkness, and, beside it, leaning against the saddle, stood a man in high boots and a short full-skirted jacket who looked like an overseer on some big estate. Judging from his upright and motionless figure, from his manners, and his behavior to the shepherds and to his horse, he was a serious, reasonable man who knew his own value; even in the darkness signs could be detected in him of military carriage and of the majestically condescending expression gained by frequent intercourse with the gentry and their stewards.

The sheep were asleep. Against the gray background of the dawn, already beginning to cover the eastern part of the sky, the silhouettes of sheep that were not asleep could be seen here and there; they stood with drooping heads, thinking. Their thoughts, tedious and oppressive, called forth by images of nothing but the broad steppe and the sky, the days and the nights, probably weighed upon them themselves, crushing them into apathy; and, standing there as though rooted to the earth, they noticed neither the presence of a stranger nor the uneasiness of the dogs.

The drowsy, stagnant air was full of the monotonous noise inseparable from a summer night on the steppes; the grasshoppers chirruped incessantly; the quails called, and the young nightingales trilled languidly half a mile away in a ravine where a stream flowed and willows grew.

The overseer had halted to ask the shepherds for a light for his pipe. He lighted it in silence and smoked the whole pipe; then, still without uttering a word, stood with his elbow on the saddle, plunged in thought. The young shepherd took no notice of him, he still lay gazing at the sky while the old man slowly looked the overseer up and down and then asked:

"Why, aren't you Panteley from Makarov's estate?"

"That's myself," answered the overseer.

"To be sure, I see it is. I didn't know you—that is a sign you will be rich. Where has God brought you from?"

"From the Kovylyevsky fields."

"That's a good way. Are you letting the land on the part-crop system?"

"Part of it. Some like that, and some we are letting on lease, and some for raising melons and cucumbers. I have just come from the mill."

A big shaggy old sheepdog of a dirty white color with woolly tufts about its nose and eyes walked three times quietly round the horse, trying to seem unconcerned in the presence of strangers, then all at once dashed suddenly from behind at the overseer with an angry aged growl; the other dogs could not refrain from leaping up too.

"Lie down, you damned brute," cried the old man, raising himself on his elbow; "blast you, you devil's creature."

When the dogs were quiet again, the old man resumed his former attitude and said quietly:

"It was at Kovyli on Ascension Day that Yefim Zhmenya died. Don't speak of it in the dark, it is a sin to mention such people. He was a wicked old man. I dare say you have heard."

"No, I haven't."

"Yefim Zhmenya, the uncle of Styopka, the blacksmith. The whole district round knew him. Aye, he was a cursed old man, he was! I knew him for sixty years, ever since Tsar Alexander who beat the French was brought from Taganrog to Moscow. We went together to meet the dead Tsar, and in those days the great highway did not run to Bahmut, but from Esaulovka to Gorodishtche, and where Kovyli is now, there were bustards' nests—there was a bustard's nest at every step. Even then I had noticed that Yefim had given his soul to damnation, and that the Evil One was in him. I have observed that if any man of the peasant class is apt to be silent, takes up with old women's jobs, and tries to live in solitude, there is no good in it, and Yefim from his youth up was always one to hold his tongue and look at you sideways, he always seemed to be sulky and bristling like a cock before a hen. To go to church or to the tavern or to lark in the street with the lads was not his fashion, he would rather sit alone or be whispering with old women. When he was still young he took jobs to look after the bees and the market gardens. Good folks would come to his market garden sometimes and his melons were whistling. One day he caught a pike, when folks were looking on, and it laughed aloud, 'Ho-ho-ho-ho!' "

"It does happen," said Panteley.

The young shepherd turned on his side and, lifting his black eyebrows, stared intently at the old man.

"Did you hear the melons whistling?" he asked.

"Hear them I didn't, the Lord spared me," sighed the old man, "but folks told me so. It is no great wonder . . . the Evil One will begin whistling in a stone if he wants to. Before the Day of Freedom a rock was humming for three days and three nights in our parts. I heard it myself. The pike laughed because Yefim caught a devil instead of a pike."

The old man remembered something. He got up quickly onto his knees and, shrinking as though from the cold, nervously thrusting his hands into his sleeves, he muttered in a rapid, womanish gabble:

"Lord, save us, and have mercy upon us! I was walking along the riverbank one day to Novopavlovka. A storm was gathering, such a tempest it was, preserve us, Holy Mother, Queen of Heaven. . . . I was hurrying on as best I could, I looked, and beside the path between the thorn bushes—the thorn was in flower at the time—there was a white bullock coming along. I wondered whose bullock it was, and what the devil had sent it there for. It was coming along and swinging its tail and moo-oo-oo! but would you believe it, friends, I overtake it, I come up close—and it's not a bullock, but Yefim—holy, holy, holy! I make the sign of the Cross while he stares at me and mutters, showing the whites of his eyes; wasn't I frightened! We came alongside, I was afraid to say a word to him—the thunder was crashing, the sky was streaked with lightning, the willows were bent right down to the water—all at once, my friends, God strike me dead that I die impenitent, a hare ran across the path . . . it ran and stopped, and said like a man: 'Good evening, peasants.' Lie down, you brute!" the old man cried to the shaggy dog, who was moving round the horse again. "Plague take you!"

"It does happen," said the overseer, still leaning on the saddle and not stirring; he said this in the hollow, toneless voice in which men speak when they are plunged in thought.

"It does happen," he repeated, in a tone of profundity and conviction.

"Ugh, he was a nasty old fellow," the old shepherd went on with somewhat less fervor. "Five years after the Freedom he was flogged by the commune at the office, so to show his spite he took and sent the throat illness upon all Kovyli. Folks died out of number, lots and lots of them, just as in cholera. . . ."

"How did he send the illness?" asked the young shepherd after a brief silence.

"We all know how, there is no great cleverness needed where there is a will to it. Yefim murdered people with viper's fat. That is such a poison that folks will die from the mere smell of it, let alone the fat."

"That's true," Panteley agreed.

"The lads wanted to kill him at the time, but the old people would not let them. It would never have done to kill him; he knew the place where the treasure is hidden, and not another soul did know. The treasures about here are charmed so that you may find them and not see them, but he did see them. At times he would walk along the riverbank or in the forest, and under the bushes and under the rocks there would be little flames, little flames . . . little flames as though from brimstone. I have seen them myself. Everyone expected that Yefim would show people the places or dig the treasure up himself, but he—as the saying is, like a dog in the manger—so he died without digging it up himself or showing other people."

The overseer lit a pipe, and for an instant lighted up his big mustaches and his sharp, stern-looking, and dignified nose. Little circles of light danced from his hands to his cap, raced over the saddle along the horse's back, and vanished in its mane near its ears.

"There are lots of hidden treasures in these parts," he said.

And slowly stretching, he looked round him, resting his eyes on the whitening east, and added:

"There must be treasures."

"To be sure," sighed the old man, "one can see from every sign there are treasures, only there is no one to dig them, brother. No one knows the real places; besides, nowadays, you must remember, all the treasures are under a charm. To find them and see them you must have a talisman, and without a talisman you can do nothing, lad. Yefim had talismans, but there was no getting anything out of him, the bald devil. He kept them, so that no one could get them."

The young shepherd crept two paces nearer to the old man and, propping his head on his fists, fastened his fixed stare upon him. A childish expression of terror and curiosity gleamed in his dark eyes, and seemed in the twilight to stretch and flatten out the large features of his coarse young face. He was listening intently.

"It is even written in the Scriptures that there are lots of treasures hidden here," the old man went on; "it is so for sure . . . and no mistake about it. An old soldier of Novopavlovka was shown at Ivanovka a writing, and in this writing it was printed about the place of the treasure and even how many pounds of gold was in it and the sort of vessel it was in; they would have found the treasures long ago by that writing, only the treasure is under a spell, you can't get at it."

"Why can't you get at it, grandfather?" asked the young man.

"I suppose there is some reason, the soldier didn't say. It is under a spell . . . you need a talisman."

The old man spoke with warmth, as though he were pouring out his soul before the overseer. He talked through his nose and, being unaccustomed to talk much and rapidly, stuttered; and, conscious of his defects, he tried to adorn his speech with gesticulations of the hands and head and thin shoulders, and at every movement his hempen shirt crumpled into folds, slipped upward, and displayed his back, black with age and sunburn. He kept pulling it down, but it slipped up again at once. At last, as though driven out of all patience by the rebellious shirt, the old man leaped up and said bitterly:

"There is fortune, but what is the good of it if it is buried in the earth? It is just riches wasted with no profit to anyone, like chaff or sheep's dung, and yet there are riches there, lad, fortune enough for all the country round, but not a soul sees it! It will come to this, that the gentry will dig it up or the government will take it away. The gentry have begun digging the barrows. . . . They scented something! They are envious of the peasants' luck! The government, too, is looking after itself. It is written in the law that if any peasant finds the treasure he is to take it to the authorities! I dare say, wait till you get it! There is a brew but not for you!"

The old man laughed contemptuously and sat down on the ground. The overseer listened with attention and agreed, but from his silence and the expression of his figure it was evident that what the old man told him was not new to him, that he had thought it all over long ago, and knew much more than was known to the old shepherd.

"In my day, I must own, I did seek for fortune a dozen times," said the old man, scratching himself nervously. "I looked in the right places, but I must have come on treasures under a charm. My father looked for it, too, and my brother, too—but not a thing did they find, so they died without luck. A monk revealed to my brother Ilya—the Kingdom of Heaven be his—that in one place in the fortress of Taganrog there was a treasure under three stones, and that that treasure was under a charm, and in those days—it was, I remember, in the year '38—an Armenian used to live at Matvyeev Barrow who sold talismans. Ilya bought a talisman, took two other fellows with him, and went to Taganrog. Only when he got to the place in the fortress, brother, there was a soldier with a gun, standing at the very spot. . . ."

A sound suddenly broke on the still air, and floated in all directions over the steppe. Something in the distance gave a menacing bang, crashed against stone, and raced over the steppe, uttering, "Tah! tah! tah! tah!" When the sound had died away the old man looked inquiringly at Panteley, who stood motionless and unconcerned.

"It's a bucket broken away at the pits," said the young shepherd after a moment's thought.

It was by now getting light. The Milky Way had turned pale and gradually melted like snow, losing its outlines; the sky was becoming dull and dingy, so that you could not make out whether it was clear or covered thickly with clouds, and only from the bright leaden streak in the east and from the stars that lingered here and there could one tell what was coming.

The first noiseless breeze of morning, cautiously stirring the spurges and the brown stalks of last year's grass, fluttered along the road.

The overseer roused himself from his thoughts and tossed his head. With both hands he shook the saddle, touched the girth, and, as though he could not make up his mind to mount the horse, stood still again, hesitating.

"Yes," he said, "your elbow is near, but you can't bite it. There is fortune, but there is not the wit to find it."

And he turned facing the shepherds. His stern face looked sad and mocking, as though he were a disappointed man.

"Yes, so one dies without knowing what happiness is like . . ." he said emphatically, lifting his left leg into the stirrup. "A younger man may live to see it, but it is time for us to lay aside all thought of it."

Stroking his long mustaches covered with dew, he seated himself heavily on the horse and screwed up his eyes, looking into the distance, as though he had forgotten something or left something unsaid. In the bluish distance where the furthest visible hillock melted into the mist nothing was stirring; the ancient barrows, once watchmounds and tombs, which rose here and there above the horizon and the boundless steppe had a sullen and deathlike look; there was a feeling of endless time and utter indifference to man in their immobility and silence; another thousand years would pass, myriads of men would die, while they would still stand as they had stood, with no regret for the dead nor interest in the living, and no soul would ever know why they stood there, and what secret of the steppes was hidden under them.

The rooks, awakening, flew one after another in silence over the earth. No meaning was to be seen in the languid flight of those long-lived birds, nor in the morning which is repeated punctually every twenty-four hours, nor in the boundless expanse of the steppe.

The overseer smiled and said:

"What space, Lord, have mercy upon us! You would have a hunt to find treasure in it! Here," he went on, dropping his voice and making a serious face, "here there are two treasures buried for a certainty. The gentry don't know of them, but the old peasants, particularly the soldiers, know all about them. Here, somewhere on that ridge [the overseer pointed with his whip] robbers one time attacked a caravan of gold; the gold was being taken from Petersburg to the Emperor Peter, who was building a fleet at the time at Voronezh. The robbers killed the men with the caravan and buried the gold, but did not find it again afterward. Another treasure was buried by our Cossacks of the Don. In the year '12 they carried off lots of plunder of all sorts from the French, goods and gold and silver. When they were going homeward they heard on the way that the government wanted to take away all the gold and silver from them. Rather than give up their plunder like that to the government for nothing, the brave fellows took and buried it, so that their children, anyway, might get it; but where they buried it no one knows."

"I have heard of those treasures," the old man muttered grimly.

"Yes . . ." Panteley pondered again. "So it is . . ."

A silence followed. The overseer looked dreamily into the distance, gave a laugh and pulled the rein, still with the same expression as though he had forgotten something or left something unsaid. The horse reluctantly started at a walking pace. After riding a hundred paces Panteley shook his head resolutely, roused himself from his thoughts, and, lashing his horse, set off at a trot.

The shepherds were left alone.

"That was Panteley from Makarov's estate," said the old man. "He gets a hundred and fifty a year and provisions found, too. He is a man of education. . . ."

The sheep, waking up—there were about three thousand of them—began without zest to while away the time, nipping at the low, half-trampled grass. The sun had not yet risen, but by now all the barrows could be seen and, like a cloud in the distance, Saur's

Grave with its peaked top. If one clambered up on that tomb one could see the plain from it, level and boundless as the sky, one could see villages, manor houses, the settlements of the Germans and of the Molokani, and a longsighted Kalmuck could even see the town and the railway station. Only from there could one see that there was something else in the world besides the silent steppe and the ancient barrows, that there was another life that had nothing to do with buried treasure and the thoughts of sheep.

The old man felt beside him for his crook—a long stick with a hook at the upper end—and got up. He was silent and thoughtful. The young shepherd's face had not lost the look of childish terror and curiosity. He was still under the influence of what he had heard in the night, and impatiently awaiting fresh stories.

"Grandfather," he asked, getting up and taking his crook, "what did your brother Ilya do with the soldier?"

The old man did not hear the question. He looked absentmindedly at the young man, and answered, mumbling with his lips:

"I keep thinking, Sanka, about that writing that was shown to that soldier at Ivanovka. I didn't tell Panteley—God be with him—but you know in that writing the place was marked out so that even a woman could find it. Do you know where it is? At Bogata Bylotchka, at the spot, you know, where the ravine parts like a goose's foot into three little ravines; it is the middle one."

"Well, will you dig?"

"I will try my luck. . . ."

"And, Grandfather, what will you do with the treasure when you find it?"

"Do with it?" laughed the old man. "H'm! . . . If only I could find it, then. . . . I would show them all. . . . H'm! . . . I should know what to do. . . ."

And the old man could not answer what he would do with the treasure if he found it. That question had presented itself to him that morning probably for the first time in his life, and judging from the expression of his face, indifferent and uncritical, it did not seem to him important and deserving of consideration. In Sanka's brain another puzzled question was stirring: why was it only old men searched for hidden treasure, and what was the use of earthly happiness to people who might die any day of old age? But Sanka could not put this perplexity into words, and the old man could scarcely have found an answer to it.

An immense crimson sun came into view surrounded by a faint haze. Broad streaks of light, still cold, bathing in the dewy grass, lengthening out with a joyous air as though to prove they were not weary of their task, began spreading over the earth. The silvery wormwood, the blue flowers of the pig's onion, the yellow mustard, the cornflowers—all burst into gay colors, taking the sunlight for their own smile.

The old shepherd and Sanka parted and stood at the further sides of the flock. Both stood like posts, without moving, staring at the ground and thinking. The former was haunted by thoughts of fortune, the latter was pondering on what had been said in the night; what interested him was not the fortune itself, which he did not want and could not imagine, but the fantastic fairy-tale character of human happiness.

A hundred sheep started and, in some inexplicable panic as at a signal, dashed away from the flock; and as though the thoughts of the sheep—tedious and oppressive—had for a moment infected Sanka also, he, too, dashed aside in the same inexplicable animal panic, but at once he recovered himself and shouted:

"You crazy creatures! You've gone mad, plague take you!"

When the sun, promising long hours of overwhelming heat, began to bake the earth, all living things that in the night had moved and uttered sounds were sunk in drowsiness. The old shepherd and Sanka stood with their crooks on opposite sides of the flock, stood without stirring, like fakirs at their prayers, absorbed in thought. They did not heed each other; each of them was living in his own life. The sheep were pondering, too.

1887

ANYUTA

In the cheapest room of a big block of furnished apartments Stepan Klochkov, a medical student in his third year, was walking to and fro, zealously cramming anatomy. His mouth was dry and his forehead perspiring from the unceasing effort to learn it by heart.

In the window, covered by patterns of frost, sat on a stool the girl who shared his room—Anyuta, a thin little brunette of five and twenty, very pale, with mild gray eyes. Sitting with bent back she was busy embroidering with red thread the collar of a man's shirt. She was working against time. . . . The clock in the passage struck two drowsily, yet the little room had not been put to rights for the morning. Crumpled bedclothes, pillows thrown about, books, clothes, a big filthy slop pail filled with soapsuds in which cigarette ends were swimming, and the litter on the floor—all seemed as though purposely jumbled together in one confusion. . . .

"The right lung consists of three parts . . ." Klochkov repeated. "Boundaries! Upper part on anterior wall of thorax reaches the fourth or fifth rib, on the lateral surface, the fourth rib . . . behind to the *spina scapulæ* . . ."

Klochkov raised his eyes to the ceiling, striving to visualize what he had just read. Unable to form a clear picture of it, he began feeling his upper ribs through his waistcoat.

"These ribs are like the keys of a piano," he said. "One must familiarize oneself with them somehow, if one is not to get muddled over them. One must study them in the skeleton and the living body. . . . I say, Anyuta, let me pick them out."

Anyuta put down her sewing, took off her blouse, and straightened herself up. Klochkov sat down facing her, frowned, and began counting her ribs.

"H'm! . . . One can't feel the first rib; it's behind the shoulder blade. . . . This must be the second rib. . . . Yes . . . this is the third . . . this is the fourth. . . . H'm! . . . yes. . . . Why are you wriggling?"

"Your fingers are cold!"

"Come, come . . . it won't kill you. Don't twist about. That must be the third rib, then . . . this is the fourth. . . . You look such a skinny thing, and yet one can hardly feel your ribs. That's the second . . . that's the third. . . . Oh, this is muddling, and one can't see it clearly. . . . I must draw it. . . . Where's my crayon?"

Klochkov took his crayon and drew on Anyuta's chest several parallel lines corresponding with the ribs.

"First-rate. That's all straightforward. . . . Well, now I can sound you. Stand up!"

Anyuta stood up and raised her chin. Klochkov began sounding her, and was so absorbed in this occupation that he did not notice how Anyuta's lips, nose, and fingers turned blue with cold. Anyuta shivered, and was afraid the student, noticing it, would stop drawing and sounding her, and then, perhaps, might fail in his exam.

"Now it's all clear," said Klochkov when he had finished. "You sit like that and don't rub off the crayon, and meanwhile I'll learn up a little more."

And the student again began walking to and fro, repeating to himself. Anyuta, with black stripes across her chest, looking as though she had been tattooed, sat thinking, huddled up and shivering with cold. She said very little as a rule; she was always silent, thinking and thinking. . . .

In the six or seven years of her wanderings from one furnished room to another, she had known five students like Klochkov. Now they had all finished their studies, had gone out into the world, and, of course, like respectable people, had long ago forgotten her. One of them was living in Paris, two were doctors, the fourth was an artist, and the fifth was said to be already a professor. Klochkov was the sixth. . . . Soon he, too, would finish his studies and go out into the world. There was a fine future before him, no doubt, and Klochkov probably would become a great man, but the present was anything but bright; Klochkov had no tobacco and no tea, and there were only four lumps of sugar left. She must make haste and finish her embroidery, take it to the woman who had ordered it, and with the quarter ruble she would get for it, buy tea and tobacco.

"Can I come in?" asked a voice at the door.

Anyuta quickly threw a woollen shawl over her shoulders. Fetisov, the artist, walked in.

"I have come to ask you a favor," he began, addressing Klochkov, and glaring like a wild beast from under the long locks that hung over his brow. "Do me a favor; lend me your young lady just for a couple of hours! I'm painting a picture, you see, and I can't get on without a model."

"Oh, with pleasure," Klochkov agreed. "Go along, Anyuta."

"The things I've had to put up with there," Anyuta murmured softly.

"Rubbish! The man's asking you for the sake of art, and not for any sort of nonsense. Why not help him if you can?"

Anyuta began dressing.

"And what are you painting?" asked Klochkov.

"Psyche; it's a fine subject. But it won't go, somehow. I have to keep painting from different models. Yesterday I was painting one with blue legs. 'Why are your legs blue?' I asked her. 'It's my stockings stain them,' she said. And you're still cramming! Lucky fellow! You have patience."

"Medicine's a job one can't get on with without grinding."

"H'm! . . . Excuse me, Klochkov, but you do live like a pig! It's awful the way you live!"

"How do you mean! I can't help it. . . . I only get twelve rubles a month from my father, and it's hard to live decently on that."

"Yes . . . yes . . ." said the artist, frowning with an air of disgust; "but, still, you might live better. . . . An educated man is in duty bound to have taste, isn't he? And goodness knows what it's like here! The bed not made, the slops, the dirt . . . yesterday's porridge in the plates. . . . Tfoo!"

"That's true," said the student in confusion; "but Anyuta has had no time today to tidy up; she's been busy all the while."

When Anyuta and the artist had gone out Klochkov lay down on the sofa and began learning, lying down; then he accidentally dropped asleep, and waking up an hour later, propped his head on his fists and sank into gloomy reflection. He recalled the artist's words that an educated man was in duty bound to have taste, and his surroundings actually struck him now as loathsome and revolting. He saw, as it were in his mind's eye, his own future, when he would see his patients in his consulting room, drink tea in a large dining room in the company of his wife, a real lady. And now that slop-pail in which the cigarette ends were swimming looked incredibly disgusting. Anyuta, too, rose before his imagination—a plain, slovenly, pitiful figure . . . and he made up his mind to part with her at once, at all costs.

When, in coming back from the artist's, she took off her coat, he got up and said to her seriously:

"Look here, my good girl . . . sit down and listen. We must part! The fact is, I don't want to live with you any longer."

Anyuta had come back from the artist's worn out and exhausted. Standing so long as a model had made her face look thin and sunken, and her chin sharper than ever. She said nothing in answer to the student's words, only her lips began to tremble.

"You know we should have to part sooner or later, anyway," said the student. "You're a nice, good girl, and not a fool; you'll understand. . . ."

Anyuta put on her coat again, in silence wrapped up her embroidery in paper, gathered together her needles and thread: she found the screw of paper with the four lumps of sugar in the window, and laid it on the table by the books.

"That's . . . your sugar . . ." she said softly, and turned away to conceal her tears.

"Why are you crying?" asked Klochkov.

He walked about the room in confusion, and said:

"You are a strange girl, really. . . . Why, you know we shall have to part. We can't stay together forever."

She had gathered together all her belongings, and turned to say goodbye to him, and he felt sorry for her.

"Shall I let her stay on here another week?" he thought. "She really may as well stay, and I'll tell her to go in a week"; and, vexed at his own weakness, he shouted to her roughly:

"Come, why are you standing there? If you are going, go; and if you don't want to, take off your coat and stay! You can stay!"

Anyuta took off her coat, silently, stealthily, then blew her nose also stealthily, sighed, and noiselessly returned to her invariable position on her stool by the window.

The student drew his textbook to him and began again pacing from corner to corner. "The right lung consists of three parts," he repeated; "the upper part, on anterior wall of thorax, reaches the fourth or fifth rib. . . ."

In the passage some one shouted at the top of his voice: "Grigory! The samovar!"

1886

THE WITCH

It was approaching nightfall. The sexton, Savély Gykin, was lying in his huge bed in the hut adjoining the church. He was not asleep, though it was his habit to go to sleep at the same time as the hens. His coarse red hair peeped from under one end of the greasy patchwork quilt, made up of colored rags, while his big unwashed feet stuck out from the other. He was listening. His hut adjoined the wall that encircled the church and the solitary window in it looked out upon the open country. And out there a regular battle was going on. It was hard to say who was being wiped off the face of the earth, and for the sake of whose destruction nature was being churned up into such a ferment; but, judging from the unceasing malignant roar, someone was getting it very hot. A victorious force was in full chase over the fields, storming in the forest and on the church roof, battering spitefully with its fists upon the windows, raging and tearing, while something vanquished was howling and wailing. . . . A plaintive lament sobbed at the window, on the roof, or in the stove. It sounded not like a call for help, but like a cry of misery, a consciousness that it was too late, that there was no salvation. The snowdrifts were covered with a thin coating of ice; tears quivered on them and on the trees; a dark slush of mud and melting snow flowed along the roads and paths. In short, it was thawing, but through the dark night the heavens failed to see it, and flung flakes of fresh snow upon the melting earth at a terrific rate. And the wind staggered like a drunkard. It would not let the snow settle on the ground, and whirled it round in the darkness at random.

Savély listened to all this din and frowned. The fact was that he knew, or at any rate suspected, what all this racket outside the window was tending to and whose handiwork it was.

"I know!" he muttered, shaking his finger menacingly under the bedclothes; "I know all about it."

On a stool by the window sat the sexton's wife, Raïssa Nilovna. A tin lamp standing on another stool, as though timid and distrustful of its powers, shed a dim and flickering light on her broad shoulders, on the handsome, tempting-looking contours of her person, and on her thick plait, which reached to the floor. She was making sacks out of coarse hempen stuff. Her hands moved nimbly, while her whole body, her eyes, her eyebrows, her full lips, her white neck were as still as though they were asleep, absorbed in the monotonous, mechanical toil. Only from time to time she raised her head to rest her weary neck, glanced for a moment toward the window, beyond which the snowstorm was raging, and bent again over her sacking. No desire, no joy, no grief, nothing was expressed by her handsome face with its turned-up nose and its dimples. So a beautiful fountain expresses nothing when it is not playing.

But at last she had finished a sack. She flung it aside, and, stretching luxuriously, rested her motionless, lackluster eyes on the window. The panes were swimming with drops like tears, and white with short-lived snowflakes which fell on the window, glanced at Raïssa, and melted. . . .

"Come to bed!" growled the sexton. Raïssa remained mute. But suddenly her eyelashes flickered and there was a gleam of attention in her eye. Savély, all the time watching her expression from under the quilt, put out his head and asked:

"What is it?"

"*Only from time to time she raised her head to rest her weary neck, glanced for a moment toward the window, beyond which the snowstorm was raging, and bent again over her sacking. No desire, no joy, no grief, nothing was expressed by her handsome face with its turned-up nose and its dimples. So a beautiful fountain expresses nothing when it is not playing.*"

"Nothing. . . . I fancy someone's coming," she answered quietly.

The sexton flung the quilt off with his arms and legs, knelt up in bed, and looked blankly at his wife. The timid light of the lamp illuminated his hirsute, pockmarked countenance and glided over his rough, matted hair.

"Do you hear?" asked his wife.

Through the monotonous roar of the storm he caught a scarcely audible thin and jingling monotone like the shrill note of a gnat when it wants to settle on one's cheek and is angry at being prevented.

"It's the post," muttered Savély, squatting on his heels.

Two miles from the church ran the posting road. In windy weather, when the wind was blowing from the road to the church, the inmates of the hut caught the sound of bells.

"Lord! fancy people wanting to drive about in such weather," sighed Raïssa.

"It's government work. You've to go whether you like or not."

The murmur hung in the air and died away.

"It has driven by," said Savély, getting into bed.

But before he had time to cover himself up with the bedclothes he heard a distinct sound of the bell. The sexton looked anxiously at his wife, leapt out of bed, and walked, waddling, to and fro by the stove. The bell went on ringing for a little, then died away again as though it had ceased.

"I don't hear it," said the sexton, stopping, and looking at his wife with his eyes screwed up.

But at that moment the wind rapped on the window and with it floated a shrill jingling note. Savély turned pale, cleared his throat, and flopped about the floor with his bare feet again.

"The postman is lost in the storm," he wheezed out, glancing malignantly at his wife. "Do you hear? The postman has lost his way! . . . I . . . I know! Do you suppose I . . . don't understand?" he muttered. "I know all about it, curse you!"

"What do you know?" Raïssa asked quietly, keeping her eyes fixed on the window.

"I know that it's all your doing, you she-devil! Your doing, damn you! This snowstorm and the post going wrong, you've done it all—you!"

"You're mad, you silly," his wife answered calmly.

"I've been watching you for a long time past and I've seen it. From the first day I married you I noticed that you'd bitch's blood in you!"

"Tfoo!" said Raïssa, surprised, shrugging her shoulders and crossing herself. "Cross yourself, you fool!"

"A witch is a witch," Savély pronounced in a hollow, tearful voice, hurriedly blowing his nose on the hem of his shirt; "though you are my wife, though you are of a clerical family, I'd say what you are even at confession. . . . Why, God have mercy upon us! Last year on the Eve of the Prophet Daniel and the Three Young Men there was a snowstorm, and what happened then? The mechanic came in to warm himself. Then on St. Alexey's Day the ice broke on the river and the district policeman turned up, and he was chatting with you all night . . . the damned brute! And when he came out in the morning and I looked at him, he had rings under his eyes and his cheeks were hollow! Eh? During the August fast there were two storms and each time the huntsman turned up. I saw it all, damn him! Oh, she is redder than a crab now, aha!"

"You didn't see anything."

"Didn't I! And this winter before Christmas on the Day of the Ten Martyrs of Crete, when the storm lasted for a whole day and night—do you remember?—the marshal's clerk was lost, and turned up here, the hound. . . . Tfoo! To be tempted by the clerk! It was worth upsetting God's weather for him! A driveling scribbler not a foot from the ground, pimples all over his mug and his neck awry! If he were good-looking, anyway—but he, tfoo! he is as ugly as Satan!"

The sexton took breath, wiped his lips, and listened. The bell was not to be heard, but the wind banged on the roof, and again there came a tinkle in the darkness.

And it's the same thing now!" Savély went on. "It's not for nothing the postman is lost! Blast my eyes if the postman isn't looking for you! Oh, the devil is a good hand at his work; he is a fine one to help! He will turn him round and round and bring him here. I know, I see! You can't conceal it, you devil's bauble, you heathen wanton! As soon as the storm began I knew what you were up to."

"Here's a fool!" smiled his wife. "Why, do you suppose, you thickhead, that I make the storm?"

"H'm! . . . Grin away! Whether it's your doing or not, I only know that when your blood's on fire there's sure to be bad weather, and when there's bad weather there's bound to be some crazy fellow turning up here. It happens so every time! So it must be you!"

To be more impressive the sexton put his finger to his forehead, closed his left eye, and said in a singsong voice:

"Oh, the madness! oh, the unclean Judas! If you really are a human being and not a witch, you ought to think what if he is not the mechanic, or the clerk, or the huntsman, but the devil in their form! Ah! You'd better think of that!"

"Why, you are stupid, Savély," said his wife, looking at him compassionately. "When Father was alive and living here, all sorts of people used to come to him to be cured of the ague: from the village, and the hamlets, and the Armenian settlement. They came almost every day, and no one called them devils. But if anyone once a year comes in bad weather to warm himself, you wonder at it, you silly, and take all sorts of notions into your head at once."

His wife's logic touched Savély. He stood with his bare feet wide apart, bent his head, and pondered. He was not firmly convinced yet of the truth of his suspicions, and his wife's genuine and unconcerned tone quite disconcerted him. Yet after a moment's thought he wagged his head and said:

"It's not as though they were old men or bandy-legged cripples; it's always young men who want to come for the night. . . . Why is that? And if they only wanted to warm themselves— But they are up to mischief. No, woman; there's no creature in this world as cunning as your female sort! Of real brains you've not an ounce, less than a starling, but for devilish slyness—oo-oo-oo! The Queen of Heaven protect us! There is the postman's bell! When the storm was only beginning I knew all that was in your mind. That's your witchery, you spider!"

"Why do you keep on at me, you heathen?" His wife lost her patience at last. "Why do you keep sticking to it like pitch?"

"I stick to it because if anything—God forbid—happens tonight . . . do you hear? . . . if anything happens tonight, I'll go straight off tomorrow morning to Father Nikodim and tell him all about it. 'Father Nikodim,' I shall say, 'graciously excuse me, but she is a witch.' 'Why so?' 'H'm! do you want to know why? Certainly . . .' And I shall tell him. And woe to you, woman! Not only at the dread Seat of Judgment, but in your earthly life you'll be punished, too! It's not for nothing there are prayers in the breviary against your kind!"

Suddenly there was a knock at the window, so loud and unusual that Savély turned pale and almost dropped backward with fright. His wife jumped up, and she, too, turned pale.

"For God's sake, let us come in and get warm!" they heard in a trembling deep bass. "Who lives here? For mercy's sake! We've lost our way."

"Who are you?" asked Raïssa, afraid to look at the window.

"The post," answered a second voice.

"You've succeeded with your devil's tricks," said Savély with a wave of his hand. "No mistake; I am right! Well, you'd better look out!"

The sexton jumped on to the bed in two skips, stretched himself on the feather mattress, and sniffing angrily, turned with his face to the wall. Soon he felt a draft of cold air on his back. The door creaked and the tall figure of a man, plastered over with snow from head to foot, appeared in the doorway. Behind him could be seen a second figure as white.

"Am I to bring in the bags?" asked the second in a hoarse bass voice.

"You can't leave them there." Saying this, the first figure began untying his hood, but gave it up, and pulling it off impatiently with his cap, angrily flung it near the stove. Then taking off his greatcoat, he threw that down beside it, and without saying good evening, began pacing up and down the hut.

He was a fair-haired young postman wearing a shabby uniform and black rusty-looking high boots. After warming himself by walking to and fro, he sat down at the table, stretched out his muddy feet toward the sacks, and leaned his chin on his fist. His pale face, reddened in places by the cold, still bore vivid traces of the pain and terror he had just been through. Though distorted by anger and bearing traces of recent suffering, physical and moral, it was handsome in spite of the melting snow on the eyebrows, mustaches, and short beard.

"It's a dog's life!" muttered the postman, looking round the walls and seeming hardly able to believe that he was in the warmth. "We were nearly lost! If it had not been for your light, I don't know what would have happened. Goodness only knows when it will all be over! There's no end to this dog's life! Where have we come?" he asked, dropping his voice and raising his eyes to the sexton's wife.

"To the Gulyaevsky Hill on General Kalinovsky's estate," she answered, startled and blushing.

"Do you hear, Stepan?" The postman turned to the driver, who was wedged in the doorway with a huge mailbag on his shoulders. "We've got to Gulyaevsky Hill."

"Yes . . . we're a long way out." Jerking out these words like a hoarse sigh, the driver went out and soon after returned with another bag, then went out once more and this time brought the postman's sword on a big belt, of the pattern of that long flat blade with which Judith is portrayed by the bedside of Holofernes in cheap woodcuts. Laying the bags along the wall, he went out into the outer room, sat down there, and lighted his pipe.

"Perhaps you'd like some tea after your journey?" Raïssa inquired.

"How can we sit drinking tea?" said the postman, frowning. "We must make haste and get warm, and then set off, or we shall be late for the mail train. We'll stay ten minutes and then get on our way. Only be so good as to show us the way."

"What an infliction it is, this weather!" sighed Raïssa.

"H'm, yes. . . . Who may you be?"

"We? We live here, by the church. . . . We belong to the clergy. . . . There lies my husband. Savély, get up and say good evening! This used to be a separate parish till eighteen months ago. Of course, when the gentry lived here there were more people, and it was worthwhile to have the services. But now the gentry have gone, and I need not tell you there's nothing for the clergy to live on. The nearest village is Markovka, and that's over three miles away. Savély is on the retired list now, and has got the watchman's job; he has to look after the church. . . ."

And the postman was immediately informed that if Savély were to go to the general's lady and ask her for a letter to the bishop, he would be given a good berth. "But he doesn't go to the general's lady because he is lazy and afraid of people. We belong to the clergy all the same . . ." added Raïssa.

"What do you live on?" asked the postman.

"There's a kitchen garden and a meadow belonging to the church. Only we don't get much from that," sighed Raïssa. "The old skinflint, Father Nikodim, from the next village celebrates here on St. Nicolas's Day in the winter and on St. Nicolas's Day in the summer, and for that he takes almost all the crops for himself. There's no one to stick up for us!"

"You are lying," Savély growled hoarsely. "Father Nikodim is a saintly soul, a luminary of the Church; and if he does take it, it's the regulation!"

"You've a cross one!" said the postman, with a grin. "Have you been married long?"

"It was three years ago the last Sunday before Lent. My father was sexton here in the old days, and when the time came for him to die, he went to the Consistory and asked them to send some unmarried man to marry me that I might keep the place. So I married him."

"Aha, so you killed two birds with one stone!" said the postman, looking at Savély's back. "Got wife and job together."

Savély wriggled his leg impatiently and moved closer to the wall. The postman moved away from the table, stretched, and sat down on the mailbag. After a moment's thought he squeezed the bags with his hands, shifted his sword to the other side, and lay down with one foot touching the floor.

"It's a dog's life," he muttered, putting his hands behind his head and closing his eyes. "I wouldn't wish a wild Tatar such a life."

Soon everything was still. Nothing was audible except the sniffing of Savély and the slow, even breathing of the sleeping postman, who uttered a deep prolonged "h-h-h" at every breath. From time to time there was a sound like a creaking wheel in his throat, and his twitching foot rustled against the bag.

Savély fidgeted under the quilt and looked round slowly. His wife was sitting on the stool, and with her hands pressed against her cheeks was gazing at the postman's face. Her face was immovable, like the face of someone frightened and astonished.

"Well, what are you gaping at?" Savély whispered angrily.

"What is it to you? Lie down!" answered his wife without taking her eyes off the flaxen head.

Savély angrily puffed all the air out of his chest and turned abruptly to the wall. Three minutes later he turned over restlessly again, knelt up on the bed, and with his hands on the pillow looked askance at his wife. She was still sitting motionless, staring at the visitor. Her cheeks were pale and her eyes were glowing with a strange fire. The sexton cleared his throat, crawled on his stomach off the bed, and going up to the postman, put a handkerchief over his face.

"What's that for?" asked his wife.

"To keep the light out of his eyes."

"Then put out the light!"

Savély looked distrustfully at his wife, put out his lips toward the lamp, but at once thought better of it and clasped his hands.

"Isn't that devilish cunning?" he exclaimed. "Ah! Is there any creature slyer than womankind?"

"Ah, you long-skirted devil!" hissed his wife, frowning with vexation. "You wait a bit!"

And settling herself more comfortably, she stared at the postman again.

It did not matter to her that his face was covered. She was not so much interested in his face as in his whole appearance, in the novelty of this man. His chest was broad and powerful, his hands were slender and well formed, and his graceful, muscular legs were much comelier than Savély's stumps. There could be no comparison, in fact.

"Though I am a long-skirted devil," Savély said after a brief interval, "they've no business to sleep here. . . . It's government work; we shall have to answer for keeping them. If you carry the letters, carry them, you can't go to sleep. . . . Hey! you!" Savély shouted into the outer room. "You, driver. . . . What's your name? Shall I show you the way? Get up; postmen mustn't sleep!"

And Savély, thoroughly roused, ran up to the postman and tugged him by the sleeve.

"Hey, Your Honor, if you must go, go; and if you don't, it's not the thing. . . . Sleeping won't do."

The postman jumped up, sat down, looked with blank eyes round the hut, and lay down again.

"But when are you going?" Savély pattered away. "That's what the post is for—to get there in good time, do you hear? I'll take you."

The postman opened his eyes. Warmed and relaxed by his first sweet sleep, and not yet quite awake, he saw as through a mist the white neck and the immovable, alluring eyes of the sexton's wife. He closed his eyes and smiled as though he had been dreaming it all.

"Come, how can you go in such weather!" he heard a soft feminine voice; "you ought to have a sound sleep and it would do you good!"

"And what about the post?" said Savély anxiously. "Who's going to take the post? Are you going to take it, pray, you?"

The postman opened his eyes again, looked at the play of the dimples on Raïssa's face, remembered where he was, and understood Savély. The thought that he had to go out into the cold darkness sent a chill shudder all down him, and he winced.

"I might sleep another five minutes," he said, yawning. "I shall be late, anyway. . . ."

"We might be just in time," came a voice from the outer room. "All days are not alike; the train may be late for a bit of luck."

The postman got up, and stretching lazily began putting on his coat.

Savély positively neighed with delight when he saw his visitors were getting ready to go.

"Give us a hand," the driver shouted to him as he lifted up a mailbag.

The sexton ran out and helped him drag the postbags into the yard. The postman began undoing the knot in his hood. The sexton's wife gazed into his eyes, and seemed trying to look right into his soul.

"You ought to have a cup of tea . . ." she said.

"I wouldn't say no . . . but, you see, they're getting ready," he assented. "We are late, anyway."

"Do stay," she whispered, dropping her eyes and touching him by the sleeve.

The postman got the knot undone at last and flung the hood over his elbow, hesitating. He felt it comfortable standing by Raïssa.

"What a . . . neck you've got! . . ." And he touched her neck with two fingers. Seeing that she did not resist, he stroked her neck and shoulders.

"I say, you are . . ."

"You'd better stay . . . have some tea."

"Where are you putting it?" The driver's voice could be heard outside. "Lay it crossways."

"You'd better stay. . . . Hark how the wind howls."

And the postman, not yet quite awake, not yet quite able to shake off the intoxicating sleep of youth and fatigue, was suddenly overwhelmed by a desire for the sake of which mailbags, postal trains . . . and all things in the world, are forgotten. He glanced at the door in a frightened way, as though he wanted to escape or hide himself, seized Raïssa round the waist, and was just bending over the lamp to put out the light, when he heard the tramp of boots in the outer room, and the driver appeared in the doorway. Savély peeped in over his shoulder. The postman dropped his hands quickly and stood still as though irresolute.

"It's all ready," said the driver. The postman stood still for a moment, resolutely threw up his head as though waking up completely, and followed the driver out. Raïssa was left alone.

"Come, get in and show us the way!" she heard.

One bell sounded languidly, then another, and the jingling notes in a long delicate chain floated away from the hut.

When little by little they had died away, Raïssa got up and nervously paced to and fro. At first she was pale, then she flushed all over. Her face was contorted with hate, her breathing was tremulous, her eyes gleamed with wild, savage anger, and, pacing up and down as in a cage, she looked like a tigress menaced with red-hot iron. For a moment she stood still and looked at her abode. Almost half of the room was filled up by the bed, which stretched the length of the whole wall and consisted of a dirty feather bed, coarse gray pillows, a quilt, and nameless rags of various sorts. The bed was a shapeless ugly mass which suggested the shock of hair that always stood up on Savély's head whenever it occurred to him to oil it. From the bed to the door that led into the cold outer room stretched the dark stove surrounded by pots and hanging clouts. Everything, including the absent Savély himself, was dirty, greasy, and smutty to the last degree, so that it was strange to see a woman's white neck and delicate skin in such surroundings.

Raïssa ran up to the bed, stretched out her hands as though she wanted to fling it all about, stamp it underfoot, and tear it to shreds. But then, as though frightened by contact with the dirt, she leapt back and began pacing up and down again.

When Savély returned two hours later, worn out and covered with snow, she was undressed and in bed. Her eyes were closed, but from the slight tremor that ran over her face he guessed that she was not asleep. On his way home he had vowed inwardly to wait till next day and not to touch her, but he could not resist a biting taunt at her.

"Your witchery was all in vain: he's gone off," he said, grinning with malignant joy.

His wife remained mute, but her chin quivered. Savély undressed slowly, clambered over his wife, and lay down next to the wall.

"Tomorrow I'll let Father Nikodim know what sort of wife you are!" he muttered, curling himself up.

Raïssa turned her face to him and her eyes gleamed.

"The job's enough for you, and you can look for a wife in the forest, blast you!" she said. "I am no wife for you, a clumsy lout, a slugabed, God forgive me!"

"Come, come . . . go to sleep!"

"How miserable I am!" sobbed his wife. "If it weren't for you, I might have married a merchant or some gentleman! If it weren't for you, I should love my husband now! And you haven't been buried in the snow, you haven't been frozen on the high road, you Herod!"

Raïssa cried for a long time. At last she drew a deep sigh and was still. The storm still raged without. Something wailed in the stove, in the chimney, outside the walls, and it seemed to Savély that the wailing was within him, in his ears. This evening had completely confirmed him in his suspicions about his wife. He no longer doubted that his wife, with the aid of the Evil One, controlled the winds and the post sledges. But to add to his grief, this mysteriousness, this supernatural, weird power gave the woman beside him a peculiar, incomprehensible charm of which he had not been conscious before. The fact that in his stupidity he unconsciously threw a poetic glamour over her made her seem, as it were, whiter, sleeker, more unapproachable.

"Witch!" he muttered indignantly. "Tfoo, horrid creature!"

Yet, waiting till she was quiet and began breathing evenly, he touched her head with his finger . . . held her thick plait in his hand for a minute. She did not feel it. Then he grew bolder and stroked her neck.

"Leave off!" she shouted, and prodded him on the nose with her elbow with such violence that he saw stars before his eyes.

The pain in his nose was soon over, but the torture in his heart remained.

1886

THE TWO VOLODYAS

"Let me; I want to drive myself! I'll sit by the driver!" Sofya Lvovna said in a loud voice. "Wait a minute, driver; I'll get up on the box beside you."

She stood up in the sledge, and her husband, Vladimir Nikititch, and the friend of her childhood, Vladimir Mihalovitch, held her arms to prevent her falling. The three horses were galloping fast.

"I said you ought not to have given her brandy," Vladimir Nikititch whispered to his companion with vexation. "What a fellow you are, really!"

The colonel knew by experience that in women like his wife, Sofya Lvovna, after a little too much wine, turbulent gaiety was followed by hysterical laughter and then tears. He was afraid that when they got home, instead of being able to sleep, he would have to be administering compresses and drops.

"Whoa!" cried Sofya Lvovna. "I want to drive myself!"

She felt genuinely gay and triumphant. For the last two months, ever since her wedding, she had been tortured by the thought that she had married Colonel Yagitch from worldly motives and, as it is said, *par dépit;* but that evening, at the restaurant, she had suddenly become convinced that she loved him passionately. In spite of his fifty-four years, he was so slim, agile, supple, he made puns and hummed to the gypsies' tunes so charmingly. Really, the older men were nowadays a thousand times more interesting than the young. It seemed as though age and youth had changed parts. The colonel was two years older than her father, but could there be any importance in that if, honestly speaking, there were infinitely more vitality, go, and freshness in him than in herself, though she was only twenty-three?

"Oh, my darling!" she thought. "You are wonderful!"

She had become convinced in the restaurant, too, that not a spark of her old feeling remained. For the friend of her childhood, Vladimir Mihalovitch, or simply Volodya, with whom only the day before she had been madly, miserably in love, she now felt nothing but complete indifference. All that evening he had seemed to her spiritless, torpid, uninteresting, and insignificant, and the *sangfroid* with which he habitually avoided paying at restaurants on this occasion revolted her, and she had hardly been able to resist saying, "If you are poor, you should stay at home." The colonel paid for all.

Perhaps because trees, telegraph posts, and drifts of snow kept flitting past her eyes, all sorts of disconnected ideas came rushing into her mind. She reflected: the bill at the restaurant had been a hundred and twenty rubles, and a hundred had gone to the gypsies, and tomorrow she could fling away a thousand rubles if she liked; and only two months ago, before her wedding, she had not had three rubles of her own, and had to ask her father for every trifle. What a change in her life!

Her thoughts were in a tangle. She recalled, how, when she was a child of ten, Colonel Yagitch, now her husband, used to make love to her aunt, and every one in the house said that he had ruined her. And her aunt had, in fact, often come down to dinner with her eyes red from crying, and was always going off somewhere; and people used to say of her that the poor thing could find no peace anywhere. He had been very handsome in those days, and had an extraordinary reputation as a lady-killer. So much so that he was known all over the town, and it was said of him that he paid a round of visits to his adorers every day like a doctor visiting his patients. And even now, in spite of his gray hair, his wrinkles, and his spectacles, his thin face looked handsome, especially in profile.

Sofya Lvovna's father was an army doctor, and had at one time served in the same regiment with Colonel Yagitch. Volodya's father was an army doctor too, and he, too, had once been in the same regiment as her father and Colonel Yagitch. In spite of many amatory adventures, often very complicated and disturbing, Volodya had done splendidly at the university, and had taken a very good degree. Now he was specializing in foreign literature, and was said to be writing a thesis. He lived with his father, the army doctor, in the barracks, and had no means of his own, though he was thirty. As children Sofya and he had lived under the same roof, though in different flats. He often came to play with her, and they had dancing and French lessons together. But when he grew up into a graceful, remarkably handsome young man, she began to feel shy of him, and then fell madly in love with him, and had loved him right up to the time when she was married to Yagitch. He, too, had been renowned for his success with women almost from the age of fourteen, and the ladies who deceived their husbands on his account excused themselves by saying that he was only a boy. Someone had told a story of him lately that when he was a student living in lodgings so as to be near the university, it always happened if one knocked at his door, that one heard his footstep, and then a whispered apology: *"Pardon, je ne suis pas seul."* Yagitch was delighted with him, and blessed him as a worthy successor, as Derchavin blessed Pushkin; he appeared to be fond of him. They would play billiards or picquet by the hour together without uttering a word, if Yagitch drove out on any expedition he always took Volodya with him, and Yagitch was the only person Volodya initiated into the mysteries of his thesis. In earlier days, when Yagitch was rather younger, they had often been in the position of rivals, but they had never been jealous of one another. In the circle in which they moved Yagitch was nicknamed Big Volodya, and his friend Little Volodya.

Besides Big Volodya, Little Volodya, and Sofya Lvovna, there was a fourth person in the sledge—Margarita Alexandrovna, or, as everyone called her, Rita, a cousin of Madame Yagitch—a very pale girl over thirty, with black eyebrows and a pince-nez, who was forever smoking cigarettes, even in the bitterest frost, and who always had her knees and the front of her blouse covered with cigarette ash. She spoke through her nose, drawling every word, was of a cold temperament, could drink any amount of wine and liquor without being drunk, and used to tell scandalous anecdotes in a languid and tasteless way. At home she spent her days reading thick magazines, covering them with cigarette ash, or eating frozen apples.

"Sonia, give over fooling," she said, drawling. "It's really silly."

As they drew near the city gates they went more slowly, and began to pass people and houses. Sofya Lvovna subsided, nestled up to her husband, and gave herself up to her thoughts. Little Volodya sat opposite. By now her lighthearted and cheerful thoughts were mingled with gloomy ones. She thought that the man sitting opposite knew that she loved him, and no doubt he believed the gossip that she married the colonel *par dépit*. She had never told him of her love; she had not wanted him to know, and had done her best to hide her feeling, but from her face she knew that he understood her perfectly—and her pride suffered. But what was most humiliating in her position was that, since her wedding, Volodya had suddenly begun to pay her attention, which he had never done before, spending hours with her, sitting silent or chattering about trifles; and even now in the sledge, though he did not talk to her, he touched her foot with his and pressed her hand a little. Evidently that was all he wanted, that she should be married; and it was evident that he despised her and that she only excited in him an interest of a special kind as though she were an immoral and disreputable woman. And when the feeling of triumph and love for her husband were mingled in her soul with humiliation and wounded pride, she was overcome by a spirit of defiance, and longed to sit on the box, to shout and whistle to the horses.

Just as they passed the nunnery the huge hundred-ton bell rang out. Rita crossed herself.

"Our Olga is in that nunnery," said Sofya Lvovna, and she, too, crossed herself and shuddered.

"Why did she go into the nunnery?" said the colonel.

"*Par dépit,*" Rita answered crossly, with obvious allusion to Sofya's marrying Yagitch. "*Par dépit* is all the fashion nowadays. Defiance of all the world. She was always laughing, a desperate flirt, fond of nothing but balls and young men, and all of a sudden off she went—to surprise everyone!"

"That's not true," said Volodya, turning down the collar of his fur coat and showing his handsome face. "It wasn't a case of *par dépit;* it was simply horrible, if you like. Her brother Dmitri was sent to penal servitude, and they don't know where he is now. And her mother died of grief."

He turned up his collar again.

"Olga did well," he added in a muffled voice. "Living as an adopted child, and with such a paragon as Sofya Lvovna—one must take that into consideration too!"

Sofya Lvovna heard a tone of contempt in his voice, and longed to say something rude to him, but she said nothing. The spirit of defiance came over her again; she stood up again and shouted in a tearful voice:

"I want to go to the early service! Driver, back! I want to see Olga."

They turned back. The nunnery bell had a deep note, and Sofya Lvovna fancied there was something in it that reminded her of Olga and her life. The other church bells began ringing too. When the driver stopped the horses, Sofya Lvovna jumped out of the sledge and, unescorted and alone, went quickly up to the gate.

"Make haste, please!" her husband called to her. "It's late already."

She went in at the dark gateway, then by the avenue that led from the gate to the chief church. The snow crunched under her feet, and the ringing was just above her head, and seemed to vibrate through her whole being. Here was the church door, then three steps down, and an anteroom with icons of the saints on both sides, a fragrance of juniper and incense, another door, and a dark figure opening it and bowing very low. The service had not yet begun. One nun was walking by the icon screen and lighting the candles on the tall standard candlesticks, another was lighting the chandelier. Here and there, by the columns and the side chapels, there stood black, motionless figures. "I suppose they must remain standing as they are now till the morning," thought Sofya Lvovna, and it seemed to her dark, cold, and dreary—drearier than a graveyard. She looked with a feeling of dreariness at the still, motionless figures and suddenly felt a pang at her heart. For some reason, in one short nun, with thin shoulders and a black kerchief on her head, she recognized Olga, though when Olga went into the nunnery she had been plump and had looked taller. Hesitating and extremely agitated, Sofya Lvovna went up to the nun, and looking over her shoulder into her face, recognized her as Olga.

"Olga!" she cried, throwing up her hands, and could not speak from emotion. "Olga!"

The nun knew her at once; she raised her eyebrows in surprise, and her pale, freshly washed face, and even, it seemed, the white headcloth that she wore under her wimple, beamed with pleasure.

"What a miracle from God!" she said, and she, too, threw up her thin, pale little hands.

Sofya Lvovna hugged her and kissed her warmly, and was afraid as she did so that she might smell of spirits.

"We were just driving past, and we thought of you," she said, breathing hard, as though she had been running. "Dear me! How pale you are! I . . . I'm very glad to see you. Well, tell me how are you? Are you dull?"

Sofya Lvovna looked round at the other nuns, and went on in a subdued voice:

"There've been so many changes at home . . . you know, I'm

married to Colonel Yagitch. You remember him, no doubt. . . . I am very happy with him."

"Well, thank God for that. And is your father quite well?"

"Yes, he is quite well. He often speaks of you. You must come and see us during the holidays, Olga, won't you?"

"I will come," said Olga, and she smiled. "I'll come on the second day."

Sofya Lvovna began crying, she did not know why, and for a minute she shed tears in silence, then she wiped her eyes and said:

"Rita will be very sorry not to have seen you. She is with us too. And Volodya's here. They are close to the gate. How pleased they'd be if you'd come out and see them. Let's go out to them; the service hasn't begun yet."

"Let us," Olga agreed. She crossed herself three times and went out with Sofya Lvovna to the entrance.

"So you say you're happy, Sonitchka?" she asked when they came out at the gate.

"Very."

"Well, thank God for that."

The two Volodyas, seeing the nun, got out of the sledge and greeted her respectfully. Both were visibly touched by her pale face and her black monastic dress, and both were pleased that she had remembered them and come to greet them. That she might not be cold, Sofya Lvovna wrapped her up in a rug and put one half of her fur coat round her. Her tears had relieved and purified her heart, and she was glad that this noisy, restless, and, in reality, impure night should unexpectedly end so purely and serenely. And to keep Olga by her a little longer she suggested:

"Let us take her for a drive! Get in, Olga; we'll go a little way."

The men expected the nun to refuse—saints don't dash about in three-horse sledges; but to their surprise, she consented and got into the sledge. And while the horses were galloping to the city gate all were silent, and only tried to make her warm and comfortable, and each of them was thinking of what she had been in the past and what she was now. Her face was now passionless, inexpressive, cold, pale, and transparent, as though there were water, not blood, in her veins. And two or three years ago she had been plump and rosy, talking about her suitors and laughing at every trifle.

Near the city gate the sledge turned back; when it stopped ten minutes later near the nunnery, Olga got out of the sledge. The bell had begun to ring more rapidly.

"The Lord save you," said Olga, and she bowed low as nuns do.

"Mind you come, Olga."

"I will, I will."

She went and quickly disappeared through the gateway. And when after that they drove on again, Sofya Lvovna felt very sad. Everyone was silent. She felt dispirited and weak all over. That she should have made a nun get into a sledge and drive in a company hardly sober seemed to her now stupid, tactless, and almost sacrilegious. As the intoxication passed off, the desire to deceive herself passed away also. It was clear to her now that she did not love her husband, and never could love him, and that it all had been foolishness and nonsense. She had married him from interested motives, because, in the words of her school friends, he was madly rich, and because she was afraid of becoming an old maid like Rita, and because she was sick of her father, the doctor, and wanted to annoy Volodya. If she could have imagined when she got married, that it would be so oppressive, so dreadful, and so hideous, she would not have consented to the marriage for all the wealth in the world. But now there was no setting it right. She must make up her mind to it.

They reached home. Getting into her warm, soft bed, and pulling the bedclothes over her, Sofya Lvovna recalled the dark church, the smell of incense, and the figures by the columns, and she felt frightened at the thought that these figures would be standing there all the while she was asleep. The early service would be very, very long; then there would be "the hours," then the mass, then the service of the day. . . .

"But of course there is a God—there certainly is a God; and I shall have to die, so that sooner or later one must think of one's soul, of eternal life, like Olga. Olga is saved now; she has settled all questions for herself. . . . But if there is no God? Then her life is wasted. But how is it wasted? Why is it wasted?"

And a minute later the thought came into her mind again:

"There is a God; death must come; one must think of one's soul. If Olga were to see death before her this minute she would not be afraid. She is prepared. And the great thing is that she has already solved the problem of life for herself. There is a God . . . yes. . . . But is there no other solution except going into a monastery? To go into the monastery means to renounce life, to spoil it . . ."

Sofya Lvovna began to feel rather frightened; she hid her head under her pillow.

"I mustn't think about it," she whispered. "I mustn't . . ."

Yagitch was walking about on the carpet in the next room with a soft jingle of spurs, thinking about something. The thought occurred to Sofya Lvovna that this man was near and dear to her only for one reason—that his name, too, was Vladimir. She sat up in bed and called tenderly:

"Volodya!"

"What is it?" her husband responded.

"Nothing."

She lay down again. She heard a bell, perhaps the same nunnery bell. Again she thought of the vestibule and the dark figures, and thoughts of God and of inevitable death strayed through her mind, and she covered her ears that she might not hear the bell. She thought that before old age and death there would be a long, long life before her, and that day by day she would have to put up with being close to a man she did not love, who had just now come into the bedroom and was getting into bed, and would have to stifle in her heart her hopeless love for the other young, fascinating, and, as she thought, exceptional man. She looked at her husband and tried to say good night to him, but suddenly burst out crying instead. She was vexed with herself.

"Well, now then for the music!" said Yagitch.

She was not pacified till ten o'clock in the morning. She left off crying and trembling all over, but she began to have a splitting headache. Yagitch was in haste to go to the late mass, and in the next room was grumbling at his orderly, who was helping him to dress. He came into the bedroom once with the soft jingle of his spurs to fetch something, and then a second time wearing his epaulettes, and his orders on his breast, limping slightly from rheumatism; and it struck Sofya Lvovna that he looked and walked like a bird of prey.

She heard Yagitch ring the telephone bell.

"Be so good as to put me on to the Vassilevsky barracks," he said; and a minute later: "Vassilevsky barracks? Please ask Doctor Salimovitch to come to the telephone . . ." And a minute later: "With whom am I speaking? Is it you, Volodya? Delighted. Ask your father to come to us at once, dear boy; my wife is rather shattered after yesterday. Not at home, you say? H'm! . . . Thank you. Very good. I shall be much obliged. . . . *Merci.*"

Yagitch came into the bedroom for the third time, bent down to his wife, made the sign of the Cross over her, gave her his hand to kiss (the women who had been in love with him used to kiss his hand and he had got into the habit of it), and saying that he should be back to dinner, went out.

At twelve o'clock the maid came in to announce that Vladimir Mihalovitch had arrived. Sofya Lvovna, staggering with fatigue and headache, hurriedly put on her marvelous new lilac dressing gown trimmed with fur, and hastily did up her hair after a fashion. She was conscious of an inexpressible tenderness in her heart, and was trembling with joy and with fear that he might go away. She wanted nothing but to look at him.

Volodya came dressed correctly for calling, in a swallowtail coat and white tie. When Sofya Lvovna came in he kissed her hand and expressed his genuine regret that she was ill. Then when they had sat down, he admired her dressing gown.

"I was upset by seeing Olga yesterday," she said. "At first I felt it dreadful, but now I envy her. She is like a rock that cannot be shattered; there is no moving her. But was there no other solution for her, Volodya? Is burying oneself alive the only solution of the problem of life? Why, it's death, not life!"

At the thought of Olga, Volodya's face softened.

"Here, you are a clever man, Volodya," said Sofya Lvovna. "Show me how to do what Olga has done. Of course, I am not a believer and should not go into a nunnery, but one can do something equivalent. Life isn't easy for me," she added after a brief pause. "Tell me what to do. . . . Tell me something I can believe in. Tell me something, if it's only one word."

"One word? By all means: tararaboomdeeay."

"Volodya, why do you despise me?" she asked hotly. "You talk to me in a special, fatuous way, if you'll excuse me, not as one talks to one's friends and women one respects. You are so good at your work, you are fond of science; why do you never talk of it to me? Why is it? Am I not good enough?"

Volodya frowned with annoyance and said:

"Why do you want science all of a sudden? Don't you perhaps want constitutional government? Or sturgeon and horseradish?"

"Very well, I am a worthless, trivial, silly woman with no convictions. I have a mass, a mass of defects. I am neurotic, corrupt, and I ought to be despised for it. But you, Volodya, are ten years older than I am, and my husband is thirty years older. I've grown up before your eyes, and if you would, you could have made anything you liked of me—an angel. But you"—her voice quivered—"treat me horribly. Yagitch has married me in his old age, and you . . ."

"Come, come," said Volodya, sitting nearer her and kissing both her hands. "Let the Schopenhauers philosophize and prove whatever they like, while we'll kiss these little hands."

"You despise me, and if only you knew how miserable it makes me," she said uncertainly, knowing beforehand that he would not believe her. "And if you only knew how I want to change, to begin another life! I think of it with enthusiasm!" and tears of enthusiasm actually came into her eyes. "To be good, honest, pure, not to be lying; to have an object in life."

"Come, come, come, please don't be affected! I don't like it!" said Volodya, and an ill-humored expression came into his face. "Upon my word, you might be on the stage. Let us behave like simple people."

To prevent him from getting cross and going away, she began defending herself, and forced herself to smile to please him; and again she began talking of Olga, and of how she longed to solve the problem of her life and to become something real.

"Ta-ra-ra-boomdee-ay," he hummed. "Ta-ra-ra-boomdee-ay!"

And all at once he put his arm round her waist, while she, without knowing what she was doing, laid her hands on his shoulders and for a minute gazed with ecstasy, almost intoxication, at his clever, ironical face, his brow, his eyes, his handsome beard.

"You have known that I love you for ever so long," she confessed to him, and she blushed painfully, and felt that her lips were twitching with shame. "I love you. Why do you torture me?"

She shut her eyes and kissed him passionately on the lips, and for a long while, a full minute, could not take her lips away, though she knew it was unseemly, that he might be thinking the worse of her, that a servant might come in.

"Oh, how you torture me!" she repeated.

When half an hour later, having got all that he wanted, he was sitting at lunch in the dining room, she was kneeling before him, gazing greedily into his face, and he told her that she was like a little dog waiting for a bit of ham to be thrown to it. Then he sat her on his knee, and dancing her up and down like a child, hummed:

"Ta-ra-ra-boomdee-ay. . . . Ta-ra-ra-boomdee-ay."

And when he was getting ready to go she asked him in a passionate whisper:

"When? Today? Where?" And held out both hands to his mouth as though she wanted to seize his answer in them.

"Today it will hardly be convenient," he said after a minute's thought. "Tomorrow, perhaps."

And they parted. Before dinner Sofya Lvovna went to the nunnery to see Olga, but there she was told that Olga was reading the psalter somewhere over the dead. From the nunnery she went to her father's and found that he, too, was out. Then she took another sledge and drove aimlessly about the streets till evening. And for some reason she kept thinking of the aunt whose eyes were red with crying, and who could find no peace anywhere.

And at night they drove out again with three horses to a restaurant out of town and listened to the gypsies. And driving back past the nunnery again, Sofya Lvovna thought of Olga, and she felt aghast at the thought that for the girls and women of her class there was no solution but to go on driving about and telling lies, or going into a nunnery to mortify the flesh. . . . And next day she met her lover, and again Sofya Lvovna drove about the town alone in a hired sledge thinking about her aunt.

A week later Volodya threw her over. And after that life went on as before, uninteresting, miserable, and sometimes even agonizing. The colonel and Volodya spent hours playing billiards and picquet, Rita told anecdotes in the same languid, tasteless way, and Sofya Lvovna went about alone in hired sledges and kept begging her husband to take her for a good drive with three horses.

Going almost every day to the nunnery, she wearied Olga, complaining of her unbearable misery, weeping, and feeling as she did so that she brought with her into the cell something impure, pitiful, shabby. And Olga repeated to her mechanically, as though a lesson learnt by rote, that all this was of no consequence, that it would all pass and God would forgive her.

1893

WARD NO. 6

I

In the hospital yard there stands a small lodge surrounded by a perfect forest of burdocks, nettles, and wild hemp. Its roof is rusty, the chimney is tumbling down, the steps at the front door are rotting away and overgrown with grass, and there are only traces left of the stucco. The front of the lodge faces the hospital; at the back it looks out into the open country, from which it is separated by the gray hospital fence with nails on it. These nails, with their points upward, and the fence, and the lodge itself, have that peculiar, desolate, godforsaken look which is only found in our hospital and prison buildings.

If you are not afraid of being stung by the nettles, come by the narrow footpath that leads to the lodge, and let us see what is going on inside. Opening the first door, we walk into the entry. Here along the walls and by the stove every sort of hospital rubbish lies littered about. Mattresses, old tattered dressing gowns, trousers, blue striped shirts, boots and shoes no good for anything—all these remnants are piled up in heaps, mixed up and crumpled, moldering, and giving out a sickly smell.

The porter, Nikita, an old soldier wearing rusty good-conduct stripes, is always lying on the litter with a pipe between his teeth. He has a grim, surly, battered-looking face, overhanging eyebrows which give him the expression of a sheepdog of the steppes, and a red nose; he is short and looks thin and scraggy, but he is of imposing deportment and his fists are vigorous. He belongs to the class of simple-hearted, practical, and dull-witted people, prompt in carrying out orders, who like discipline better than anything in the world, and so are convinced that it is their duty to beat people. He showers blows on the face, on the chest, on the back, on whatever comes first, and is convinced that there would be no order in the place if he did not.

Next you come into a big, spacious room which fills up the whole lodge except for the entry. Here the walls are painted a dirty blue, the ceiling is as sooty as in a hut without a chimney—it is evident that in the winter the stove smokes and the room is full of fumes. The windows are disfigured by iron gratings on the inside. The wooden floor is gray and full of splinters. There is a stench of sour cabbage, of smoldering wicks, of bugs, and of ammonia, and for the first minute this stench gives you the impression of having walked into a menagerie. . . .

There are bedsteads screwed to the floor. Men in blue hospital dressing gowns, and wearing nightcaps in the old style, are sitting and lying on them. These are the lunatics.

There are five of them in all here. Only one is of the upper class, the rest are all artisans. The one nearest the door—a tall, lean workman with shining red whiskers and tearstained eyes—sits with his head propped on his hand, staring at the same point. Day and night he grieves, shaking his head, sighing and smiling bitterly. He takes a part in conversation and usually makes no answer to questions; he eats and drinks mechanically when food is offered him. From his agonizing, throbbing cough, his thinness, and the flush on his cheeks, one may judge that he is in the first stage of consumption. Next to him is a little, alert, very lively old man, with a pointed beard and curly black hair like a negro's. By day he walks up and down the ward from window to window, or sits on his bed, cross-legged like a

Turk, and, ceaselessly as a bullfinch whistles, softly sings and titters. He shows his childish gaiety and lively character at night also when he gets up to say his prayers—that is, to beat himself on the chest with his fists, and to scratch with his fingers at the door. This is the Jew Moiseika, an imbecile, who went crazy twenty years ago when his hat factory was burnt down.

And of all the inhabitants of Ward No. 6, he is the only one who is allowed to go out of the lodge, and even out of the yard into the street. He has enjoyed this privilege for years, probably because he is an old inhabitant of the hospital—a quiet, harmless imbecile, the buffoon of the town, where people are used to seeing him surrounded by boys and dogs. In his wretched gown, in his absurd nightcap, and in slippers, sometimes with bare legs and even without trousers, he walks about the streets, stopping at the gates and little shops, and begging for a copper. In one place they will give him some kvass, in another some bread, in another a copper, so that he generally goes back to the ward feeling rich and well fed. Everything that he brings back Nikita takes from him for his own benefit. The soldier does this roughly, angrily turning the Jew's pockets inside out, and calling God to witness that he will not let him go into the street again, and that breach of the regulations is worse to him than anything in the world.

Moiseika likes to make himself useful. He gives his companions water, and covers them up when they are asleep; he promises each of them to bring him back a kopeck, and to make him a new cap; he feeds with a spoon his neighbor on the left, who is paralyzed. He acts in this way, not from compassion nor from any considerations of a humane kind, but through imitation, unconsciously dominated by Gromov, his neighbor on the right hand.

Ivan Dmitritch Gromov, a man of thirty-three, who is a gentleman by birth, and has been a court usher and provincial secretary, suffers from the mania of persecution. He either lies curled up in bed, or walks from corner to corner as though for exercise; he very rarely sits down. He is always excited, agitated, and overwrought by a sort of vague, undefined expectation. The faintest rustle in the entry or shout in the yard is enough to make him raise his head and begin listening: whether they are coming for him, whether they are looking for him. And at such times his face expresses the utmost uneasiness and repulsion.

I like his broad face with its high cheekbones, always pale and unhappy, and reflecting, as though in a mirror, a soul tormented by conflict and long-continued terror. His grimaces are strange and abnormal, but the delicate lines traced on his face by profound, genuine suffering show intelligence and sense, and there is a warm and healthy light in his eyes. I like the man himself, courteous, anxious to be of use, and extraordinarily gentle to everyone except Nikita. When anyone drops a button or a spoon, he jumps up from his bed quickly and picks it up; every day he says good morning to his companions, and when he goes to bed he wishes them good night.

Besides his continually overwrought condition and his grimaces, his madness shows itself in the following way also. Sometimes in the evenings he wraps himself in his dressing gown, and, trembling all over, with his teeth chattering, begins walking rapidly from corner to corner and between the bedsteads. It seems as though he is in a violent fever. From the way he suddenly stops and glances at his companions, it can be seen that he is longing to say something very important, but, apparently reflecting that they would not listen, or would not understand him, he shakes his head impatiently and goes on pacing up and down. But soon the desire to speak gets the upper hand of every consideration, and he will let himself go and speak fervently and passionately. His talk is disordered and feverish like delirium, disconnected, and not always intelligible, but, on the other hand, something extremely fine may be felt in it, both in the words and the voice. When he talks you recognize in him the lunatic and the man. It is difficult to reproduce on paper his insane talk. He speaks of the baseness of mankind, of violence trampling on justice, of the glorious life which will one day be upon earth, of the window gratings, which remind him every minute of the stupidity and cruelty of oppressors. It makes a disorderly, incoherent potpourri of themes old but not yet out of date.

II

Some twelve or fifteen years ago an official called Gromov, a highly respectable and prosperous person, was living in his own house in the principal street of the town. He had two sons, Sergey and Ivan. When Sergey was a student in his fourth year he was taken ill with galloping consumption and died, and his death was, as it were, the first of a whole series of calamities which suddenly showered on the Gromov family. Within a week of Sergey's funeral the old father was put on trial for fraud and misappropriation, and he died of typhoid in the prison hospital soon afterward. The house, with all their belongings, was sold by auction, and Ivan Dmitritch and his mother were left entirely without means.

Hitherto in his father's lifetime, Ivan Dmitritch, who was studying in the University of Petersburg, had received an allowance of sixty or seventy rubles a month, and had had no conception of poverty; now he had to make an abrupt change in his life. He had to spend his time from morning to night giving lessons for next to nothing, to work at copying, and with all that to go hungry, as all his earnings were sent to keep his mother. Ivan Dmitritch could not stand such a life; he lost heart and strength, and, giving up the university, went home.

Here, through interest, he obtained the post of teacher in the district school, but could not get on with his colleagues, was not liked by the boys, and soon gave up the post. His mother died. He was for six months without work, living on nothing but bread and water; then he became a court usher. He kept this post until he was dismissed owing to his illness.

He had never even in his young student days given the impression of being perfectly healthy. He had always been pale, thin, and given to catching cold; he ate little and slept badly. A single glass of wine went to his head and made him hysterical. He always had a craving for society, but, owing to his irritable temperament and suspiciousness, he never became very intimate with anyone, and had no friends. He always spoke with contempt of his fellow townsmen, saying that their coarse ignorance and sleepy animal existence seemed to him loathsome and horrible. He spoke in a loud tenor, with heat, and invariably either with scorn and indignation, or with wonder and enthusiasm, and always with perfect sincerity. Whatever one talked to him about he always brought it round to the same subject: that life was dull and stifling in the town; that the townspeople had no lofty interests, but lived a dingy, meaningless life, diversified by violence, coarse profligacy, and hypocrisy; that scoundrels were well fed and clothed, while honest men lived from hand to mouth; that they needed schools, a progressive local paper, a theater, public lectures, the coordination of the intellectual elements; that society must see its failings and be horrified. In his criticisms of people he laid on the colors thick, using only black and white, and no fine shades; mankind was divided for him into honest men and scoundrels: there was nothing in between. He always spoke with passion and enthusiasm of women and of love, but he had never been in love.

In spite of the severity of his judgments and his nervousness, he was liked, and behind his back was spoken of affectionately as Vanya. His innate refinement and readiness to be of service, his good breeding, his moral purity, and his shabby coat, his frail appearance and family misfortunes, aroused a kind, warm, sorrowful feeling. Moreover, he was well educated and well read; according to the townspeople's notions, he knew everything, and was in their eyes something like a walking encyclopædia.

He had read a great deal. He would sit at the club, nervously pulling at his beard and looking through the magazines and books; and from his face one could see that he was not reading, but devouring the pages without giving himself time to digest what he read. It must be supposed that reading was one of his morbid habits, as he fell upon anything that came into his hands with equal avidity, even last year's newspapers and calendars. At home he always read lying down.

III

One autumn morning Ivan Dmitritch, turning up the collar of his greatcoat and splashing through the mud, made his way by side streets and back lanes to see some artisan, and to collect some payment that was owing. He was in a gloomy mood, as he always was in the morning. In one of the side streets he was met by two convicts in fetters and four soldiers with rifles in charge of them. Ivan Dmitritch had very often met convicts before, and they had always excited feelings of compassion and discomfort in him; but now this meeting made a peculiar, strange impression on him. It suddenly seemed to him for some reason that he, too, might be put into fetters and led through the mud to prison like that. After visiting the artisan, on the way home he met near the post office a police superintendent of his acquaintance, who greeted him and walked a few paces along the street with him, and for some reason this seemed to him suspicious. At home he could not get the convicts or the soldiers with their rifles out of his head all day, and an unaccountable inward agitation prevented him from reading or concentrating his mind. In the evening he did not light his lamp, and at night he could not sleep, but kept thinking that he might be arrested, put into fetters, and thrown into prison. He did not know of any harm he had done, and could be certain that he would never be guilty of murder, arson, or theft in the future either; but was it not easy to commit a crime by accident, unconsciously, and was not false witness always possible, and, indeed, miscarriage of justice? It was not without good reason that the agelong experience of the simple people teaches that beggary and prison are ills none can be safe from. A judicial mistake is very possible as legal proceedings are conducted nowadays, and there is nothing to be wondered at in it. People who have an official, professional relation to other men's sufferings—for instance, judges, police officers, doctors—in course of time, through habit, grow so callous that they cannot, even if they wish it, take any but a formal attitude to their clients; in this respect they are not different from the peasant who slaughters sheep and calves in the backyard, and does not notice the blood. With this formal, soulless attitude to human personality the judge needs but one thing—time—in order to deprive an innocent man of all rights of property, and to condemn him to penal servitude. Only the time spent on performing certain formalities for which the judge is paid his salary, and then—it is all over. Then you may look in vain for justice and protection in this dirty, wretched little town a hundred and fifty miles from a railway station! And, indeed, is it not absurd even to think of justice when every kind of violence is accepted by society as a rational and consistent necessity, and every act of mercy—for instance, a verdict of acquittal—calls forth a perfect outburst of dissatisfied and revengeful feeling?

In the morning Ivan Dmitritch got up from his bed in a state of horror, with cold perspiration on his forehead, completely convinced that he might be arrested any minute. Since his gloomy thoughts of yesterday had haunted him so long, he thought, it must be that there was some truth in them. They could not, indeed, have come into his mind without any grounds whatever.

A policeman walking slowly passed by the windows: that was not for nothing. Here were two men standing still and silent near the house. Why were they silent? And agonizing days and nights followed for Ivan Dmitritch. Everyone who passed by the windows or came into the yard seemed to him a spy or a detective. At midday the chief of the police usually drove down the street with a pair of horses; he was going from his estate near the town to the police department; but Ivan Dmitritch fancied every time that he was driving especially quickly, and that he had a peculiar expression: it was evident that he was in haste to announce that there was a very important criminal in the town. Ivan Dmitritch started at every ring at the bell and knock at the gate, and was agitated whenever he came upon anyone new at his landlady's; when he met police officers and gendarmes he smiled and began whistling so as to seem unconcerned. He could not sleep for whole nights in succession expecting to be arrested, but he snored loudly and sighed as though in deep sleep, that his landlady might think he was asleep; for if he could not sleep it meant that he was tormented by the stings of conscience—what a piece of evidence! Facts and common sense persuaded him that all these terrors were nonsense and morbidity, that if one looked at the matter more broadly there was nothing really terrible in arrest and imprisonment—so long as the conscience is at ease; but the more sensibly and logically he reasoned, the more acute and agonizing his mental distress became. It might be compared with the story of a hermit who tried to cut a dwelling-place for himself in a virgin forest; the more zealously he worked with his ax, the thicker the forest grew. In the end Ivan Dmitritch, seeing it was useless, gave up reasoning altogether, and abandoned himself entirely to despair and terror.

He began to avoid people and to seek solitude. His official work had been distasteful to him before: now it became unbearable to him. He was afraid they would somehow get him into trouble, would put a bribe in his pocket unnoticed and then denounce him, or that he would accidentally make a mistake in official papers that would appear to be fraudulent, or would lose other people's money. It is strange that his imagination had never at other times been so agile and inventive as now, when every day he thought of thousands of different reasons for being seriously anxious over his freedom and honor; but, on the other hand, his interest in the outer world, in books in particular, grew sensibly fainter, and his memory began to fail him.

In the spring when the snow melted there were found in the ravine near the cemetery two half-decomposed corpses—the bodies of an old woman and a boy bearing the traces of death by violence. Nothing was talked of but these bodies and their unknown murderers. That people might not think he had been guilty of the crime,

Ivan Dmitritch walked about the streets, smiling, and when he met acquaintances he turned pale, flushed, and began declaring that there was no greater crime than the murder of the weak and defenseless. But this duplicity soon exhausted him, and after some reflection he decided that in his position the best thing to do was to hide in his landlady's cellar. He sat in the cellar all day and then all night, then another day, was fearfully cold, and waiting till dusk, stole secretly like a thief back to his room. He stood in the middle of the room till daybreak, listening without stirring. Very early in the morning, before sunrise, some workmen came into the house. Ivan Dmitritch knew perfectly well that they had come to mend the stove in the kitchen, but terror told him that they were police officers disguised as workmen. He slipped stealthily out of the flat, and, overcome by terror, ran along the street without his cap and coat. Dogs raced after him barking, a peasant shouted somewhere behind him, the wind whistled in his ears, and it seemed to Ivan Dmitritch that the force and violence of the whole world was massed together behind his back and was chasing after him.

He was stopped and brought home, and his landlady sent for a doctor. Doctor Andrey Yefimitch, of whom we shall have more to say hereafter, prescribed cold compresses on his head and laurel drops, shook his head, and went away, telling the landlady he should not come again, as one should not interfere with people who are going out of their minds. As he had not the means to live at home and be nursed, Ivan Dmitritch was soon sent to the hospital, and was there put into the ward for venereal patients. He could not sleep at night, was full of whims and fancies, and disturbed the patients, and was soon afterward, by Andrey Yefimitch's orders, transferred to Ward No. 6.

Within a year Ivan Dmitritch was completely forgotten in the town, and his books, heaped up by his landlady in a sledge in the shed, were pulled to pieces by boys.

IV

Ivan Dmitritch's neighbor on the left hand is, as I have said already, the Jew Moiseika; his neighbor on the right hand is a peasant so rolling in fat that he is almost spherical, with a blankly stupid face, utterly devoid of thought. This is a motionless, gluttonous, unclean animal who has long ago lost all powers of thought or feeling. An acrid, stifling stench always comes from him.

Nikita, who has to clean up after him, beats him terribly with all his might, not sparing his fists; and what is dreadful is not his being beaten—that one can get used to—but the fact that this stupefied creature does not respond to the blows with a sound or a movement, nor by a look in the eyes, but only sways a little like a heavy barrel.

The fifth and last inhabitant of Ward No. 6 is a man of the artisan class who had once been a sorter in the post office, a thinnish, fair little man with a good-natured but rather sly face. To judge from the clear, cheerful look in his calm and intelligent eyes, he has some pleasant idea in his mind, and has some very important and agreeable secret. He has under his pillow and under his mattress something that he never shows anyone, not from fear of its being taken from him and stolen, but from modesty. Sometimes he goes to the window, and turning his back to his companions, puts something on his breast, and bending his head, looks at it; if you go up to him at such a moment, he is overcome with confusion and snatches something off his breast. But it is not difficult to guess his secret.

"Congratulate me," he often says to Ivan Dmitritch; "I have been presented with the Stanislav order of the second degree with the star. The second degree with the star is only given to foreigners, but for some reason they want to make an exception for me," he says with a smile, shrugging his shoulders in perplexity. "That I must confess I did not expect."

"I don't understand anything about that," Ivan Dmitritch replies morosely.

"But do you know what I shall attain to sooner or later?" the former sorter persists, screwing up his eyes slyly. "I shall certainly get the Swedish 'Polar Star.' That's an order it is worth working for, a white cross with a black ribbon. It's very beautiful."

Probably in no other place is life so monotonous as in this ward. In the morning the patients, except the paralytic and the fat peasant, wash in the entry at a big tub and wipe themselves with the skirts of their dressing gowns; after that they drink tea out of tin mugs which Nikita brings them out of the main building. Everyone is allowed one mugful. At midday they have soup made out of sour cabbage and boiled grain, in the evening their supper consists of grain left from dinner. In the intervals they lie down, sleep, look out of the window, and walk from one corner to the other. And so every day. Even the former sorter always talks of the same orders.

Fresh faces are rarely seen in Ward No. 6. The doctor has not taken in any new mental cases for a long time, and the people who are fond of visiting lunatic asylums are few in this world. Once every two months Semyon Lazaritch, the barber, appears in the ward. How he cuts the patients' hair, and how Nikita helps him to do it, and what a trepidation the lunatics are always thrown into by the arrival of the drunken, smiling barber, we will not describe.

No one even looks into the ward except the barber. The patients are condemned to see day after day no one but Nikita.

A rather strange rumor has, however, been circulating in the hospital of late.

It is rumored that the doctor has begun to visit Ward No. 6.

V

A strange rumor!

Dr. Andrey Yefimitch Ragin is a strange man in his way. They say that when he was young he was very religious, and prepared himself for a clerical career, and that when he had finished his studies at the high school in 1863 he intended to enter a theological academy, but that his father, a surgeon and doctor of medicine, jeered at him and declared point-blank that he would disown him if he became a priest. How far this is true I don't know, but Andrey Yefimitch himself has more than once confessed that he has never had a natural bent for medicine or science in general.

However that may have been, when he finished his studies in the medical faculty he did not enter the priesthood. He showed no special devoutness, and was no more like a priest at the beginning of his medical career than he is now.

His exterior is heavy, coarse like a peasant's, his face, his beard, his flat hair, and his coarse, clumsy figure, suggest an overfed, intemperate, and harsh innkeeper on the high road. His face is surly-looking and covered with blue veins, his eyes are little, and his nose is red. With his height and broad shoulders he has huge hands and feet; one would think that a blow from his fist would knock the life out of anyone, but his step is soft, and his walk is cautious and insinuating; when he meets anyone in a narrow passage he is always the first to stop and make way, and to say, not in a bass, as one would expect, but in a high, soft tenor: "I beg your pardon!" He has a little swelling on his neck which prevents him from wearing stiff starched collars, and so he always goes about in soft linen or cotton shirts. Altogether he does not dress like a doctor. He wears the same suit for ten years, and the new clothes, which he usually buys at a Jewish shop, look as shabby and crumpled on him as his old ones; he sees patients and dines and pays visits all in the same coat; but this is not due to niggardliness, but to complete carelessness about his appearance.

When Andrey Yefimitch came to the town to take up his duties the "institution founded to the glory of God" was in a terrible condition. One could hardly breathe for the stench in the wards, in the passages, and in the courtyards of the hospital. The hospital servants, the nurses, and their children slept in the wards together with the patients. They complained that there was no living for beetles, bugs, and mice. The surgical wards were never free from erysipelas. There

". . . his step is soft, and his walk is cautious and insinuating; when he meets anyone in a narrow passage he is always the first to stop and make way . . ."

were only two scalpels and not one thermometer in the whole hospital; potatoes were kept in the baths. The superintendent, the housekeeper, and the medical assistant robbed the patients, and of the old doctor, Andrey Yefimitch's predecessor, people declared that he secretly sold the hospital alcohol, and that he kept a regular harem consisting of nurses and female patients. These disorderly proceedings were perfectly well known in the town, and were even exaggerated, but people took them calmly; some justified them on the ground that there were only peasants and working men in the hospital, who could not be dissatisfied, since they were much worse off at home than in the hospital—they couldn't be fed on woodcocks! Others said in excuse that the town alone, without help from the Zemstvo, was not equal to maintaining a good hospital; thank God for having one at all, even a poor one. And the newly formed Zemstvo did not open infirmaries either in the town or the neighborhood, relying on the fact that the town already had its hospital.

After looking over the hospital Andrey Yefimitch came to the conclusion that it was an immoral institution and extremely prejudicial to the health of the townspeople. In his opinion the most sensible thing that could be done was to let out the patients and close the hospital. But he reflected that his will alone was not enough to do this, and that it would be useless; if physical and moral impurity were driven out of one place, they would only move to another; one must wait for it to wither away of itself. Besides, if people open a hospital and put up with having it, it must be because they need it; superstition and all the nastiness and abominations of daily life were necessary, since in process of time they worked out to something sensible, just as manure turns into black earth. There was nothing on earth so good that it had not something nasty about its first origin.

When Andrey Yefimitch undertook his duties he was apparently not greatly concerned about the irregularities at the hospital. He only asked the attendants and nurses not to sleep in the wards, and had two cupboards of instruments put up; the superintendent, the housekeeper, the medical assistant, and the erysipelas remained unchanged.

Andrey Yefimitch loved intelligence and honesty intensely, but he had no strength of will nor belief in his right to organize an intelligent and honest life about him. He was absolutely unable to give orders, to forbid things, and to insist. It seemed as though he had taken a vow never to raise his voice and never to make use of the imperative. It was difficult for him to say "Fetch" or "Bring"; when he wanted his meals he would cough hesitatingly and say to the cook, "How about tea? . . ." or "How about dinner? . . ." To dismiss the superintendent or to tell him to leave off stealing, or to abolish the unnecessary parasitic post altogether, was absolutely beyond his powers. When Andrey Yefimitch was deceived or flattered, or accounts he knew to be cooked were brought him to sign, he would turn as red as a crab and feel guilty, but yet he would sign the accounts. When the patients complained to him of being hungry or of the roughness of the nurses, he would be confused and mutter guiltily: "Very well, very well, I will go into it later. . . . Most likely there is some misunderstanding. . . ."

At first Andrey Yefimitch worked very zealously. He saw patients every day from morning till dinnertime, performed operations, and even attended confinements. The ladies said of him that he was attentive and clever at diagnosing diseases, especially those of women and children. But in process of time the work unmistakably wearied him by its monotony and obvious uselessness. Today one sees thirty patients, and tomorrow they have increased to thirty-five, the next day forty, and so on from day to day, from year to year, while the mortality in the town did not decrease and the patients did not leave off coming. To be any real help to forty patients between morning and dinner was not physically possible, so it could but lead to deception. If twelve thousand patients were seen in a year it meant, if one looked at it simply, that twelve thousand men were deceived. To put those who were seriously ill into wards, and to treat them according to the principles of science, was impossible, too, because though there were principles there was no science; if he were to put aside philosophy and pedantically follow the rules as other doctors did, the things above all necessary were cleanliness and ventilation instead of dirt, wholesome nourishment instead of broth made of stinking, sour cabbage, and good assistants instead of thieves; and, indeed, why hinder people dying if death is the normal and legitimate end of everyone? What is gained if some shopkeeper or clerk lives an extra five or ten years? If the aim of medicine is by drugs to alleviate suffering, the question forces itself on one: why alleviate it? In the first place, they say that suffering leads man to perfection; and in the second, if mankind really learns to alleviate its sufferings with pills and drops, it will completely abandon religion and philosophy, in which it has hitherto found not merely protection from all sorts of trouble, but even happiness. Pushkin suffered terrible agonies before his death, poor Heine lay paralyzed for several years; why, then, should not some Andrey Yefimitch or Matryona Savishna be ill, since their lives had nothing of importance in them, and would have been entirely empty and like the life of an amoeba except for suffering?

Oppressed by such reflections, Andrey Yefimitch relaxed his efforts and gave up visiting the hospital every day.

VI

His life was passed like this. As a rule he got up at eight o'clock in the morning, dressed, and drank his tea. Then he sat down in his study to read, or went to the hospital. At the hospital the outpatients were sitting in the dark, narrow little corridor waiting to be seen by the doctor. The nurses and the attendants, tramping with their boots over the brick floors, ran by them; gaunt-looking patients in dressing gowns passed; dead bodies and vessels full of filth were carried by; the children were crying, and there was a cold draft. Andrey Yefimitch knew that such surroundings were torture to feverish, consumptive, and impressionable patients; but what could be done? In the consulting room he was met by his assistant, Sergey Sergeyitch—

a fat little man with a plump, well-washed shaven face, with soft, smooth manners, wearing a new loosely cut suit, and looking more like a senator than a medical assistant. He had an immense practice in the town, wore a white tie, and considered himself more proficient than the doctor, who had no practice. In the corner of the consulting room there stood a large icon in a shrine with a heavy lamp in front of it, and near it a candle stand with a white cover on it. On the walls hung portraits of bishops, a view of the Svyatogorsky Monastery, and wreaths of dried cornflowers. Sergey Sergeyitch was religious, and liked solemnity and decorum. The icon had been put up at his expense; at his instructions some one of the patients read the hymns of praise in the consulting room on Sundays, and after the reading Sergey Sergeyitch himself went through the wards with a censer and burned incense.

There were a great many patients, but the time was short, and so the work was confined to the asking of a few brief questions and the administration of some drugs, such as castor oil or volatile ointment. Andrey Yefimitch would sit with his cheek resting in his hand, lost in thought and asking questions mechanically. Sergey Sergeyitch sat down too, rubbing his hands, and from time to time putting in his word.

"We suffer pain and poverty," he would say, "because we do not pray to the merciful God as we should. Yes!"

Andrey Yefimitch never performed any operation when he was seeing patients; he had long ago given up doing so, and the sight of blood upset him. When he had to open a child's mouth in order to look at its throat, and the child cried and tried to defend itself with its little hands, the noise in his ears made his head go round and brought tears to his eyes. He would make haste to prescribe a drug, and motion to the woman to take the child away.

He was soon wearied by the timidity of the patients and their incoherence, by the proximity of the pious Sergey Sergeyitch, by the portraits on the walls, and by his own questions, which he had asked over and over again for twenty years. And he would go away after seeing five or six patients. The rest would be seen by his assistant in his absence.

With the agreeable thought that, thank God, he had no private practice now, and that no one would interrupt him, Andrey Yefimitch sat down to the table immediately on reaching home and took up a book. He read a great deal and always with enjoyment. Half his salary went on buying books, and of the six rooms that made up his abode three were heaped up with books and old magazines. He liked best of all works on history and philosophy; the only medical publication to which he subscribed was *The Doctor*, of which he always read the last pages first. He would always go on reading for several hours without a break and without being weary. He did not read as rapidly and impulsively as Ivan Dmitritch had done in the past, but slowly and with concentration, often pausing over a passage which he liked or did not find intelligible. Near the books there always stood a decanter of vodka, and a salted cucumber or a pickled apple lay beside it, not on a plate, but on the baize tablecloth. Every half hour he would pour himself out a glass of vodka and drink it without taking his eyes off the book. Then without looking at it he would feel for the cucumber and bite off a bit.

At three o'clock he would go cautiously to the kitchen door, cough, and say, "Daryushka, what about dinner? . . ."

After his dinner—a rather poor and untidily served one—Andrey Yefimitch would walk up and down his rooms with his arms folded, thinking. The clock would strike four, then five, and still he would be walking up and down thinking. Occasionally the kitchen door would creak, and the red and sleepy face of Daryushka would appear.

"Andrey Yefimitch, isn't it time for you to have your beer?" she would ask anxiously.

"No, it's not time yet . . ." he would answer. "I'll wait a little. . . . I'll wait a little. . . ."

Toward the evening the postmaster, Mihail Averyanitch, the only man in town whose society did not bore Andrey Yefimitch, would come in. Mihail Averyanitch had once been a very rich landowner, and had served in the cavalry, but had come to ruin, and was forced by poverty to take a job in the post office late in life. He had a hale and hearty appearance, luxuriant gray whiskers, the manners of a well-bred man, and a loud, pleasant voice. He was good-natured and emotional, but hot-tempered. When anyone in the post office made a protest, expressed disagreement, or even began to argue, Mihail Averyanitch would turn crimson, shake all over, and shout in a voice of thunder, "Hold your tongue!" so that the post office had long enjoyed the reputation of an institution which it was terrible to visit. Mihail Averyanitch liked and respected Andrey Yefimitch for his culture and the loftiness of his soul; he treated the other inhabitants of the town superciliously, as though they were his subordinates.

"Here I am," he would say, going in to Andrey Yefimitch. "Good evening, my dear fellow! I'll be bound, you are getting sick of me, aren't you?"

"On the contrary, I am delighted," said the doctor. "I am always glad to see you."

The friends would sit on the sofa in the study and for some time would smoke in silence.

"Daryushka, what about the beer?" Andrey Yefimitch would say.

They would drink their first bottle still in silence, the doctor brooding and Mihail Averyanitch with a gay and animated face, like a man who has something very interesting to tell. The doctor was always the one to begin the conversation.

"What a pity," he would say quietly and slowly, not looking his friend in the face (he never looked anyone in the face)—"what a great pity it is that there are no people in our town who are capable of carrying on intelligent and interesting conversation, or care to do so. It is an immense privation for us. Even the educated class do not rise above vulgarity; the level of their development, I assure you, is not a bit higher than that of the lower orders."

"Perfectly true. I agree."

"You know, of course," the doctor went on quietly and deliberately, "that everything in this world is insignificant and uninteresting except the higher spiritual manifestations of the human mind. Intellect draws a sharp line between the animals and man, suggests the divinity of the latter, and to some extent even takes the place of the immortality which does not exist. Consequently the intellect is the only possible source of enjoyment. We see and hear of no trace of intellect about us, so we are deprived of enjoyment. We have books, it is true, but that is not at all the same as living talk and converse. If you will allow me to make a not quite apt comparison: books are the printed score, while talk is the singing."

"Perfectly true."

A silence would follow. Daryushka would come out of the kitchen and with an expression of blank dejection would stand in the doorway to listen, with her face propped on her fist.

"Eh!" Mihail Averyanitch would sigh. "To expect intelligence of this generation!"

And he would describe how wholesome, entertaining, and interesting life had been in the past. How intelligent the educated class in Russia used to be, and what lofty ideas it had of honor and friendship; how they used to lend money without an IOU, and it was thought a disgrace not to give a helping hand to a comrade in need; and what campaigns, what adventures, what skirmishes, what comrades, what women! And the Caucasus, what a marvelous country! The wife of a battalion commander, a queer woman, used to put on an officer's uniform and drive off into the mountains in the evening, alone, without a guide. It was said that she had a love affair with some princeling in the native village.

"Queen of Heaven, Holy Mother . . ." Daryushka would sigh.

"And how we drank! And how we ate! And what desperate liberals we were!"

Andrey Yefimitch would listen without hearing; he was musing as he sipped his beer.

"I often dream of intellectual people and conversation with them," he said suddenly, interrupting Mihail Averyanitch. "My father gave me an excellent education, but under the influence of the ideas of the sixties made me become a doctor. I believe if I had not obeyed him then, by now I should have been in the very center of the intellectual movement. Most likely I should have become a member of some university. Of course, intellect, too, is transient and not eternal, but you know why I cherish a partiality for it. Life is a vexatious trap; when a thinking man reaches maturity and attains to full consciousness he cannot help feeling that he is in a trap from which there is no escape. Indeed, he is summoned without his choice by fortuitous circumstances from nonexistence into life . . . what for? He tries to find out the meaning and object of his existence; he is told nothing, or he is told absurdities; he knocks and it is not opened to him; death comes to him—also without his choice. And so, just as in prison men held together by common misfortune feel more at ease when they are together, so one does not notice the trap in life when people with a bent for analysis and generalization meet together and pass their time in the interchange of proud and free ideas. In that sense the intellect is the source of an enjoyment nothing can replace."

"Perfectly true."

Not looking his friend in the face, Andrey Yefimitch would go on, quietly and with pauses, talking about intellectual people and conversation with them, and Mihail Averyanitch would listen attentively and agree: "Perfectly true."

"And you do not believe in the immortality of the soul?" he would ask suddenly.

"No, honored Mihail Averyanitch; I do not believe it, and have no grounds for believing it."

"I must own I doubt it too. And yet I have a feeling as though I should never die. Oh, I think to myself: 'Old fogey, it is time you were dead!' But there is a little voice in my soul says: 'Don't believe it; you won't die.'"

Soon after nine o'clock Mihail Averyanitch would go away. As he put on his fur coat in the entry he would say with a sigh:

"What a wilderness fate has carried us to, though, really! What's most vexatious of all is to have to die here. Ech! . . ."

VII

After seeing his friend out Andrey Yefimitch would sit down at the table and begin reading again. The stillness of the evening, and afterward of the night, was not broken by a single sound, and it seemed as though time were standing still and brooding with the doctor over the book, and as though there were nothing in existence but the books and the lamp with the green shade. The doctor's coarse, peasantlike face was gradually lighted up by a smile of delight and enthusiasm over the progress of the human intellect. Oh, why is not man immortal? he thought. What is the good of the brain centers and convolutions, what is the good of sight, speech, self-consciousness, genius, if it is all destined to depart into the soil, and in the end to grow cold together with the earth's crust, and then for millions of years to fly with the earth round the sun with no meaning and no object? To do that there was no need at all to draw man with his lofty, almost godlike intellect out of nonexistence, and then, as though in mockery, to turn him into clay. The transmutation of substances! But what cowardice to comfort oneself with that cheap substitute for immortality! The unconscious processes that take place in nature are lower even than the stupidity of man, since in stupidity there is, anyway, consciousness and will, while in those processes there is absolutely nothing. Only the coward who has more fear of death than dignity can comfort himself with the fact that his body will in time live again in the grass, in the stones, in the toad. To find one's immortality in the transmutation of substances is as strange as to prophesy a brilliant future for the case after a precious violin has been broken and become useless.

When the clock struck, Andrey Yefimitch would sink back into his chair and close his eyes to think a little. And under the influence of the fine ideas of which he had been reading he would, unawares, recall his past and his present. The past was hateful—better not to think of it. And it was the same in the present as in the past. He knew that at the very time when his thoughts were floating together with the cooling earth round the sun, in the main building beside his abode people were suffering in sickness and physical impurity: someone perhaps could not sleep and was making war upon the insects, someone was being infected by erysipelas, or moaning over too tight a bandage; perhaps the patients were playing cards with the nurses and drinking vodka. According to the yearly return, twelve thousand people had been deceived; the whole hospital rested as it had done twenty years ago on thieving, filth, scandals, gossip, on gross quackery, and, as before, it was an immoral institution extremely injurious to the health of the inhabitants. He knew that Nikita knocked the patients about behind the barred windows of Ward No. 6, and that Moiseika went about the town every day begging alms.

On the other hand, he knew very well that a magical change had taken place in medicine during the last twenty-five years. When he was studying at the university he had fancied that medicine would soon be overtaken by the fate of alchemy and metaphysics; but now when he was reading at night the science of medicine touched him and excited his wonder, and even enthusiasm. What unexpected brilliance, what a revolution! Thanks to the antiseptic system operations were performed such as the great Pirogov had considered impossible even *in spe*. Ordinary Zemstvo doctors were venturing to perform the resection of the kneecap; of abdominal operations only one percent was fatal; while stone was considered such a trifle that they did not even write about it. A radical cure for syphilis had been discovered. And the theory of heredity, hypnotism, the discoveries of Pasteur and of Koch, hygiene based on statistics, and the work of Zemstvo doctors!

Psychiatry with its modern classification of mental diseases, methods of diagnosis, and treatment, was a perfect Elborus in comparison with what had been in the past. They no longer poured cold water on the heads of lunatics nor put strait-waistcoats upon them; they treated them with humanity, and even, so it was stated in the papers, got up balls and entertainments for them. Andrey Yefimitch knew that with modern tastes and views such an abomination as Ward No. 6 was possible only a hundred and fifty miles from a railway in a little town where the mayor and all the town council were half-illiterate tradesmen who looked upon the doctor as an oracle who must be believed without any criticism even if he had poured molten lead into their mouths; in any other place the public and the newspapers would long ago have torn this little Bastille to pieces.

"But, after all, what of it?" Andrey Yefimitch would ask himself, opening his eyes. "There is the antiseptic system, there is Koch, there is Pasteur, but the essential reality is not altered a bit; ill health and mortality are still the same. They get up balls and entertainments for the mad, but still they don't let them go free; so it's all nonsense and vanity, and there is no difference in reality between the best Vienna clinic and my hospital." But depression and a feeling akin to envy prevented him from feeling indifferent; it must have been owing to exhaustion. His heavy head sank on to the book, he put his hands under his face to make it softer, and thought: "I serve in a pernicious institution and receive a salary from people whom I am deceiving. I am not honest, but then, I of myself am nothing, I am only part of an inevitable social evil: all local officials are pernicious and receive their salary for doing nothing. . . . And so for my dishonesty it is not I who am to blame, but the times. . . . If I had been born two hundred years later I should have been different. . . ."

When it struck three he would put out his lamp and go into his bedroom; he was not sleepy.

VIII

Two years before, the Zemstvo in a liberal mood had decided to allow three hundred rubles a year to pay for additional medical service in the town till the Zemstvo hospital should be opened, and the district doctor, Yevgeny Fyodoritch Hobotov, was invited to the town to assist Andrey Yefimitch. He was a very young man—not yet thirty—tall and dark, with broad cheekbones and little eyes; his forefathers had probably come from one of the many alien races of Russia. He arrived in the town without a farthing, with a small portmanteau, and a plain young woman whom he called his cook. This woman had a baby at the breast. Yevgeny Fyodoritch used to go about in a cap with a peak, and in high boots, and in the winter wore a sheepskin. He made great friends with Sergey Sergeyitch, the medical assistant, and with the treasurer, but held aloof from the other officials, and for some reason called them aristocrats. He had only one book in his lodgings, *The Latest Prescriptions of the Vienna Clinic for 1881*. When he went to a patient he always took this book with him. He played billiards in the evening at the club: he did not like cards. He was very fond of using in conversation such expressions as "endless bobbery," "canting soft soap," "shut up with your finicking. . . ."

He visited the hospital twice a week, made the round of the wards, and saw outpatients. The complete absence of antiseptic treatment and the cupping roused his indignation, but he did not introduce any new system, being afraid of offending Andrey Yefimitch. He regarded his colleague as a sly old rascal, suspected him of being a man of large means, and secretly envied him. He would have been very glad to have his post.

IX

On a spring evening toward the end of March, when there was no snow left on the ground and the starlings were singing in the hospital garden, the doctor went out to see his friend the postmaster as far as the gate. At that very moment the Jew Moiseika, returning with his booty, came into the yard. He had no cap on, and his bare feet were thrust into galoshes; in his hand he had a little bag of coppers.

"Give me a kopeck!" he said to the doctor, smiling, and shivering with cold. Andrey Yefimitch, who could never refuse anyone anything, gave him a ten-kopeck piece.

"How bad that is!" he thought, looking at the Jew's bare feet with their thin red ankles. "Why, it's wet."

And stirred by a feeling akin both to pity and disgust, he went into the lodge behind the Jew, looking now at his bald head, now at his ankles. As the doctor went in, Nikita jumped up from his heap of litter and stood at attention.

"Good day, Nikita," Andrey Yefimitch said mildly. "That Jew should be provided with boots or something, he will catch cold."

"Certainly, Your Honor. I'll inform the superintendent."

"Please do; ask him in my name. Tell him that I asked."

The door into the ward was open. Ivan Dmitritch, lying propped on his elbow on the bed, listened in alarm to the unfamiliar voice, and suddenly recognized the doctor. He trembled all over with anger, jumped up, and with a red and wrathful face, with his eyes starting out of his head, ran out into the middle of the road.

"The doctor has come!" he shouted, and broke into a laugh. "At last! Gentlemen, I congratulate you. The doctor is honoring us with a visit! Cursed reptile!" he shrieked, and stamped in a frenzy such as had never been seen in the ward before. "Kill the reptile! No, killing's too good. Drown him in the midden-pit!"

Andrey Yefimitch, hearing this, looked into the ward from the entry and asked gently: "What for?"

"What for?" shouted Ivan Dmitritch, going up to him with a menacing air and convulsively wrapping himself in his dressing gown. "What for? Thief!" he said with a look of repulsion, moving his lips as though he would spit at him. "Quack! Hangman!"

"Calm yourself," said Andrey Yefimitch, smiling guiltily. "I assure you I have never stolen anything; and as to the rest, most likely you greatly exaggerate. I see you are angry with me. Calm yourself, I beg, if you can, and tell me coolly what are you angry for?"

"What are you keeping me here for?"

"Because you are ill."

"Yes, I am ill. But you know dozens, hundreds of madmen are walking about in freedom because your ignorance is incapable of distinguishing them from the sane. Why am I and these poor wretches to be shut up here like scapegoats for all the rest? You, your assistant, the superintendent, and all your hospital rabble, are immeasurably inferior to every one of us morally; why then are we shut up and you not? Where's the logic of it?"

"Morality and logic don't come in, it all depends on chance. If anyone is shut up he has to stay, and if anyone is not shut up he can walk about, that's all. There is neither morality nor logic in my being a doctor and your being a mental patient, there is nothing but idle chance."

"That twaddle I don't understand . . ." Ivan Dmitritch brought out in a hollow voice, and he sat down on his bed.

Moiseika, whom Nikita did not venture to search in the presence of the doctor, laid out on his bed pieces of bread, bits of paper, and little bones, and, still shivering with cold, began rapidly in a singsong voice saying something in Yiddish. He most likely imagined that he had opened a shop.

"Let me out," said Ivan Dmitritch, and his voice quivered.

"I cannot."

"But why, why?"

"Because it is not in my power. Think, what use will it be to you if I do let you out? Go. The townspeople or the police will detain you or bring you back."

"Yes, yes, that's true," said Ivan Dmitritch, and he rubbed his forehead. "It's awful! But what am I to do, what?"

Andrey Yefimitch liked Ivan Dmitritch's voice and his intelligent young face with its grimaces. He longed to be kind to the young man and soothe him; he sat down on the bed beside him, thought, and said:

"You ask me what to do. The very best thing in your position would be to run away. But, unhappily, that is useless. You would be taken up. When society protects itself from the criminal, mentally deranged, or otherwise inconvenient people, it is invincible. There is only one thing left for you: to resign yourself to the thought that your presence here is inevitable."

"It is no use to anyone."

"So long as prisons and madhouses exist someone must be shut up in them. If not you, I. If not I, some third person. Wait till in the distant future prisons and madhouses no longer exist, and there will be neither bars on the windows nor hospital gowns. Of course, that time will come sooner or later."

Ivan Dmitritch smiled ironically.

"You are jesting," he said, screwing up his eyes. "Such gentlemen as you and your assistant Nikita have nothing to do with the future, but you may be sure, sir, better days will come! I may express myself cheaply, you may laugh, but the dawn of a new life is at hand; truth and justice will triumph, and—our turn will come! I shall not live to see it, I shall perish, but some people's great-grandsons will see it. I greet them with all my heart and rejoice, rejoice with them! Onward! God be your help, friends!"

With shining eyes Ivan Dmitritch got up, and stretching his hands toward the window, went on with emotion in his voice:

"From behind these bars I bless you! Hurrah for truth and justice! I rejoice!"

"I see no particular reason to rejoice," said Andrey Yefimitch, who thought Ivan Dmitritch's movement theatrical, though he was delighted by it. "Prisons and madhouses there will not be, and truth, as you have just expressed it, will triumph; but the reality of things, you know, will not change, the laws of nature will still remain the same. People will suffer pain, grow old, and die just as they do now. However magnificent a dawn lighted up your life, you would yet in the end be nailed up in a coffin and thrown into a hole."

"And immortality?"

"Oh, come, now!"

"You don't believe in it, but I do. Somebody in Dostoevsky or Voltaire said that if there had not been a God men would have invented Him. And I firmly believe that if there is no immortality the great intellect of man will sooner or later invent it."

"Well said," observed Andrey Yefimitch, smiling with pleasure; "it's a good thing you have faith. With such a belief one may live happily even shut up within walls. You have studied somewhere, I presume?"

"Yes, I have been at the university, but did not complete my studies."

"You are a reflecting and a thoughtful man. In any surroundings you can find tranquillity in yourself. Free and deep thinking which strives for the comprehension of life, and complete contempt for the foolish bustle of the world—those are two blessings beyond any that man has ever known. And you can possess them even though you lived behind threefold bars. Diogenes lived in a tub, yet he was happier than all the kings of the earth."

"Your Diogenes was a blockhead," said Ivan Dmitritch morosely. "Why do you talk to me about Diogenes and some foolish comprehension of life?" he cried, growing suddenly angry and leaping up. "I love life; I love it passionately. I have the mania of persecution, a continual agonizing terror; but I have moments when I am overwhelmed by the thirst for life, and then I am afraid of going mad. I want dreadfully to live, dreadfully!"

He walked up and down the ward in agitation, and said, dropping his voice:

"When I dream I am haunted by phantoms. People come to me, I hear voices and music, and I fancy I am walking through woods or by the seashore, and I long so passionately for movement, for interests. . . . Come, tell me, what news is there?" asked Ivan Dmitritch; "what's happening?"

"Do you wish to know about the town or in general?"

"Well, tell me first about the town, and then in general."

"Well, in the town it is appallingly dull. . . . There's no one to say a word to, no one to listen to. There are no new people. A young doctor called Hobotov has come here recently."

"He had come in my time. Well, he is a low cad, isn't he?"

"Yes, he is a man of no culture. It's strange, you know. . . . Judging by every sign, there is no intellectual stagnation in our capital cities; there is a movement—so there must be real people there too; but for some reason they always send us such men as I would rather not see. It's an unlucky town!"

"Yes, it is an unlucky town," sighed Ivan Dmitritch, and he laughed. "And how are things in general? What are they writing in the papers and reviews?"

It was by now dark in the ward. The doctor got up, and, standing, began to describe what was being written abroad and in Russia, and the tendency of thought that could be noticed now. Ivan Dmitritch listened attentively and put questions, but suddenly, as though recalling something terrible, clutched at his head and lay down on the bed with his back to the doctor.

"What's the matter?" asked Andrey Yefimitch.

"You will not hear another word from me," said Ivan Dmitritch rudely. "Leave me alone."

"Why so?"

"I tell you, leave me alone. Why the devil do you persist?"

Andrey Yefimitch shrugged his shoulders, heaved a sigh, and went out. As he crossed the entry he said: "You might clear up here, Nikita . . . there's an awfully stuffy smell."

"Certainly, Your Honor."

"What an agreeable young man!" thought Andrey Yefimitch, going back to his flat. "In all the years I have been living here I do believe he is the first I have met with whom one can talk. He is capable of reasoning and is interested in just the right things."

While he was reading, and afterward, while he was going to bed, he kept thinking about Ivan Dmitritch, and when he woke next morning he remembered that he had the day before made the acquaintance of an intelligent and interesting man, and determined to visit him again as soon as possible.

X

Ivan Dmitritch was lying in the same position as on the previous day, with his head clutched in both hands and his legs drawn up. His face was not visible.

"Good day, my friend," said Andrey Yefimitch. "You are not asleep, are you?"

"In the first place, I am not your friend," Ivan Dmitritch articulated into the pillow; "and in the second, your efforts are useless; you will not get one word out of me."

"Strange," muttered Andrey Yefimitch in confusion. "Yesterday we talked peacefully, but suddenly for some reason you took offense and broke off all at once. . . . Probably I expressed myself awkwardly, or perhaps gave utterance to some idea which did not fit in with your convictions. . . ."

"Yes, a likely idea!" said Ivan Dmitritch, sitting up and looking at the doctor with irony and uneasiness. His eyes were red. "You can go and spy and probe somewhere else, it's no use your doing it here. I knew yesterday what you had come for."

"A strange fancy," laughed the doctor. "So you suppose me to be a spy?"

"Yes, I do. . . . A spy or a doctor who has been charged to test me—it's all the same—"

"Oh excuse me, what a queer fellow you are really!"

The doctor sat down on the stool near the bed and shook his head reproachfully.

"But let us suppose you are right," he said, "let us suppose that I am treacherously trying to trap you into saying something so as to betray you to the police. You would be arrested and then tried. But would you be any worse off being tried and in prison than you are here? If you are banished to a settlement, or even sent to penal servitude, would it be worse than being shut up in this ward? I imagine it would be no worse. . . . What, then, are you afraid of?"

These words evidently had an effect on Ivan Dmitritch. He sat down quietly.

It was between four and five in the afternoon—the time when Andrey Yefimitch usually walked up and down his rooms, and Daryushka asked whether it was not time for his beer. It was a still, bright day.

"I came out for a walk after dinner, and here I have come, as you see," said the doctor. "It is quite spring."

"What month is it? March?" asked Ivan Dmitritch.

"Yes, the end of March."

"Is it very muddy?"

"No, not very. There are already paths in the garden."

"It would be nice now to drive in an open carriage somewhere into the country," said Ivan Dmitritch, rubbing his red eyes as though he were just awake, "then to come home to a warm, snug study, and . . . and to have a decent doctor to cure one's headache. . . . It's so long since I have lived like a human being. It's disgusting here! Insufferably disgusting!"

After his excitement of the previous day he was exhausted and listless, and spoke unwillingly. His fingers twitched, and from his face it could be seen that he had a splitting headache.

"There is no real difference between a warm, snug study and this ward," said Andrey Yefimitch. "A man's peace and contentment do not lie outside a man, but in himself."

"What do you mean?"

"The ordinary man looks for good and evil in external things— that is, in carriages, in studies—but a thinking man looks for it in himself."

"You should go and preach that philosophy in Greece, where it's warm and fragrant with the scent of pomegranates, but here it is not suited to the climate. With whom was it I was talking of Diogenes? Was it with you?"

"Yes, with me yesterday."

"Diogenes did not need a study or a warm habitation; it's hot there without. You can lie in your tub and eat oranges and olives. But bring him to Russia to live: he'd be begging to be let indoors in May, let alone December. He'd be doubled up with the cold."

"No. One can be insensible to cold as to every other pain. Marcus Aurelius says: 'A pain is a vivid idea of pain; make an effort of will to change that idea, dismiss it, cease to complain, and the pain will disappear.' That is true. The wise man, or simply the reflecting, thoughtful man, is distinguished precisely by his contempt for suffering; he is always contented and surprised at nothing."

"Then I am an idiot, since I suffer and am discontented and surprised at the baseness of mankind."

"You are wrong in that; if you will reflect more on the subject you will understand how insignificant is all that external world that agitates us. One must strive for the comprehension of life, and in that is true happiness."

"Comprehension . . ." repeated Ivan Dmitritch, frowning. "External, internal. . . . Excuse me, but I don't understand it. I only know," he said, getting up and looking angrily at the doctor—"I only know that God has created me of warm blood and nerves, yes, indeed! If organic tissue is capable of life it must react to every stimulus. And I do! To pain I respond with tears and outcries, to baseness with indignation, to filth with loathing. To my mind, that is just what is called life. The lower the organism, the less sensitive it is, and the more feebly it reacts to stimulus; and the higher it is, the more responsively and vigorously it reacts to reality. How is it you don't know that? A doctor, and not know such trifles! To despise suffering, to be always contented, and to be surprised at nothing, one must reach this condition"—and Ivan Dmitritch pointed to the peasant who was a mass of fat—"or to harden oneself by suffering to such a point that one loses all sensibility to it—that is, in other words, to cease to live. You must excuse me, I am not a sage or a philosopher," Ivan Dmitritch continued with irritation, "and I don't understand anything about it. I am not capable of reasoning."

"On the contrary, your reasoning is excellent."

"The Stoics, whom you are parodying, were remarkable people, but their doctrine crystallized two thousand years ago and has not advanced, and will not advance, an inch forward, since it is not practical or living. It had a success only with the minority which spends its life in savoring all sorts of theories and ruminating over them; the majority did not understand it. A doctrine which advocates indifference to wealth and to the comforts of life, and a contempt for suffering and death, is quite unintelligible to the vast majority of men, since that majority has never known wealth or the comforts of life; and to despise suffering would mean to it despising life itself, since the whole existence of man is made up of the sensations of hunger, cold, injury, loss, and a Hamletlike dread of death. The whole of life lies in these sensations; one may be oppressed by it, one may hate it, but one cannot despise it. Yes, so, I repeat, the doctrine of the Stoics can never have a future; from the beginning of time up to today you see continually increasing the struggle, the sensibility to pain, the capacity of responding to stimulus."

Ivan Dmitritch suddenly lost the thread of his thoughts, stopped, and rubbed his forehead with vexation.

"I meant to say something important, but I have lost it," he said. "What was I saying? Oh, yes! This is what I mean: one of the Stoics sold himself into slavery to redeem his neighbor, so, you see, even a Stoic did react to stimulus, since, for such a generous act as the destruction of oneself for the sake of one's neighbor, he must have had a soul capable of pity and indignation. Here in prison I have forgotten everything I have learned, or else I could have recalled something else. Take Christ, for instance: Christ responded to reality by weeping, smiling, being sorrowful and moved to wrath, even overcome by misery. He did not go to meet His sufferings with a smile, He did not despise death, but prayed in the Garden of Gethsemane that this cup might pass Him by."

Ivan Dmitritch laughed and sat down.

"Granted that a man's peace and contentment lie not outside but in himself," he said, "granted that one must despise suffering and not be surprised at anything, yet on what ground do you preach the theory? Are you a sage? A philosopher?"

"No, I am not a philosopher, but everyone ought to preach it because it is reasonable."

"No, I want to know how it is that you consider yourself competent to judge of 'comprehension,' contempt for suffering, and so on. Have you ever suffered? Have you any idea of suffering? Allow me to ask you, were you ever thrashed in your childhood?"

"No, my parents had an aversion for corporal punishment."

"My father used to flog me cruelly; my father was a harsh, sickly government clerk with a long nose and a yellow neck. But let us talk of you. No one has laid a finger on you all your life, no one has scared you nor beaten you; you are as strong as a bull. You grew up under your father's wing and studied at his expense, and then you dropped at once into a sinecure. For more than twenty years you have lived rent free with heating, lighting, and service all provided, and had the right to work how you pleased and as much as you pleased, even to do nothing. You were naturally a flabby, lazy man, and so you have tried to arrange your life so that nothing should disturb you or make you move. You have handed over your work to the assistant and the rest of the rabble while you sit in peace and warmth, save money, read, amuse yourself with reflections, with all sorts of lofty nonsense, and" (Ivan Dmitritch looked at the doctor's red nose) "with boozing; in fact, you have seen nothing of life, you know absolutely nothing of it, and are only theoretically acquainted with reality; you despise suffering and are surprised at nothing for a very simple reason: vanity of vanities, the external and the internal, contempt for life, for suffering and for death, comprehension, true happiness—that's the philosophy that suits the Russian sluggard best. You see a peasant beating his wife, for instance. Why interfere? Let him beat her, they will both die sooner or later, anyway; and, besides, he who beats injures by his blows, not the person he is beating, but himself. To get drunk is stupid and unseemly, but if you drink you die, and if you don't drink you die. A peasant woman comes with toothache . . . well, what of it? Pain is the idea of pain, and besides, 'there is no living in this world without illness; we shall all die, and so, go away, woman, don't hinder me from thinking and drinking vodka.' A young man asks advice, what he is to do, how he is to live; anyone else would think before answering, but you have got the answer ready: strive for 'comprehension' or for true happiness. And what is that fantastic 'true happiness'? There's no answer, of course. We are kept here behind barred windows, tortured, left to rot; but that is very good and reasonable, because there is no difference at all between this ward and a warm, snug study. A convenient philosophy. You can do nothing, and your conscience is clear, and you feel you are wise. . . . No, sir, it is not philosophy, it's not thinking, it's not breadth of vision, but laziness, fakirism, drowsy stupefaction. Yes," cried Ivan Dmitritch, getting angry again, "you despise suffering, but I'll be bound if you pinch your finger in the door you will howl at the top of your voice."

"And perhaps I shouldn't howl," said Andrey Yefimitch, with a gentle smile.

"Oh, I dare say! Well, if you had a stroke of paralysis, or supposing some fool or bully took advantage of his position and rank to insult you in public, and if you knew he could do it with impunity, then you would understand what it means to put people off with comprehension and true happiness."

"That's original," said Andrey Yefimitch, laughing with pleasure and rubbing his hands. "I am agreeably struck by your inclination for drawing generalizations, and the sketch of my character you have just drawn is simply brilliant. I must confess that talking to you gives me great pleasure. Well, I've listened to you, and now you must graciously listen to me."

XI

The conversation went on for about an hour longer, and apparently made a deep impression on Andrey Yefimitch. He began going to the ward every day. He went there in the mornings and after dinner, and often the dusk of evening found him in conversation with Ivan Dmitritch. At first Ivan Dmitritch held aloof from him, suspected him of evil designs, and openly expressed his hostility. But afterward he got used to him, and his abrupt manner changed to one of condescending irony.

Soon it was all over the hospital that the doctor, Andrey Yefimitch, had taken to visiting Ward No. 6. No one—neither Sergey Sergeyitch, nor Nikita, nor the nurses—could conceive why he went there, why he stayed there for hours together, what he was talking about, and why he did not write prescriptions. His actions seemed strange. Often Mihail Averyanitch did not find him at home, which had never happened in the past, and Daryushka was greatly perturbed, for the doctor drank his beer now at no definite time, and sometimes was even late for dinner.

One day—it was at the end of June—Dr. Hobotov went to see Andrey Yefimitch about something. Not finding him at home, he proceeded to look for him in the yard; there he was told that the old doctor had gone to see the mental patients. Going into the lodge and stopping in the entry, Hobotov heard the following conversation:

"We shall never agree, and you will not succeed in converting me to your faith," Ivan Dmitritch was saying irritably; "you are utterly ignorant of reality, and you have never known suffering, but have only like a leech fed beside the sufferings of others, while I have been in continual suffering from the day of my birth till today. For that reason, I tell you frankly, I consider myself superior to you and more competent in every respect. It's not for you to teach me."

"I have absolutely no ambition to convert you to my faith," said Andrey Yefimitch gently, and with regret that the other refused to understand him. "And that is not what matters, my friend; what matters is not that you have suffered and I have not. Joy and suffering are passing; let us leave them, never mind them. What matters is that you and I think; we see in each other people who are capable of thinking and reasoning, and that is a common bond between us however different our views. If you knew, my friend, how sick I am of the universal senselessness, ineptitude, stupidity, and with what delight I always talk with you! You are an intelligent man, and I enjoyed your company."

Hobotov opened the door an inch and glanced into the ward; Ivan Dmitritch in his nightcap and the doctor Andrey Yefimitch were sitting side by side on the bed. The madman was grimacing, twitching, and convulsively wrapping himself in his gown, while the doctor sat motionless with bowed head, and his face was red and look helpless and sorrowful. Hobotov shrugged his shoulders, grinned, and glanced at Nikita. Nikita shrugged his shoulders too.

Next day Hobotov went to the lodge, accompanied by the assistant. Both stood in the entry and listened.

"I fancy our old man has gone clean off his chump!" said Hobotov as he came out of the lodge.

"Lord have mercy upon us sinners!" sighed the decorous Sergey Sergeyitch, scrupulously avoiding the puddles that he might not muddy his polished boots. "I must own, honored Yevgeny Fyodoritch, I have been expecting it for a long time."

XII

After this Andrey Yefimitch began to notice a mysterious air in all around him. The attendants, the nurses, and the patients looked at him inquisitively when they met him, and then whispered together. The superintendent's little daughter Masha, whom he liked to meet in the hospital garden, for some reason ran away from him now when he went up with a smile to stroke her on the head. The postmaster no longer said, "Perfectly true," as he listened to him, but in unaccountable confusion muttered, "Yes, yes, yes . . ." and looked at him with a grieved and thoughtful expression; for some reason he took to advising his friend to give up vodka and beer, but as a man of delicate feeling he did not say this directly, but hinted it, telling him first about the commanding officer of his battalion, an excellent man, and then about the priest of the regiment, a capital fellow, both of whom drank and fell ill, but on giving up drinking completely regained their health. On two or three occasions Andrey Yefimitch was visited by his colleague Hobotov, who also advised him to give up spirituous liquors, and for no apparent reason recommended him to take bromide.

In August Andrey Yefimitch got a letter from the mayor of the town asking him to come on very important business. On arriving at the town hall at the time fixed, Andrey Yefimitch found there the military commander, the superintendent of the district school, a member of the town council, Hobotov, and a plump, fair gentleman who was introduced to him as a doctor. This doctor, with a Polish surname difficult to pronounce, lived at a pedigree stud-farm twenty miles away, and was now on a visit to the town.

"There's something that concerns you," said the member of the town council, addressing Andrey Yefimitch after they had all greeted one another and sat down to the table. "Here Yevgeny Fyodoritch says that there is not room for the dispensary in the main building, and that it ought to be transferred to one of the lodges. That's of no consequence—of course it can be transferred, but the point is that the lodge wants doing up."

"Yes, it would have to be done up," said Andrey Yefimitch after a moment's thought. "If the corner lodge, for instance, were fitted up as a dispensary, I imagine it would cost at least five hundred rubles. An unproductive expenditure!"

Everyone was silent for a space.

"I had the honor of submitting to you ten years ago," Andrey Yefimitch went on in a low voice, "that the hospital in its present form is a luxury for the town beyond its means. It was built in the forties, but things were different then. The town spends too much on unnecessary buildings and superfluous staff. I believe with a different system two model hospitals might be maintained for the same money."

"Well, let us have a different system, then!" the member of the town council said briskly.

"I have already had the honor of submitting to you that the medical department should be transferred to the supervision of the Zemstvo."

"Yes, transfer the money to the Zemstvo and they will steal it," laughed the fair-haired doctor.

"That's what it always comes to," the member of the council assented, and he also laughed.

Andrey Yefimitch looked with apathetic, lusterless eyes at the fair-haired doctor and said: "One should be just."

Again there was silence. Tea was brought in. The military commander, for some reason much embarrassed, touched Andrey Yefimitch's hand across the table and said: "You have quite forgotten us, Doctor. But of course you are a hermit: you don't play cards and don't like women. You would be dull with fellows like us."

They all began saying how boring it was for a decent person to live in such a town. No theater, no music, and at the last dance at the club there had been about twenty ladies and only two gentlemen. The young men did not dance, but spent all the time crowding round the refreshment bar or playing cards.

Not looking at anyone and speaking slowly in a low voice, Andrey Yefimitch began saying what a pity, what a terrible pity it was that the townspeople should waste their vital energy, their hearts, and their minds on cards and gossip, and should have neither the power nor the inclination to spend their time in interesting conversation and reading, and should refuse to take advantage of the enjoyments of the mind. The mind alone was interesting and worthy of attention, all the rest was low and petty. Hobotov listened to his colleague attentively and suddenly asked:

"Andrey Yefimitch, what day of the month is it?"

Having received an answer, the fair-haired doctor and he, in the tone of examiners conscious of their lack of skill, began asking Andrey Yefimitch what was the day of the week, how many days there were in the year, and whether it was true that there was a remarkable prophet living in Ward No. 6.

In response to the last question Andrey Yefimitch turned rather red and said: "Yes, he is mentally deranged, but he is an interesting young man."

They asked him no other questions.

When he was putting on his overcoat in the entry, the military commander laid a hand on his shoulder and said with a sigh:

"It's time for us old fellows to rest!"

As he came out of the hall, Andrey Yefimitch understood that it had been a committee appointed to inquire into his mental condition. He recalled the questions that had been asked him, flushed crimson, and for some reason, for the first time in his life, felt bitterly grieved for medical science.

"My God . . ." he thought, remembering how these doctors had just examined him; "why, they have only lately been hearing lectures on mental pathology; they had passed an examination—what's the explanation of this crass ignorance? They have not a conception of mental pathology!"

And for the first time in his life he felt insulted and moved to anger.

In the evening of the same day Mihail Averyanitch came to see him. The postmaster went up to him without waiting to greet him, took him by both hands, and said in an agitated voice:

"My dear fellow, my dear friend, show me that you believe in my genuine affection and look on me as your friend!" And preventing Andrey Yefimitch from speaking, he went on, growing excited: "I love you for your culture and nobility of soul. Listen to me, my dear fellow. The rules of their profession compel the doctors to conceal the truth from you, but I blurt out the plain truth like a soldier. You are not well! Excuse me, my dear fellow, but it is the truth; everyone about you has been noticing it for a long time. Dr. Yevgeny Fyodoritch has just told me that it is essential for you to rest and distract your mind for the sake of your health. Perfectly true! Excellent! In a day or two I am taking a holiday and am going away for a sniff of a different atmosphere. Show that you are a friend to me, let us go together! Let us go for a jaunt as in the good old days."

"I feel perfectly well," said Andrey Yefimitch after a moment's thought. "I can't go away. Allow me to show you my friendship in some other way."

To go off with no object, without his books, without his Daryushka, without his beer, to break abruptly through the routine of life, established for twenty years—the idea for the first minute struck him as wild and fantastic, but he remembered the conversation at the Zemstvo committee and the depressing feelings with which he had returned home, and the thought of a brief absence from the town in which stupid people looked on him as a madman was pleasant to him.

"And where precisely do you intend to go?" he asked.

"To Moscow, to Petersburg, to Warsaw. . . . I spent the five happiest years of my life in Warsaw. What a marvelous town! Let us go, my dear fellow!"

XIII

A week later it was suggested to Andrey Yefimitch that he should have a rest—that is, send in his resignation—a suggestion he received with indifference, and a week later still, Mihail Averyanitch and he were sitting in a posting carriage driving to the nearest railway station. The days were cool and bright, with a blue sky and a transparent distance. They were two days driving the hundred and fifty miles to the railway station, and stayed two nights on the way. When at the posting station the glasses given them for their tea had not been properly washed, or the drivers were slow in harnessing the horses, Mihail Averyanitch would turn crimson, and quivering all over would shout:

"Hold your tongue! Don't argue!"

And in the carriage he talked without ceasing for a moment, describing his campaigns in the Caucasus and in Poland. What adventures he had had, what meetings! He talked loudly and opened his eyes so wide with wonder that he might well be thought to be lying. Moreover, as he talked he breathed in Andrey Yefimitch's face and laughed into his ear. This bothered the doctor and prevented him from thinking or concentrating his mind.

In the train they traveled, from motives of economy, third class in a nonsmoking compartment. Half the passengers were decent people. Mihail Averyanitch soon made friends with everyone, and moving from one seat to another, kept saying loudly that they ought not to travel by these appalling lines. It was a regular swindle! A very different thing riding on a good horse: one could do over seventy miles a day and feel fresh and well after it. And our bad harvests were due to the draining of the Pinsk marshes; altogether, the way things were done was dreadful. He got excited, talked loudly, and would not let others speak. This endless chatter to the accompaniment of loud laughter and expressive gestures wearied Andrey Yefimitch.

"Which of us is the madman?" he thought with vexation. "I, who try not to disturb my fellow passengers in any way, or this egoist who thinks that he is cleverer and more interesting than anyone here, and so will leave no one in peace?"

In Moscow Mihail Averyanitch put on a military coat without epaulettes and trousers with red braid on them. He wore a military cap and overcoat in the street, and soldiers saluted him. It seemed to Andrey Yefimitch, now, that his companion was a man who had flung away all that was good and kept only what was bad of all the characteristics of a country gentleman that he had once possessed. He liked to be waited on even when it was quite unnecessary. The matches would be lying before him on the table, and he would see them and shout to the waiter to give him the matches; he did not hesitate to appear before a maidservant in nothing but his underclothes; he used the familiar mode of address to all footmen indiscriminately, even old men, and when he was angry called them fools and blockheads. This, Andrey Yefimitch thought, was like a gentleman, but disgusting.

First of all Mihail Averyanitch led his friend to the Iversky Madonna. He prayed fervently, shedding tears and bowing down to the earth, and when he had finished, heaved a deep sigh and said:

"Even though one does not believe it makes one somehow easier when one prays a little. Kiss the icon, my dear fellow."

Andrey Yefimitch was embarrassed and he kissed the image, while Mihail Averyanitch pursed up his lips and prayed in a whisper, and again tears came into his eyes. Then they went to the Kremlin and looked there at the Tsar cannon and the Tsar bell, and even touched them with their fingers, admired the view over the river, visited St. Savior's and the Rumyantsev museum.

They dined at Tyestov's. Mihail Averyanitch looked a long time at the menu, stroking his whiskers, and said in the tone of a gourmand accustomed to dine in restaurants:

"We shall see what you give us to eat today, angel!"

XIV

The doctor walked about, looked at things, ate and drank, but he had all the while one feeling: annoyance with Mihail Averyanitch. He longed to have a rest from his friend, to get away from him, to hide himself, while the friend thought it was his duty not to let the doctor move a step away from him, and to provide him with as many distractions as possible. When there was nothing to look at he entertained him with conversation. For two days Andrey Yefimitch endured it, but on the third he announced to his friend that he was ill and wanted to stay at home for the whole day; his friend replied that in that case he would stay too—that really he needed rest, for he was run off his legs already. Andrey Yefimitch lay on the sofa, with his face to the back, and clenching his teeth, listened to his friend, who assured him with heat that sooner or later France would certainly thrash Germany, that there were a great many scoundrels in Moscow, and that it was impossible to judge of a horse's quality by its outward appearance. The doctor began to have a buzzing in his ears and palpitations of the heart, but out of delicacy could not bring himself to beg his friend to go away or hold his tongue. Fortunately Mihail Averyanitch grew weary of sitting in the hotel room, and after dinner he went out for a walk.

As soon as he was alone Andrey Yefimitch abandoned himself to a feeling of relief. How pleasant to lie motionless on the sofa and to know that one is alone in the room! Real happiness is impossible without solitude. The fallen angel betrayed God probably because he longed for solitude, of which the angels know nothing. Andrey Yefimitch wanted to think about what he had seen and heard during the last few days, but he could not get Mihail Averyanitch out of his head.

"Why, he has taken a holiday and come with me out of friend-ship, out of generosity," thought the doctor with vexation; "nothing could be worse than this friendly supervision. I suppose he is good-natured and generous and a lively fellow, but he is a bore. An insufferable bore. In the same way there are people who never say anything but what is clever and good, yet one feels that they are dull-witted people."

For the following days Andrey Yefimitch declared himself ill and would not leave the hotel room; he lay with his face to the back of the sofa, and suffered agonies of weariness when his friend enter-tained him with conversation, or rested when his friend was absent. He was vexed with himself for having come, and with his friend, who grew every day more talkative and more free-and-easy; he could not succeed in attuning his thoughts to a serious and lofty level.

"This is what I get from the real life Ivan Dmitritch talked about," he thought, angry at his own pettiness. "It's of no consequence, though. . . . I shall go home, and everything will go on as before. . . ."

It was the same thing in Petersburg too; for whole days together he did not leave the hotel room, but lay on the sofa and only got up to drink beer.

Mihail Averyanitch was all haste to get to Warsaw.

"My dear man, what should I go there for?" said Andrey Yefimitch in an imploring voice. "You go alone and let me get home! I entreat you!"

"On no account," protested Mihail Averyanitch. "It's a marvelous town."

Andrey Yefimitch had not the strength of will to insist on his own way, and much against his inclination went to Warsaw. There he did not leave the hotel room, but lay on the sofa, furious with himself, with his friend, and with the waiters, who obstinately refused to understand Russian; while Mihail Averyanitch, healthy, hearty, and full of spirits as usual, went about the town from morning to night, looking for his old acquaintances. Several times he did not return home at night. After one night spent in some unknown haunt he returned home early in the morning, in a violently excited condition, with a red face and tousled hair. For a long time he walked up and down the rooms muttering something to himself, then stopped and said:

"Honor before everything."

After walking up and down a little longer he clutched his head in both hands and pronounced in a tragic voice: "Yes, honor before everything! Accursed be the moment when the idea first entered my head to visit this Babylon! My dear friend," he added, addressing the doctor, "you may despise me, I have played and lost; lend me five hundred rubles!"

Andrey Yefimitch counted out five hundred rubles and gave them to his friend without a word. The latter, still crimson with shame and anger, incoherently articulated some useless vow, put on his cap, and went out. Returning two hours later he flopped into an easy chair, heaved a loud sigh, and said:

"My honor is saved. Let us go, my friend; I do not care to remain another hour in this accursed town. Scoundrels! Austrian spies!"

By the time the friends were back in their own town it was November, and deep snow was lying in the streets. Dr. Hobotov had Andrey Yefimitch's post; he was still living in his old lodgings, waiting for Andrey Yefimitch to arrive and clear out of the hospital apartments. The plain woman whom he called his cook was already established in one of the lodges.

Fresh scandals about the hospital were going the round of the town. It was said that the plain woman had quarreled with the superintendent, and that the latter had crawled on his knees before her begging forgiveness. On the very first day he arrived Andrey Yefimitch had to look out for lodgings.

"My friend," the postmaster said to him timidly, "excuse an indiscreet question: what means have you at your disposal?"

Andrey Yefimitch, without a word, counted out his money and said: "Eighty-six rubles."

"I don't mean that," Mihail Averyanitch brought out in confusion, misunderstanding him; "I mean, what have you to live on?"

"I tell you, eighty-six rubles . . . I have nothing else."

Mihail Averyanitch looked upon the doctor as an honorable man, yet he suspected that he had accumulated a fortune of at least twenty thousand. Now learning that Andrey Yefimitch was a beggar, that he had nothing to live on, he was for some reason suddenly moved to tears and embraced his friend.

XV

Andrey Yefimitch now lodged in a little house with three windows. There were only three rooms besides the kitchen in the little house.

The doctor lived in two of them which looked into the street, while Daryushka and the landlady with her three children lived in the third room and the kitchen. Sometimes the landlady's lover, a drunken peasant who was rowdy and reduced the children and Daryushka to terror, would come for the night. When he arrived and established himself in the kitchen and demanded vodka, they all felt very uncomfortable, and the doctor would be moved by pity to take the crying children into his room and let them lie on his floor, and this gave him great satisfaction.

He got up as before at eight o'clock, and after his morning tea sat down to read his old books and magazines: he had no money for new ones. Either because the books were old, or perhaps because of the change in his surroundings, reading exhausted him, and did not grip his attention as before. That he might not spend his time in idleness he made a detailed catalog of his books and gummed little labels on their backs, and this mechanical, tedious work seemed to him more interesting than reading. The monotonous, tedious work lulled his thoughts to sleep in some unaccountable way, and the time passed quickly while he thought of nothing. Even sitting in the kitchen, peeling potatoes with Daryushka or picking over the buckwheat grain, seemed to him interesting. On Saturdays and Sundays he went to church. Standing near the wall and half closing his eyes, he listened to the singing and thought of his father, of his mother, of the university, of the religions of the world; he felt calm and melancholy, and as he went out of the church afterward he regretted that the service was so soon over. He went twice to the hospital to talk to Ivan Dmitritch. But on both occasions Ivan Dmitritch was unusually excited and ill-humored; he bade the doctor leave him in peace, as he had long been sick of empty chatter, and declared, to make up for all his sufferings, he asked from the damned scoundrels only one favor—solitary confinement. Surely they would not refuse him even that? On both occasions when Andrey Yefimitch was taking leave of him and wishing him good night, he answered rudely and said:

"Go to hell!"

And Andrey Yefimitch did not know now whether to go to him for the third time or not. He longed to go.

In old days Andrey Yefimitch used to walk about his rooms and think in the interval after dinner, but now from dinnertime till evening tea he lay on the sofa with his face to the back and gave himself up to trivial thoughts which he could not struggle against. He was mortified that after more than twenty years of service he had been given neither a pension nor any assistance. It is true that he had not done his work honestly, but, then, all who are in the Service get a pension without distinction whether they are honest or not. Contemporary justice lies precisely in the bestowal of grades, orders, and pensions, not for moral qualities or capacities, but for service whatever it may have been like. Why was he alone to be an exception? He had no money at all. He was ashamed to pass by the shop and look at the woman who owned it. He owed thirty-two rubles for beer already. There was money owing to the landlady also. Daryushka sold old clothes and books on the sly, and told lies to the landlady, saying that the doctor was just going to receive a large sum of money.

He was angry with himself for having wasted on traveling the thousand rubles he had saved up. How useful that thousand rubles would have been now! He was vexed that people would not leave him in peace. Hobotov thought it his duty to look in on his sick colleague from time to time. Everything about him was revolting to Andrey Yefimitch—his well-fed face and vulgar, condescending tone, and his use of the word "colleague," and his high top boots; the most revolting thing was that he thought it was his duty to treat Andrey Yefimitch, and thought that he really was treating him. On every visit he brought a bottle of bromide and rhubarb pills.

Mihail Averyanitch, too, thought it his duty to visit his friend and entertain him. Every time he went in to Andrey Yefimitch with an affectation of ease, laughed constrainedly, and began assuring him that he was looking very well today, and that, thank God, he was on the high road to recovery, and from this it might be concluded that he looked on his friend's condition as hopeless. He had not yet repaid his Warsaw debt, and was overwhelmed by shame; he was constrained, and so tried to laugh louder and talk more amusingly. His anecdotes and descriptions seemed endless now, and were an agony both to Andrey Yefimitch and himself.

In his presence Andrey Yefimitch usually lay on the sofa with his face to the wall, and listened with his teeth clenched; his soul was oppressed with rankling disgust, and after every visit from his friend he felt as though this disgust had risen higher, and was mounting into his throat.

To stifle petty thoughts he made haste to reflect that he himself, and Hobotov, and Mihail Averyanitch, would all sooner or later perish without leaving any trace on the world. If one imagined some spirit flying by the earthly globe in space in a million years he would see nothing but clay and bare rocks. Everything—culture and the moral law—would pass away and not even a burdock would grow out of them. Of what consequence was shame in the presence of a shopkeeper, of what consequence was the insignificant Hobotov or the wearisome friendship of Mihail Averyanitch? It was all trivial and nonsensical.

But such reflections did not help him now. Scarcely had he imagined the earthly globe in a million years, when Hobotov in his high top boots or Mihail Averyanitch with his forced laugh would appear from behind a bare rock, and he even heard the shamefaced whisper: "The Warsaw debt. . . . I will repay it in a day or two, my dear fellow, without fail. . . ."

XVI

One day Mihail Averyanitch came after dinner when Andrey Yefimitch was lying on the sofa. It so happened that Hobotov arrived at the same time with his bromide. Andrey Yefimitch got up heavily and sat down, leaning both arms on the sofa.

"You have a much better color today than you had yesterday, my dear man," began Mihail Averyanitch. "Yes, you look jolly. Upon my soul, you do!"

"It's high time you were well, dear colleague," said Hobotov, yawning. "I'll be bound, you are sick of this bobbery."

"And we shall recover," said Mihail Averyanitch cheerfully. "We shall live another hundred years! To be sure!"

"Not a hundred years, but another twenty," Hobotov said reassuringly. "It's all right, all right, colleague; don't lose heart. . . . Don't go piling it on!"

"We'll show what we can do," laughed Mihail Averyanitch, and he slapped his friend on the knee. "We'll show them yet! Next summer, please God, we shall be off to the Caucasus, and we will ride all over it on horseback—trot, trot, trot! And when we are back from the Caucasus I shouldn't wonder if we will all dance at the wedding." Mihail Averyanitch gave a sly wink. "We'll marry you, my dear boy, we'll marry you. . . ."

Andrey Yefimitch felt suddenly that the rising disgust had mounted to his throat, his heart began beating violently.

"That's vulgar," he said, getting up quickly and walking away to the window. "Don't you understand that you are talking vulgar nonsense?"

He meant to go on softly and politely, but against his will he suddenly clenched his fists and raised them above his head.

"Leave me alone," he shouted in a voice unlike his own, blushing crimson and shaking all over. "Go away, both of you!"

Mihail Averyanitch and Hobotov got up and stared at him first with amazement and then with alarm.

"Go away, both!" Andrey Yefimitch went on shouting. "Stupid people! Foolish people! I don't want either your friendship or your medicines, stupid man! Vulgar! Nasty!"

Hobotov and Mihail Averyanitch, looking at each other in bewilderment, staggered to the door and went out. Andrey Yefimitch snatched up the bottle of bromide and flung it after them; the bottle broke with a crash on the door frame.

"Go to the devil!" he shouted in a tearful voice, running out into the passage. "To the devil!"

When his guests were gone Andrey Yefimitch lay down on the sofa, trembling as though in a fever, and went on for a long while repeating: "Stupid people! Foolish people!"

When he was calmer, what occurred to him first of all was the thought that poor Mihail Averyanitch must be feeling fearfully ashamed and depressed now, and that it was all dreadful. Nothing like this had ever happened to him before. Where was his intelligence and his tact? Where was his comprehension of things and his philosophical indifference?

The doctor could not sleep all night for shame and vexation with himself, and at ten o'clock next morning he went to the post office and apologized to the postmaster.

"We won't think again of what has happened," Mihail Averyanitch, greatly touched, said with a sigh, warmly pressing his hand. "Let bygones by bygones. Lyubavkin," he suddenly shouted so loud that all the postmen and other persons present started, "hand a chair; and you wait," he shouted to a peasant woman who was stretching out a registered letter to him through the grating. "Don't you see that I am busy? We will not remember the past," he went on, affectionately addressing Andrey Yefimitch; "sit down, I beg you, my dear fellow."

For a minute he stroked his knees in silence, and then said:

"I have never had a thought of taking offense. Illness is no joke, I understand. Your attack frightened the doctor and me yesterday, and we had a long talk about you afterward. My dear friend, why won't you treat your illness seriously? You can't go on like this. . . . Excuse me speaking openly as a friend," whispered Mihail Averyanitch. "You live in the most unfavorable surroundings, in a crowd, in uncleanliness, no one to look after you, no money for proper treatment. . . . My dear friend, the doctor and I implore you with all our hearts, listen to our advice: go into the hospital! There you will have wholesome food and attendance and treatment. Though, between ourselves, Yevgeny Fyodoritch is *mauvais ton*, yet he does understand his work, you can fully rely upon him. He has promised me he will look after you."

Andrey Yefimitch was touched by the postmaster's genuine sympathy and the tears which suddenly glittered on his cheeks.

"My honored friend, don't believe it!" he whispered, laying his hand on his heart; "don't believe them. It's all a sham. My illness is only that in twenty years I have only found one intelligent man in the whole town, and he is mad. I am not ill at all, it's simply that I have got into an enchanted circle which there is no getting out of. I don't care; I am ready for anything."

"Go into the hospital, my dear fellow."

"I don't care if it were into the pit."

"Give me your word, my dear man, that you will obey Yevgeny Fyodoritch in everything."

"Certainly I will give you my word. But I repeat, my honored friend, I have got into an enchanted circle. Now everything, even the genuine sympathy of my friends, leads to the same thing—to my ruin. I am going to my ruin, and I have the manliness to recognize it."

"My dear fellow, you will recover."

"What's the use of saying that?" said Andrey Yefimitch, with irritation. "There are few men who at the end of their lives do not experience what I am experiencing now. When you are told that you have something such as diseased kidneys or enlarged heart, and you begin being treated for it, or are told you are mad or a criminal—that is, in fact, when people suddenly turn their attention to you—you may be sure you have got into an enchanted circle from which you will not escape. You will try to escape and make things worse. You had better give in, for no human efforts can save you. So it seems to me."

Meanwhile the public was crowding at the grating. That he might not be in their way, Andrey Yefimitch got up and began to take leave.

Mihail Averyanitch made him promise on his honor once more, and escorted him to the outer door.

Toward evening on the same day Hobotov, in his sheepskin and his high top boots, suddenly made his appearance, and said to Andrey Yefimitch in a tone as though nothing had happened the day before:

"I have come on business, colleague. I have come to ask you whether you would not join me in a consultation. Eh?"

Thinking that Hobotov wanted to distract his mind with an outing, or perhaps really to enable him to earn something, Andrey Yefimitch put on his coat and hat, and went out with him into the street. He was glad of the opportunity to smooth over his fault of the previous day and to be reconciled, and in his heart thanked Hobotov, who did not even allude to yesterday's scene and was evidently sparing him. One would never have expected such delicacy from this uncultured man.

"Where is your invalid?" asked Andrey Yefimitch.

"In the hospital. . . . I have long wanted to show him to you. A very interesting case."

They went into the hospital yard, and going round the main building, turned toward the lodge where the mental cases were kept, and all this, for some reason, in silence. When they went into the lodge Nikita as usual jumped up and stood at attention.

"One of the patients here has a lung complication," Hobotov said in an undertone, going into the yard with Andrey Yefimitch. "You wait here, I'll be back directly. I am going for a stethoscope."

And he went away.

XVII

It was getting dusk. Ivan Dmitritch was lying on his bed with his face thrust into his pillow; the paralytic was sitting motionless, crying quietly and moving his lips. The fat peasant and the former sorter were asleep. It was quiet.

Andrey Yefimitch sat down on Ivan Dmitritch's bed and waited. But half an hour passed, and instead of Hobotov, Nikita came into the ward with a dressing gown, some underlinen, and a pair of slippers in a heap on his arm.

"Please change your things, Your Honor," he said softly. "Here is your bed; come this way," he added, pointing to an empty bedstead which had obviously recently been brought into the ward. "It's all right; please God, you will recover."

Andrey Yefimitch understood it all. Without saying a word he crossed to the bed to which Nikita pointed and sat down; seeing that Nikita was standing waiting, he undressed entirely and he felt ashamed. Then he put on the hospital clothes; the drawers were very short, the shirt was long, and the dressing gown smelt of smoked fish.

"Please God, you will recover," repeated Nikita, and he gathered up Andrey Yefimitch's clothes into his arms, went out, and shut the door after him.

"No matter . . ." thought Andrey Yefimitch, wrapping himself in his dressing gown in a shamefaced way and feeling that he looked like a convict in his new costume. "It's no matter. . . . It does not matter whether it's a dress coat or a uniform or this dressing gown. . . ."

But how about his watch? And the notebook that was in the side pocket? And his cigarettes? Where had Nikita taken his clothes? Now perhaps to the day of his death he would not put on trousers, a waistcoat, and high boots. It was all somehow strange and even incomprehensible at first. Andrey Yefimitch was even now convinced that there was no difference between his landlady's house and Ward No. 6, that everything in this world was nonsense and vanity of vanities. And yet his hands were trembling, his feet were cold, and he was filled with dread at the thought that soon Ivan Dmitritch would get up and see that he was in a dressing gown. He got up and walked across the room and sat down again.

Here he had been sitting already half an hour, an hour, and he was miserably sick of it: was it really possible to live here a day, a week, and even years like these people? Why, he had been sitting here, had walked about and sat down again; he could get up and look out of the window and walk from corner to corner again, and then what? Sit so all the time, like a post, and think? No, that was scarcely possible.

Andrey Yefimitch lay down, but at once got up, wiped the cold sweat from his brow with his sleeve and felt that his whole face smelt of smoked fish. He walked about again.

"It's some misunderstanding . . ." he said, turning out the palms of his hands in perplexity. "It must be cleared up. There is a misunderstanding. . . ."

Meanwhile Ivan Dmitritch woke up; he sat up and propped his cheeks on his fists. He spat. Then he glanced lazily at the doctor, and apparently for the first minute did not understand; but soon his sleepy face grew malicious and mocking.

"Aha! so they have put you in here, too, old fellow?" he said in a voice husky from sleepiness, screwing up one eye. "Very glad to see you. You sucked the blood of others, and now they will suck yours. Excellent!"

"It's a misunderstanding . . ." Andrey Yefimitch brought out, frightened by Ivan Dmitritch's words; he shrugged his shoulders and repeated: "It's some misunderstanding. . . ."

Ivan Dmitritch spat again and lay down.

"Cursed life," he grumbled, "and what's bitter and insulting, this life will not end in compensation for our sufferings, it will not end with apotheosis as it would in an opera, but with death; peasants will come and drag one's dead body by the arms and the legs to the cellar. Ugh! Well, it does not matter. . . . We shall have our good time in the other world. . . . I shall come here as a ghost from the other world and frighten these reptiles. I'll turn their hair gray."

Moiseika returned, and, seeing the doctor, held out his hand.

"Give me one little kopeck," he said.

XVIII

Andrey Yefimitch walked away to the window and looked out into the open country. It was getting dark, and on the horizon to the right a cold crimson moon was mounting upward. Not far from the hospital fence, not much more than two hundred yards away, stood a tall white house shut in by a stone wall. This was the prison.

"So this is real life," thought Andrey Yefimitch, and he felt frightened.

The moon and the prison, and the nails on the fence, and the faraway flames at the bone-charring factory were all terrible. Behind him there was the sound of a sigh. Andrey Yefimitch looked round and saw a man with glittering stars and orders on his breast, who was smiling and slyly winking. And this, too, seemed terrible.

Andrey Yefimitch assured himself that there was nothing special about the moon or the prison, that even sane persons wear orders, and that everything in time will decay and turn to earth, but he was suddenly overcome with desire; he clutched at the grating with both hands and shook it with all his might. The strong grating did not yield.

Then that it might not be so dreadful he went to Ivan Dmitritch's bed and sat down.

"I have lost heart, my dear fellow," he muttered, trembling and wiping away the cold sweat, "I have lost heart."

"You should be philosophical," said Ivan Dmitritch ironically.

"My God, my God. . . . Yes, yes. . . . You were pleased to say once that there was no philosophy in Russia, but that all people, even the paltriest, talk philosophy. But you know the philosophizing of the paltriest does not harm anyone," said Andrey Yefimitch in a tone as if he wanted to cry and complain. "Why, then, that malignant laugh, my friend, and how can these paltry creatures help philosophizing if they are not satisfied? For an intelligent, educated man, made in God's image, proud and loving freedom, to have no alternative but to be a doctor in a filthy, stupid, wretched little town, and to spend his whole life among bottles, leeches, mustard plasters! Quackery, narrowness, vulgarity! Oh, my God!"

"You are talking nonsense. If you don't like being a doctor you should have gone in for being a statesman."

"I could not, I could not do anything. We are weak, my dear friend. . . . I used to be indifferent. I reasoned boldly and soundly, but at the first coarse touch of life upon me I have lost heart. . . . Prostration. . . . We are weak, we are poor creatures . . . and you, too, my dear friend, you are intelligent, generous, you drew in good impulses with your mother's milk, but you had hardly entered upon life when you were exhausted and fell ill. . . . Weak, weak!"

Andrey Yefimitch was all the while at the approach of evening tormented by another persistent sensation besides terror and the feeling of resentment. At last he realized that he was longing for a smoke and for beer.

"I am going out, my friend," he said. "I will tell them to bring a light; I can't put up with this. . . . I am not equal to it. . . ."

Andrey Yefimitch went to the door and opened it, but at once Nikita jumped up and barred his way.

"Where are you going? You can't, you can't!" he said. "It's bedtime."

"But I'm only going out for a minute to walk about the yard," said Andrey Yefimitch.

"You can't, you can't; it's forbidden. You know that yourself."

"But what difference will it make to anyone if I do go out?" asked Andrey Yefimitch, shrugging his shoulders. "I don't understand. Nikita, I must go out!" he said in a trembling voice. "I must."

"Don't be disorderly, it's not right," Nikita said peremptorily.

"This is beyond everything," Ivan Dmitritch cried suddenly, and he jumped up. "What right has he not to let you out? How dare they keep us here? I believe it is clearly laid down in the law that no one can be deprived of freedom without trial! It's an outrage! It's tyranny!"

"Of course it's tyranny," said Andrey Yefimitch, encouraged by

Ivan Dmitritch's outburst. "I must go out, I want to. He has no right! Open, I tell you."

"Do you hear, you dull-witted brute?" cried Ivan Dmitritch, and he banged on the door with his fist. "Open the door, or I will break it open! Torturer!"

"Open the door," cried Andrey Yefimitch, trembling all over; "I insist!"

"Talk away!" Nikita answered through the door, "talk away. . . ."

"Anyhow, go and call Yevgeny Fyodoritch! Say that I beg him to come for a minute!"

"His Honor will come of himself tomorrow."

"They will never let us out," Ivan Dmitritch was going on meanwhile. "They will leave us to rot here! Oh, Lord, can there really be no hell in the next world, and will these wretches be forgiven? Where is justice? Open the door, you wretch! I am choking!" he cried in a hoarse voice, and flung himself upon the door. "I'll dash out my brains, murderers!"

Nikita opened the door quickly, and roughly with both his hands and his knee shoved Andrey Yefimitch back, then swung his arm and punched him in the face with his fist. It seemed to Andrey Yefimitch as though a huge salt wave enveloped him from his head downward and dragged him to the bed; there really was a salt taste in his mouth: most likely the blood was running from his teeth. He waved his arms as though he were trying to swim out and clutched at a bedstead, and at the same moment felt Nikita hit him twice on the back.

Ivan Dmitritch gave a loud scream. He must have been beaten too.

Then all was still, the faint moonlight came through the grating, and a shadow like a net lay on the floor. It was terrible. Andrey Yefimitch lay and held his breath: he was expecting with horror to be struck again. He felt as though someone had taken a sickle, thrust it into him, and turned it round several times in his breast and bowels. He bit the pillow from pain and clenched his teeth, and all at once through the chaos in his brain there flashed the terrible, unbearable thought that these people, who seemed now like black shadows in the moonlight, had to endure such pain day by day for years. How could it have happened that for more than twenty years he had not known it and had refused to know it? He knew nothing of pain, had no conception of it, so he was not to blame, but his conscience, as inexorable and as rough as Nikita, made him turn cold from the crown of his head to his heels. He leapt up, tried to cry out with all his might, and to run in haste to kill Nikita, and then Hobotov, the superintendent and the assistant, and then himself; but no sound came from his chest, and his legs would not obey him. Gasping for breath, he tore at the dressing gown and the shirt on his breast, rent them, and fell senseless on the bed.

XIX

Next morning his head ached, there was a droning in his ears and a feeling of utter weakness all over. He was not ashamed at recalling his weakness the day before. He had been cowardly, had even been afraid of the moon, had openly expressed thoughts and feelings such as he had not expected in himself before; for instance, the thought that the paltry people who philosophized were really dissatisfied. But now nothing mattered to him.

He ate nothing; he drank nothing. He lay motionless and silent.

"It is all the same to me, he thought when they asked him questions. "I am not going to answer. . . . It's all the same to me."

After dinner Mihail Averyanitch brought him a quarter pound of tea and a pound of fruit pastilles. Daryushka came too and stood for a whole hour by the bed with an expression of dull grief on her face. Dr. Hobotov visited him. He brought a bottle of bromide and told Nikita to fumigate the ward with something.

Toward evening Andrey Yefimitch died of an apoplectic stroke. At first he had a violent shivering fit and a feeling of sickness;

something revolting as it seemed, penetrating through his whole body, even to his fingertips, strained from his stomach to his head and flooded his eyes and ears. There was a greenness before his eyes. Andrey Yefimitch understood that his end had come, and remembered that Ivan Dmitritch, Mihail Averyanitch, and millions of people believed in immortality. And what if it really existed? But he did not want immortality, and he thought of it only for one instant. A herd of deer, extraordinarily beautiful and graceful, of which he had been reading the day before, ran by him; then a peasant woman stretched out her hand to him with a registered letter. . . . Mihail Averyanitch said something, then it all vanished, and Andrey Yefimitch sank into oblivion forever.

The hospital porters came, took him by his arms and legs, and carried him away to the chapel.

There he lay on the table, with open eyes, and the moon shed its light upon him at night. In the morning Sergey Sergeyitch came, prayed piously before the crucifix, and closed his former chief's eyes.

Next day Andrey Yefimitch was buried. Mihail Averyanitch and Daryushka were the only people at the funeral.

1892

A PLAY

МОСКОВСКИЙ ХУДОЖЕСТВЕННЫЙ ТЕАТР.

„ТРИ СЕСТРЫ"

ПЬЕСЫ А. П. ЧЕХОВА

ПОД РЕДАКЦИЕЙ

Вл. Ив. НЕМИРОВИЧА ДАНЧЕНКО

ПЕТЕРБУРГ.

1919.

The cover of the album commemorating the original production of The Three Sisters, *with a portrait of Anton Chekhov by Sergei Bekhonen, 1919.*

THE
THREE SISTERS

Characters

ANDREI SERGEYEVICH PROZOROFF

NATALYA IVANOVNA, his fiancée, afterward his wife.

OLGA

MASHA   } his sisters.

IRINA

FYODOR ILYCH KULYGIN, a high-school teacher, husband of
MASHA.

LIEUTENANT COLONEL ALEXANDR IGNATYEVICH VERSHININ,
battery commander.

BARON NIKOLAI LVOVICH TUZENBACH, lieutenant.

VASSILY VASSILYEVICH SOLYONY, captain.

IVAN ROMANOVICH CHEBUTYKIN, army doctor.

ALEXI PETROVICH FEDOTIK, second lieutenant.

VLADIMIR KARLOVICH RODE, second lieutenant.

FERAPONT, an old porter from the District Board.

ANFISA, the nanny, an old woman of eighty.

SCENE

The action takes place in a provincial town.

Act I

*The Prozoroffs' House—a parlor. Mid-day. The table
is being set for breakfast.*

OLGA, IRINA, *and* MASHA.

OLGA: Well. I'm going to tell you. It's funny the way time does
pass. Here we are. The same day. One year later. Irina. And the
anniversaries. Irina's birthday and the day of Father's death.
Which now will always be linked. And it snowed then. It was
bitter cold, I thought that I would not survive it, you lay in a faint.
And one year has passed and we can remember it with ease. You
in a white dress, your face shining. (*The clock strikes.*) And the
clock was striking then, it's striking *now*. (*Pause.*) When we went
to the cemetery. To the martial music. In honor of our father. And
the ceremonial salutes. Guns for a general. Commanded a brigade.
Yet so few mourners. Didn't you think? Walking. Heavy rain and
snow.

IRINA: Must you?

(CHEBUTYKIN, TUZENBACH, *and* SOLYONY *can be seen in the reception
room.*)

OLGA: But today. Mmm. Today it is warm. We keep the windows
open though the birches still are closed. You know. Eleven years

ago. When we left Moscow. (*Pause.*) Eleven years ago. When he was given the brigade. When we left Moscow. At this time. The beginning of May, I remember it. As *so* warm. As if it were yesterday. Do you know—when I woke this morning, I saw the spring light. My soul responded to that light. As that light which we'd left, and I was filled with *passion*. To be back again.

CHEBUTYKIN: . . . in *Hell* . . .

TUZENBACH: It's garbage, what it is.

(MASHA *whistles a song quietly.*)

OLGA: Masha. Please don't whistle. *Please.*

MASHA: . . . Don't whistle?

OLGA: Please. My head is splitting, I've grown old *working*, and I'm sorry if I seem to *carp*, but I need some *quiet*, you know . . . ?

MASHA: . . . some quiet.

OLGA: . . . and a rest. From the *gymnasium* and *lessons* and four years of teaching constantly until I'm going to die because each lesson is a cup of my blood drained. Eh? And only one thought in my heart.

IRINA: To write a close to everything here and to go to Moscow.

OLGA: Yes. That's right. (*Pause.*) That's right. As soon as possible.

(CHEBUTYKIN *and* TUZENBACH *laugh offstage.*)

IRINA: And Brother to get his diploma and move off, the sole remainder being Masha.

OLGA: Who will come to Moscow the entire summer. Every year.

IRINA: Then, God grant, everything will come 'round right.

OLGA: Amen.

IRINA: A lovely day today.

OLGA: Yes, it is.

IRINA: My soul feels so light—do you know? This morning? I remembered that it was my birthday? And I felt such joy. And such *thoughts* moving me—of *Mama.*

OLGA: . . . Rest in peace.

IRINA: Rest in peace . . . and . . . such wonderful thoughts— such *memories* . . .

OLGA: Oh, darling. You are so beautiful today. You are radiant. Masha is shining, Andrei himself would look good, only he's gotten so terribly fat, hasn't he?

MASHA: Yes.

OLGA: Doesn't suit him.

MASHA: No.

OLGA: But I . . .

MASHA: . . . that's right . . .

OLGA: . . . I have grown old. I have grown very old. And thin— from being cross all of the time . . . with the girls at the gymnasium. Of whom I today am free. (*Pause.*) Thank God. And make me younger. I feel younger today. I do. And it all is God—I know it. Life is good. It . . . Life all flows from God, and I am only twenty-eight years old. And I don't have a bad life . . .

MASHA: . . . no.

OLGA: Only it seems. If I were *married* . . . in love with my husband. Married, do you know . . . ?

TUZENBACH (*to* SOLYONY): What garbage, excuse me, I'm sick of listening to you. (*Entering parlor.*) Forgot to *inform* you that our new battery commander, Vershinin, will today be paying you a visit.

OLGA: Very glad.

IRINA: Is he old?

TUZENBACH: Not overly. Forty-five? Forty? Seems a decent sort. Not stupid. Not at all. Talks a bit, though . . .

IRINA: An interesting man?

TUZENBACH: As I said. Not bad. Got a wife, mother-in-law—two girls. Second marriage. Everywhere he goes he tells you that he's got a wife and the two girls. He'll say it to you, too. You watch him. And his wife's a piece of work. Long schoolgirl braid; she's given to philosophy and *"says"* things, don't'cha know. And tries to take her wee life now and then. We think to spite her husband. Another man'd ditch 'er. *I* would—he bears it and complains.

SOLYONY (*entering with* CHEBUTYKIN): One arm, I can lift fifty pounds. Eh? With *two* arms, I can lift . . . five times that. We can conclude that two people, that the strength of two, is not twice but *three* times, perhaps more, more . . .

CHEBUTYKIN (*reading a newspaper*): For *hair* loss . . . two parts *naphthalene* . . . to . . . what is this? To ten parts alcohol. Dissolve. And apply daily . . . *Note* it! Do we note it? I was saying . . . putcher cork into your bottle and you take your Small Glass Tube. Alright—a tiny pinch of common or everyday *alum* . . .

IRINA: Ivan *Romanych* . . . my dear *Romanych* . . .

CHEBUTYKIN: Yes, my fount of joy?

IRINA: Why am I so completely happy today . . . ?

CHEBUTYKIN: Tell me . . .

IRINA: I am borne by sails. Beneath the softest sky. White birds overhead, flying by me . . . why . . . ?

CHEBUTYKIN (*kissing her hands*):   The lovely birds of white . . .

IRINA: When I got up today. I got up and washed, and I got up and it seemed clear to me. Everything in the world. It was all clear to me—the way one ought to live. My dear Ivan Romanych—shall I tell you?

CHEBUTYKIN: Yes.

IRINA: By toil. We must live by toil. By the sweat of our brow. Each person must. This is the whole meaning of life. All happiness. *All* happiness. That laborer, do you see, up at dawn—who pounds stones in the streets, a shepherd, a, a *teacher*—in the cold dark—lighting the stove—who works with *children*. A . . . a railroad engineer . . . a, any, don't you see. Better to be a beast, an ox, a dray horse pulling in the street—*as long as one works*—than to be a woman of our class, rising at noon, to have her coffee brought her and to lie around, to spend two hours dressing . . . the revolving horror of a life with no work in it—I love to work. Ivan Romanych, as a parched man in the desert longs for water, I long to work. And if I do *not* work, Ivan Romanych, if I do not find that work, and toil—deny me your friendship—discard me. (*Pause.*) Reject me.

CHEBUTYKIN (*tenderly*):   I swear it.

IRINA: *Will* you . . . ?

CHEBUTYKIN: Yes. Yes.

OLGA: Father trained us to get up at seven. So Irina now rises at seven, lies in bed til nine—her face screwed up, "thinking." About things . . .

IRINA: No, no, you see, you are used to thinking of me as a little girl, and so you find it strange if I seem serious.

OLGA: Mmm.

IRINA: I'm twenty years *old* . . .

TUZENBACH: No, it's not strange to long for labor. (*Sighs*.) *Oh*, God . . . no, I understand it—I, if I may speak of myself, haven't worked a day in my life. Born in Petersburg—a city of the cold and idle, into a family that knew neither worry nor work— I'd come home, I remember, I'd come home from military school, the footman, he would pull my boots off. No, I would be "acting up," you know, with him, I would treat him with insolence and my mother would *beam*. She'd look on me with benevolence, and of course, I was amazed when I found others who reacted differently. They shielded me, they *hid* me from the fact of labor. But they did not serve me, neither did they *protect* me—because the time has come—the juggernaut is bearing down upon us. And that storm is brooding. Brooding. Very near—preparing to fall upon us, that powerful storm, that healthy storm which will cleanse from our society the sloth, the indifference. The scorn of labor, the boredom—*I* shall work, not only shall *I* work—in twenty-five, in thirty years, we *all* shall work. Each person shall work. Every one.

CHEBUTYKIN: I won't work.

TUZENBACH: You don't count.

SOLYONY: In twenty-five years you'll be dead—thank God—two, three more years, you'll die of a stroke, or I'll, I don't know, I'll fly off the handle one day, and jump up and shoot you dead.

CHEBUTYKIN: Yes. Literally true—I've never done a thing—not one—never lifted a finger, any single thing could be called work. Not since I left the university, and never read a book. Read the newspapers. (*Takes out a newspaper.*) Look here, there is a, for example, fellow called *Dobroliudov*, writer—*but*—what he's been *writing*, I could not tell you—*God* only knows— (*Sound of knocking.*) Uh . . . huh . . . calling me downstairs. Yes. Someone there for me—back presently. Wait—eh? (*Exits.*)

IRINA: Something occurred to him.

TUZENBACH: It seems. Left rather pensive.

IRINA: Mmm.

TUZENBACH: You watch—he'll come back and bring you up some "offering."

IRINA: How distasteful.

OLGA: Isn't it?

IRINA: Horrible.

OLGA: Always the fool he is.

MASHA (*sings*):   An oak of green
In Lokomoryeh
A chain of gold
Upon the oak
A chain of gold
Upon the oak—
. . . A chain of gold
. . . upon the oak.

OLGA: You out of sorts today? (MASHA *hums, puts on her hat.*) Are you out of sorts today? Where are you going?

MASHA: Home.

IRINA: . . . You're going *home* . . . ?

TUZENBACH: You're leaving a *birthday* . . . ?

MASHA: All the same to me. I'll be back this evening. (*Kisses* IRINA.) Again, always, be healthy, be happy. In the old days. When Father was alive—we would have half the garrison come to our birthdays—didn't we? And what a lot of commotion. But what do we have today, a person and a half and it is dead as the bottom of the sea. Me, yes, I'll go—I'm down today—I'm so out of sorts and not cheerful, so pay me no attention—it's alright. We'll talk later my darling—now goodbye. I think I'd better go.

IRINA: You are so . . .

OLGA: No, I understand you, Masha.

SOLYONY: If a man, if a man *philosophizes*, then it is, it is, it is *philosophizing*—or we can say that it is "sophistry"—but if a *woman*, if a *woman* should take to *philosophizing*, then it is, it is a case of "tap me on the head."

MASHA (*pause*): What *can* that mean? What *can* that mean, you horrid man . . . ? What did you mean by that?

SOLYONY: Nothing.

MASHA: You didn't?

SOLYONY: "Hardly had he cried 'alack'
Before the bear was on his back . . ."

MASHA (*to* OLGA): Do you think you might stop crying?

(*Enter* ANFISA *and* FERAPONT *with a cake.*)

ANFISA: Come in, come in, little father—are your feet clean? Yes. Here—from the District Board, from Mikhail Ivanych Protopopov—a . . . a "pie."

IRINA: Thank you. Do thank him for me.

FERAPONT: What?

IRINA: THANK HIM.

OLGA: Nanny, dear—give him some pie.

FERAPONT: What?

IRINA: *THANK HIM!!!!!*

OLGA: Will you give him some pie? Ferapont, please, go along, you'll get your pie in there.

FERAPONT: What?

ANFISA: Come along, little one, come along now. (*Exits.*)

MASHA: I don't like Protopopov—Mikhail Potapych or *Ivanych* or whatever he is. I don't like him. Who invited him?

IRINA: I didn't invite him.

MASHA: Well, *fine* . . .

(*Enter* CHEBUTYKIN, *followed by a soldier with a silver samovar—murmur of astonishment.*)

OLGA (*exiting*): A *samovar*—oh, God . . . oh, no . . .

IRINA: Ivan Romanych, my dove, what is it you're doing?

TUZENBACH: I told you.

MASHA: Ivan Romanych, no, you have no shame . . .

CHEBUTYKIN: My dearest ones, my good, my only ones . . . those that are to me the dearest objects in the world. I am a lonely, worthless man, an old man, soon I will be sixty—there is nothing of the good in me except my love for you. If it were not for you, I would have left off living many years ago. (*To* IRINA:) My darling child—I've known you since the day that you were born. I bore you in my arms, I loved your sainted mother . . .

IRINA: Yes. But why such lavish presents?

CHEBUTYKIN: Lavish presents . . . lavish presents . . . *Damn* it, then, take, take that samovar away. "Such lavishness . . ." (*To orderly:*) Put it in there . . .

ANFISA (*passing through the parlor*): My dears—An "unknown colonel"—got his topcoat off already—coming in here, come to call—Arinushka, now, you be sweet—you mind, now—oh, Lord, and we need breakfast, too . . .

TUZENBACH: Vershinin, I would think . . .

VERSHININ (*entering, to* MASHA *and* IRINA): I have the honor to present myself: Vershinin—I am so very glad to be here with you—oh, Lord, *look* at you . . .

IRINA: Sit down, please. We're so glad to have you.

VERSHININ: And I, how glad am I to be here, can you know? I don't think you can know. Yes. Three girls. There are three of you. And, looking back, no, I can't see the faces, but I remember—so strongly—Colonel Prozoroff and his three little girls . . . (*Pause.*) How time passes. Oh, Lord, the ways in which time . . . (*Pause.*)

TUZENBACH: Alexandr Ignatyevich is from Moscow.

IRINA: You are from Moscow, you're from Moscow?

VERSHININ: Yes. I am. Your late father, when he commanded Moscow battery I was an officer in his brigade. (*To* MASHA:) Yes. Now I begin to remember you. Yes, I do.

MASHA: I don't remember you.

IRINA: Olga. Olga. Ol . . . will you come in here . . . ?

(OLGA *enters.*)

IRINA: It seems Lieutenant Colonel Vershinin is from *Moscow*.

VERSHININ: And you must be Olga Sergeyevna—"the oldest daughter." And you, you must be *Maria*, and you are the youngest, and you are *Irina*. Isn't that it?

OLGA: You're from Moscow?

VERSHININ: Many years. Studied there, entered the service. Served in Moscow many years. Finally received my command here, transferred here—as you see—but, you know, it is so *vague*, really, so vague—only I remember, there were *three* of you. Just an impression, really, while your father, when I close my eyes—I have him right before me. In my memory, as if he were alive. I used to call on you.

OLGA: . . . you.

VERSHININ: Alexandr Ignatyevich.

OLGA: Alexandr Ignatyevich.

VERSHININ: Yes.

OLGA: I *remarked* it, because we're returning there . . .

IRINA: We're moving back to Moscow—our plan is to be installed by autumn—back on . . .

OLGA: . . . yes.

IRINA: Old Basmannaya Street.

OLGA: "Back on the old street . . ."

(*The two girls laugh.*)

MASHA: And out of the blue. We meet a fellow townsman. Oh. Wait, wait, wait. Olga—Olga. They said, at our house, they used to say "the lovesick major . . ." You were . . .

VERSHININ: Yes.

MASHA: But you were still a lieutenant—but they called you "the lovesick major." You were stuck on some . . . some . . .

VERSHININ: "The lovesick major . . ."

MASHA: But you had a moustache. (*Pause.*) How old you've grown. Oh, my Lord . . .

VERSHININ: Well. You see. When I was "the lovesick major" I was young. I was young. And in love.

MASHA: . . . yes.

VERSHININ: And I . . . it's not the same now, you see.

OLGA: But, you haven't gone gray—do you know? You're "old," but you're *not* old . . .

VERSHININ: Well, that is it then.

OLGA: You're somehow . . .

VERSHININ: I'm forty-three. How long since you left Moscow?

OLGA: Eleven years. Oh—Masha, Masha. Stop it now, stop it now, or I'll start in too . . . (*Crying.*)

MASHA: No, I'm fine—and you lived on what street?

VERSHININ: Old Basmannaya.

OLGA: So did we . . .

VERSHININ: At one time I'd lived on Nemetskaya Street. And from there I could walk down to the barracks. I used to *walk* it . . . there is this bridge on the way . . . the water roars beneath it. Every day, I'd take that walk . . . I'd take that walk and something in the lonely place . . . or in *me*, you see, would, would grow quite sad. (*Pause.*) While here—a broad, open, a *lovely* river.

OLGA: Well, except it's vicious cold, and the *mosquitos* . . .

VERSHININ: *Oh* no, *oh* no. A good and a healthy Slavic climate. The *forest*, the *river*, the *birches* you have! Which, to me, are, in their modest selves, most beautiful trees. How blessed you are to live here. In this magnificent country, and why, I'm puzzled by it, though, is the railway depot forty miles off. Why is that? No one can tell me why that is so.

SOLYONY: Why is that?

VERSHININ: Yes.

SOLYONY: In fact, because, *because, had it been nearer* . . . (*Pause.*) It would *not* have been forty miles off. (*Pause.*)

TUZENBACH: And they say wit has disappeared.

OLGA: No, no. I remember you!

VERSHININ: I knew your sainted mother.

CHEBUTYKIN: . . . Kingdom of Heaven unto her . . .

IRINA: She is buried in Moscow.

OLGA: At the Nova-Devichyeh.

MASHA: And I'm beginning to forget her face. Already. Could you have imagined that? In the same way that we will be forgotten.

VERSHININ: Yes. They'll forget us.

MASHA: Will they not?

VERSHININ: Yes. Which is the nature of the world. And that is our *fate* and there's nothing to be done. And that which seems to us now so significant, so "important," a time will come . . . it will certainly come, when it will be forgotten. (*Pause.*) And do you know, I believe, I find it quite interesting, I do, *that we cannot know* that we have *no* way of foretelling what *specifically* will be seen as important and what as, as pitiful and comic. *Copernicus*, let us say. Christopher Columbus—did not their work and lives, at first, seem laughable, misguided, and beneath contempt? While the works of those long forgotten were held to be universal truth? I think so. And it so could happen, could it not, that our present life, of which we think so well, to which we are so reconciled, will come, in time, to be seen as *unwise*, uncomfortable, strange. *Unclean* perhaps, perhaps even sinful.

TUZENBACH: Well, we don't know. *Do* we? Neither do we know that our life will not be called elevated. And thought of with great respect—you see—we have no . . . *tortures, executions*, no . . . *invasions* . . .

VERSHININ: And yet.

TUZENBACH: Yes, and yet, yes. How much suffering . . .

SOLYONY: Kitty, kitty, kitty, kitty, eat your vittles and philosophize a bit . . .

TUZENBACH: Vassily Vassilych. I require you, with all courtesy, to please leave me alone. You understand me?

SOLYONY: Kitty, kitty, kitty.

TUZENBACH: Yes. How tedious. (*To* VERSHININ:) However.

VERSHININ: Yes.

TUZENBACH: However.

VERSHININ: Yes.

TUZENBACH: That suffering which we observe.

VERSHININ: Yes.

TUZENBACH: And there is so much of it.

VERSHININ: There is.

TUZENBACH: Is it not possible.

VERSHININ: Yes.

TUZENBACH: That it's *nature*.

VERSHININ: That's to say the nature of the suffering today.

TUZENBACH: Yes. Does it not speak to the possibility of a, an *uplift* in the moral tenor of the times? Don't you *think?*

VERSHININ: Yes. I do.

CHEBUTYKIN: You have said, Baron, that our life today might be called *elevated*. How is it, then, that, all the same, the people are short. (*Stands.*) *I'm* short . . . look how short I am. Then I must thank you, you see, for your holding out to me this consolation . . .

(*Violin plays offstage.*)

MASHA: Our brother Andrei.

IRINA: Our scholar. Picked out to be a professor. Papa was a military man . . .

MASHA: Yes.

IRINA: But his son has chosen differently.

MASHA: Though in accord with Papa's wishes.

IRINA: Yes.

OLGA: Well, and it's his turn to bear a little teasing these days, for it seems he has fallen slightly in love.

IRINA: A certain local miss.

Original cast members of The Three Sisters: *Olga Knipper Chekhova (Masha), M. H. Germanova (Olga), and M. A. Zhdanova (Irina).*

OLGA: Yes.

IRINA: Who will be with us today, in all possibility.

MASHA: You know. She dresses herself—she dresses herself as if she were a pig. It's not that it's ugly. It's just, it's pathetic. Little yellow "skirts," you know, with "fringe," this "fringelike" affair, and that *trim red blouse.* Her cheeks glowing. So "scrubbed." I . . . don't *say* that Andrei's in love with her. No, say he may be diverting himself. But don't say that our brother has no taste. *Additionally,* I heard that she is marrying Protopopov, of the District Board. Joy to their union. Andrei—Andrei . . . come here, dearest. My brother, Andrei Sergeyevich.

VERSHININ: Vershinin.

ANDREI: Prozoroff. Delighted. You're posted here as battery commander.

VERSHININ: I am.

ANDREI: I congratulate you.

OLGA: Come from Moscow.

ANDREI: And that is a pity. As now my good sisters will give you no peace.

VERSHININ: We've already had time to let them tire of me.

IRINA: Look at this magnificent little frame—Andrei gave it to me. He gave it to me today, and he made it himself. (*Pause.*)

VERSHININ: I . . . yes, a, a frame.

IRINA: And that sweet little one above the piano, he made that one too.

OLGA: Here is what he is. Our boy. A *scholar,* a *master* of the *violin,* an *artificer* of all sorts of . . . in short, a jack-of-all-trades,

Andrei, don't go, and always, and this is your manner too, you're always walking away. Come here . . .

MASHA: Come here, come on, then.

ANDREI: Please. Leave me alone. Please.

MASHA: And now we've angered you. Oh . . . You're so *sensitive!* You are. Alexandr Ignatyevich here, used to be called a *lovesick* major, and did he take on about it? No.

VERSHININ: No.

MASHA: And you. We'll call you, the demon um um um, the demon lover, no, the lovestruck fiddler, no . . .

IRINA: The puppy-love professor.

MASHA: No, the . . .

IRINA: He's in love. Andrei's in love . . .

CHEBUTYKIN: "For this alone has Nature placed us in the world— for *love!*"

ANDREI: Alright. Fine. Thank you.

CHEBUTYKIN: "Just for love . . ."

ANDREI: Thank you. Enough. Alright. Oh, Lord. I am so tired. I am not quite myself, as they say. Up until four reading. Shut my eyes. Couldn't sleep. Everything racing through my mind. Then there's the early sun and the bedroom's bursting with light. You know, this summer I think that while I'm here I'm going to translate this one book from the English.

VERSHININ: You read English?

ANDREI: Our *father,* his spirit rest in peace, saddled us with an education. *Since his death (pause)* since his death, I've noticed, and they must be connected, that I've put on weight. I've gained all of this weight. In the past year. As if I had been, as if my body had been freed from fetters. Yes. We all speak French, German, and English. My sisters and I, Irina knowing some Italian, too, into the bargain. (*Pause.*) And what a price we paid.

MASHA: To speak three languages in this town is not an accomplishment. It is a deformity.

VERSHININ: Well, *no.*

MASHA: Yes.

VERSHININ: *Really* . . .

MASHA: Yes.

VERSHININ: How can that be. How can there be a town so dull but that it cannot be enlivened by intelligence?

MASHA: Look around you.

VERSHININ: No, truly . . . say there are one hundred thousand people. A town of a hundred thousand backward, coarse, uneducated. And there, in the midst of that town, three such as yourselves. Now. *As you live your lives*—it goes without saying that you will not overcome the mass. The gray mass which surrounds you—you will be subsumed. For this is how life works. *But* you shall not be without influence—to the contrary. Your influence *will, will* imperceptibly but certainly make itself felt. And *after* you, perhaps, another three, like yourselves, another three, six, twelve more, each, you see, adding their influence—over time—such that, over time, you will be the majority. In two, three hundred years. Such that life on earth will have become unutterably beautiful. Men need such a life. We do not have it, but we dream of it. We anticipate it. We wait. We wonder. We prepare for it. For the need to know. More than our ancestors—more than those who've gone before . . . more than they know . . . hah hah . . . hah . . . and you say that *you* are mired in redundancy.

MASHA (*taking off her hat*):   I'm going to stay for breakfast.

IRINA: You know. I wish that someone had been here to *write that down*.

TUZENBACH: You say that after many years life on earth will become beautiful. Yes. I think so. But in order to *partake*, if I may say, to partake now of that beauty, to "participate" in it now, though it be from afar, we must *plan* for it, we must *work* for it. We must . . .

VERSHININ: Yes, yes. Well, I *think* so. What a *raft* of flowers you have here. Your home is so beautiful. All my life I have been banging about small, dingy flats with the two chairs, the couch, the samovar and the same smoking stove, all of my life. I have lacked *precisely* these flowers. *Oh*, well, then; *oh* well . . . *oh* my . . .

TUZENBACH: Yes. One must work. I know, you're thinking "Yes. A sentimental German." On my mother's grave, I am a *Russian*. My *name's* German, I am a Russian, I don't even *speak* German. My father's Russian *Orthodox*, and *he* even, you see, is not fluent in German.

VERSHININ: I have thought. I have often thought what if we could begin our lives anew. If we could *remember* the life we've lived and use that as a draft, as a rough draft, if you will. Do you see. Learning from our mistakes—arranging *everything*, as we know its result, you see; to *please*, to *complement*, as one would decorate a house, or this apartment, with *flowers*. And light—with a sense of the whole. My wife is unwell. I have two small girls. If I were to start again, if I were to, I would not marry, no, I'd . . .

(*Enter* KULYGIN.)

KULYGIN (*to* IRINA):   Dear sister. May I congratulate you. Upon your name day. May I *wish* you, with all that at my command.

Health, happiness, and all the customary wishes one addresses to a lady of your years. Then let me offer you this little "pamphlet." I wrote it. It is the history of the last fifty years of our academy. A little "tract"; scribbled from want of other idleness. But, but, but read it, do. Ladies and gentlemen. (*To* VERSHININ:) Kulygin— instructor at our academy and civil counselor. (*To* IRINA:) *In* this book you will find a roster of all those having completed our course in the last half century. That you will find in here. *Feci quod potui, faciant meliora potentes.* I hope my book amuses you. (*Kisses* MASHA.)

IRINA (*of book*):   You gave me one at Easter.

KULYGIN: Ha. Well. Then I suppose you have superfluity. Dear *Colonel,* if you will permit me. (*Gives him the book.*) And, perhaps someday, in an hour of boredom, my poor book . . .

VERSHININ: Thank you. I thank you very much. I am so glad to've met you . . .

OLGA: Are you going? *No* . . .

IRINA: No, no, stay, please. For breakfast, at least—please.

OLGA: Please—oblige us.

VERSHININ: Well. (*Pause.*) It seems I have found myself involved in a *birthday* . . . (*pause*) . . . a birthday.

OLGA (*inviting him into the next room*):   Come with me.

VERSHININ: Yes. I will . . . (*Exiting.*) Congratulations . . . (*Exits.*)

KULYGIN: Today, ladies and gentlemen, is Sunday. Sunday is a day of rest. Let us rest, therefore, and each, in that way appropriate to his age and rank, rejoice and make merry. We'll take the carpets up and store them away til the winter comes—with Persian powder or with naphthalene—*Romans* enjoyed health because they knew this rule: *mens sana in corpore sano*, they understood both *work* and *rest*. And, so, their lives *flowed*, along certain prescribed *forms*. Our headmaster has said that the chief thing in a life is form. That which loses its form ends. But that which *possesses* it, do you see? And in our daily lives it is the same. Masha, my wife, loves me. My wife loves me. The *window* curtains, which, just as the carpets . . . must . . . Today I have a high heart! Masha— a cheerful heart. At four o'clock we're to be at the headmaster's. Who has arranged the outing for the faculty families.

MASHA: No, I'm not . . . No. I'm not going. (*Pause.*)

KULYGIN: . . . Darling.

MASHA: No.

KULYGIN: My darling. Why?

MASHA: No. I, uh. Fine. I'll tell you later. No. I'll go. Alright. I'll go. Alright? I'll go. If you'll not PLAGUE me . . . will you. Please . . . ? (*Walks away.*)

KULYGIN: . . . and, afterwards . . . we'll spend the evening at the headmaster's. Who does, who is so social. Despite it all. Isn't he? An excellent man. I think. A good soul. An excellent man. At the conference yesterday, he says, he says, "Tired, Fyodor Ilych . . . *tired.*" (*Pause.*) "Tired . . ." (*Looks at the clock on the wall, then at his watch.*) Your clock is seven minutes fast. "Yes . . ." he says . . . "tired . . ."

(*A violin plays offstage.*)

OLGA (*reemerging*): Gentlemen. If you please. Be so good as to be seated. Your breakfast. A pie.

KULYGIN: Oh. Olga, my dear Olga. *Olga.* Yesterday I worked from morning til eleven o'clock at night. And, yes, I was fatigued—yes, I was. But today, I feel happy . . . my dear. (*Exits.*)

CHEBUTYKIN: . . . a *pie.*

OLGA: Yes.

CHEBUTYKIN: Magnificent.

MASHA: But no drinking. No drinking today. Do you hear me? It's no good for you to drink.

CHEBUTYKIN: Please. I'm over it. Would you please? For the last two years. My little mother. Two years. What's it going to hurt?

MASHA: No drinking. Don't you *dare* to do it. And, oh God, protect me. The whole evening. Bored to madness by the headmaster.

TUZENBACH: Don't go.

MASHA: Mmm.

TUZENBACH: In your place I wouldn't.

CHEBUTYKIN: Don't you go. My pumpkin.

MASHA: Fine. "Don't go." The cursed life of one of the damned. (*Exits to reception room.*)

CHEBUTYKIN: Now, *Masha* . . . (*Also exits.*)

SOLYONY (*going into the reception room*):   Cluck, cluck, cluck, cluck.

TUZENBACH: Fine, Vassily Vassilych. That will do.

KULYGIN (*reentering*):   To your health, Colonel. Yes. I'm an academic . . . yes. I am "one of our own" here. Masha's husband. Here at the house. One of "les nôtres." What a woman. So kind.

VERSHININ: Some of the pepper vodka. (*To* OLGA:) Your health. Yes. I feel so good here.

(*Only* IRINA *and* TUZENBACH *remain in the parlor.*)

IRINA: Masha's out of sorts today.

TUZENBACH: Mmm.

IRINA: At eighteen she married one who seemed to her the most intelligent of men. Now . . .

TUZENBACH: Yes?

IRINA: . . . he is a *kind* man. He may be the kindest of men—but he's not the most intelligent.

OLGA (*offstage*):   On, Andrei . . . do come, finally . . .

ANDREI (*offstage*):   . . . I'm coming.

TUZENBACH: What are you thinking about?

IRINA: I am thinking . . . I do not like your Solyony. I don't like him, and I'm frightened of him. All that he says are stupid things.

TUZENBACH: Yes. He's strange.

IRINA (*to herself*):   . . . strange . . .

TUZENBACH: I'm sorry for him. He annoys me, too. But I pity him.

IRINA: Do you?

TUZENBACH: Yes. I think he's shy. When we're alone he can be quite . . . engaging . . . quite intelligent. Tender, even, perhaps. In company he is crude, as you say, and coarse. No. Don't go. (*Pause.*) Let them go in. We'll join them in a while. Let me be near you for a moment yet. And tell me. What you're thinking of. (*Pause.*) And here you are. Twenty years old. And I am not yet thirty. How many days lie before us? (*Pause.*) A procession of days. Full of love. Full of my love for you.

IRINA: Nikolai Lvovich . . .

TUZENBACH: . . . my feeling is that *love* . . . that *struggle*, that a thirst for *labor*—why can we not say "a thirst" . . . ? . . . all the things in life . . . have merged with my love for you. Oh—

296 ◆ ANTON CHEKHOV

with my love for you—and your *beauty*. And life seems so beautiful—what . . . ?

IRINA: I'm thinking of what you're saying.

TUZENBACH: . . . yes . . . ?

IRINA: You say that "life is beautiful." Yes. It seems so to you. But for my sisters. And for me. It has not yet been so. We . . . (*Pause.*) Do you know what it is to be *cloyed?* To become *jaded?* To live as it . . . oh, now I'm crying—what does *that* accomplish? (*Pause.*) Work. "Work" . . . you see . . . ? Through *work* . . . it's through work that one can find happiness. And if one does *not* work . . . and that's why we are unhappy. *Isn't* it? Because we have nothing to do. We are born of people who despise work.

(*Enter* NATALYA IVANOVNA.)

NATALYA: Yes. They're at breakfast. And I'm late. (*Looks at herself in the mirror. To herself:*) My hair. Is. Good. Enough. (*To* IRINA:) Dearest Irina Sergeyevna. My congratulations. (*Kisses her.*) Here is a kiss . . . and what a slew of guests we have. They'll make me self-conscious . . . so many of them. I swear that they will. *Baron* . . .

OLGA (*entering*): . . . at last . . .

NATALYA: Congratulations on your *birthday* girl . . . on your . . . *"birthday"* girl . . . but, do you know, you just have so much "company" . . .

OLGA: . . . we . . .

NATALYA: . . . it makes people *"shy"* . . .

OLGA: . . . it's only the old . . . Oh, Lord.

NATALYA: What?

OLGA: No.

NATALYA: What?

OLGA: Your belt.

NATALYA: What?

OLGA: You're wearing a green belt.

NATALYA: . . . yes.

OLGA: . . . that.

NATALYA: That isn't good?

OLGA (*pause*):   No.

NATALYA: Is it "bad luck"?

OLGA: Is it bad luck? Is it "bad luck . . . ?" Noo . . .

NATALYA: Then . . . ? (*Pause.*) *What?* It doesn't "go" . . .

OLGA: No, it . . .

NATALYA: What?

OLGA: It looks *strange*.

NATALYA: It looks strange. Why? (*Pause.*) Why? The "color."

OLGA: Yes.

NATALYA: Because it's *green* . . .

OLGA: Because . . .

NATALYA: It isn't "green" you know.

OLGA: It isn't? (*They exit to reception room.*)

NATALYA: No.

OLGA: What *is* it?

NATALYA: What is it? *Gray . . . Putty,* sort of . . .

OLGA: It's *"gray"?*

KULYGIN: And you, Irina. To you, a fine fiancé, and a healthy marriage. The time for which, I think I may say, is . . .

CHEBUTYKIN: Natalya Ivanovna, to you, too, I wish such a fiancé.

KULYGIN: Natalya Ivanovna already possesses such a . . .

MASHA: Well. I'll *take* a wee dram, then. Yes. I will. A life of knock-down jollity and ease, and God damn me to hell if it isn't so.

KULYGIN: *Zéro pour conduite.*

VERSHININ (*of liquor*):   This is delicious. And it's made of what?

SOLYONY: Bat's blood.

VERSHININ: . . . it's . . . ?

IRINA: Oh, God. *Must* we?

OLGA: For supper we have: roast turkey. Sweet potato pie. With apples . . . thank God that I have the time . . . *DO* come this evening. Everyone.

VERSHININ: May I come too?

IRINA: Please.

NATALYA: Yes. We do things simply here.

CHEBUTYKIN: "For love it is that for which a loving God has put us in the world . . ."

ANDREI: Isn't it "cloying"? Don't you think?

(FEDOTIK *and* RODE *enter with flowers.*)

FEDOTIK: . . . breakfast *already* is it . . . ?

RODE: Yes. Breakfast. Yes. Breakfast.

FEDOTIK: One moment. (*Takes a snapshot.*) One more . . . hold that please . . . One . . . *Two* . . . (*Takes a snapshot.*)

RODE: CONGRATULATIONS. What do I *not* wish you? What a day! May you have it *all*. Everything! This morning. I was out. On a walk. With the *academy* boys, you know?

FEDOTIK: And now you may move.

RODE: You may know, I teach gymnastics there.

FEDOTIK: Irina Sergeyevna: you may move now. (*Pause.*) How attractive you are today. Here, by the way, is a "top" . . . I want you to hear the sound that it makes.

IRINA: Oh, yes. (*To all, of the top:*) You *hear* this . . . ?

MASHA: "An oak of green, in Lokomoryeh. A chain of gold *upon* the oak . . ." A golden chain upon it. What in the *world* would you think I am saying that for? That phrase. Did this ever happen to you? Been inside my head since *morning*, it's been stuck to me.

KULYGIN: Thirteen at table . . . ?

RODE: But can it be we attach weight to superstition?

KULYGIN: "Thirteen at table, then two of the thirteen are in Love." ⏤And could one of that two, God save the mark, be *you* . . . Ivan Romanych . . . ? Be *you!!!?*

CHEBUTYKIN: I am an old sinner. Why, however, why Natalya Ivanovna should be blushing *eludes* me . . .

(NATALYA *runs out of the room.* ANDREI *follows.*)

ANDREI: Oh, please . . . No, no. It's not important. Please.

NATALYA: No. They make me feel . . . I'm sorry. I feel so *ashamed* . . . and, and, and . . . now I've left the *table!* Oh, Lord. I'm sorry. I can't . . . I can't . . . (*Covers her face with her hand.*)

ANDREI: My dearest. Please. Please. You don't have to *upset* yourself . . . they're . . . *please.* They're *joking.* They're speaking out of *love* for you. They *are.* My *darling* . . . my good one . . . What are they but kind, warmhearted people? *Nothing.* They love me, and they love you. Yes. Come here. Come here . . . they can't see us . . .

NATALYA: I, I, I, I don't know how to, to . . .

ANDREI: . . . what?

NATALYA: To "comport" myself. In company.

ANDREI: Oh, no. Oh. My darling young one. Believe me. I feel so . . . I am so full of love for you . . . no, they can't see us. No, they can't. Oh, go, who led to, to you . . . ! What a mystery. I love you. I love you. Marry me. Be my wife. I love you as no one ever . . . listen to me, as no man . . . (*He kisses her. Two workmen enter and watch them kissing.*)

Act II

The same set as Act I.

Eight o'clock in the evening. Offstage, on the street, the sound of an accordion playing. Enter NATALYA *in a dressing gown, carrying a candle into the dark room. She stops at the door leading to Andrei's room.*

NATALYA: Andriushka . . . ? Andriushka . . . ? Are you? Are you reading? . . . are you awake . . . ?

(*She goes to an adjacent door, opens it.* ANDREI *comes out of her room and sees her looking in at the other door.*)

I was just checking the fire is out. You know . . . *Shrovetide,* and the servants are . . . do you think I'm foolish?

ANDREI: Natalya . . .

NATALYA: To be "concerned." Do you think it's silly of me? But yesterday evening. *Midnight,* I was walking through the dining room, and there was a candle burning. On the tablecloth. I *worry* . . . and I . . . who *lit* it, who left it *burning* . . . (*Puts her candle down.*) What, what time is it?

ANDREI (*looks at the clock*):   Past eight. Quarter past eight.

NATALYA: A quarter past eight . . . Irina isn't back . . .

ANDREI: No.

NATALYA: Irina is not back. Olga isn't back. No. Oh. Lord. They work so hard. They're at the *teacher's* meeting . . . Irina is at the *telegraph* . . . this morning I said to her *"Darling . . ."* I said to your sister . . . "Take *care* of yourself . . . Irina. My *jewel . . ."* And did she listen? . . . a quarter past eight . . .

ANDREI: Yes.

NATALYA: I am afraid our Bobik isn't well. Why is he cold? Why is he so cold? Yesterday he's burning, and today he's cold. I'm frightened, I . . .

ANDREI: It's nothing, Natalya . . .

NATALYA: It *is* . . .

ANDREI: The boy is healthy.

NATALYA: *Is* he? (*Pause.*) In *any* case. The *diet.* Let him *eat* it, you see. I'm, I'm so afraid for him. The mummers are coming at nine. I wish they weren't. Andrei . . . ?

ANDREI: . . . but we invited them.

NATALYA: This morning. My angel. Woke up and looked at me, he *looked* at me, and . . . *"smiled."* And I saw such *recognition.* In that smile. He . . .

ANDREI: . . . he "knew" you.

NATALYA: And, yes, and *"Bobik,"* I said. *"Morning,* darling!" And he *laughed.* You know. What *don't* they understand? They understand it all. I think. I think they do. So, I'll, Andriushka, I'll have them send the mummers away when they come.

ANDREI: But . . .

NATALYA: Yes?

ANDREI: You see?

NATALYA: Yes?

ANDREI: My *sisters* . . . they've . . . they've *sent* for them . . .

NATALYA: . . . I'll . . .

ANDREI: . . . n'as it is their *house* . . .

NATALYA: No, no, no, I'll tell them too. I'll tell them what I did. They're so kind. *Aren't* they? I find them exceptional. (*Exiting.*) For supper I've told them to lay out some yoghurt . . .

(ANDREI *starts to interject.*)

Doctor says . . . *yes*, I know, but if you don't *eat* it, how are you going to lose the weight? No. He's cold. Bobik is cold in that room. It's the *room*, and we must find him another one til it turns warm. *Irina's* room! It's *perfect* for a child. It's *dry*, it's *sunny*, and why couldn't she move in with Olga for a while? You know? She's never here during the day. Isn't that true? Andriushka. You're so quiet.

ANDREI: . . . just thinking.

NATALYA: And there was something I wanted to tell you. Oh. Oh yes. Ferapont. From the District Board. Is here for you.

ANDREI: Alright.

NATALYA: Send him in?

ANDREI: Yes. (*She exits.* FERAPONT *enters.*) "Captain of my Soul." How are we?

FERAPONT: The chairman has sent down some papers.

ANDREI: *Has* he.

FERAPONT: And this book. (*Hands them to* ANDREI.)

ANDREI: Uh huh. And what brings you here so dispunctually.

FERAPONT (*pause*):   What?

ANDREI: Why are you here so late?

FERAPONT: . . . I'm late . . . ?

ANDREI: It's past *eight.*

FERAPONT: Yes, sir. It is. Sir. When I arrived here, it was *light.*
They kept putting me off. "The master's *busy* . . ." "Oh. Well.
If he's *'busy'* . . . then, you know, I'll, I'll, I'll . . . *wait."* I'm
sorry . . . ?

ANDREI: What? What? Nothing. Never mind. Tomorrow we're off
in the morning. But I'll stop in. Things to do. *Don't* we? So good
to have an "occupation."

FERAPONT: Sir?

ANDREI: Good to have somewhere to *go. Isn't* it? (*Pause.*) Old one.
(*Pause.*) Eh? Our *life.* And I say: "Go understand it." *"Explain"* it
to me. When I can take up a *book* . . . out of *boredom,* at *random,* and my hand falls upon, my old, my *university* lectures. Isn't
that "odd," then? I think so. Who is it that thinks so? The secretary of the District Board, of which board Protopopov sits as
chairman, while I revel in the honor of working as secretary *to* that
board, and while the highest honor to which I might in my delu-
sion aspire is to be nominated to sit with those dignitaries. I fall
asleep each night fantasizing that I am a Russian *Treasure,* you see,
a renowned light of the university whose name is synonymous
with *learning, courage, insight* . . .

FERAPONT: What?

ANDREI: Well. If you could *hear*, would I be *talking* to you . . . ? (*Pause.*) I need somebody to talk to. My *wife* doesn't understand. If I talked to my *sisters* they'd laugh me to scorn. I think they would. Who's going to listen to me? I don't care for *clubs* . . . but I would sit with *joy*, I would, at *Tyestov's*, or Slavyansky *Bazaar*, yes, I would. At any Moscow . . .

FERAPONT: A contractor was telling me that in Moscow, the other day, some men were eating *blinis*, and one man ate forty blinis. And died, is what he said. (*Pause.*) . . . Thirty or forty.

ANDREI: . . . there you are. (*Pause.*) In the grand dining room. Of a great Moscow restaurant. You know no one. And no one knows you. At The Same Time, you understand, there is a feeling of *belonging*. Yes. I use that word. Here, everyone knows everyone. And to what end, for we're all strangers. And so lonely. So . . .

FERAPONT: What? (*Pause.*) And the same man was saying—well, he might be lying, who's to say? That they have stretched a *hawser* crost the whole of Moscow. (*Pause.*)

ANDREI: What for?

FERAPONT: What?

ANDREI: For what purpose?

FERAPONT: I do not have the honor to know. And the man was saying.

ANDREI: What a load of garbage. Have you *been* to Moscow?

FERAPONT: Can't say that I have. For it did not fit with God's Will to guide me there. (*Pause.*) May I go now?

ANDREI: Well, yes. You may. God bless you. Come back tomorrow for the papers. Will you. Now go along. Goodbye.

(FERAPONT *exits.*)

Yes. To "work" at a thing. (*Pause.*) Isn't it? (*Exits.*)

(*Enter* MASHA *and* VERSHININ. *While they go on with their discourse, a maid enters and lights candles.*)

MASHA: I don't know. (*Pause.*) I don't know. Habit is a contributory factor, I know. When we lost our orderlies, you know, when Father died, we'd come to be so used to them. No, in any case, though, perhaps not in other places, but here, in *our* town, I've always found that the most decent people were the military.

VERSHININ: Would you like some tea?

MASHA: They'll serve the tea soon. They married me off at eighteen. Frightened of my husband. In awe of him. There he was, a *teacher*. There *I* was. I'd barely finished school. He seemed so *learned*. Do you know? So *wise*, to me. And so *important*. Regrettably, those feelings have changed.

VERSHININ: . . . have changed. Yes.

MASHA: And I'm not speaking specifically, or, or I'm not speaking *exclusively* of just my husband. I'm inured to him. But I *am* speaking of the nonmilitary portion of the population, when I find them coarse, ill-bred, ill-mannered, lacking in *grace; so* many civilians, and I am *disturbed* by this behavior, which is insufficiently polite, and . . . *gracious*. And to be among his *"teachers"* is torture for me.

VERSHININ: . . . it's . . . yes.

MASHA: It's *torture*. (*Pause.*)

VERSHININ: But I would observe that, civilian *or* military . . . in this town, it's much the same.

MASHA: Is it?

VERSHININ: It's the same. I think. If you listen to the educated class—in the service or not. A man. And his life is jaded. And he has worn out his *aims* . . . and he has worn out his *horses*, you see? And, and he has worn out his *wife*, and he has *used them up*, and the Russian Man deems a life of . . . "thought" in which . . .

MASHA: . . . yes . . .

VERSHININ: . . . in which he might . . .

MASHA: . . . "recapture," yes.

VERSHININ: . . . that is right . . . *regain* his spirits . . . he deems such . . . "philosophy" "not quite the thing." . . . He has grown jaded with his wife, his *children*, with the very, the very, the food he *eats*, until it all tastes of the pan, and the pan tastes of . . .

MASHA: Well. Yes. We're out of spirits today.

VERSHININ: I am out of spirits. I've had no dinner. I've had nothing since morning. My daughter is ill, I'm sick with anger at the kind of *mother* that fate has blessed her with, this morning, *shrieking* at me, from seven o'clock this morning, until I slammed the door at nine. You let me plague you with this. I talk to *no* one about this. Only you. Don't be cross with me. I have, please, I have no one. After you. (*Pause.*) No one.

(*Sound offstage.*)

MASHA: Did you hear that? Our stove rumbled. In the chimney. Just like that. It did. Just before Father died.

VERSHININ: What is that? A superstition?

MASHA: Yes.

VERSHININ: How romantic that is. What a wonderful woman you are. Magnificent. A wonderful . . . you are a wonderful woman. Even in the dark, here, I see your eyes. Sparkling . . .

MASHA (*moves*): There's more light over here.

VERSHININ: I love you. (*Pause.*) I love you. I love you. I love the way you move. I love your eyes. I dream about you. *Constantly*. You are the first thought and the last thought in my day.

MASHA: No, no, you've got me laughing. You know, you . . . *terrify* me. Don't . . . take it back. Someone is coming . . .

(*Enter* TUZENBACH *and* IRINA.)

TUZENBACH: I have a German name. I have a triple surname. Yes. I do. The Baron Tuzenbach-Kron-Altschauer. But am I a German? No. I am a Russian. Russian Orthodox, like you. Nothing of the German is left in me. Patience. Patience, perhaps. Or call it "stubbornness." With which I pursue you. Each evening, as I see you home.

IRINA: . . . I'm tired . . . how tired I am.

TUZENBACH: . . . and every day. As I *will* see you home. As I *will:* come by the telegraph office. At the end of day. And see you home. How many years shall I see you home? Ten years? Twenty? How long? Til you banish me. (*Sees* MASHA *and* VER-SHININ.) Oh yes. It's you. Home at last.

IRINA: Thank God I'm home. (*Pause.*) Woman comes in. She wants to telegraph her brother in Saratov. That her son has died. (*Pause.*) Can't remember the address. She sends it just like that: "Saratov." She's *crying* . . . I was so *rude* to her . . . "I haven't the *time*, you see?" Oh, Lord. It all comes out wrong. (*Pause. Sighs.*) We're having the mummers this evening.

MASHA: Yes.

IRINA (*sighs*): Oh *God*, I'm tired.

TUZENBACH: Back from your post.

IRINA: . . . yes.

TUZENBACH: Such a young, Unhappy Little Thing.

IRINA: I hate that office.

MASHA: You're losing weight?

IRINA: Am I?

MASHA: And, yes, you are, your face has lost its softness. You look like a young boy.

TUZENBACH: No, that's the hairstyle.

IRINA: I'm going to have to find a new position.

MASHA: . . . are you?

IRINA: Yes. It is *toil*, you see, without poetry. Not quite what I dreamed of.

MASHA: . . . Mmm.

IRINA: . . . without *thought* . . . with . . . (*Sound of knocking.*) The doctor . . . (*To* TUZENBACH:) Knock back to him. Will you? (TUZENBACH *knocks on the floor.* IRINA *sighs.*) He'll come up now. We are going to have to do something, you know. He and Andrei went to the club and they lost again. They say Andrei lost over two hundred rubles.

MASHA: . . . Mmm.

IRINA: Two weeks *past*, he lost, in *December* he lost. I wish to God
that he'd get it done and lose *everything*. Lose *everything*. Then,
maybe, we'd *quit* this town. Oh, Lord. My dearest God. I dream of
Moscow. Every night. It's an obsession. Just like a mad woman.
Til June. I am supposed to wait til June. "We move in June." But
we have *February*, we have *March*, we have . . . *April* . . . we
. . . almost half a *year*. We have *May* . . .

MASHA: We have these, Natalya doesn't know he's lost.

IRINA: To her it's all the same. (*Sighs.*)

(CHEBUTYKIN *comes in, sits down. He takes out a newspaper.*)

MASHA: And here he is. Has he paid his rent?

IRINA: No. Not for eight months. No.

MASHA: Slipped his mind.

IRINA: . . . seems . . . (*They laugh.*)

MASHA: Oh. Doesn't he sit like a *Pasha*.

(*Everyone laughs. Pause.*)

IRINA: Alexandr Ignatyevich?

VERSHININ (*sighs*): Oh, *I* don't know . . . do we not have *tea*. I
would give all that is in my power to *bestow* for half a glass of tea. I

CHEBUTYKIN: Irina Sergeyevna . . . ?

VERSHININ: . . . haven't had a crumb since morning.

IRINA: . . . yes . . . what?

CHEBUTYKIN: "Be. So. Good . . ." Would you descend to be so good as to come here to me? *Venez ici.* (*She goes to him.*) I cannot live without you.

VERSHININ: No. No tea. Then, if we cannot have tea, may we enjoy the comforts of Philosophy.

TUZENBACH: Yes. Treating of what?

VERSHININ: Treating of . . . can we not "daydream," as it were, of what life will be in three hundred years.

TUZENBACH: Immediately. People will move in hot-air balloons. *Fashions* will change. We will see the discovery and the development of the Sixth *Sense* . . .

VERSHININ: Yes.

TUZENBACH: But "life" . . .

VERSHININ: . . . "life," eyes.

TUZENBACH: *Life* will remain the same. Dark. Full of mysteries. Dark. Difficult. Unhappy. In a thousand years, too.

VERSHININ: . . . yes?

TUZENBACH: Man, man will sigh the same way and exclaim "Oh, Lord, I do not understand. It's so hard." Just as now. And free death. (*Pause.*) And yearn to live. Exactly as now. (*Pause.*)

VERSHININ: . . . but it is not, for it seems to me that it is, that *change,* and that the process of *changing,* alters every aspect of our life, little by little . . . so that, in accumulation, you see, in two or three hundred, in a thousand years—no, the date is not the point. "AT SOME TIME . . ." life will have *changed.* How can we say that it will not—as it is changing now?—into a new, a *happy* life—a life of betterment. Not that we live to *see* it, for we will not, but that now, in our suffering, in our . . . "philoso-

Konstantin Stanislavsky, the groundbreaking director and actor, whose thoughtful interpretations of Chekhov's plays helped establish the short story writer as a dramatist. In the first production of The Three Sisters, *he played Lieutenant Colonel Vershinin.*

phizing," in our lives *we are creating it.* And *this, this* is the purpose of our being—*this,* if you will, is our happiness. (*Pause.*)

(MASHA *laughs softly.*)

TUZENBACH: What?

MASHA: I don't know. I've been like this all day.

VERSHININ: . . . no, I have somewhat of the *groundwork* . . . but I lack your "refinement," in education, not having attended the academy. I do read. I read quite a bit, if not, perhaps, after any "system," and, so, do not, perhaps, read *what I should* . . . Meanwhile, the more I live, the more I want to know. And as I grow. Toward Death, and my hair grays, I become old, and I perceive how little, how very little I know. (*Pause.*) What do I know? One thing. It seems, and beyond contradiction: that, that, and I *ache,* you see, to demonstrate it: that there *is* no happiness. That there will *be* no happiness for us. But that *work,* that *work* (and we *must* work) will create happiness. For our, for, for our *descendants.* Which is *not* our lot; but may belong to them.

(FEDOTIK *and* RODE *appear and strum guitars.*)

TUZENBACH: Then one ought not even to dream of happiness.

VERSHININ: No.

TUZENBACH: No. Ah—but, if I'm "happy" . . . ?

VERSHININ (*pause*):   No.

TUZENBACH: . . . I'm not . . . ? Ha. Then we do not understand one another. How, then am I to convince you?

(MASHA *laughs softly.*)

Ah. Yes. *Laughter.* One million years, two million years, eighteen million years, and life will be the same. Life doesn't change. Life flows in its own ways, regardless of how we regard it. It has its own laws. With which we have no business. Or—however—which laws we can never know. (*Pause.*) Birds of passage. *Cranes,* for example; they "fly." Irrespective of what "thoughts," high or low, they may have running through their heads. They fly on. They do not know *why,* they don't know *where;* and they will fly no matter what philosopher-birds might emerge among them. Which the cranes would let philosophize as they might, while they continue to fly.

MASHA: . . . and the meaning?

TUZENBACH: The meaning? There! It's snowing! Yes. What is the meaning. (*Pause.*)

MASHA: This is the meaning: that a person must have a religion. He must seek a faith, or else his life is empty . . . it . . . it . . . to not *question,* you see? . . . why *children* are born . . . why the *cranes* fly . . . why . . . why the *stars* revolve over us . . . either one *feels* what one lives for, or else, wait a moment, or else everything is *pointless.* Do you see . . . ?

VERSHININ: But what a pity when Youth goes.

MASHA: In Gogol somewhere it says: living in the world, Ladies and Gentlemen, is Hell.

TUZENBACH: As I say. Disputing with you is *hard.* "Ladies and gentlemen."

CHEBUTYKIN (*of the newspaper*): Balzac was married. (*Pause.*) In Berdichev. (*Pause.*) I'm going to put it in my diary. (*Writes.*) Balzac . . . married . . . (*Pause.*) in Berdichev. (*Sighs.*)

IRINA (*laying out a hand of solitaire, to herself*): Balzac was married in Berdichev.

TUZENBACH: . . . the die is cast.

IRINA: . . . hmmm . . .

TUZENBACH: Maria Sergeyevna. I've sent in my papers.

MASHA: Yes. I've heard. I can't approve.

TUZENBACH: Why?

MASHA: I don't like civilians.

TUZENBACH (*sighs*): It's all the same to me. I'm not what one calls "that fine figure of a Military Man." No. Mmm. I'm not. (*Sighs.*) Well. I am going to go to work. Work. Do you work? *If only for one day.* Such that I return home and fall exhausted the *moment* I touch the bed. "Sleeping tight" . . . as workers do. (*Exits.*)

FEDOTIK (*to* IRINA): I was just on Moskovskaya Street. At Pyshivkovs. N'I picked up these colored *pencils* for you.

IRINA: No. I'm grown up.

FEDOTIK: Take them.

IRINA: You're used to seeing me and thinking of me as a *child* . . . but I've grown *up*.

FEDOTIK: . . . I got this *penknife*, too . . .

IRINA: May I see it? (FEDOTIK *hands the objects to her.*) Oh, it's *lovely* . . .

FEDOTIK: Isn't it? And I bought one for myself, too. Almost the same thing, not quite. Look: here's your major blade, and here's another blade, and here's a *third* . . .

IRINA: . . . no . . .

FEDOTIK: Yes. This is to clean your *ears* . . . a little *scissors* . . .

RODE: Doctor. How old are you?

CHEBUTYKIN: Thirty-two. (*Laughter.*)

FEDOTIK (*looking at the game of solitaire*): I'll show you another way to work it out. Gimme the cards.

(*A samovar is brought in.* ANFISA *is by the samovar. A little later* NATALYA *comes in and fusses around the table.* SOLYONY *enters and, having greeted the others, sits down at the table.*)

VERSHININ: *Lord*, what a wind!!!

MASHA: I am so sick of winter. I've quite forgotten what summer is like.

IRINA (*of cards*): It's going to come out.

MASHA: And what will that mean?

IRINA: That we will be in Moscow.

FEDOTIK: Oh. No. Your eight is on the two of spades. Won't come out. No Moscow.

CHEBUTYKIN (*of newspaper*): A raging epidemic of smallpox.

ANFISA: Masha. Now. Drink your tea up, Little One. (*To* VER-SHININ:) Begging your pardon, your Honor, and your forgiveness, as I have forgotten your Patronymic . . .

MASHA: Bring the tea here, Nanny, if you want me to drink it.

IRINA: Nanny!

ANFISA: Yes. Nanny's coming.

NATALYA: Suckling Babies, do you know, understand *perfectly*. Did you know that? "Hello, *Bobik!*" I said, "My darling . . ." and he looked at me. In that way. And you think it's the mother in me speaking, but I assure you. I saw what I saw. *Extraordinary* child.

SOLYONY: If he were mine, I'd cut him up and boil him and eat him.

NATALYA: *Oh,* that man . . .

MASHA: Happy is he who marks not whether it is summer or winter. And it seems to me that if I were in Moscow it would be one, but *here* . . . the *weather* . . .

VERSHININ: Just the other day. Do you know? I was reading the diaries of that Frenchman who'd been convicted for the Panama fraud. He'd written his book in prison. He writes of the *bird.* He writes of the *small* things, which he saw through his window. Things he had never seen before he'd been incarcerated. All the small things. With such joy. Now, of course, that he has been set free, he'll never notice them again. Just as you, when you live in Moscow . . .

MASHA: . . . yes?

VERSHININ: Yes. When you live in Moscow, you won't see it. (*Pause.*) There *is* no happiness, and no one possesses it. All that exists is longing.

TUZENBACH (*reenters, looks at a box on the table*): But where's the candy?

IRINA: Solyony.

TUZENBACH: Ate it?

IRINA: Yes.

TUZENBACH: He ate all of it? (IRINA *nods.*)

ANFISA (*serving the tea*): A letter for you, Little Father.

VERSHININ: A letter for me? (*Takes it, reads.*) Yes. Of course. Forgive me. Maria Sergeyevna. I must go. I won't have any tea . . . (*gets up*) . . . always the same thing.

MASHA: What is it? If it's not private.

VERSHININ: The wife's poisoned herself once again. I have to go. I'll get out quietly. Oh, Lord. It's so *tawdry*. (*Pause.*) My dear woman. My dear, my sweet woman . . . forgive me. (*Exits.*)

ANFISA: And where's he off to now, and I've just served the tea . . . Yes. That man is a villain.

MASHA: Oh, *spare* him, will you please? May we have some *peace* from you?

ANFISA: *Sweetheart* . . . what . . . ?   Have   I   *offended* you . . . ?

ANDREI (*offstage*):   Anfisa . . .

ANFISA (*mimicking*):   "Anfisa . . . Anfisa . . ." Calling. Calling. Sitting out there . . . (*Exits.*)

MASHA (*by the table*):   Do suffer me to take a seat. Yes. Oh, well. Sprawled all over it. Your *cards*, your *tea*.

IRINA: Oh, Masha, don't scold us . . .

MASHA: Yes. Fine. I'm a scold. Don't *deal* with me. Don't *traffic* with me. Don't . . .

CHEBUTYKIN (*sitting*):   "Don't deal with me, don't traffic with me . . ."

MASHA: And you, sixty years old and spewing nonsense like a child, and who the hell knows what.

NATALYA: Masha.

MASHA: *Yes.*

NATALYA: Darling Masha . . .

MASHA: *What?*

NATALYA: Why must you employ such expressions? Why? With your lovely appearance. Your . . . *"carriage,"* you would, and I tell you frankly, be simply *enchanting*, yes, and quite appreciated in correct society. If you would only mind your speech. *Je vous prie—pardonnez-moi, Marie, mais vous avez des manières un peu grossières.*

TUZENBACH: Ha. I tell you what I need. If someone could give, if someone . . . I think we have some *cognac* here.

NATALYA: *Il paraît que mon Bobik déjà ne dort pas.* He's awake . . . my boy isn't well today, n'I must go to him. You'll all excuse me . . . ? (*Exits.*)

IRINA: Where is Alexandr Ignatyevich?

MASHA: Gone home.

IRINA: Has he?

MASHA: Something "unusual" about the wife again.

TUZENBACH (*to* SOLYONY):   Always alone. Sitting. Sitting, thinking. *What* are you thinking about? Well. Let's make up. Will you? Have a drink with me. Today I am going to play the piano all night. I will play all *sorts* of rubbish. *Yes, I will.*

SOLYONY: So why do you say "make up"? Have we been quarreling?

TUZENBACH: You know. Yes. You always, *you* know what I mean. You seem to have the feeling—you know that you do, that something has "occurred." Isn't that so? Isn't it? You're a strange man. And you must admit it.

SOLYONY (*declaiming*):   Yes. I am strange.
But are we all not strange
If one were, for the briefest nonce,

> To peek behind this drape of
> Normalcy, Good Don Alekko . . .

TUZENBACH: And what has Don Alekko got to do with it?

SOLYONY: When I'm with someone face to face, I'm fine. With two people . . . I'm fine. In company, however, I'm a fool. It's as simple as that. I'm glum and shy and spew all *sorts* of idiocy, *and for all that,* are you listening, I'm content that I am more *honest,* and more *noble* than many, and than *very* many, and I can establish it.

TUZENBACH: . . . I'm angry with you all the time.

SOLYONY: . . . all of the time?

TUZENBACH: Well, yes, I think you pick on me. When we're in company. You pick on me, and yet, and yet, you *do.* You mistreat me, and yet I'm drawn to you. Why is that? Why is that?

SOLYONY: . . . well . . .

TUZENBACH: I'm going to get drunk. Drink with me.

SOLYONY: Thrilled. (*They drink.*) *I,* Baron . . .

TUZENBACH: . . . yes?

SOLYONY: Have never nurtured the slightest complaint against you.

TUZENBACH: . . . no . . .

SOLYONY: But I possess . . . I possess . . .

TUZENBACH: . . . yes?

SOLYONY: . . . the *mien* . . . the *personality,* you see, of a *swashbuckler.*

TUZENBACH: . . . you do?

SOLYONY: . . . I am *impetuous* and *brash* . . . yes, I do . . . in my *manner*, in *demeanor* . . . I bear it in my face. Like *Lermontov*, whom, it is said, and I agree, I resemble, and who . . .

TUZENBACH: I'm resigning.

SOLYONY: You are?

TUZENBACH: I'm sending in my resignation. Today. Yes. I am. Five years I've been debating. And I've made up my mind, I am going to work. To *work*, you see . . .

SOLYONY (*declaiming*): "Be not embroiled in *Wrath*, Alekko, and Forswear thy dreams . . ."

(ANDREI *enters*.)

TUZENBACH: . . . I shall work.

SOLYONY: "For *Dreams* . . . for Dreams are but the . . ."

CHEBUTYKIN (*going into the parlor with* IRINA): You should have seen the meal they laid out. *Caucasian*. Absolutely Caucasian. Magnificent. Soup with *onions* . . . Cheremsha.

IRINA: . . . Cheremsha?

CHEBUTYKIN: A meat-and-potato stew . . .

SOLYONY: Burdock.

CHEBUTYKIN: Yes?

SOLYONY: A burdock stew.

CHEBUTYKIN: Yes?

SOLYONY: Burdock is not a meat. (*Pause.*) "*Burdock* . . ."

CHEBUTYKIN: Yes . . .

SOLYONY: Is a *plant*.

CHEBUTYKIN: *Burdock*.

SOLYONY: Yes. It's a plant, akin to the turnip.

CHEBUTYKIN: Yes. I know. *Cheremsha*, however.

SOLYONY: . . . yes?

CHEBUTYKIN: Is a lamb stew. (*Pause*.)

SOLYONY (*to himself*):   Cheremsha is a lamb stew . . . (*To* CHEBUTYKIN:) But I am telling you that burdock . . .

CHEBUTYKIN: . . . yes . . . ?

SOLYONY: That *Cheremsha* is burdock.

CHEBUTYKIN: Yes, and I'm telling you that Cheremsha is lamb.

SOLYONY: And I'm telling *you* that Cheremsha is *burdock* and that burdock is a *plant*, and that Cheremsha is a plant, and it is burdock.

CHEBUTYKIN: And why should I, why should I dispute with *you*, who have never *been*, never *been* . . . have you ever been in the Caucasus . . . ?

SOLYONY: . . . I.

CHEBUTYKIN: Have you ever been in the Caucasus? You have never been in the Caucasus, and you have never *touched* Cheremsha.

SOLYONY: I've never *touched* it, as it is a turnip *stew*, a plant which I *detest*, the very *smell* of which . . .

ANDREI: Gentlemen . . .

SOLYONY: One moment . . . makes me nauseous, and I *ask* you, would I be *ignorant* of the *identity* of a substance which, the very *sight* of it, had the ability to cause me such distress?

CHEBUTYKIN: I . . .

SOLYONY: . . . seriously. I ask you.

ANDREI: Gentlemen.

SOLYONY: Your proposition's ludicrous upon the *face* of it.

NATALYA (*reentering*): . . . gentlemen . . . (*Exits.*)

SOLYONY: Respond to *that*.

ANDREI: Gentlemen. *Enough*. I beg you . . . *enough*.

TUZENBACH: When are the mummers coming?

IRINA: They promised by nine. Any time now.

TUZENBACH (*embraces* ANDREI *and sings and dances*): "Oh my bower, Oh my bower, Oh my bower new."

ANDREI (*singing and dancing*): "Bright paint and latticed maplewood."

CHEBUTYKIN: "Good strong and pleasant maplewood . . ."

TUZENBACH: Oh the *hell* with it. Let's just get drunk. Andriushka: let's drink *Brüderschaft*. Let us drink to that. You and me. Andriushka. To Moscow. Yes. To the university!

SOLYONY: Which one?

TUZENBACH: What?

SOLYONY: Which one? (*Pause.*) Moscow has two universities. (*Pause.*)

ANDREI: Moscow has one university.

SOLYONY: And I'm telling you two.

ANDREI: Fine. Alright. Two, three, so much the better for Moscow.

SOLYONY: No. Two. Not three. Two. Being the number of universities in Moscow. The *old*, and the *new*. And if my words displease you, if they "irritate," you see, I needn't *stay*, I can *remove* myself. (*Exits.*)

TUZENBACH: Bravo. He outdoes his very self. Bravo, our own Solyony. Ladies and gentlemen, I'm sitting down to play.

MASHA: The baron's drunk . . .

TUZENBACH: I'm preparing to play . . .

MASHA: The baron's drunk, the baron's drunk, he's drunk.

(*Enter* NATALYA.)

NATALYA (*to* CHEBUTYKIN): Ivan Romanych . . . (*She says something to* CHEBUTYKIN, *then goes out quietly.*)

(CHEBUTYKIN *touches* TUZENBACH *on the shoulder, whispers something to him.*)

IRINA: What is it?

CHEBUTYKIN: Time to go. Take care.

IRINA: Ah. Yes. Oh. One moment . . . the mummers?

ANDREI: Oh. They've been canceled. (*Pause.*) Natalya, you see (*pause*) Natalya says Bobik is not well and, so, you see, *I* don't know . . . *I* don't care . . . it's all the same to me . . .

IRINA: . . . Bobik isn't well . . . ?

MASHA: Well, then the *hell* with it. We're kicked out, and we've *got* to *go*. Ain't that the thing of it? Companions . . . ? (*To* IRINA:) Saying that it's not our Bobik who is unwell, but someone else . . . isn't that so . . . ? (*Taps forehead.*) In this portion right here . . . the *shrew*.

(ANDREI *goes to his room through the door on the right.* CHEBUTYKIN *follows him. In the reception room people are saying goodbye.*)

FEDOTIK: What a pity. I was so counting on spending a lovely evening. (*Pause.*) But if the little thing is sick, of course. I'll bring something *by* for him tomorrow, a *"toy"* . . .

RODE: I *purposefully* took a long nap after dinner, as I'd intended to *dance* all night, it's nine *o'clock,* for the Lord's sake . . .

MASHA: . . . on the street. We'll hash it all out there.

(*Everyone exits.* CHEBUTYKIN *and* ANDREI *enter quietly.*)

CHEBUTYKIN: I had, had not *time* to marry. Life flashed by me like *lightning*. And . . . (*pause*) and I deeply loved your dear mother. Your mother, who, of course, *was* married . . . so . . .

ANDREI: Men shouldn't marry.

CHEBUTYKIN: No?

ANDREI: It's . . . (*Pause.*) It's boring.

CHEBUTYKIN: Is it?

ANDREI: Yes.

CHEBUTYKIN: Aha. (*Pause.*) The *other* hand . . .

ANDREI: Yes?

CHEBUTYKIN: Loneliness.

ANDREI: Mmm.

CHEBUTYKIN: Philosophize all you like. But *loneliness* . . . devastating. Do you see? Dear fellow. Yes. It is. Though, and in this, you're right; set one against the other, and what do you have?

ANDREI: Well.

CHEBUTYKIN: Yes.

ANDREI: Let's go now, shall we . . . ?

CHEBUTYKIN: All the time in the world.

ANDREI: Let's go now, though.

CHEBUTYKIN: Why?

ANDREI (*pause*): I don't want my wife to stop me going.

CHEBUTYKIN: Mmm.

ANDREI: No, no, no. I'm not going to play today. *No*. I'm not. I'm not *up* to it . . . that's *right*. (*Pause*.) Ivan Romanych.

CHEBUTYKIN: Yes.

ANDREI: What do I take for a shortness of breath?

CHEBUTYKIN: I don't *remember*, and I don't think that I ever knew.

ANDREI: Let's get out through the kitchen.

(*They exit. A ring, another ring. Voices are heard offstage, laughter.*)

IRINA (*entering*): What's that, who's there . . . ?

ANFISA (*in a whisper*): The mummers.

IRINA: *Nanny*. Tell them there's no one home. Please ask them . . . (ANFISA *starts to exit*) . . . their pardon. (*Pause*.)

(SOLYONY *enters.*)

SOLYONY: . . . why . . . why is . . . where is everyone . . . ?

IRINA: Gone home.

SOLYONY: Odd. (*Pause.*) Are you alone?

IRINA: Yes. (*Pause.*) Goodbye.

SOLYONY: You know, I believed I behaved, just now, without suffi-
cient restraint. And that I acted tactlessly. But you can understand
me. I feel that. You are so far above the average of . . . *intelligence*, of . . . you are *pure*. I think that you are *elevated*. You
perceive the truth. And you, alone, can understand me. And my
love. I *profoundly*, I *endlessly* . . . adore . . .

IRINA: Oh. Go away. (*Pause.*) Go away. *Goodbye.*

SOLYONY: . . . I cannot live without you. My angel. My *bliss*. My
darling. You magnificent, you wonderful, such eyes, which no
mortal . . .

IRINA: I said Stop It. (*Pause.*)

SOLYONY: I am speaking of my love for you. For the first time.

IRINA: . . . Vassily Vassilych . . .

SOLYONY: And, as I do, it is as if I am not on the earth. Or, I *am*
on the earth, for, for the first time, and that, *previously* . . .

IRINA: VASSILY VASSILYCH . . . (*Pause.*)

SOLYONY: Yes. (*Pause.*) I see. One cannot make oneself dear to
someone else by force. (*Pause.*) I see. (*Pause.*) Of course, yes.
(*Pause.*) As long as there are no *rivals;* you see? For a *rival* is an
obstacle which may be overcome. Eh? a *rival* . . . a rival may be
killed, he may, my *God*, I love you. My *Bliss*, my . . .

(NATALYA *passes, with a candle. She looks behind one door and passes by the door, looking for her husband's room.*)

NATALYA: . . . weeellll, that's *Andrei*—let him read . . . Vassily Vassilych. I beg your pardon. Please excuse my undress. I didn't know you were still . . .

SOLYONY: . . . it's all one, believe me.

NATALYA: I . . .

SOLYONY: Goodbye . . . (*Exits.*)

NATALYA: You must be tired, my dear. Mmm? Ought to get you to bed earlier. Mmm . . .

IRINA: Is Bobik sleeping?

NATALYA: Asleep. Barely, but yes. Restlessly.

IRINA: Mmm.

NATALYA: I meant, by the way, dearest, I meant to bring it up to you, but you're *out*, or I've been *busy*, eh?

IRINA: Yes?

NATALYA: . . . but he's been *cold*, you see, in his room, Bobik . . . it seems to me. His *nursery* is always cold. It's damp, and your room would be so nice for a child. So warm, and would you do this and move into Olga's room for me . . . ? A little while. My dearest . . . ? (*Pause.*)

IRINA: What?

(*Sleighbells are heard approaching the house.*)

NATALYA: That you and Olga would move in together. In her room. A while. A little while. To give Bobik your room. For the warmth. My angel. I said to him today, *"Bobik:* You're *mine.* Mine. Mine. Mine." And he responded to me. With those eyes . . . ? You know? He looked at me. With those eyes of his. (*A ring.*) Well, mustn't that be *Olga?* Mmm. How late she is . . .

(*The maid goes up to* NATALYA, *whispers in her ear.*)

NATALYA: Protopopov . . . ? What a funny man! *"Protopopov"* has come. To ask me to go for a *troika* ride. Ha! How bizarre these men are. *Aren't* they . . . ? (*Pause.*) Aren't they . . . ? (*A ring.*) Someone's come. Yes. I suppose I *could* go riding—for a quarter hour. (*A ring.*) And that must be Olga.

(NATALYA *and the maid exit. Enter* KULYGIN, VERSHININ, *and* OLGA.)

KULYGIN: Well, *here's* one for you . . . said that they'd be having a soiree. What do you make of it . . . ?

VERSHININ: I left not half an hour ago, and the mummers were coming.

IRINA: Everyone's gone.

KULYGIN: Masha's gone, too? (*Pause.*) Where did she go? Protopopov's downstairs in a *troika.* (*Pause.*) Waiting for whom?

IRINA: Oh. Please. No questions. I'm so tired.

KULYGIN: Ah. You capricious girl.

OLGA: The meeting's just ended. I'm sick-tired. (*Pause.*) My head is splitting. The headmistress is ill. I'm doing *her* job . . . Andrei squandered two hundred fifty rubles at cards yesterday, the whole town's talking about it.

KULYGIN: . . . yes. I was tired by the meeting too.

VERSHININ: Well. The wife took a funny way to frighten me a bit. She's almost killed herself . . . (*Sighs.*) But it came 'round alright. So . . . well. (*Pause.*) And we're *resting* now . . . are we . . . ? No "soiree"? No. And, so, we're off, I suppose. Yes. Well, then, permit me to wish you the best. Fyodor Ilych . . . ? Will you come with me? We'll go somewhere. Eh? Can't go "home" mmm. No. Come with me.

KULYGIN: No.

VERSHININ: Please.

KULYGIN: I'm *exhausted*. No. I'm not coming. (*He gets up.*) Has my wife gone home?

IRINA: Must have.

KULYGIN (*kisses her hand*): Goodbye. Tomorrow, and the day after tomorrow. We can rest. Goodbye. I really need some tea. Thought we were going to spend the evening . . . (*Pause.*) *Refreshments* . . . oh well. *O fallacem hominum spem.* Which we find is the accusative case, exclamatory . . . (*Exits.*)

VERSHININ (*following*): I'll come too.

OLGA: Oh, *God*, my head. And Andrei has lost a fortune. And the whole *town's* gossiping about it. I have to lie down. Two days' rest. Tomorrow I'm free. And the day after tomorrow I'm free. Oh. My God. My head. Why do you do this to me . . . ? (*Exits.*)

IRINA: All gone.

NATALYA (*entering*): Just going out half an hour. Then I will be back. (*Exits.*)

IRINA (*pause*): Moscow. (*Pause.*) Oh, Lord. Could we go to Moscow . . .

Act III

Olga and Irina's room. To the left and right, screened off beds. It is past two o'clock in the morning. Outside, a fire alarm is being sounded. MASHA *is lying on the couch in a black dress. Enter* ANFISA *and* OLGA.

ANFISA: Well, now, they're under the stairs. "Have the Gracious Goodness to come up," I say. "Who *acts* like that . . . ?" And they say, *"Father.* Where *are* you . . . ? We don't know where he *is* . . ." God forbid. "He's *burned"* they say. "He's burned up!!!" How do they *think* these things? Out in the yard, we've got some there, too. *Also* uncovered. Undressed.

OLGA (*taking clothes out of the wardrobe*): Take . . . yes . . . take the little gray one. Take *this* one. Take the skirt, too, Nanny. Oh. My God. The whole of Kirsanovsky Lane's burnt down.

ANFISA: Lord.

OLGA: Burnt down to the ground. Take this one, too. The poor Vershinins. Nearly lost their house.

ANFISA: . . . God bless them . . .

OLGA: . . . and let them spend the night here.

ANFISA: Yes.

OLGA: Mustn't go home.

ANFISA: No.

OLGA: And poor Fedotik. Everything burnt. (*Pause.*) Quite lost.

ANFISA: Good if you called Ferapont.

OLGA: Mmm. Yes.

ANFISA: Or Oliushka, or I won't be able to carry it all.

OLGA (*sound of a ring*):   Come in. Whoever is there . . .

(*Through the door the red glare of the fire is visible. The sound of a fire brigade passing is heard.*)

How horrible . . .

(*Enter* FERAPONT.)

Take this downstairs. The Kolotilin girls. They're standing under the stairs.

FERAPONT: Yes, miss.

OLGA: Give it to them.

FERAPONT: Yes, miss.

OLGA: Go.

FERAPONT: In the year twelve, Moscow was burnt too.

OLGA: . . . would . . . ?

FERAPONT: . . . was it *not?* Eh? And *weren't* the French surprised? We . . .

OLGA: Would you go, please?

FERAPONT: Yes, miss.

OLGA: Nanny.

ANFISA: Yes?

OLGA: Give it all away. We don't need any of it. Give it all away. Oh, Lord. I'm tired. I can hardly stand. Don't let the Vershinins go home. Put the girls in the parlor. Alexandr Ignatyevich can go down to the baron's room too. Or he can stay here. And the doctor is drunk, as it falls out, and must be alone . . . and Vershinin . . .

ANFISA: Yes . . . ?

OLGA: . . . his wife in the parlor too.

ANFISA: Oliushka, dear. (*Pause.*) Oliushka . . . (*Pause.*)

OLGA: Yes?

ANFISA: Oliushka.

OLGA: Yes.

ANFISA: Don't put me out.

OLGA: What?

ANFISA: Please don't put me out.

OLGA: What are you saying? No one's putting you out.

ANFISA: . . . my Golden Child, you know. I work and slave. I must grow weak, I'm "old," and everyone will say "Put her out. What good can she do?" But where would I go? Eighty-two years old, my next name day, and God willing that . . . "Go on, GO!" To an old woman . . . but, but . . .

OLGA: Nanny . . .

ANFISA: . . . where would I *go?*

OLGA: Nanny, dear, please. Please. You're tired. Rest. My good one. Shhhh. You're white as a . . . no one is putting you out.

(*Enter* NATALYA.)

NATALYA: Well. They're saying we should take up a subscription. For the victims. As we should. Right away. For the fire victims. Excellent idea. As the poor should be helped. It is the duty of the rich, and he who gives quickly gives twice. Bobik and Sofotchka are sleeping away. Just as if nothing had occurred. Aren't they . . . ? Oh. *Such* a lot of people in the house. Wherever one turns. And influenza in town and I'm terrified the children will get it.

OLGA (*looking out the window*): We can't see the fire from here. So peaceful.

NATALYA (*in front of a mirror*): Yes. I must look a fright. They say I've put on weight. Well. *That's* not true . . . No. Not a bit of it. And Masha sleeping. She's exhausted. *Isn't* she? . . . poor thing. (*To* ANFISA:) How *dare* you sit in my presence? How *dare* you??? Get up! Get out of here! Get UP!! (ANFISA *exits*.) HOW CAN YOU KEEP THAT *HAG?* I swear to the *Lord*, I don't understand you.

OLGA: . . . forgive me . . . what? (*Pause.*) What?

NATALYA: What *use* is she? Why is she *here?* She's . . . why is she here . . . ? She's a *peasant*, she shouldn't be in the house. She should be in the *country* somewhere. What are you "playing" at . . . ? A house must run on *order*. Like a *machine*. Do you understand? It cannot have a superfluous part. *You* understand me. Poor thing. Poor tired thing. Our headmistress is tired. Yessss. When my Sofotchka grows up and goes to the academy, then I must live in fear of you. *Won't* I . . . ?

OLGA: I won't be the headmistress.

NATALYA: Yes. You will. Olyetchka. It's been decided.

OLGA: It's beyond me.

NATALYA: What?

OLGA: I shall decline.

NATALYA: Why?

OLGA: I can't. It's beyond my strength. (*Pause.*) You were so rude to Nanny just now . . . I . . . forgive me . . . I'm . . . I don't have the *strength* . . . to *endure* . . . it all went dark. For one moment.

NATALYA: Oh, God. Olga. Forgive me. I'm sorry.

OLGA: . . . it . . .

NATALYA: . . . so sorry I've *upset* you . . .

OLGA: We, if you would understand me, we were brought up strangely. It's true, but I cannot bear, bear to see such treatment. I can't *bear* it. Do you hear me? It makes me *heartsick* . . .

NATALYA: I'm sorry, I . . .

OLGA: . . . the slightest rudeness. A harsh word, a thoughtless word . . .

NATALYA: I often say what's uncalled for. It's true.

OLGA: . . . it so *disturbs* me . . .

NATALYA: But you must agree, my dear, she really should live in the country.

OLGA: She's been with us thirty years.

NATALYA: But she cannot *work* anymore. I don't . . . I, I don't understand it. Either I don't understand or you don't wish me to. She cannot *work* anymore. She just sleeps or sits.

OLGA: Let her sit, then.

NATALYA: What do you mean?

OLGA: Let her sit.

NATALYA: But she's a *servant*. (*Pause.*) I don't *understand* you,
Olga. I don't *understand* you. I have a maid. I have a *nanny* . . .
I have a wet nurse . . . why in the world would we need this old
woman . . . ? *Why*. What *for*?

(*Sound of an alarm offstage.*)

OLGA: I've aged ten years tonight.

NATALYA: *Olga*. (*Pause.*) It's essential for us to come to an understanding. You're at the academy all day. While I am at the house.
(*Pause.*) You have your *teaching*. I have my *domestic* duties. If I say
something touching the help . . . (*Pause.*) If I say something
treating of the *help* . . . then I know what I'm speaking of. Do
you understand me? And I want her gone. I want her to be out of
here. By tomorrow night. *OUT* of here. I'm here all day, and I say
so. That *hag*. She's a *thief* . . . she's . . . I know what she is.
You don't. YOU AREN'T HERE. And I won't have you, I will
not *stand* for this behavior on your part. Do you . . . (*Pause.*)
You know . . . really . . . I think if you don't move downstairs we are likely always to be quarreling. Don't you think? It's
not right.

(*Enter* KULYGIN.)

KULYGIN: Where's Masha? It's time to go home. The fire's dying
down. They say. (*Stretches.*) Only one block lost. What a wind,
though. We thought the whole town would go. Oh, Lord, I'm
tired. Olyetchka, my dear, you know, often I've thought, if it

wasn't Masha, I'd have married *you* . . . you are so good . . . (*Pause.*) I'm tired to my bones. (*He listens.*)

OLGA: What?

KULYGIN: Seems that our doctor's on a, somewhat of a *bender*. And it seems he's coming here . . . yes? Hear it? *Oh* yes. Alright. (*Pause.*) Don't give me away. (*He starts to hide himself in the wardrobe. To himself:*) Our *doctor* . . .

OLGA: Two years he hasn't been drinking.

KULYGIN: Mmm . . .

OLGA: . . . all of a sudden now . . .

(CHEBUTYKIN *enters, goes to the washstand, and starts washing his hands.*)

CHEBUTYKIN: The devil, the devil, the devil "take" them. Take the *lot* of them. What do they think I am. "A doctor." What am I supposed to do? Well. He's supposed to *recognize* and *treat* and *cure* all sorts of . . . what? *Disease* and *maladies*. While I know absolutely nothing. I remember nothing, if I learnt it, and I *know* nothing.

(OLGA *and* NATALYA *exit.*)

Last Wednesday. The woman in Zasp. The doctor treated her. She died. It was my fault. Twenty-five *years* ago . . . Yes. Yes. *Then*. But now? I am nothing. What am I? Nothing. No profession. And no arms. No legs. Nothing. Not a man. Not a man. But not to *exist* . . . Dear Lord, forgive me and the people at the club. Talking of *Shakespeare, Werther* . . . talking of them . . . talking to me of them. *I* haven't read them. And yet I'm nodding at them. I'm nodding at them. Why? WHY IN THE WORLD AM I

PRETENDING? *WHY?* That woman? I *butchered* her. I killed her. *All* of it. How can one sort it out? How? When one is *puking* at the *sordidness* of this life. This loathsome *self*, leading a life . . . and so I started drinking . . .

(IRINA, VERSHININ, *and* TUZENBACH *enter.* TUZENBACH *is wearing civilian clothes, very new.*)

IRINA: We can sit here. No one will come in here.

VERSHININ: The soldiers saved the town.

IRINA: Yes.

VERSHININ: Weren't for the soldiers, the town would have burnt. Good. Good men. Lovely men.

KULYGIN: Ladies and gentlemen. What is the hour?

TUZENBACH: Going on four.

KULYGIN: Mmm.

TUZENBACH: Getting light soon.

IRINA: Everyone's in the reception room. Nobody's going home. And your Solyony's in there too. Doctor. You ought to be in bed.

CHEBUTYKIN: Quite right, miss. (*Pause.*) Quite right.

IRINA: . . . yes.

CHEBUTYKIN: *Thank* you, miss.

KULYGIN: Got swackered. Yes. You did. Ivan Romanych. *Good* boy. Good for you. That's my lad! *Vino veritas*, as the Old Folks explained it.

TUZENBACH: Everyone's asking me to engineer a benefit for the fire victims.

IRINA: How would we?

TUZENBACH: No—no, it could be done. If we wanted to do it.

IRINA: We . . .

TUZENBACH: Maria Sergeyevna plays the piano. She plays superbly.

KULYGIN: Superbly.

IRINA: . . . she . . .

KULYGIN: . . . like twenty angels.

IRINA: She hasn't touched the piano in years.

TUZENBACH: . . . no, I.

IRINA: For years.

TUZENBACH: No, I . . . I . . . this is not a musical town. It is not a town "schooled in music," but I give you my word that *she*, you see, plays magnificently. She does.

IRINA: Maria Sergeyevna.

TUZENBACH: Almost on a professional level.

KULYGIN: I love her, Baron. I love her. Masha. She is so.

TUZENBACH: . . . what must that be? To be so *gifted*. To play so . . . "well." And know that no one can appreciate it. What must that be like?

KULYGIN: Yes. She plays well. But.

TUZENBACH: . . . she does.

KULYGIN: . . . would it be proper? For her to take part? In a concert?

TUZENBACH (*pause*): Why not?

KULYGIN: Well, what do I know. Perhaps it would be fine. Perhaps. I don't know anything. You see. What do I know? But our head-master . . . a fine man, an intelligent man . . . he has such "views." Do you understand me? And, it is not "his business," of course, but perhaps I could refer it to him . . .

(CHEBUTYKIN *picks up and examines a peculiar clock.*)

VERSHININ: I got all filthy at the fire. I look like something. What do I look like? Nothing on earth. I heard yesterday. There is talk that they may transfer the brigade. Yes. To *Poland*, perhaps, or China.

TUZENBACH: Yes. I heard that too.

VERSHININ: Mmm.

TUZENBACH: *That* would empty the town . . .

IRINA: . . . and we would be going away too . . .

(CHEBUTYKIN *drops the clock.*)

CHEBUTYKIN: Smashed to flinders. (*Pause.*)

KULYGIN: Zero for conduct, Ivan Romanych.

IRINA: That was Mama's clock.

CHEBUTYKIN: Perhaps. Perhaps that was Mama's clock. And per-haps it was hers and perhaps it appears that I broke it. Perhaps it *seems* that I did. And perhaps we do not exist—to think these things. And if we did not think them, do *they* exist? Do they? And is it not true that no one knows *anything*, finally? Is that not the case? (*By the door.*) What are you looking at? Natalya's in there flirting with Protopopov. *You* don't see it. You're in *here*. She's in *there*. That's the nature of phenomena. She's in there. Flirting with

Protopopov. Would you find it diverting to accept this little *plum . . . ?*

VERSHININ: Thank you. (*Laughs.*) How *odd* this all is, finally.

CHEBUTYKIN: Mmm.

VERSHININ: I ran home. When the fire broke out. I raced home. As I got there, I saw the house was safe. But my girls, my little girls—they were out on the threshold. Dressed in their thin underclothes. Their mother wasn't there. Everywhere people running. Horses, dogs running . . . I saw on their faces such terror. Such terror. It broke my heart. My *God*, the things those little girls will have to face in the course of their lives. (*Pause.*) What they will have to live through. And I came here. (*Pause.*) And here is their mother. (*Alarm.*) My little girls. Were stranded at the threshold.

(MASHA *enters, sits.*)

And the street was red with fire. And there was. That terrible noise. And I thought: long ago . . . long ago . . . that *something like this* has occurred. (*Pause.*) There was a raid. An enemy . . . "invaded" . . . they looted. And killed and plundered. (*Pause.*) In a savage time. And I thought: in essence, what difference is there? Between that time and this? Between that and this. (*Pause.*) Between what *was* and *is* . . . ? And then more time will pass. Two, and three hundred years. Will have passed. And *our* life. Our . . . "shouting" . . . will be looked back on with the same . . . "incredulity" as that which *we* have. Looking at the past. How odd it seems. How *awkward*. How strange. (*Pause.*) Yes. Forgive me. It seems that I'm "going on again." I am philosophizing. (*Pause.*) Listen to me. It seems . . . what if . . . as if everyone in the town were sleeping. Can you feel that? As if that were so? As if only we three in the town were awake. Truly awake. But. In each generation. As time passed. More would come. Gradually. Constantly. Until the *people*, you see, gradually, would come 'round to think your way. Until this state of "wakefulness," over the years, until it came to be, you see . . . the "norm." Until that norm *itself* was surpassed. In "time" . . . do you see . . . ? In "time" . . . and people. Who were born. Looked back . . . they looked back . . . (*Pause.*) *Ha.* (*Pause.*) *Lord*, I want to live . . . I'm in a mood, I know it . . . I would like to live to see it . . . *HA.* But I want to live . . . (*Sings.*) "All ages are in thrall to love. The very spheres Adore her."

(MASHA *sings along with him a bit. Enter* FEDOTIK, *who sings along and dances.*)

FEDOTIK: "Burnt *Out*, Burnt *Down*, burnt out all *Around* . . ." (*Pause.*) Quite completely burnt.

IRINA: Why are you singing about it?

FEDOTIK: . . . quite completely burnt. All gone. Guitar's gone. All of the photographs burnt. All of my letters. I wanted to give you one of my notebooks. (*Sighs.*) They're all burnt too.

(*Enter* SOLYONY.)

IRINA: No. No, please. Vassily Vassilych, *please*. Not now.

SOLYONY: I . . .

IRINA: You . . . you can't come in.

SOLYONY: . . . I can't come in . . .

IRINA: No.

SOLYONY: The baron can. The baron can come in, but I can't . . . ?

VERSHININ: Well, I have to go in any case. How are they doing with the fire?

SOLYONY: It's subsiding. .

VERSHININ: . . . Mmm.

SOLYONY: They say. No. I'm sorry. I find it *odd*. How is it that the *baron* comes in, and I can't?

VERSHININ (*singing*): ta tum ta tum ta tum ta tum . . . the very Spheres.

(MASHA *sings along with him.*)

VERSHININ (*to* SOLYONY): We'll go in to the foyer.

SOLYONY: Well. Fine. If that's the answer. "Yes. It all could be a bit more clear. But that would irk the Geese, I fear . . ."

(*He makes clucking noises at* TUZENBACH. *Exits with* VERSHININ *and* FEDOTIK.)

IRINA: Solyony has smoked up the room. The baron's asleep. Baron! . . . the baron's asleep.

TUZENBACH: . . . waking. Oh, God I'm tired. (*Pause.*) The brickyard. You see, that's a day's work. I'm not joking with you. And I don't say it in jest. I *will* be working. In the brickyard, soon. I've already been speaking to a man. (*To* IRINA:) You are so pale. Do you know? You enchant me. *So* beautiful. Your pale complexion lightens the dark air. How sad you are. I see it in your face. Yes. You are sad. My darling. You are discontented. Discontented with life. Live with me. Come with me, *work* with me. Live with me . . .

MASHA: Nikolai Lvovich.

TUZENBACH: Yes.

MASHA: Get out of here.

TUZENBACH (*laughs*): *There* you are.

MASHA: Yes.

TUZENBACH: Alright. Oh, Lord. Alright. I'm going. Goodbye, I look at you now, and the *past* comes back to me. I see you *long* ago. Long ago on your *birthday*. So long ago. Bright. Young. You spoke of the "joys of Labor." Yes, you did. And how *right* life seemed to me then. How *right* it seemed. That Happy Life. You're crying. Off you go. Go to bed, now. It's morning. It's almost light. The new day is coming. Oh. If I could give my life to you . . . (*Pause.*) I *give* it! Yes!

MASHA: Nikolai Lvovich.

TUZENBACH: Yes?

MASHA: That's enough.

TUZENBACH: Yes?

MASHA: Yes. Go away.

TUZENBACH: I'm going. (*Exits.*)

MASHA: Fyodor?

KULYGIN: Mmm.

MASHA: Are you sleeping?

KULYGIN: Eh?

MASHA: Go home. You ought to go home.

KULYGIN: My dear, sweet Masha. Dear girl . . .

IRINA: She's exhausted.

KULYGIN: . . . mmm?

IRINA: *Fedya* . . .

KULYGIN: Yes.

IRINA: Go and let her rest.

KULYGIN: Yes. In a moment. *My. Good. Wife.* My only one. My nice "wife." I love you, my . . .

MASHA: *Amo. Amas. Amat. Amamus, amatis, amant.*

KULYGIN: Isn't it. You amaze me. Seven years of marriage and it seems to me that we met *yesterday. Yesterday*, eh? Seven years. And what a woman. What am I? *Content.* Yes. That is the world which we're speaking of. A man who is content. Who . . .

MASHA: And I'm sick. I'm sick. I'm tired. A woman who is both, and are you listening. *Tired* and *sick.* And what else? What else has been done? To *plague* me, and to occupy my *thoughts* . . . with *worry.* All day. Every day, a nail in my shoe: he's mortgaged the house, Andrei. Our Andriushka. Has mortgaged our *house.* The house where the *four* of us live. He mortgaged it. His wife's taken the money . . . FROM OUR HOUSE—which belongs, not to him alone, but to the *four* of us; and she's taken the money. How . . . how can an honest man . . .

KULYGIN: Shhhh, Masha . . .

MASHA: *What?*

KULYGIN: . . . why . . .

MASHA: Why *what?*

KULYGIN: He's in *debt.* Andriushka's in *debt.* He owes . . .

MASHA: He's in "debt" is he . . . ?

KULYGIN: What do you need it for?

MASHA: What do I need it for? *What?*

KULYGIN: The money.

MASHA: It's *mine*. (*Pause.*) It's mine.

KULYGIN: Are we poor? Eh? I work. I teach. I give *lessons*. We have a good life. An honest life. Your needs . . .

MASHA: I wasn't speaking of our needs.

KULYGIN: What are you speaking of?

MASHA: I'm speaking of injustice. (*Pause.*) Go, Fyodor. Go.

KULYGIN (*kisses her*):   You're tired.

MASHA: I told you that.

KULYGIN: You rest. Rest a half hour or so. I'll wait for you. I'll sit out there. You rest. Sleep. I am content. I'll wait for you. (*Exiting.*) Oh, yes . . .

IRINA: How petty Andrei has become. How small. He is *wrung out* by that woman. He was going to be a *professor*. Now he's boasting that he's been accepted as a member of the District Board. A member of the Wondrous Board. Of which board Protopopov is the chairman. And our Andrei's all elated he's a member of the ranks. The whole town's laughing at him. He sees nothing. And *here:* everyone is running to the fire. Where is our Andrei . . . ? In his room. Tuning his fiddle. Oh. Oh. I can't bear it any more. No. Please. I can't.

(OLGA *enters.*)

Put me out. Put me out. Put me out of here. I can't *bear* it.

OLGA: What *is* it? *Darling*. What *is* it . . . ?

IRINA: Where has it all gone? My *God*, where has it gone? I've lost *everything*. Where has it gone? It's lost in my head. I . . . I keep forgetting . . . I . . . the Italian for "window," for "ceiling" . . . HOW CAN I HAVE LOST IT? And life is passing. Every day. And *everything* we have is going by. And we will never go to Moscow. I see we won't go.

OLGA: . . . my dear . . .

IRINA: Oh! My unhappy life. I can't work anymore. I can't work anymore. I worked at the telegraph. And now I'm in an office. For the town. I hate my useless work. I hate it. I hate it. I'm almost twenty-four. I've been working so long. I've grown old working. I'm so tired. My brain is tired. My memory. I've become thin. And ugly. My mind has grown old. And nothing pleases me. Time passes. I feel myself . . . moving "off" from it. Farther and farther. From a beautiful life. Into some . . . (*Pause*.) Why am I still alive? Why haven't I ended it? I don't understand, I . . .

OLGA: Shhhh. Darling. Don't cry. Shhhh. You're killing me.

IRINA: I'm not crying. I'm not. Now . . . now . . . No. I'm not crying anymore. I'm done.

OLGA: . . . my darling.

IRINA: . . . I . . .

OLGA: My darling. I tell you. I'm telling you. As a sister—I'm telling you. As your best friend: (*pause*) marry the baron. (*Pause*.) You respect him. You do. You "value" him. And it is *true:* he isn't handsome. But he's good. He's decent. And he's pure . . . as you know. Shhhh. Why . . . yes . . . why do we marry? For "love"? I think not. Finally, no. For *duty*. Yes. I think, in any case, that *I* would. Without love . . . ? Yes. *Whomever*. If he was decent. If he was *pure* . . . an *old* man, even. Yes. For the *important* thing . . .

IRINA: You know . . . I just keep waiting. I just kept on. Waiting for our move. "In *Moscow,*" I thought. "I'd meet my *real* man." My "destined" man. I dreamed of him. I loved him. I waited for him . . . what stupid folly.

OLGA (*embraces her*): I know. I know. I know. My darling. My *dear.* I know. (*Pause.*) I know. When the baron resigned and came to us without his uniform . . .

IRINA: . . . yes.

OLGA: I know . . . he looked so *dowdy* . . .

IRINA: . . . yes.

OLGA: . . . so dowdy. I started crying. What could I say to him? "Why are you crying?" he said. But, but . . . wait a moment. Darling . . . *"But."* If this good man, if this "decent" man should want to *marry* you, I would be happy. I would be so happy. Because, you see, this is *different* . . . you see . . . because . . .

(NATALYA, *carrying a candle, enters and walks across the stage.*)

MASHA: I think she set the fire.

OLGA: Oh *Masha* . . .

MASHA: . . . Mmm.

OLGA: You're the family clown.

MASHA: Mmm. My sisters? My Clown Soul. My Jolly Soul is heavy, do you want to know? It is. Hear my confession. For I am in torment and my Guilty Knowledge sears my Heart. My sinful Mystery. My secret which screams to be told. I am in love and I love someone. I love a man. You have just seen him. The man that I love. Vershinin.

OLGA: Stop it.

MASHA: I . . .

OLGA: Stop it. I don't want to hear it.

MASHA: What am I to do? You tell me. He was *strange* to me. At first. I *thought* about him. Often. I felt sorry for him. I . . . I "grew to love him." I did. I grew to love him. His *voice* . . . his *ways* . . . his *misfortunes* . . . his two little *girls* . . .

OLGA: No no *no!* I can't hear. I Cannot Hear What You Are Saying. *NO*. It's *shameful*. It's *foolishness*. I won't hear it.

MASHA: You won't hear it? Olga? You won't hear it? Why? I love him. He loves me. It's my Fate, do you see? This love. It's as simple as that. Yes. Yes, it's frightening. Yes. But it's *mine*. It's what I *am*. Yes. My darling. Yes. It's *life* s'what it is. We *live* it, and look what it does to us. We read a novel, and it's clear. It's so *spelled out*. This *isn't* clear. *Nothing* is clear. And *no* one has a final *true* idea of anything. It's "life." We have to *decide*. Each of us. We. Have. To *DECIDE*: what *is*, what it *means*, what we *want*. My darling sisters. (*Pause*.) That's what the thing is. And now I've confessed. And I'll be silent. (*Pause*.) As the grave. (*Pause*.) Silence.

(*Enter* ANDREI, *followed by* FERAPONT.)

ANDREI: *What?* I don't understand you.

FERAPONT: Andrei Sergeyevich. I have explained it to you. Ten times. I . . .

ANDREI: One moment. *Firstly:* you may call me "Your Honor."

FERAPONT: Andrei Ser . . .

ANDREI: *Not* Andrei Sergeyevich . . .

FERAPONT: . . . I . . .

ANDREI: "Your *Honor*."

FERAPONT: I . . .

ANDREI: "Your *Honor*." (*Pause*.)

FERAPONT: Your Honor . . . Your Honor. The firemen. Asking permission to get down to the river through the garden. (*Pause*.) They want to cut across the garden, else they'll have to go around—the . . . uh . . . "long way."

ANDREI: Alright. Tell them yes. (*Pause*. FERAPONT *does not leave*.) Al*right!* (FERAPONT *exits*.) *God*, am I sick of the . . . Where's Olga? (OLGA *comes out from behind a screen*.) I need you. Where is your key to the cupboard? That little key . . . ? (*She hands him the key*. IRINA *goes behind the screen*.) *Vast*. Vast fire. Overwhelming. Burning down now. Burning itself out. (*Pause*.) Ferapont. Fine, now I've gotten myself, made a fool of myself, n'front of him. "Your Honor." What is it? Olga? What is it? Let's have it out. It's enough, now. All of this, all of this "sulking," any moment . . . What is it? What have I done to you?

VERSHININ (*offstage, singing*): Tra traaa tra traaa . . .

MASHA (*getting up*): Tra traaa tra traaa. Olga: good*bye*. And God be with you. (*Kisses* IRINA, *goes behind the screen*.) All Restful Slumbers. Andrei: Goodbye. Goodbye. Leave us now. Everyone's so tired. You, you "have it out" tomorrow. (*Exits*.)

OLGA: Andriushka. Yes. Leave it til tomorrow. (*Goes behind the screen*.) Sleep now. Time to sleep.

ANDREI: No. I'll go. But I'm going to say it first. One moment. Please. Please. Firstly: my wife. You . . . please . . . there's something which you bear against her. Natalya. *I've* seen it. Since our wedding. Now: now: now: my wife, Natalya is, in my opinion, a fine human being. Can I say that plainer? A fine, honest, and straightforward, noble Human Being. I *respect* her, I respect those things in her, and I demand, I *demand* that others do the same. Do you see? She, my wife, is a "good woman," and all of your, your, your "grievances" against her, are, what can I call them? "whims." Now: suddenly, what? You seem to be "hurt." You're "grieved" at *my* life. That I have not, that I am not a *"professor,"* that I do not occupy my life among the "sciences" . . . this angers you. My choices. My . . . as you perceive it, *"degradation"* in my choice of work. And this *reflects* upon you. Is that it? That . . . yes. Well, I've *said* it. But I *do* work. I *do* work. Don't I? I work on the District Council. As a member of the Board. And I am proud of that work, if you want to know. And don't *require* your . . . "endorsement" of that work to be proud of it. And, as it seems, you must *withhold* that, be it so. *Thirdly,* I have mortgaged the house. And I have done so, yes, without resort to your opinion. In this I am at fault, and I ask your pardon. (*Pause.*) I was compelled to it. By debt. (*Pause.*) I . . . uh . . . I . . . a debt, a debt of thirty-five thousand rubles. (*Pause.*) I no longer play at cards—you may have remarked. That I quit that some time since. (*Pause.*) If I, and if I may suggest something. To justify myself. Perhaps. That it was in my thoughts, as it *is*, that you girls, you are the guaranteed recipients of *income*, in the form of your *annuity*. While I, as you know, as you know, have nothing. *No* . . . "income" . . . no . . .

KULYGIN (*entering*): Is *Masha* here? No . . . ? Where is *Masha* . . . ? (*Exits.*)

ANDREI: . . . and Natalya, as I have said, is an *excellent* human being. She has a good soul. She . . . (*Pause.*) She . . . (*Pause.*) My darlings. (*Pause.*) My darling sisters. I thought that we'd be happy. (*Pause.*) I didn't marry her to be unhappy. I swear to you . . . I thought . . . my darlings . . . I . . . (*He weeps. Exits.*)

KULYGIN (*reentering*):   No? She's not here? Where *is* she . . . ?
Where the devil . . . ? (*Exits.*)

(*The stage is empty. Sound of an alarm. Sound of knocking.*)

IRINA (*behind the screen*):   Olga . . . What is that?

OLGA: It's Doctor Ivan Romanych.

IRINA: *What?*

OLGA: It's Doctor Ivan Romanych. Knocking on the floor.

IRINA: Why is he doing that?

OLGA: He's drunk.

IRINA: . . . what a night. (*Pause.*)

OLGA: *What?*

IRINA (*looks out from behind the screen*):   Olga . . .

OLGA: What?

IRINA: Did you hear?

OLGA: . . . did I . . . ?

IRINA: . . . that the brigade is being transferred.

OLGA: I heard it. Yes. It's only gossip.

IRINA: . . . because we'd be all alone. (*Pause.*) Olga.

OLGA: Yes.

IRINA: We'd be all alone. (*Pause.*) Olga.

OLGA: Yes.

IRINA: Olga . . . (*Pause.*) The *baron* . . .

OLGA: Yes. The baron?

IRINA: He is a good man?

OLGA: Yes.

IRINA: He's a good man. (*Pause.*) I can marry him.

OLGA: Yes?

IRINA: I'll marry him.

OLGA: You will.

IRINA: I'll agree to marry him. Only. Can we go to Moscow? Can we leave here? Olga? Please (*Pause.*) Olga . . .

Act IV

The old garden of the Prozoroff house. A long avenue of firs, at the end of which a river is visible. On the other side of the river, a forest. On the right, the terrace of the house; here, bottles and glasses on the table—it is evident that champagne has just been drunk. It is twelve o'clock noon. From the street, passersby walk through the garden to the river occasionally; five or so soldiers walk through rapidly.

CHEBUTYKIN, in a benign mood which does not leave him throughout the entire act, is sitting in an armchair in the garden waiting to be called; he is in a military cap and has a stick. IRINA, KULYGIN, with a decoration around his neck and no moustache, and TUZENBACH, standing on the terrace, are seeing off FEDOTIK and RODE, who are walking down the steps; both officers are in field dress.

TUZENBACH (*exchanges kisses with* FEDOTIK):   You are a good man. You are a good man. *Such* a pleasure. Knowing you. (*Goes to* RODE. *Exchanges kisses.*) One more time. My dear. Farewell.

IRINA: Goodbye.

FEDOTIK: Yes. Farewell. Not goodbye, but farewell. For we will not meet again.

KULYGIN: Who can say? Who can say . . . Oh, Lord . . . I've started crying too.

IRINA: . . . *someday* . . .

FEDOTIK: Ten years? Fifteen years from now? Who will we be then? Wait . . . wait . . . wait . . . (*Takes a snapshot.*) Just once more . . .

RODE (*embraces* TUZENBACH):   No. We shall not meet again. (*Kisses Irina's hand.*) Thank you. For everything.

FEDOTIK: Please. Just a moment. Will you . . . ?

TUZENBACH: No. We'll meet again. God willing . . . *write* us . . .

RODE: . . . yes.

TUZENBACH: No. Truly. *Write* to us.

RODE: Farewell. *Trees*, farewell. *Air*, farewell, *Echo* . . . echo . . . farewell . . .

KULYGIN: And who's to say? You may get *married* there . . .

RODE: . . . in Poland . . . ?

KULYGIN: Yes. Why not? A Polish wife. To embrace you, to call you *Kokhaneh* . . .

FEDOTIK (*glances at his watch*):   Hour left. One. Hour. Left. Less. Out of our battery, only Solyony's trav'ling on the barge. And we are going with the combat unit. Hmm. Three of the companies are off today. And tomorrow the remaining three. And then the town will be at peace. Will be Left at Peace.

356 ♦ ANTON CHEKHOV

TUZENBACH: And unrelieved boredom.

RODE: Where is Maria Sergeyevna?

KULYGIN: In the garden.

FEDOTIK: We should tell her we're off.

RODE: . . . farewell.

FEDOTIK: Tell her we said goodbye.

RODE: I'm off, or else I'm going, to, I'm going to break down weeping. I am. (*Embraces* TUZENBACH *and* KULYGIN. *Kisses Irina's hand.*) Our life here has been so . . .

FEDOTIK (*to* KULYGIN): This is for you . . . (*Hands him several items.*)

RODE: . . . it has been *splendid*.

FEDOTIK (*to* KULYGIN): A souvenir.

RODE (*to himself*): . . . splendid.

FEDOTIK: . . . little *notebook,* and a *pencil* . . . well. Let's get down to the barge. (*They exit.*)

RODE (*shouting*): Yo!

KULYGIN (*pause, shouts*): Farewell.

(*At the rear of the stage,* FEDOTIK *and* RODE *meet* MASHA *and go out with her.*)

IRINA: . . . and gone.

CHEBUTYKIN: Gone. And who said goodbye to me?

IRINA: And what did you say to *them* . . . ?

CHEBUTYKIN: I forgot.

IRINA: Mmm.

CHEBUTYKIN: Well. I did. (*Shrugs.*) I'll see them soon. (*Pause.*) I'm off tomorrow too. One little day. One more day. One more year til my retirement. And then I'll return. And live out my life here. Near you. One more year til my pension. And an *involutional* change in my life. Into a life so . . . *quiet.* So "retired." Obliging, *genteel.*

IRINA: Yes. You change your life here. (*Pause.*) Yes. You should do that.

CHEBUTYKIN: Yes. One feels one should . . .

IRINA: . . . my dear.

CHEBUTYKIN (*sings*):   Tra traaa . . . tra traaa . . . "Upon this Rock you Find me . . ."

KULYGIN: Ivan Romanych . . . ?

CHEBUTYKIN: *Oh* yes . . . ?

KULYGIN: What can one do with you?

CHEBUTYKIN: Nothing. (*Pause.*) And very little of *that.*

IRINA: Fyodor's shaved his moustache. I can't bear to look at him.

KULYGIN: Why?

CHEBUTYKIN: Well. We see what your *face* looks like.

KULYGIN: Mmm.

CHEBUTYKIN: Why'd'ja do it?

KULYGIN: It's the "thing," I believe.

CHEBUTYKIN: Mmm . . . ?

KULYGIN: Headmaster's shaved his moustache. Made me an under head, and mine went too. Nobody likes it.

CHEBUTYKIN: Doesn't suit you.

KULYGIN: No. But it is "the done thing." And, so, there you are.

(*At the rear of the stage,* ANDREI *is wheeling a baby carriage.*)

IRINA: Ivan *Romanych* . . .

CHEBUTYKIN: Your servant.

IRINA: I'm concerned.

CHEBUTYKIN: For what?

IRINA: I'm worried.

CHEBUTYKIN: Of what?

IRINA: Yesterday . . .

CHEBUTYKIN: . . . yes . . . ?

IRINA: When you were *walking*. What transpired.

CHEBUTYKIN: "Transpired."

IRINA: Yes.

CHEBUTYKIN: Nothing.

IRINA: Nothing?

CHEBUTYKIN: No.

IRINA: No? On the boulevard . . . ?

CHEBUTYKIN: The boulevard?

IRINA: Yes.

CHEBUTYKIN: Nothing. (*Reads the paper.*) No—nothing, all the same . . .

KULYGIN: They're saying that Solyony and the baron.

CHEBUTYKIN (*reading*): Mmm hmm . . .

KULYGIN: "Met" yesterday . . .

CHEBUTYKIN: . . . Mmm . . .

KULYGIN: On the boulevard.

CHEBUTYKIN: Yes . . .

KULYGIN: Near the theater. And apparently.

TUZENBACH: Oh, please. *Enough* of that now. (*Goes into the house.*)

KULYGIN: Apparently . . . apparently Solyony took it on himself to *taunt* the baron . . . to . . . "taunt" him. And he, the baron, took "offense." And "said" something, which Solyony . . .

CHEBUTYKIN: . . . what stupid gossip.

KULYGIN: D'you know that that derives from "God's Sibs," which is to say "siblings," which is the name given to the midwives of the seventeenth century. In England. *Of* which profession the brother of a quite good friend of mine wrote a doctoral dissertation while we were at university, which paper I was privileged to read and find quite the most boring compendium it has ever fallen to my lot to see. They say Solyony is in love with Irina, and he has, understandably, then, come to loathe the baron. A fine girl. Irina. Not unlike my Masha. No. Giv'n to *reflection,* you are, with, though, as we know, a gentler disposition . . . well, no, though, then, again, then, Masha, to be just, her disposition can be quite, I, I adore her, Masha.

(*At the rear of the garden, offstage,* Coo-eeeee, Coo-eeeee!)

IRINA (*shudders*): Huh. It all frightens me today. (*Sighs.*) I'm packed. And they're coming. After dinner. To pick up my things. And tomorrow, too. I shall be Married. And the baron and I will be off. And the day after I will be already "installed" at the school, and won't that be the start of a New Life. With God's help. I sat for the teacher's examination and I cried at the awesome "completion" of it all. (*Pause.*) They'll be coming here for the things soon.

KULYGIN: Hmm. (*Pause.*) *However* it may be, for, finally, what is "philosophy," and what is "talk"? However: from the bottom of My Heart, I wish it to you.

CHEBUTYKIN: Quite moving. My good Golden Girl. All of you. Come so far. Grown so. Who can keep pace with you? Not one who has been left behind. No. Like the old bird when the young birds fly. Well, fly, then, my dear darlings. What else is it all for? Fyodor Ilych—you were a fool to shave your moustache.

KULYGIN: Thank you. (*Sighs.*) The military, today, will have mustered and decamped. And everything will go on. As it did before they came. And Masha is a *fine* woman. A *good* woman. *Whatever* they may say; and who is there that has not had everything said about them, in the course of a full life? I love her. And I thank the fate which bore me to her. *People* . . . (*pause*) have different destinies. Within the *excise* office, we discover a certain *Kozyrioff*. He was at school with me. He was "sent down." As he could never come to terms with certain peculiarities of the Latin tongue. He is now fallen on Hard Times. I, when I see him, have been known to greet him thus: "Hail, *ut consecutivum!*" To which, when done, he replies: "Yes. *Ut consecutivum* precisely." He adds his thanks. He coughs a bit. A fellow in a bad way, no mistake about it. While I, on the other hand, may stand as an example to the contrary, and the reasons being what they may, of a man who all his life has enjoyed quite a good degree of Luck. And is a happy man. A holder of the Stanislas medal, second degree, himself, a *teacher*, who, now, himself, labors to convey that selfsame *"ut consecutivum."* And, granted, a person of some intelligence, yes—yes, but does happiness reside in that . . . ?

(*In the house, someone is playing the piano.*)

IRINA: As of tomorrow evening I need never again be subjected to that song. I need never again encounter Protopopov. That same Protopopov who came today, too, and who is out there in our parlor.

KULYGIN: Has the headmistress arrived?

IRINA: No.

KULYGIN: . . . no?

IRINA: . . . she's coming.

KULYGIN: Yes?

IRINA: Yes. She's been sent for. You know, it's been so lonely here. With Olga gone all day. So lonely. She's at the academy. She *lives* there. "The headmistress . . ." Busy all day. Important things. (*Pause.*) Important work. What do I have to do? Nothing to occupy me. Nothing. (*Pause.*) A hateful life. Yes. It is. My "room . . ." (*Pause.*) And I've decided this: if I am *destined* (*pause*) if it's *written* that I will live in Moscow . . . then I will do so. If It Is Not To *Be* (*pause*) then it was *not* so written. And it's fate. And nothing's to be done about it, it's God's will. It's true. That's what I thought. And what I have arrived at. (*Pause.*) Nikolai Lvovich asked me for my hand. He is a good man. And. As I *thought* of it, my soul *lightened*, my burden "grew light." A burden lifted, and I was, at once, I became "cheerful." And wanted to *work*. I wanted to "turn my hand" to some work. To something. But yesterday . . . (*Pause.*) Yesterday, something

. . . (*Pause.*) Something "moved me from it." Something hov'ring over me . . .

CHEBUTYKIN: Disregard it.

NATALYA (*in the window*): The headmistress . . .

KULYGIN: The headmistress has arrived.

(KULYGIN *goes into the house with* IRINA.)

CHEBUTYKIN (*reads the paper, sings softly*): "Tra traaa. Upon this Stone I sit . . ."

(MASHA *approaches. In the background,* ANDREI *is wheeling the baby carriage.*)

MASHA: And there he is. Sitting.

CHEBUTYKIN: So what?

MASHA: What?

CHEBUTYKIN: What of it?

MASHA: Nothing.

CHEBUTYKIN: Well, then.

MASHA: Did you love my mother?

CHEBUTYKIN: Yes. I loved her very much.

MASHA: Did she love you? (*Pause.*)

CHEBUTYKIN: . . . it was so long ago.

MASHA: And is my Very Own One here? That's how our old cook used to speak of her policeman. "My Very Own *One.*" S'my very own one here?

CHEBUTYKIN: He isn't here yet.

MASHA: When happiness is given to you only in *installments*, do you know? In little "bits"—and then not even that, you *coarsen*. Did you know that? And you become mean. You become terribly small. As I have. And there's our Andrei. Darling of Our Hopes. Our brother. For the Multitudes Subscribed to Raise a Bell. And Capital and Labor were expended on it. On the bell. But in the *raising* of it, it fell. And it shattered. (*Pause.*) No notice. (*Pause.*) No reason. (*Pause.*) And so it is with Andrei. Little Modern Fable.

ANDREI: When will we have quiet in the house . . . the *noise* . . .

CHEBUTYKIN: There will be quiet soon. (*Looks at his watch.*) My antique repeated. Half hour. Quarter hour . . . (*Pause.*) The "hour," of course . . . the first, the fifth, and seventh companies embark at one exactly. (*Pause.*) And, then, I go tomorrow.

ANDREI: And go until.

CHEBUTYKIN: Until?

ANDREI: Forever?

CHEBUTYKIN: Forever. Can't say. Might return. One year. Don't know. S'all one, really.

(*Somewhere, far off, sound of a harp and violin.*)

ANDREI: . . . the town.

CHEBUTYKIN: . . . yes?

ANDREI: Will be like an empty *tin*. There was some "to-do" at the theater yesterday. Everyone's talking of it in shorthand. I missed it.

CHEBUTYKIN: . . . did you.

ANDREI: What was it?

CHEBUTYKIN: Nothing. Some foolishness.

ANDREI: Yes.

CHEBUTYKIN: Solyony goading the baron. (*Pause.*) The baron felt his "honor" had been . . . one thing led to the next, and Solyony felt obliged to *challenge* him.

ANDREI: Challenge the baron . . . ?

CHEBUTYKIN: That's right.

MASHA: To a duel?

CHEBUTYKIN (*looking at his watch*): Yes. I would think, just about *now.* Half past. The Birch Grove. (*Points out the window.*) "The Birch Grove over the River." Just make it out. (*Makes shooting gestures.*) Eight. Nine. Ten! Kapang! Solyony thinks he's Lermontov. Bad verse. The whole of him. Well. Fun is fun, but this is his third duel.

MASHA: His third?

CHEBUTYKIN: Yes.

MASHA: Whose?

CHEBUTYKIN: Solyony.

MASHA: And the baron?

CHEBUTYKIN: The baron.

MASHA: Yes.

CHEBUTYKIN: What?

MASHA: No. "It's." I can't . . . haven't . . . no, I haven't finally sorted it out, but, no, it shouldn't be allowed.

CHEBUTYKIN: It shouldn't.

MASHA: He might *kill* him. Or . . . he might "wound" him . . .

CHEBUTYKIN: Who?

MASHA: . . . the baron.

CHEBUTYKIN: Well. The baron's a good man. But one *baron* more or less I mean, let's not "sentimentalize" it. (*Pause.*) Let them fight.

(*A shout offstage.*)

Svortzoff. His second.

MASHA: Where is he?

CHEBUTYKIN: In the boat.

ANDREI: It is my opinion that to aid in any way the progress of a duel, or to *countenance* it, even as a doctor . . .

CHEBUTYKIN: . . . Yes?

ANDREI: Is wrong.

CHEBUTYKIN: Yes. Well, no. It only *seems* so. For we do not abet it. We are not "of" it. (*Pause.*) We are not there. Nothing is there. We do not exist. There is no one *thinking* this. It's all just "seeming." (*Pause.*)

MASHA: And so they talk. One day, the *next* day. Always. Fall to winter. Soon it will snow, and this *talk*. No. I'm not going in the house. I'm not coming in. You'll tell me when Vershinin comes. (*Looks up.*) "The birds of Passage." Migratory birds. Moving already. Lucky ones. (*Exits.*)

ANDREI: The house empties itself. The garrison is gone. The sisters will go. *You'll* go. I'll be left alone.

CHEBUTYKIN: And your wife?

(*Enter* FERAPONT, *carrying papers.*)

ANDREI: A wife is a wife.

CHEBUTYKIN: And how is that?

ANDREI: A decent. Kind, all of the adjectives . . . a woman, you
know . . . but . . . but . . . I feel. There is something in her.
That. For want of a better word . . . (*Pause.*) You know, I so
treasure, if I may, the opportunity to be open with you. You are
the only one I truly can be frank with. (*Pause.*) I love my wife. I
do. But at times, I feel that she brings me to a level where . . .
where all I can feel is *revulsion*. And I feel *hatred* for her. And for
her petty *ways*. I do. And her *vulgarity*. And *selfishness* passing as
reason. And I don't understand. And I don't remember . . . how
it was, how, I came to "love" her, or . . .

CHEBUTYKIN (*rising*):   Waaal. (*Pause.*) My friend. I'm off tomorrow.
And it's unlikely that we will meet again. And so, I'm going to
give you some advice. (*Pause.*) Get your hat. Pick up your walking stick. Go out and walk. Never come back. Never *look* back.
And the farther off you walk, the better.

(SOLYONY *turns, crosses the back of the stage with his seconds. He sees*
CHEBUTYKIN, *stops. The seconds go on.*)

SOLYONY: Doctor. Half past twelve. It's time.

(SOLYONY *greets* ANDREI.)

CHEBUTYKIN: One moment. (*Sighs.*) Lord, I'm sick of it all. I'm
sick of you all. (*To* ANDREI:) If they ask for me, you'll say, I've
just . . . (*Gestures, as if to say, "Gone off for a moment."*)

SOLYONY: "And hardly had he cried 'alack'
Before the bear was on his back!"
And what is *your* trouble, Old Man?

CHEBUTYKIN: Mmm.

SOLYONY: How *are* you this fine day?

CHEBUTYKIN: . . . excuse me.

SOLYONY: No, no, no, he frets himself for nothing. I won't *hurt* him. I may *wing* him—like a *woodcock*, eh, to "bring him *down* . . ." (*He sprinkles eau de cologne on his hands.*) That's one whole bottle gone today. Hands smell of *death*. "And he, rebellious seeks the Tempest. As though in the Storm he could find Peace . . ."

CHEBUTYKIN: And "hardly had he cried 'alack' before the bear was on his back." (*Exits with* SOLYONY.)

(*Shouts of* Coo-eeeee *and* Yoohoo *are heard. Enter* FERAPONT *and* ANDREI.)

FERAPONT: . . . Papers to sign. The papers must be signed.

ANDREI: No, please . . . Leave me alone . . . Please . . . *No*. (*He goes off with the baby carriage.*)

FERAPONT: Well, that's what papers are *for*. What are they for, if not to be signed . . . ? (*Exits*).

(*Enter* TUZENBACH *and* IRINA; KULYGIN *walks across the stage, shouting* Coo-eeeee, Masha, Coo-eeeee.)

TUZENBACH: Well. There's the only one in town is glad the garrison is off.

IRINA: The town will be empty now.

TUZENBACH: Darling. I'll be back soon.

IRINA: Where are you going?

TUZENBACH: Just into town. To see my friends off.

IRINA: Is that true?

TUZENBACH: Yes.

IRINA: No. It's not. *Nikolai.* What was it happened yesterday?

TUZENBACH: . . . yesterday?

IRINA: In front of the theater.

TUZENBACH: My darling. My darling. I'll be back. One hour. (*He kisses her.*) My dearest one. I've worshiped you for these five years. Each time I see you. It's a revelation. I *remember* you as beautiful, and then we meet, and you are *always* more beautiful than I remember. It doesn't change. It only grows stronger. I feel like I'm falling. I do. When I look at you. And *tomorrow:* I'll take you away. To be mine. To be with me. How can that be? That happiness? All my dreams. Can that be? Everything but the one thing: that you don't love me.

IRINA: How can I? (*Pause.*) I cannot "feel" it. How can one force oneself? I told you. I will be your wife. And I will serve you. Obediently. And faithfully. But if I do not love you, how am I to love? How??? . . . (*She weeps.*) Tell me that. Not once in my life. Not once. And I long for it. And I *dream* of it. My soul is a jewelry box. And they've lost the key . . . what is it?

TUZENBACH: What is it? It's *you.* I know what you're saying. I *feel* it. All night. And I don't sleep. And I *wake.* And I am thinking of that lost, as you say, of that "lost key," and don't you think that it *torments* me? Say something to me. (*Pause.*) I said say something.

IRINA: What?

TUZENBACH: What? Anything. I'm sorry. Say something.

IRINA: I don't know what to say.

TUZENBACH (*sighs*): Isn't it funny. How these things begin? And yet we go on . . . *seeing* them. And can't stop ourselves. Going on.

IRINA: What are you talking about?

TUZENBACH: No. You're right. Today . . . today is a day to be *glad*. Or be *content*. Or see the trees around us, you know? Our *maples*. Our *birth* trees. Each with its own life. Isn't it? As if they were *watching* us. They are so permanent. *We're* so . . . but it's as if to live near them we're to have an education. (*A shout off-stage.*) I must go on. (*Pause.*) That one *there* . . . you see? It's dead. But it still sways when the wind blows. Just like the others. As it seems to me, if *I* would die, that something would go on. In some way. Do you see? (*Pause. He kisses her hand.*) Darling. Farewell. The papers you gave me are in my desk.

IRINA: I'll come with you.

TUZENBACH: No. No. *Irina* . . .

IRINA: Yes. What is it?

TUZENBACH: I. Didn't get my coffee today. They forgot to make it. Would you tell them that. (*Exits.*)

FERAPONT (*entering*): Andrei Sergeyevich. (*Pause.*) These papers aren't mine. They are "official" papers. From the *bureau*. They aren't mine . . . they aren't *my* papers.

ANDREI: What did I do with my life? I was young. I was bright and clever. Future before me. Full of Joy. I saw it. How could it be otherwise? And then it was past. Just young, just begun to live. And become old. Dull. Useless. Carping. Bitter. Failed. (*Pause.*) Fools. Cheated miserable fools. (*Pause.*) We have one hundred thousand people in this town. And not one fit to emulate. Or to admire. They *eat*. They *breed*. They *die*. They grow stupid from boredom. They drink and gamble, and they cheat at cards. The women cuckold the men, who pretend not to know. The children are raised in this sewer of hypocrisy. (*To* FERAPONT:) What do you want?

FERAPONT: What? *Papers* to sign.

ANDREI: You make me want to die. (FERAPONT *hands him the papers.*)

FERAPONT: The porter from the bureau told me in Petersburg this winter they had two hundred degrees of frost.

ANDREI: The present nauseates me. I think of the future, and I feel clean. (*Pause.*) Thinking of the future. (*Pause.*) I see: a life without drink, without the *stench* of bad cooking, without after-dinner naps . . . a life free of parasites, and . . .

FERAPONT: Two thousand people froze. They did. In Petersburg. Hmm. Or Moscow.

ANDREI: Oh, Lord.

NATALYA (*in the window*):   Could we please keep our voices down? Who is . . . ? Andriushka? Is that you? You'll wake the baby. *Il ne faut pas faire de bruit, la Sofie est dormée déjà. Vous êtes un ours.* No. If you want to shout, give the *child* and the *carriage* to someone else. Ferapont.

FERAPONT: Madame?

NATALYA: Take the carriage from the master.

FERAPONT: Yes, Madame.

ANDREI: But I'm talking quietly.

NATALYA (*behind the window, talking to her boy*): Bobik . . . *Bad* Bobik. Yes, "nonobedient . . ."

ANDREI (*glancing through the papers*): Fine, fine, alright. I'll glance through them. I'll *sign* them, and then you take them back to the Board. *Fine.*

(*Goes into the house reading the papers.* FERAPONT *pushes the carriage to the back of the garden.*)

NATALYA (*behind the window*): *Bobik.* Yes! What's your mama's name? *Bobik.* What's . . . yes. What's your mama's name? And who is that? Your aunt. *Olga.* Can you say her name? *Olga.* Yeesss . . .

(*Wandering musicians play on violin and harp.* VERSHININ, OLGA, *and* ANFISA *come out of the house and listen for a moment.* IRINA *approaches.*)

OLGA: Our garden is a turnpike. Everyone cuts through it. *Nanny.*

ANFISA: . . . my dear.

OLGA: Give the musicians something.

ANFISA (*gives money to the musicians*): Go with God. Hard life. (*Pause.*) Don't play music in the streets if you're not hungry. (*To* IRINA:) My little one. What a life. What a life you've given me. At the *academy.* My own *apartment.* With my Oliushka. The Lord has vouchsafed to me. Comfort in my last years. And not since I was born, black as I am with Sin, have I enjoyed such comfort. Apartment, paid for by the government. My own *alcove.* My own *bed.* It costs me *nothing* . . . I wake in the night and pray, and in my prayer is this: "No one, mother of God, is happier than me."

VERSHININ (*glancing at his watch*):   Olga Sergeyevna. I must go. I wish you everything . . . everything that . . . where is Maria Sergeyevna?

IRINA: Somewhere in the garden. Shall I get her?

VERSHININ: If you would. (*Looks at his watch.*) Thank you.

ANFISA: *I'll* find her. (*Exits with* IRINA.) Mashenka! Mashenka! chick, chick, chick, chick . . .

VERSHININ: Everything must end. (*Pause.*) And now we are parting. The town gave us, you could call it, a "breakfast." The mayor made a speech. Champagne. My soul was here with you. (*Pause.*) I've, you know, I've grown used to you.

OLGA: Will we meet again?

VERSHININ: I would not think so. (*Pause.*) My wife will be staying on another month . . .

OLGA: . . . yes.

VERSHININ: If she, or the little ones should *need* something . . .

OLGA: Of course. Of course. I promise you. (*Pause.*) Tomorrow there won't be one uniform in the whole town. (*Pause.*) A memory. And the new life begins. And. (*Pause.*) It never falls out our way. Does it? The way we planned. (*Pause.*) I didn't want to be headmistress. Here I am. Not in Moscow. Here . . .

VERSHININ: Well. (*Pause.*) I thank you. For everything. (*Pause.*) Thank you. And, please, know of my deep respect for you, and that . . . one moment that I will remember you.

OLGA: Oh, where is *Masha,* then . . . ?

VERSHININ: And what else can I say. By the way of farewell? What have we left unsaid? What insights of philosophy? Hmm. "Life is Hard." Does that do it? It seems to us dull. Dull and repetitious.

Without hope. And yet, as we live it, *if we wish*, it becomes clearer. (*Looks at his watch.*) So much strife. Wars. Campaigns, victories. But we've left that now. Haven't we? Left it behind. A void. Now. All of that energy. For what? And how shall we fill it? That new thing? Of course we're seeking it. The educated. Seeking *labor*. Labor. Seeking "insight" . . . (*Looks at his watch.*) I must go.

OLGA: Here she is.

(*Enter* MASHA.)

VERSHININ: I've come to say goodbye.

(OLGA *walks away a little. Pause.*)

MASHA: Farewell. (*Beat. A prolonged kiss.*)

(OLGA *clears her throat. They look to her for a moment.* MASHA *sobs.*)

VERSHININ: Write me. Don't forget me. Don't forget me. (*He kisses Olga's hands. Embraces* MASHA *again.*) Don't forget me. (*Exits.*)

(*Pause.*)

OLGA: Shhhh. Masha. Shhhh, now. Come now, darling . . .

(*Enter* KULYGIN.)

KULYGIN: It's alright. Let her cry. No. No. (*Pause.*) Masha. You're my wife. My good, kind Masha. My wife. And I reproach you with *nothing*. Do you hear me? *Nothing*. And I am content. (*To* OLGA:) As you will witness. (*To* MASHA:) We'll begin again. And no one will say one word of what has occurred. Not a word, not a *reference* . . .

MASHA: . . . I'm going mad . . .

OLGA: Calm yourself, Masha. Please. Calm yourself. Get her some water.

MASHA: I don't need it.

KULYGIN: No. She doesn't need it. She's no longer crying. No.

(*Distant sound of a shot.*)

MASHA: Why should I need anything. My life is finished. Really. I'll be calm. In just a moment. You must forgive me. My head is spinning now. My *thoughts* . . .

(*Enter* IRINA.)

OLGA: Shhh. Masha. That's a clever girl. You calm yourself now. Come up to my room.

MASHA: No I will *not*. I'm not going in there. And I'm not going in the house. No.

IRINA: Alright, then. We'll sit here. We'll be silent. (*Pause.*) I'm off tomorrow, you know.

KULYGIN: I can make myself into the German master. Would you like to see it? (*Puts on false moustache and beard. Postures.*) I took them yesterday off a boy in the second form.

MASHA: You look like him.

OLGA: You look exactly like him!

(MASHA *weeps.*)

KULYGIN: Funny, those boys.

IRINA: Come, Masha.

KULYGIN (*to himself*):   . . . I look so much like him.

(*Enter* NATALYA.)

NATALYA (*to the maid*):   Take Bobik. Andrei Sergeyevich can give him a ride. A *constant* drain, children. (*Pause.*) The *watchfulness! Irina*. Leaving us tomorrow. What a pity. Stay on one more week. (*Sees* KULYGIN, *cries out, then laughs.*) You *frightened* me, you *"Prussian."* (*To* IRINA:) No, I've become *used* to you. And now you're torn away. I'll put Andrei into your room. He can play his music in there. And little Sofie in *his* room, that angel. Angel mine. My darling, who looked at me this morning with such a *look*, which *did* speak volumes; and she said *"mama"* (*Pause.*) ". . . Mama . . ."

KULYGIN: You're blessed with a fine child.

NATALYA: Well. Then. Tomorrow. That means I shall be alone. (*Sighs.*) I'm going to take the fir trees down. The whole lane of them. Then the maple there. It looks so *vulgar* in the evening. (*To* IRINA:) Darling: that belt doesn't suit you in the least. It wants something a little less "pronounced." And over there, what do you think? A bed of *flowers*. And the scent . . . from the bed of flowers. (*To maid, pointing at the bench:*) Why is this fork here? (*Shouts.*) Why is there a *fork* lying on the *bench* here, please? (*Pause. She exits into the house.*) Why is there a *fork* on the *bench* out here, I'm asking. (*Pause.*) No . . . ?

KULYGIN: . . . and she is off.

(*Offstage, a march is being played. They listen.*)

OLGA: That's the last of the garrison.

(*Enter* CHEBUTYKIN.)

MASHA: Our people are going away. (*Pause.*) Our Family. (*Pause.*) Well. (*Pause.*) A pleasant journey. (*To* KULYGIN:) Shall we go? Where's my hat?

KULYGIN: . . . put it in the house. Shall I go fetch it?

MASHA: Thank you.

OLGA: Yes. It's time.

CHEBUTYKIN: Olga Sergeyevna?

OLGA: Yes? (*Pause.*) What? (*Pause.*) What?

CHEBUTYKIN: It's . . .

OLGA: What is it?

CHEBUTYKIN: I don't know how to tell you.

OLGA: How to tell me what? (*Pause.*) No. It can't be. No.

CHEBUTYKIN: This day has killed me . . .

MASHA: What's happened?

OLGA (*embraces* IRINA): Irina . . . I . . . darling . . . darling . . .

IRINA: What? *All* of you . . . what?

CHEBUTYKIN: The baron was killed in the duel.

IRINA (*weeps*): Yes. I knew. I knew.

CHEBUTYKIN (*sits*): Oh, *God.* I am exhausted. (*Sighs.*) (*Pause. Takes out a newspaper, reads.*) . . . They'll cry it out a bit. (*Sings*

Olga

First speech links with past, last speech link with future. (Olga as disinterested one, most moral significance in play along with Tuzenbach, whom she calls so good, really good) Olga partly takes place of mother, is head of household. Olga in IV had to leave household entirely (which no longer Prozorov household, had nothing but abject Andrei, silent, wheeling the baby-carriage, all alone — as he's said he'd be — in the household; the enclave of cultivation has simply become (the clan now) barbarian household with an hopeless cultivated slave, a few dreams (quote Uncle Vanya, quote Verschinen they will crush you out (the 3 sisters) only hope dreams may visit our grave) visiting abject completely defeated Andrei are the only remnant of strong, gathered, cultivated sisters and ... brother working away.

The American poet Randall Jarrell's handwritten notes in preparation for his translation of The Three Sisters. *In a character sketch of Olga, he notes that her first speech is a link with the past, while her last line looks to the future.*

to himself softly.) "Ta tumm ta tummm tummm tummm tummm. Upon this Stone I sit." And, finally, it's all one.

(*The sisters stand holding on to one another.*)

MASHA: Oh. Fine. Play the music. Play them off. Away they go. One of them forever. For good. And isn't it true that we are left here, looking at a life that we . . . we must "create," and . . . (*Pause.*)

IRINA: In a time. Yes. In a time. It will be clear to us. What seems now to be *punishment* will be revealed. It will. And the meaning of suffering. Until then, what do we have but work? I will work. In the school. I'll give my life to those who may *profit* from it. (*Pause.*) The autumn passes. Winter comes. And the snow covers everything. And I'll be working . . .

OLGA: . . . the music plays so *brightly*. (*Pause.*) Time passes. Everything passes. We pass. We were only here for a little while. Too little to know. How can we help but think our suffering may be *transfigured*. To some good. For those who follow us? Who may remember us. Who may *bless* us. Or bless our memory. We who are living now. My darlings. Oh. Dear sisters.

(*Music grows softer and softer.* KULYGIN *enters bringing Masha's hat.* ANDREI *wheels the baby carriage.*)

. . . oh. My dears. The music plays so brightly. You would think, in just a little while, that we . . .

CHEBUTYKIN (*reading his paper, sings*):   "Ta dummm, ta dummm, ta dummm, ta dummm . . . Upon this Stone I sit . . ." (*Sighs.*) *Oh* yes . . .

OLGA: If only we knew. If only we *knew* . . .

SUGGESTIONS FOR
FURTHER READING

BIOGRAPHY

AVILOVA, LYDIA. *Chekhov in My Life: A Love Story*. Translated with an introduction by David Magarshack. Westport, Conn.: Greenwood Press, [1950], 1971. An account of their romance by an early love of Chekhov's.

GORKY, MAKSIM. "Reminiscences of Anton Chekhov." Translated by S. S. Koteliansky and Leonard Woolf. In Maksim Gorky, *Reminiscences*. Introduction by Mark Van Doren. New York: Dover, [1921], 1946. Warm recollections by a fellow writer and close friend.

LAFFITTE, SOPHIE. *Chekhov, 1860–1904*. Translated by Moura Budberg and Gordon Latta. London: Angus & Robertson, [1971], 1974. Charming and accessible.

MAGARSHACK, DAVID. *Chekhov: A Life*. Westport, Conn.: Greenwood Press, 1952. A penetrating and insightful work of scholarship, a tour de force.

PRITCHETT, V. S. *Chekhov: A Spirit Set Free*. New York: Random House, 1988. An interesting biographical and critical study combined.

TURKOV, ANDREI (compiler). *Anton Chekhov and His Times*. Cynthia Carlile, translator of memoirs; Sharon McKee, translator of letters. Fayetteville: University of Arkansas Press, 1995. An unequaled collection of essays remembering Chekhov, plus selected correspondence.

CRITICISM

AIKEN, CONRAD. "Anton Chekhov," in *Critical Essays on Anton Chekhov.* Edited by Thomas A. Eekman. Boston: Hall, 1989, pp. 21–25. Calls Chekhov "a poet of the actual."

BOWEN, ELIZABETH. "Introduction" to *The Faber Book of Modern Stories.* London: Faber & Faber, 1937. Credits Chekhov with being an innovator of the modern short story.

BROOKS, CLEANTH, and ROBERT PENN WARREN. "Anton Chekhov: 'The Lament,'" in *Understanding Fiction.* New York: Appleton-Century-Crofts, 1959, pp. 203–10. A critic and an American poet laureate explore Chekhov's story "The Lament" (translated in this Collector's Edition as "Misery").

BUNIN, IVAN. "Chekhov," in *The Atlantic Monthly*, volume 188, number 1 (July 1951), pp. 59–63.

HOWE, IRVING. "What Can We Do With Chekhov?" in *Pequod: A Journal of Contemporary Literature and Literary Criticism*, number 34 (1992), pp. 11–15.

OATES, JOYCE CAROL. *The Edge of Impossibility: Tragic Forms in Literature.* New York: Vanguard, 1972.

O'CONNOR, FRANK. "The Slave's Son," in *Kenyon Review*, volume 25, number 1 (Winter 1963), pp. 40–54. The Irish short story master honors Chekhov's contributions to the genre.

TOLSTOY, LEO. "An Afterword to Chekhov's Story 'Darling,'" in *The Works of Leo Tolstoy.* Translated by A. Maude. London: Oxford University Press, 1929, pp. 323–27. Tolstoy's homage to a Chekhovian heroine, despite the two writers' disagreement over her importance.

WILSON, EDMUND. "Seeing Chekhov Plain," in *The New Yorker*, volume 28, number 40 (November 22, 1952), 180–98.

WOOD, JAMES. "No More Mr. Nice Guy: The Brutal Comedy of Anton Chekhov," in *The New Republic* (February 5, 1996), pp. 32–39. An insightful, impassioned essay on the tough, comical, debunking side of Chekhov, proclaiming, "All his greatness flows from his comedy, and in particular his cold eye and absolving heart."

OF RELATED INTEREST

FORNES, MARIA IRENE, ET AL. *Orchards*. New York: Knopf, 1986. Plays commissioned by The Acting Company, a national repertory theater on tour for the John F. Kennedy Center, inspired by stories of Chekhov. Includes contributions by Wendy Wasserstein, John Guare, and Spalding Gray.

PITCHER, HARVEY. *Chekhov's Leading Lady: A Portrait of the Actress Olga Knipper*. London: John Murray, 1979. Chekhov's wife's own story.

STANISLAVSKY, KONSTANTIN. *My Life in Art*. Translated by J. J. Robbins. London: Geoffrey Bles, 1924. The memoirs of Chekhov's dramatic collaborator.

CHECKLIST OF ILLUSTRATIONS

All of the illustrations in this edition are taken from the holdings of The New York Public Library's Center for the Humanities and the Library for the Performing Arts.

Cover, frontispiece, and page xii: Frontispiece photograph of Anton Chekhov, n.d., from *Izbrannye proizvedeniia* (Moscow/Leningrad: Gosudarstvennoye izdatel'stvo, 1928).
Slavic and Baltic Division

Page xiv: Photo of Evgenia Chekhova. Photographer unknown, n.d.
Billy Rose Theatre Collection

Pages xvi–xvii: Drawing of Chekhov's dacha by Sergei Bekhonen, from *Tri sestri* by Nikolai Efros (St. Petersburg: Khudozhestvennoe Izdat. svetozar, 1919).
Slavic and Baltic Division

Page xix: Photo of Anton Chekhov with P. M. Svobodin, Vladimir Davidov, and Aleksei Suvorin. Photographer unknown, n.d.
Billy Rose Theatre Collection

Page xx: Photo of Olga Knipper by Sergei Bekhonen, from *Tri sestri* by Nikolai Efros (St. Petersburg: Khudozhestvennoe Izdat. svetozar, 1919).
Slavic and Baltic Division

Page xxii: Photo of Anton Chekhov. Photographer unknown, n.d.
Billy Rose Theatre Collection

Page xxiv: Wreath by Sergei Bekhonen, from *Tri sestri* by Nikolai Efros (St. Petersburg: Khudozhestvennoe Izdat. svetozar, 1919).
Slavic and Baltic Division

Pages xxviii–xxix: Postcard to Nikolai Nikolaevich Obolensky in Anton Chekhov's hand. Undated, probably November 29 or 30, 1889.
Slavic and Baltic Division

Page xxx: Isaak Levitan's painting *Berezovaya roshcha* (1885–89) from *Isaak Ilich Levitan: albom reproduktsii* (Moscow: Gos. izd-vo izobrazitelnogo iskusstva, 1957).
Slavic and Baltic Division

Page xxxii: Vladimir Nabokov's typewritten, hand-corrected miscellaneous lecture notes on Chekhov.
Berg Collection of English and American Literature

Page xxxiii: Vladimir Nabokov's handwritten miscellaneous lecture notes on Chekhov.
Berg Collection of English and American Literature

Page xxxvi: Photo of Maria Chekhova. Photographer unknown, n.d.
Billy Rose Theatre Collection

Page xxxvii: Photo of Ivan Chekhov. Photographer unknown, n.d.
Billy Rose Theatre Collection

Page xl: Cover illustration by T. Shishmarevoi for *Rasskazy* by Anton Chekhov (Moscow: Gos. izd-vo detskoi lit-ry Ministerstva prosveshcheniia RSFSR, 1949).
Slavic and Baltic Division

Page 29: Isaak Levitan's painting *Osennii den'. sokol'niki* (1879) from *Isaak Ilich Levitan: albom reproduktsii* (Moscow: Gos. izd-vo izobrazitelnogo iskusstva, 1957).
Slavic and Baltic Division

Page 46: Illustration by T. Shishmarevoi for *Rasskazy* by Anton Chekhov (Moscow: Gos. izd-vo detskoi lit-ry Ministerstva prosveshcheniia RSFSR, 1949).
Slavic and Baltic Division

Page 56: Ilia Repin's painting *In the Sun. N. I. Repina* (1900) from *Ilia Efimovich Repin* by Olga Antonovna Liaskovskaia (Moscow: Iskusstvo, 1982).
Slavic and Baltic Division

Page 77: Ilia Repin's painting *The Girl Ada* (1882) from *Ilia Efimovich Repin* by Olga Antonovna Liaskovskaia (Moscow: Iskusstvo, 1982).
Slavic and Baltic Division

Page 97: Ilia Repin's painting *A Timid Man* (1877) from *Ilia Efimovich Repin* by Olga Antonovna Liaskovskaia (Moscow: Iskusstvo, 1982).
Slavic and Baltic Division

Page 120: Ilia Repin's watercolor *Two Female Figures (Embracing Women). Etude* (1878) from *Ilia Efimovich Repin* by Olga Antonovna Liaskovskaia (Moscow: Iskusstvo, 1982).
Slavic and Baltic Division

Page 158: Isaak Levitan's painting *Vechernii zvon* (1892) from *Isaak Ilich Levitan: albom reproduktsii* (Moscow: Gos. izd-vo izobrazitelnogo iskusstva, 1957).
Slavic and Baltic Division

Page 179: Ilia Repin's painting *Portrait of E. Duse* (1891) from *Ilia Efimovich Repin* by Olga Antonovna Liaskovskaia (Moscow: Iskusstvo, 1982).
Slavic and Baltic Division

Page 218: Illustration by Kukryniksy (composite name adopted by the three satirical artists Mikhail Kupriyanov, Porfiry Krylor, and Nikolai Sokolov) for Chekhov's story "The Man in a Case" from *Rasskazy i povesti* (Moscow: OGIZ [Gos. Izd-vo khudozhestvennoi Literatury], 1944). Opposite p. 176.
Slavic and Baltic Division

Page 268: The cover by Sergei Bekhonen of *Tri sestri* by Nikolai Efros (Petersburg: Khudozhestvennoe Izdat. svetozar, 1919).
Slavic and Baltic Division

Page 287: Photograph, by M. Sakharov and P. Orlov, of original cast members of the Moscow Art Theater production of *The Three Sisters*, from *Tri sestri* by Nikolai Efros (St. Petersburg: Khudozhestvennoe Izdat. svetozar, 1919).
Slavic and Baltic Division

Page 312: Photograph of Konstantin Stanislavsky by M. Sakharov and P. Orlov, 1918, from *Tri sestri* by Nikolai Efros (St. Petersburg: Khudozhestvennoe Izdat. svetozar, 1919).
Slavic and Baltic Division

Page 377: A page (page 1 of the notes on Olga) from Randall Jarrell's handwritten notes for a translation of *The Three Sisters*.
Berg Collection of English and American Literature

PERMISSIONS

ARTWORKS AND MANUSCRIPTS

Isaak Levitan's *Berezovaya roshcha* (1885–89), *Osennii den'. sokol'niki* (1879), and *Vechernii zvon* (1892) reproduced with the permission of the Tretyakovsky Gallery, Moscow.

Ilia Repin's *In the Sun. N. I. Repina* (1900), *The Girl Ada* (1882), and *Portrait of E. Duse* (1891) reproduced with the permission of the Tretyakovsky Gallery, Moscow.

Ilia Repin's *Two Female Figures* (*Embracing Women*) (1878), reproduced with the permission of the State Russian Museum, St. Petersburg.

Vladimir Nabokov's handwritten notes for his lectures on Chekhov, published in their entirety by Harcourt, Brace in Nabokov's *Lectures on Russian Literature*, are reproduced here by arrangement with the Estate of Vladimir Nabokov. All rights reserved.

Page 1 of the notes on Olga from Randall Jarrell's handwritten notes for a translation of *The Three Sisters*. Reproduced with the permission of Mary Jarrell, Executrix.

TEXTS

"The Student," "The Huntsman," "Peasants," "Happiness," and "The Witch": reprinted with the permission of Simon & Schuster from *The Witch and Other Stories* by Anton Chekhov, translated from the Russian by Constance Garnett. Copyright © 1918 by Macmillan Publishing Company, renewed 1946 by Constance Garnett. "Anna on the Neck" and "The Teacher of Literature": reprinted with the permission of Simon & Schuster from *The Party and Other Stories* by Anton Chekhov, translated from the Russian by Constance Garnett. Copyright © 1917 by Macmillan Publishing Company, renewed 1945 by Constance Garnett. "The Beauties" and "Misery": reprinted with the permission of Simon & Schuster from *The Schoolmistress and Other Stories* by Anton Chekhov, translated from the Russian by Constance Garnett. Copyright © 1921 by Macmillan Publishing Company, renewed 1949 by David Garnett. "The Chorus Girl": reprinted with the permission of Simon & Schuster from *The Chorus Girl and Other Stories* by Anton Chekhov, translated from the Russian by Constance Garnett. Copyright © 1920 by Macmillan Publishing Company, renewed 1948 by David Garnett. "A Happy Ending" and "Ward No. 6": reprinted with the permission of Simon & Schuster from *The Horse-Stealers and Other Stories* by Anton Chekhov, translated from the Russian by Constance Garnett. Copyright © 1921 by Macmillan Publishing Company, renewed 1949 by David Garnett. "The Darling," "Anyuta," and "The Two Volodyas": reprinted with the permission of Simon & Schuster from *The Darling and Other Stories* by Anton Chekhov, translated from the Russian by Constance Garnett. Copyright © 1916 by Macmillan Publishing Company, renewed 1944 by Constance Garnett. "Sleepy": reprinted with the permission of Simon & Schuster from *The Cook's Wedding and Other Stories* by Anton Chekhov, translated from the Russian by Constance Garnett. Copyright © 1922 by Macmillan Publishing Company, renewed 1950 by David Garnett. "Easter Eve": reprinted with the permission of Simon & Schuster from *The Bishop and Other Stories* by Anton Chekhov, translated from the Russian by Constance Garnett. Copyright © 1919 by Macmillan Publishing Company, renewed 1947 by David Garnett.

The Three Sisters by Anton Chekhov as adapted by David Mamet. Copyright © 1990 by David Mamet. Used by permission of Grove/Atlantic, Inc.